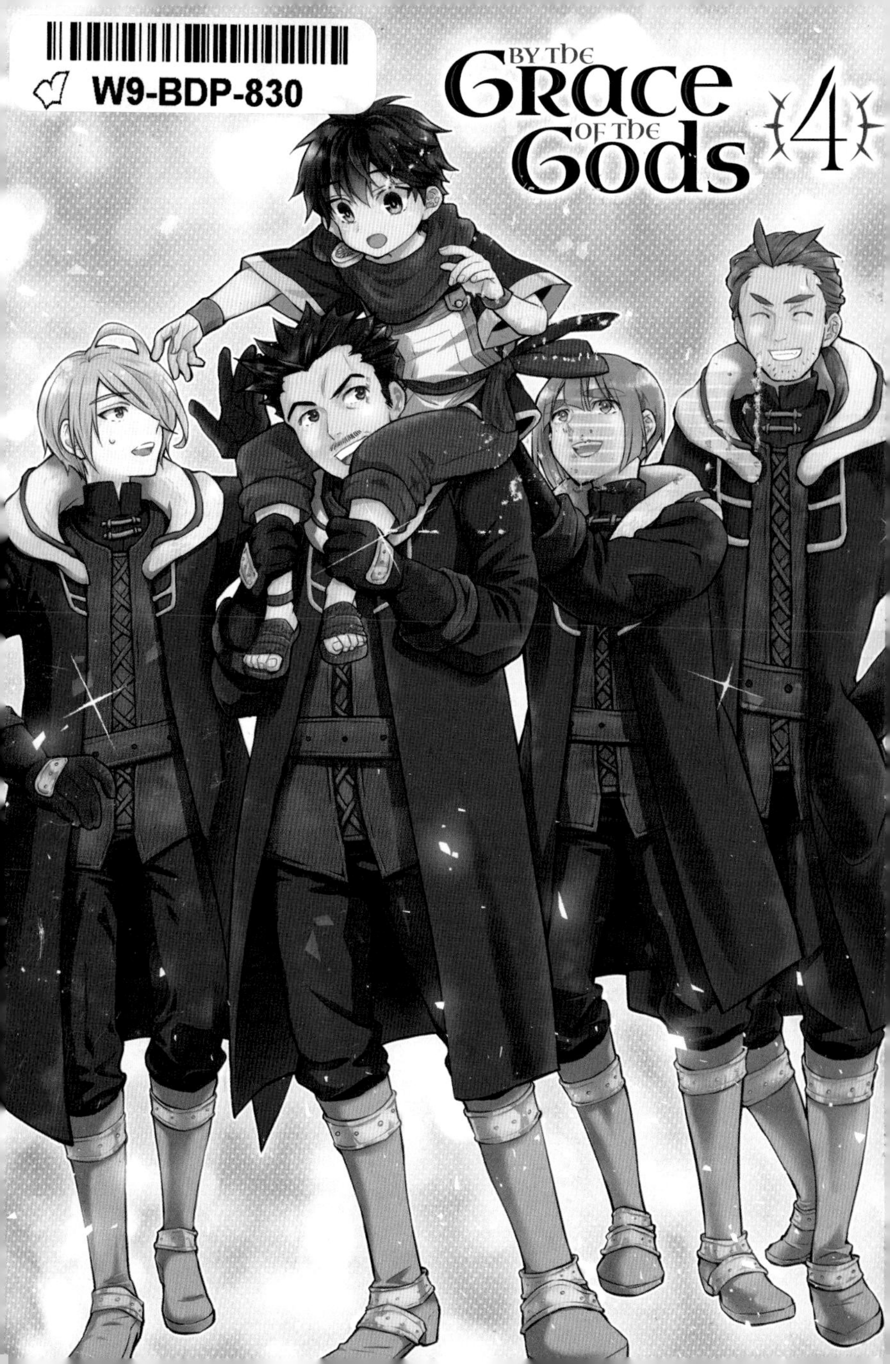
BY THE
GRACE
OF THE
GODS
4

CONTENTS

{4}

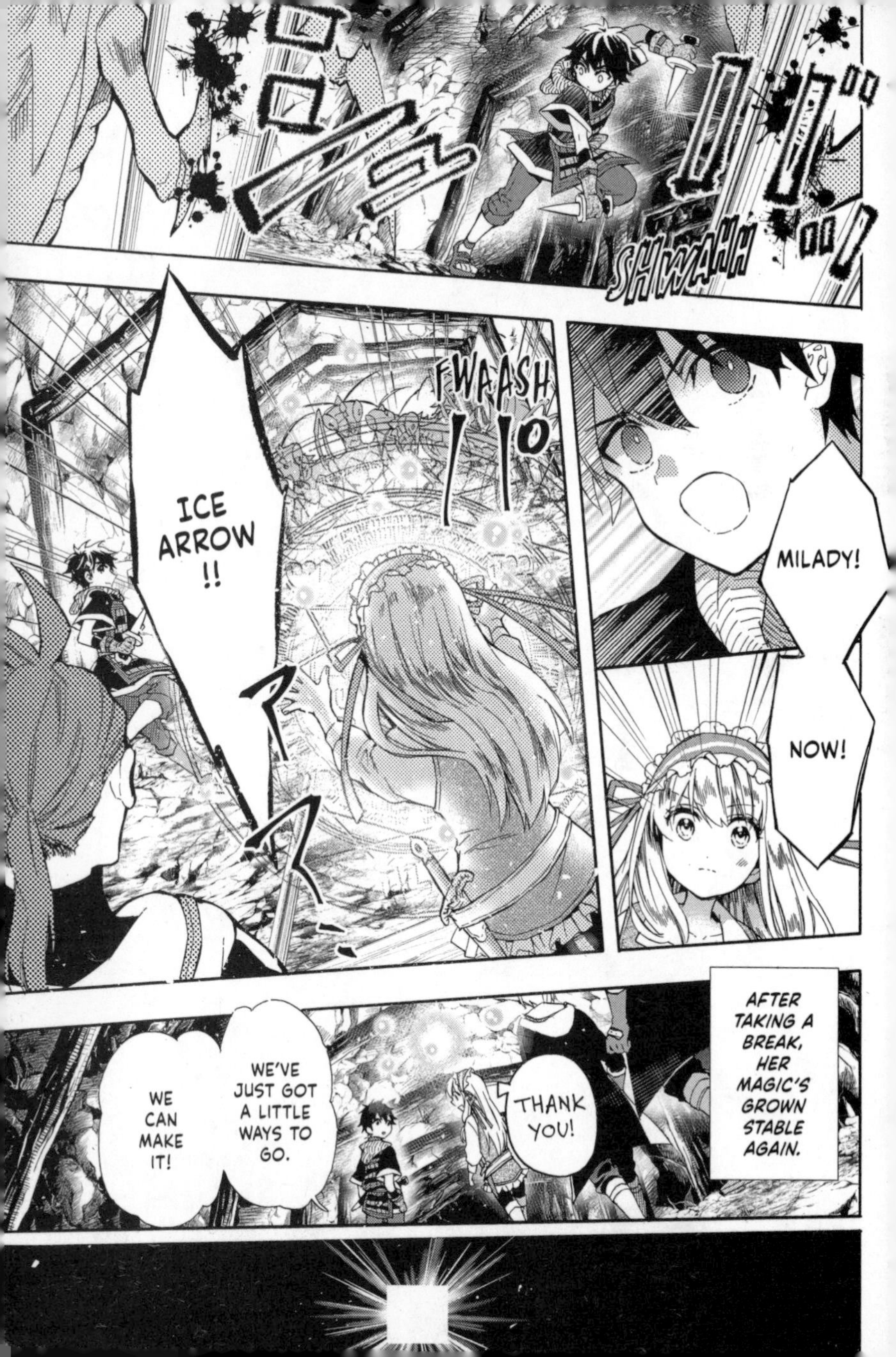
SHWAHH
MILADY!
NOW!
FWAASH
ICE ARROW !!
AFTER TAKING A BREAK, HER MAGIC'S GROWN STABLE AGAIN.
THANK YOU!
WE'VE JUST GOT A LITTLE WAYS TO GO.
WE CAN MAKE IT!

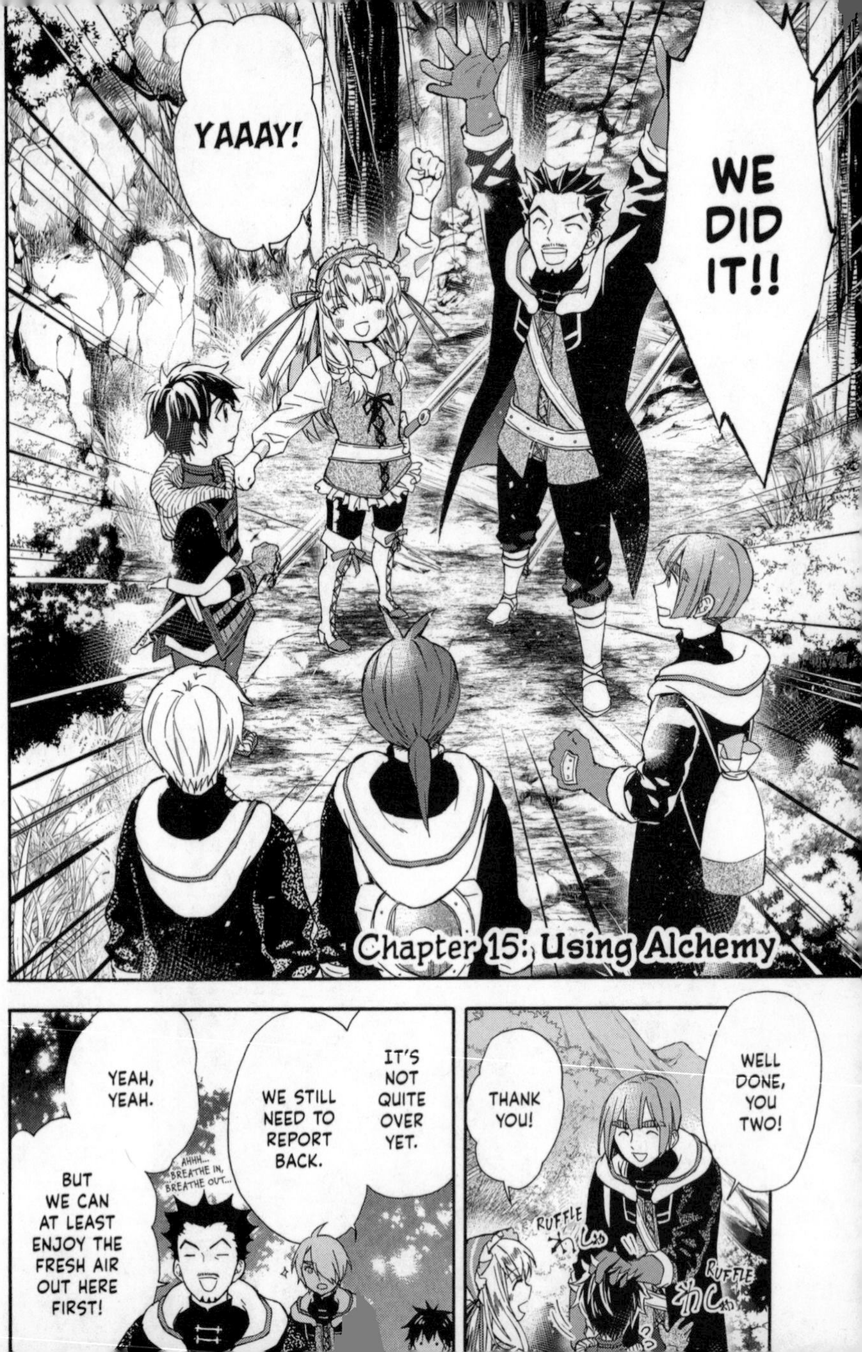
WE DID IT!!
YAAAY!
Chapter 15: Using Alchemy
WELL DONE, YOU TWO!
THANK YOU!
RUFFLE
RUFFLE
IT'S NOT QUITE OVER YET.
WE STILL NEED TO REPORT BACK.
YEAH, YEAH.
AHHH... BREATHE IN, BREATHE OUT...
BUT WE CAN AT LEAST ENJOY THE FRESH AIR OUT HERE FIRST!

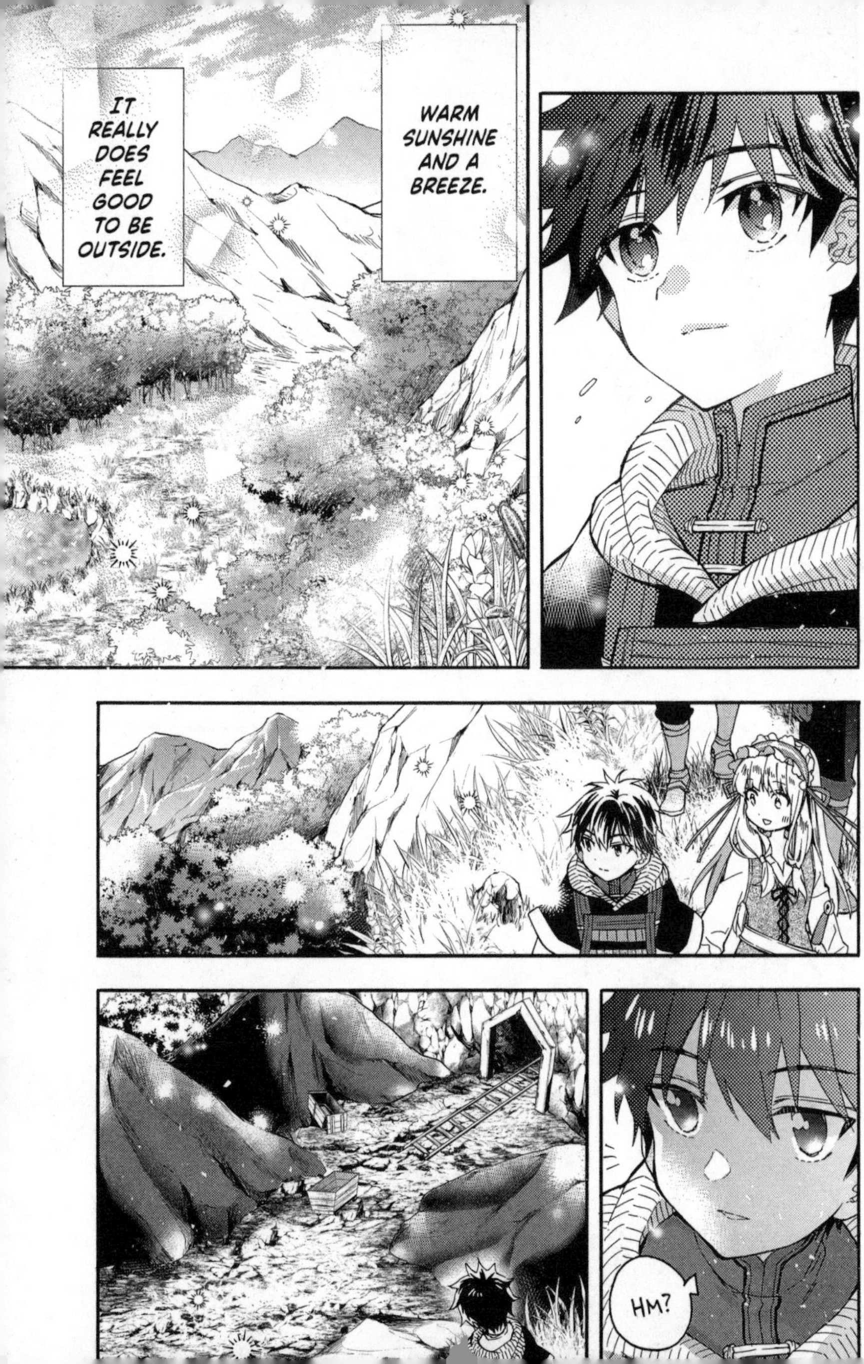
WARM SUNSHINE AND A BREEZE.
IT REALLY DOES FEEL GOOD TO BE OUTSIDE.
HM?

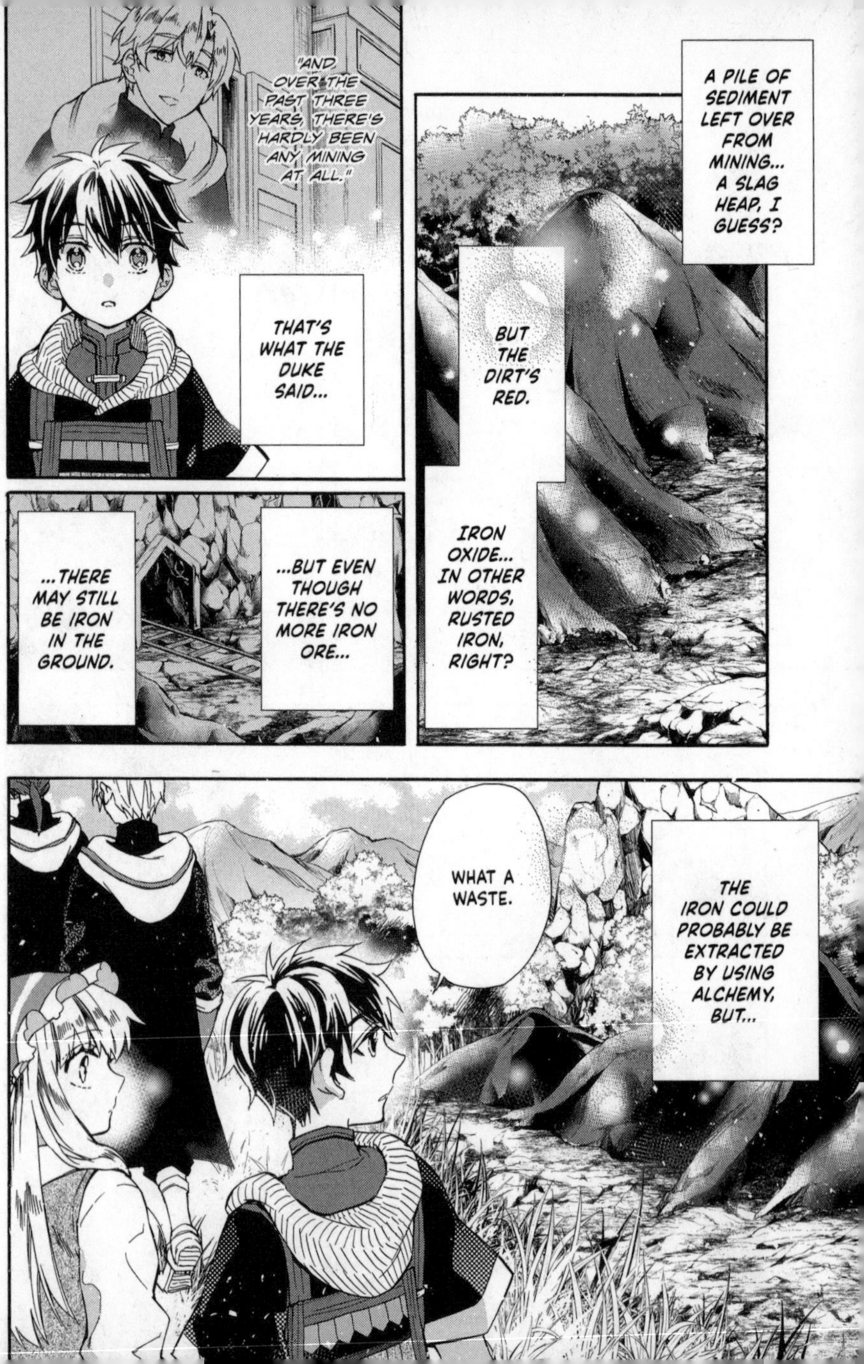
A PILE OF SEDIMENT LEFT OVER FROM MINING... A SLAG HEAP, I GUESS?
BUT THE DIRT'S RED.
IRON OXIDE... IN OTHER WORDS, RUSTED IRON, RIGHT?
"AND OVER THE PAST THREE YEARS, THERE'S HARDLY BEEN ANY MINING AT ALL."
THAT'S WHAT THE DUKE SAID...
...BUT EVEN THOUGH THERE'S NO MORE IRON ORE...
...THERE MAY STILL BE IRON IN THE GROUND.
THE IRON COULD PROBABLY BE EXTRACTED BY USING ALCHEMY, BUT...
WHAT A WASTE.

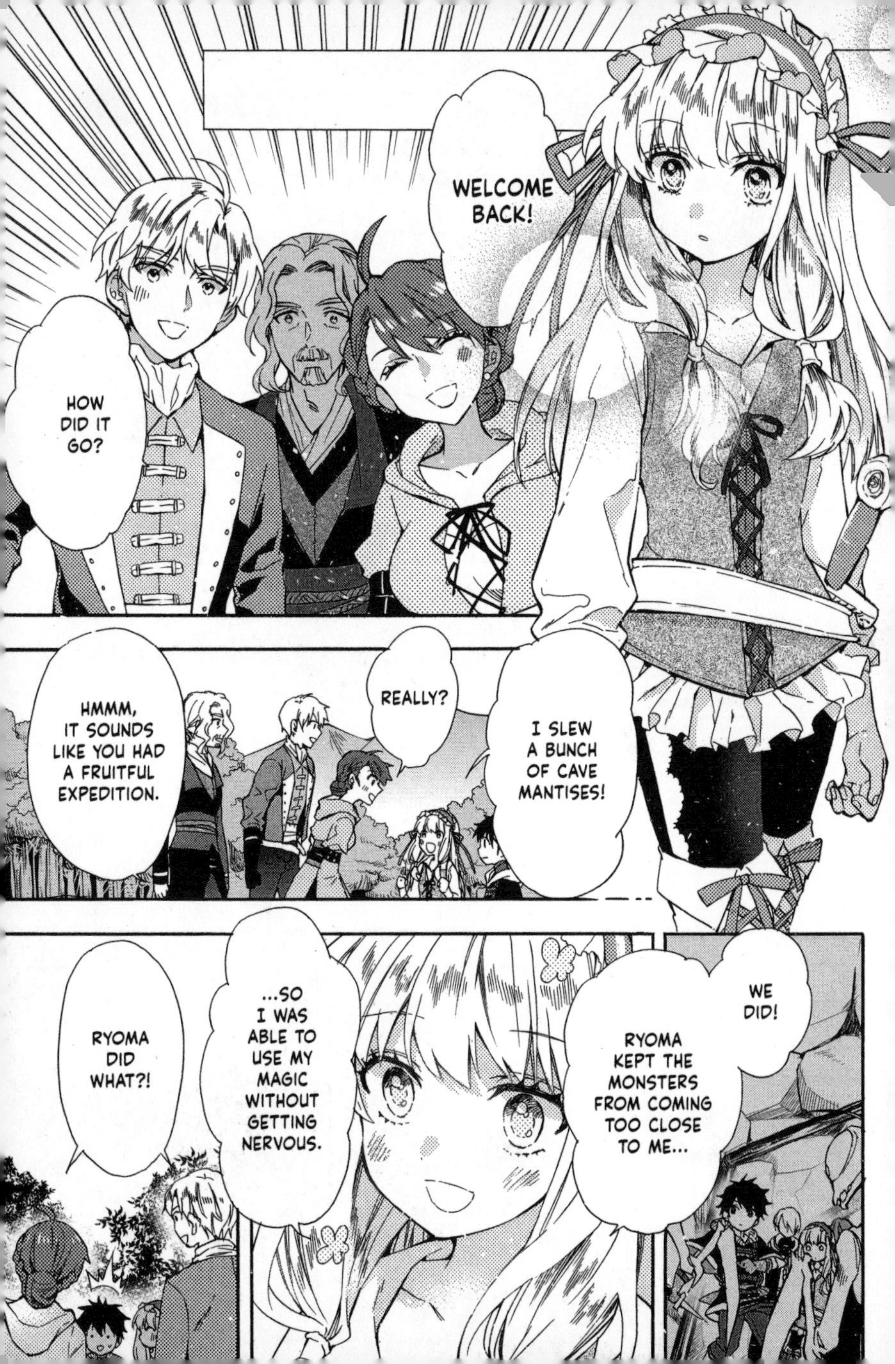
WELCOME BACK!
HOW DID IT GO?
I SLEW A BUNCH OF CAVE MANTISES!
REALLY?
HMMM, IT SOUNDS LIKE YOU HAD A FRUITFUL EXPEDITION.
WE DID!
RYOMA KEPT THE MONSTERS FROM COMING TOO CLOSE TO ME...
...SO I WAS ABLE TO USE MY MAGIC WITHOUT GETTING NERVOUS.
RYOMA DID WHAT?!

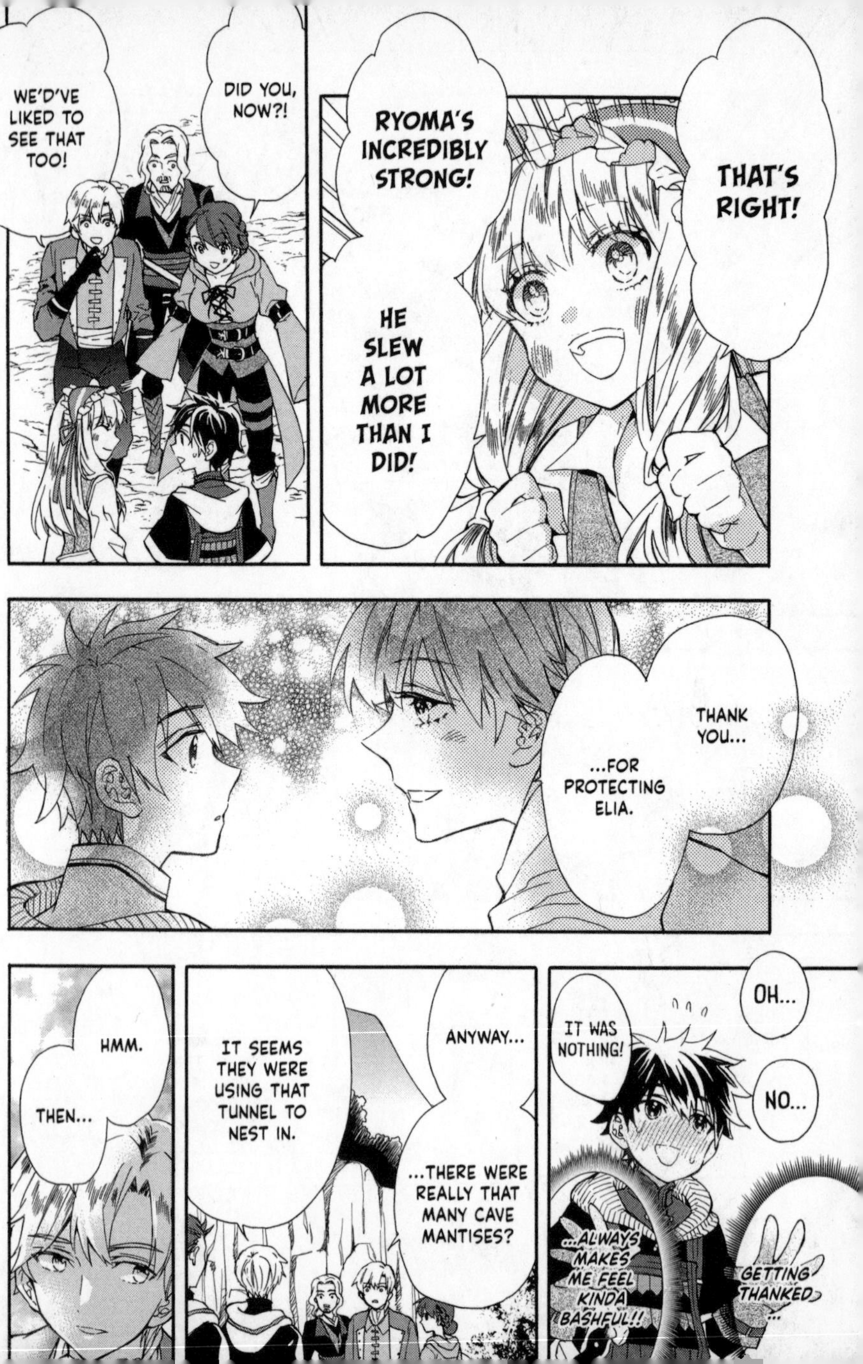
THAT'S RIGHT!
RYOMA'S INCREDIBLY STRONG!
HE SLEW A LOT MORE THAN I DID!
DID YOU, NOW?!
WE'D'VE LIKED TO SEE THAT TOO!
THANK YOU...
...FOR PROTECTING ELIA.
OH...
NO...
IT WAS NOTHING!
GETTING THANKED...
...ALWAYS MAKES ME FEEL KINDA BASHFUL!!
ANYWAY...
...THERE WERE REALLY THAT MANY CAVE MANTISES?
IT SEEMS THEY WERE USING THAT TUNNEL TO NEST IN.
HMM.
THEN...

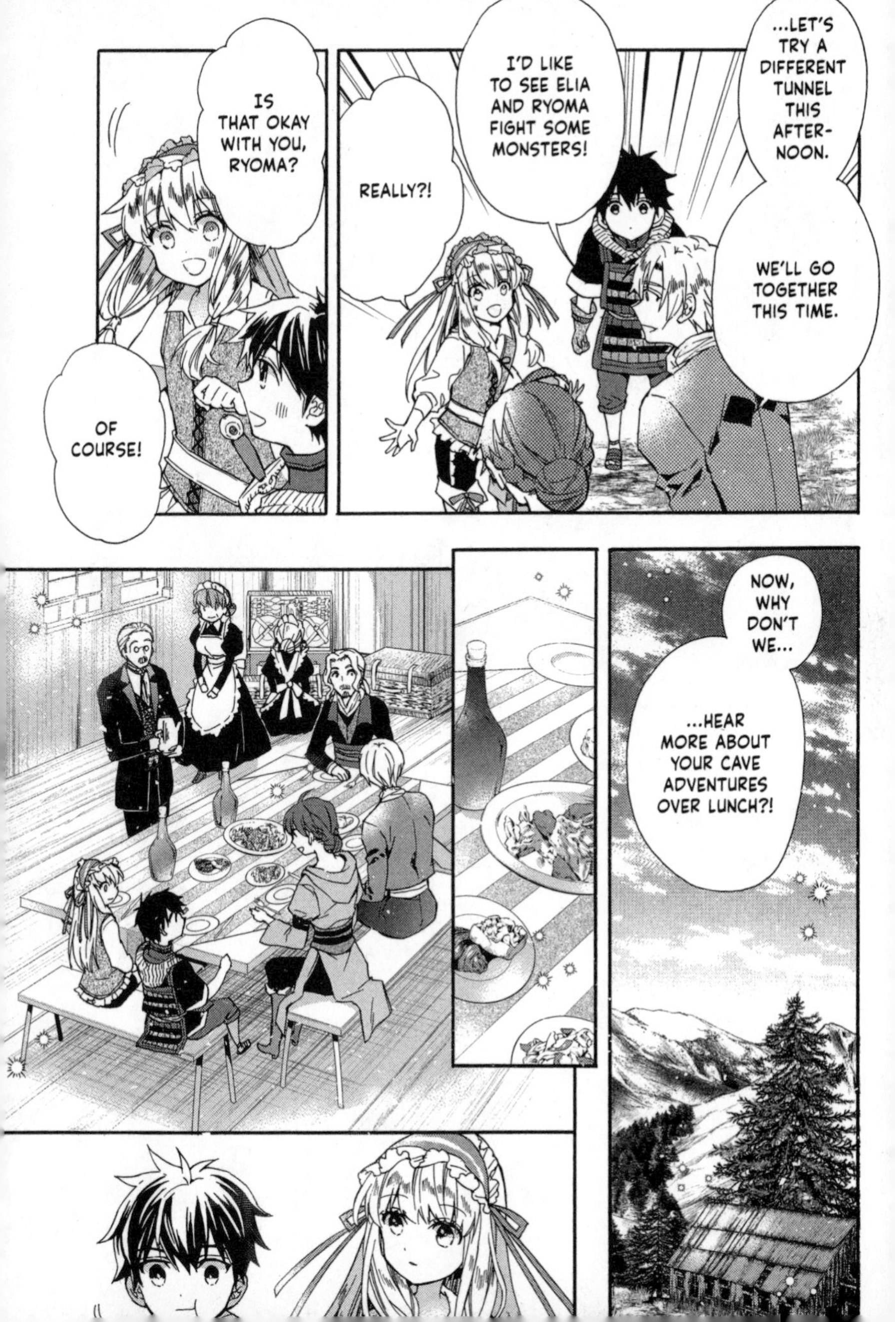
...LET'S TRY A DIFFERENT TUNNEL THIS AFTER-NOON.
WE'LL GO TOGETHER THIS TIME.
I'D LIKE TO SEE ELIA AND RYOMA FIGHT SOME MONSTERS!
REALLY?!
IS THAT OKAY WITH YOU, RYOMA?
OF COURSE!
NOW, WHY DON'T WE...
...HEAR MORE ABOUT YOUR CAVE ADVENTURES OVER LUNCH?!

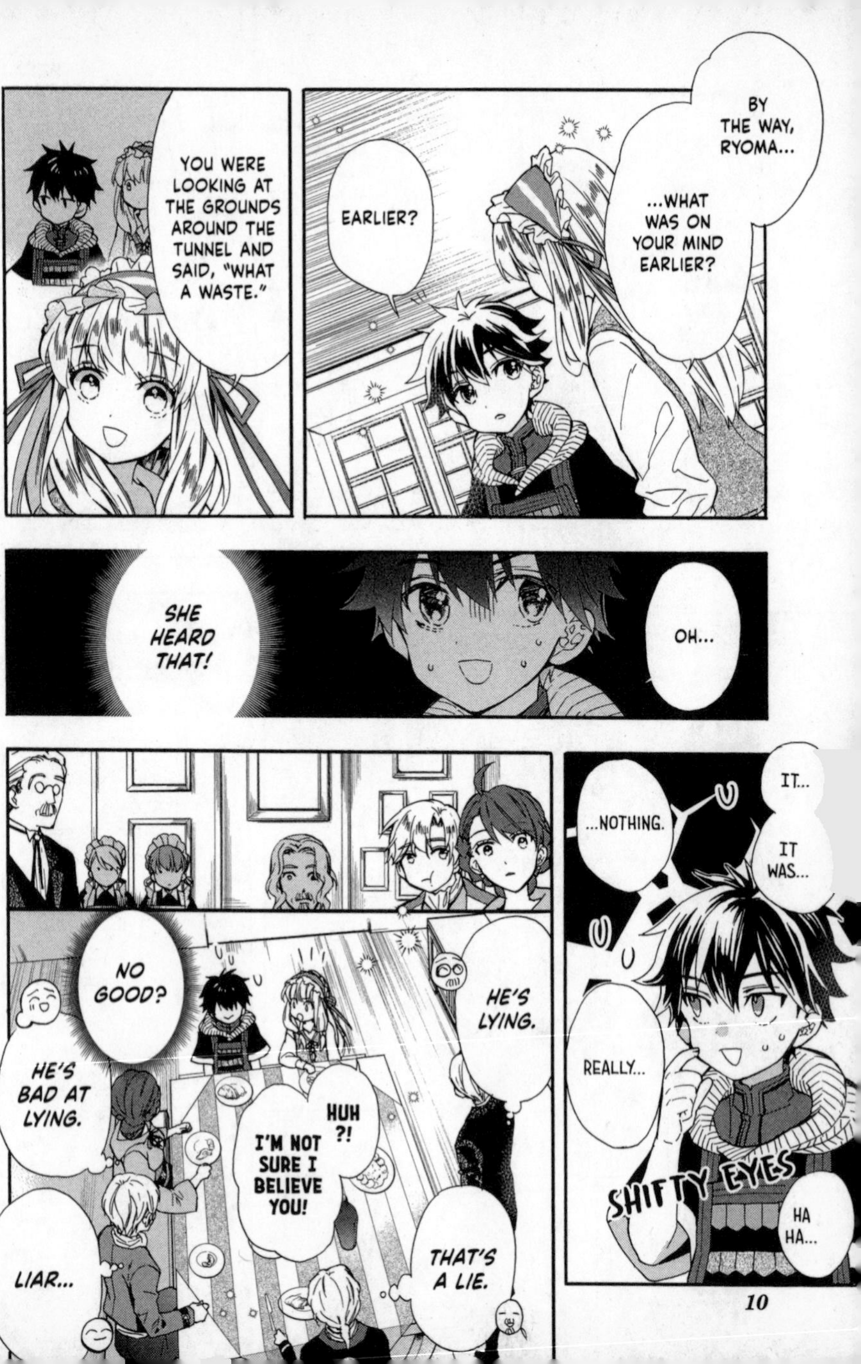
BY THE WAY, RYOMA...
...WHAT WAS ON YOUR MIND EARLIER?
EARLIER?
YOU WERE LOOKING AT THE GROUNDS AROUND THE TUNNEL AND SAID, "WHAT A WASTE."
OH...
SHE HEARD THAT!
IT...
IT WAS...
...NOTHING.
REALLY...
SHIFTY EYES
HA HA...
HE'S LYING.
HUH ?!
I'M NOT SURE I BELIEVE YOU!
NO GOOD?
HE'S BAD AT LYING.
THAT'S A LIE.
LIAR...

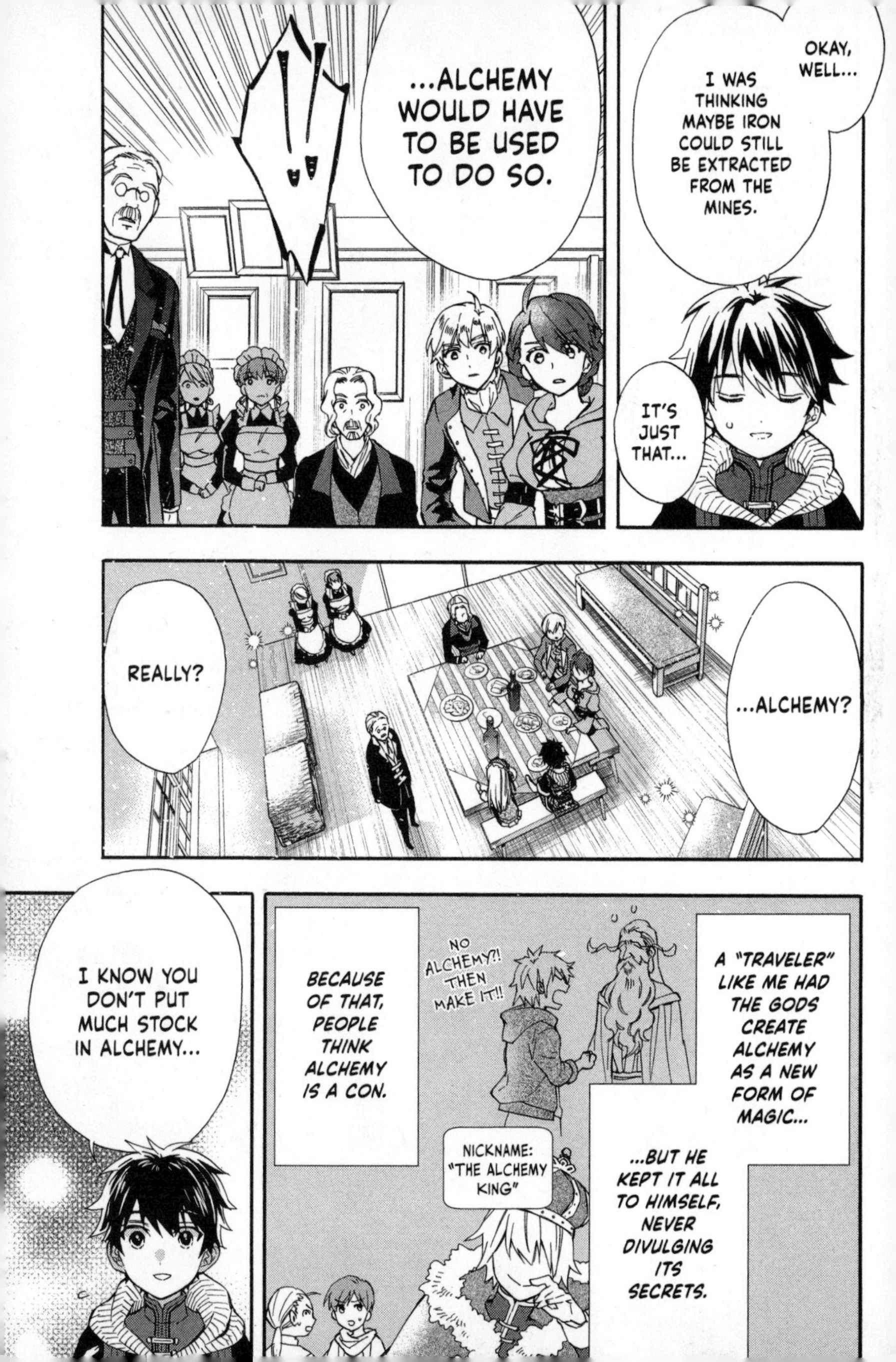
OKAY, WELL...
I WAS THINKING MAYBE IRON COULD STILL BE EXTRACTED FROM THE MINES.
IT'S JUST THAT...
...ALCHEMY WOULD HAVE TO BE USED TO DO SO.
...ALCHEMY?
REALLY?
A "TRAVELER" LIKE ME HAD THE GODS CREATE ALCHEMY AS A NEW FORM OF MAGIC...
...BUT HE KEPT IT ALL TO HIMSELF, NEVER DIVULGING ITS SECRETS.
NICKNAME: "THE ALCHEMY KING"
NO ALCHEMY?! THEN MAKE IT!!
BECAUSE OF THAT, PEOPLE THINK ALCHEMY IS A CON.
I KNOW YOU DON'T PUT MUCH STOCK IN ALCHEMY...

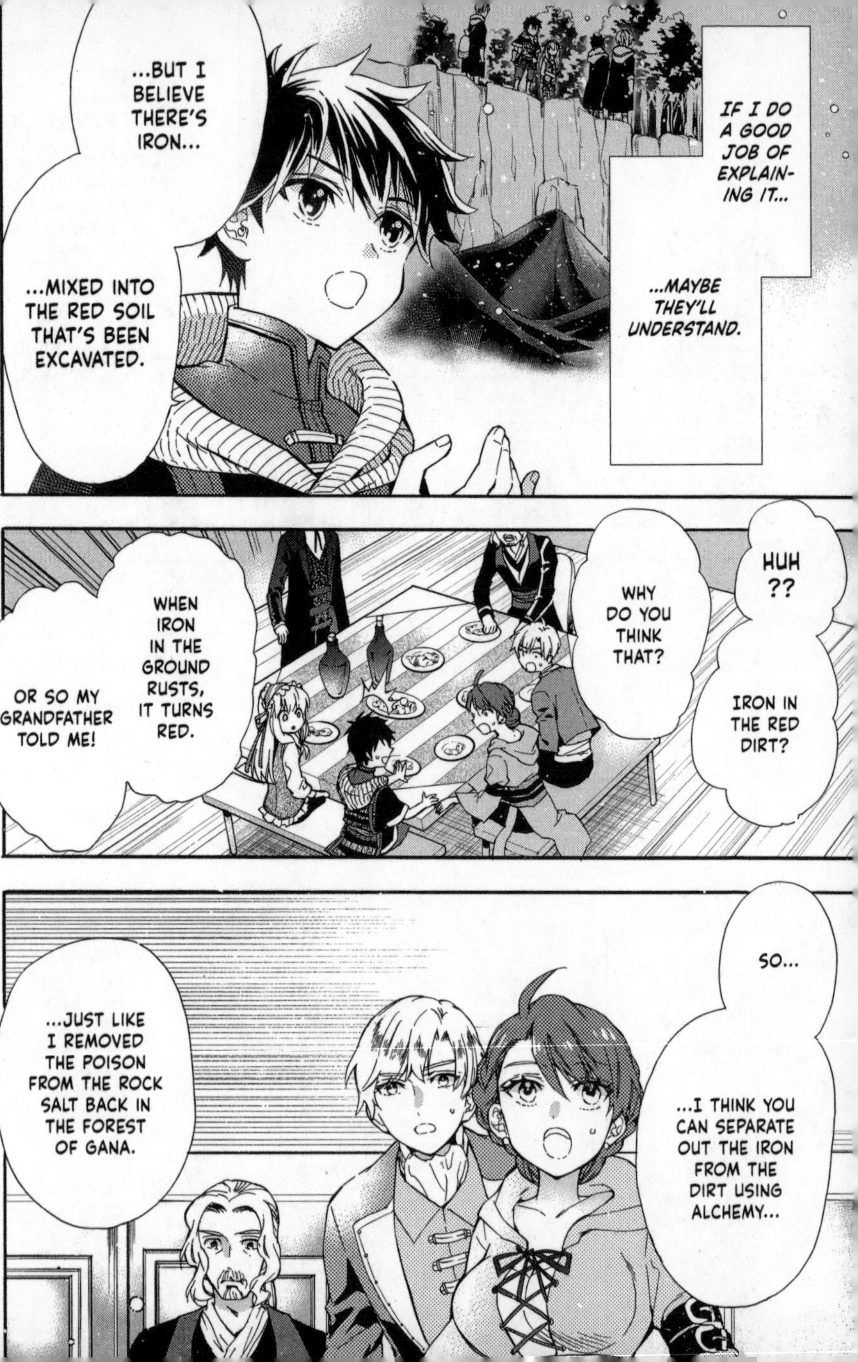
IF I DO A GOOD JOB OF EXPLAINING IT...
...MAYBE THEY'LL UNDERSTAND.
...BUT I BELIEVE THERE'S IRON...
...MIXED INTO THE RED SOIL THAT'S BEEN EXCAVATED.
HUH ??
IRON IN THE RED DIRT?
WHY DO YOU THINK THAT?
WHEN IRON IN THE GROUND RUSTS, IT TURNS RED.
OR SO MY GRANDFATHER TOLD ME!
SO...
...I THINK YOU CAN SEPARATE OUT THE IRON FROM THE DIRT USING ALCHEMY...
...JUST LIKE I REMOVED THE POISON FROM THE ROCK SALT BACK IN THE FOREST OF GANA.

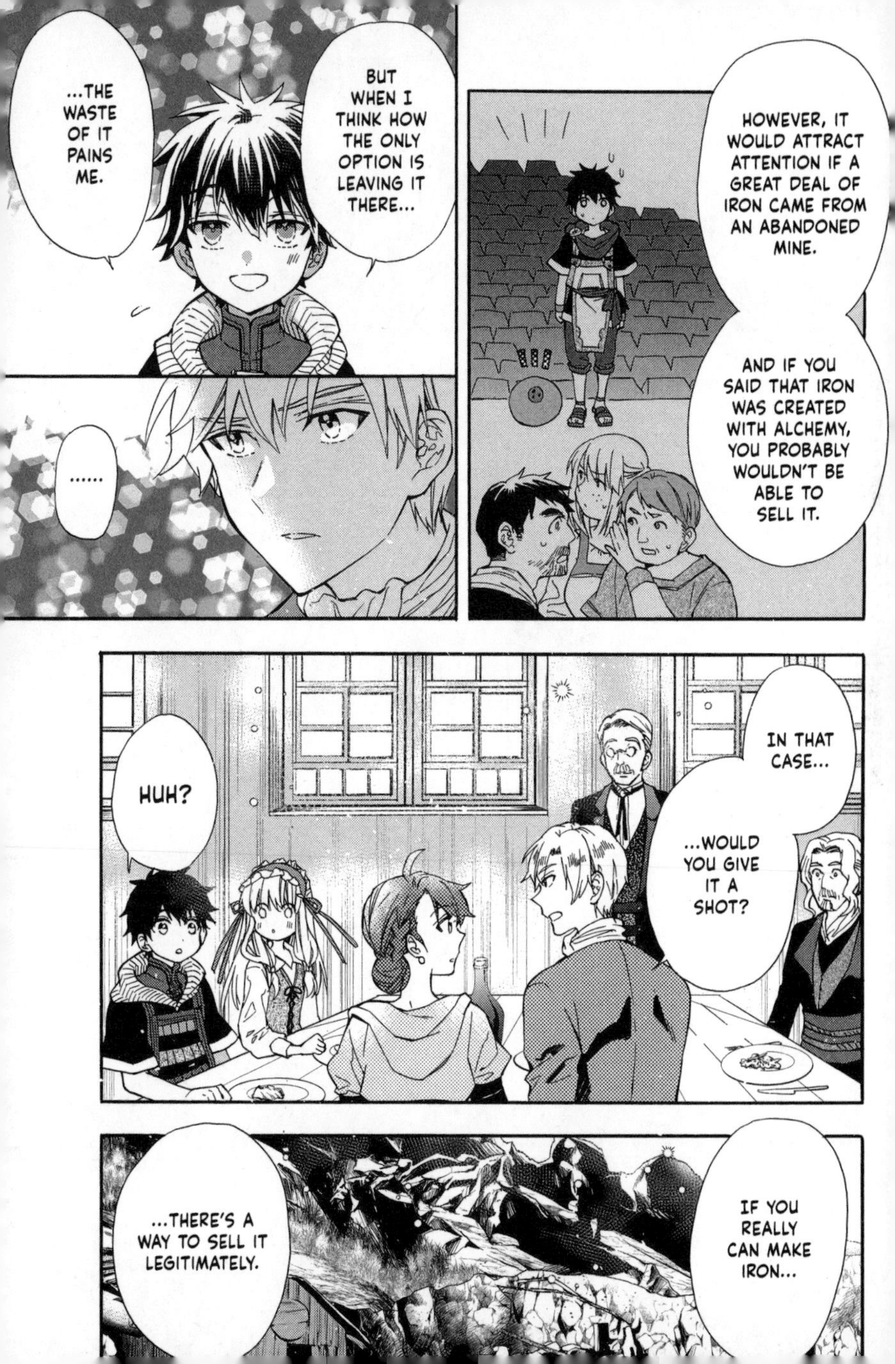
HOWEVER, IT WOULD ATTRACT ATTENTION IF A GREAT DEAL OF IRON CAME FROM AN ABANDONED MINE.
AND IF YOU SAID THAT IRON WAS CREATED WITH ALCHEMY, YOU PROBABLY WOULDN'T BE ABLE TO SELL IT.
BUT WHEN I THINK HOW THE ONLY OPTION IS LEAVING IT THERE...
...THE WASTE OF IT PAINS ME.
......
IN THAT CASE...
...WOULD YOU GIVE IT A SHOT?
HUH?
IF YOU REALLY CAN MAKE IRON...
...THERE'S A WAY TO SELL IT LEGITIMATELY.

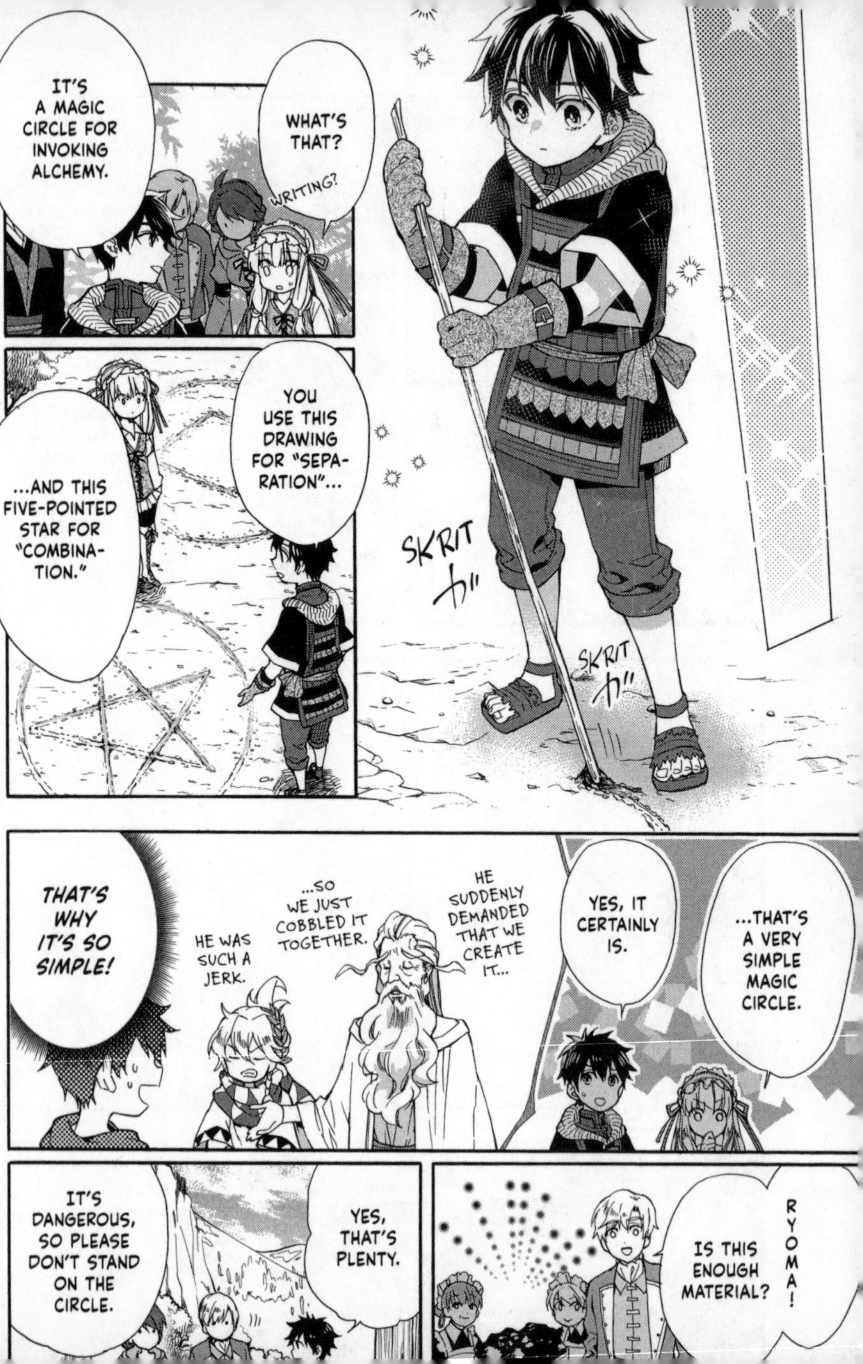
SKRIT
SKRIT
WHAT'S THAT?
WRITING?
IT'S A MAGIC CIRCLE FOR INVOKING ALCHEMY.
YOU USE THIS DRAWING FOR "SEPARATION"...
...AND THIS FIVE-POINTED STAR FOR "COMBINATION."
...THAT'S A VERY SIMPLE MAGIC CIRCLE.
YES, IT CERTAINLY IS.
HE SUDDENLY DEMANDED THAT WE CREATE IT...
...SO WE JUST COBBLED IT TOGETHER.
HE WAS SUCH A JERK.
THAT'S WHY IT'S SO SIMPLE!
RYOMA!
IS THIS ENOUGH MATERIAL?
YES, THAT'S PLENTY.
IT'S DANGEROUS, SO PLEASE DON'T STAND ON THE CIRCLE.

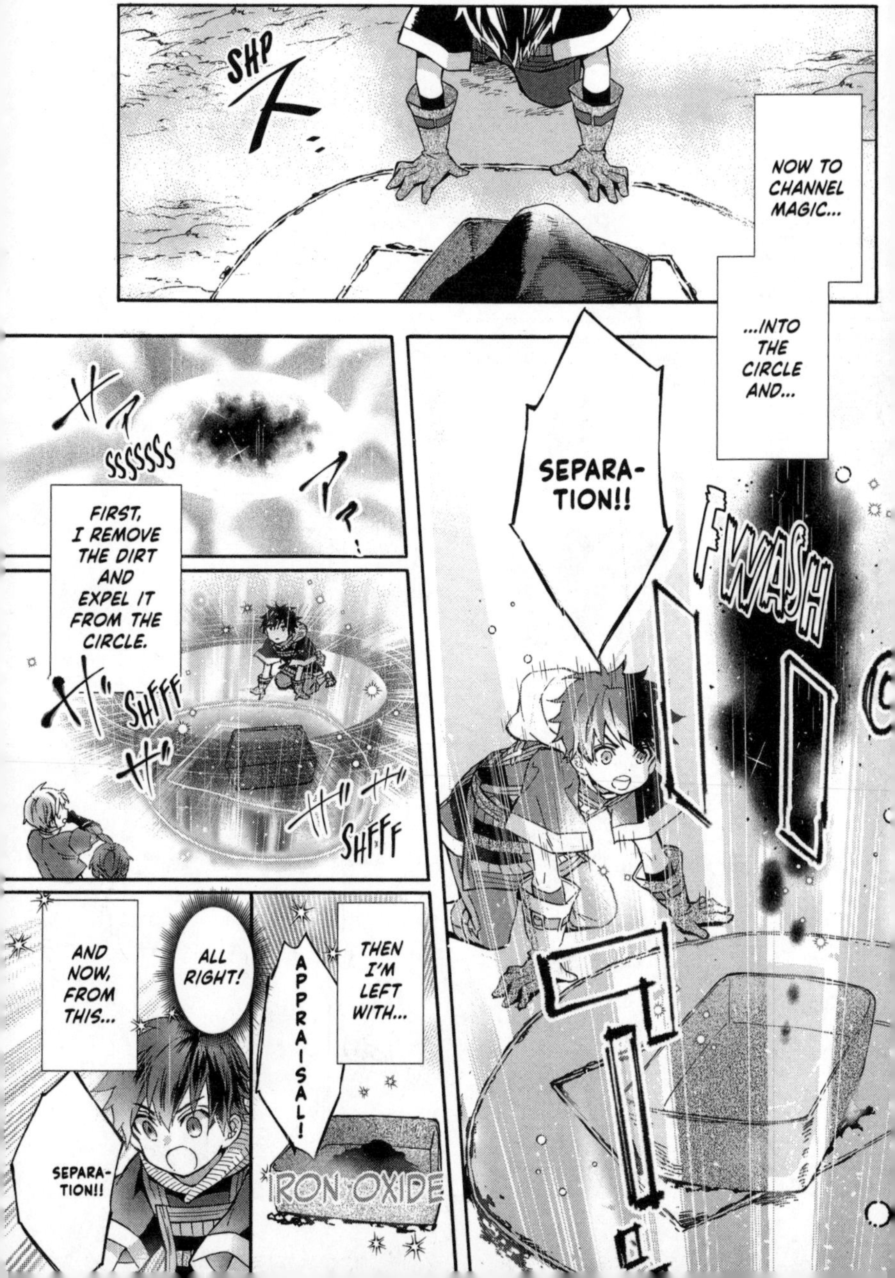
SHP
NOW TO CHANNEL MAGIC...
...INTO THE CIRCLE AND...
SEPARATION!!
FWASH
SSSSSSS
FIRST, I REMOVE THE DIRT AND EXPEL IT FROM THE CIRCLE.
SHFFF
SHFFF
THEN I'M LEFT WITH...
APPRAISAL!
IRON OXIDE
AND NOW, FROM THIS...
ALL RIGHT!
SEPARATION!!

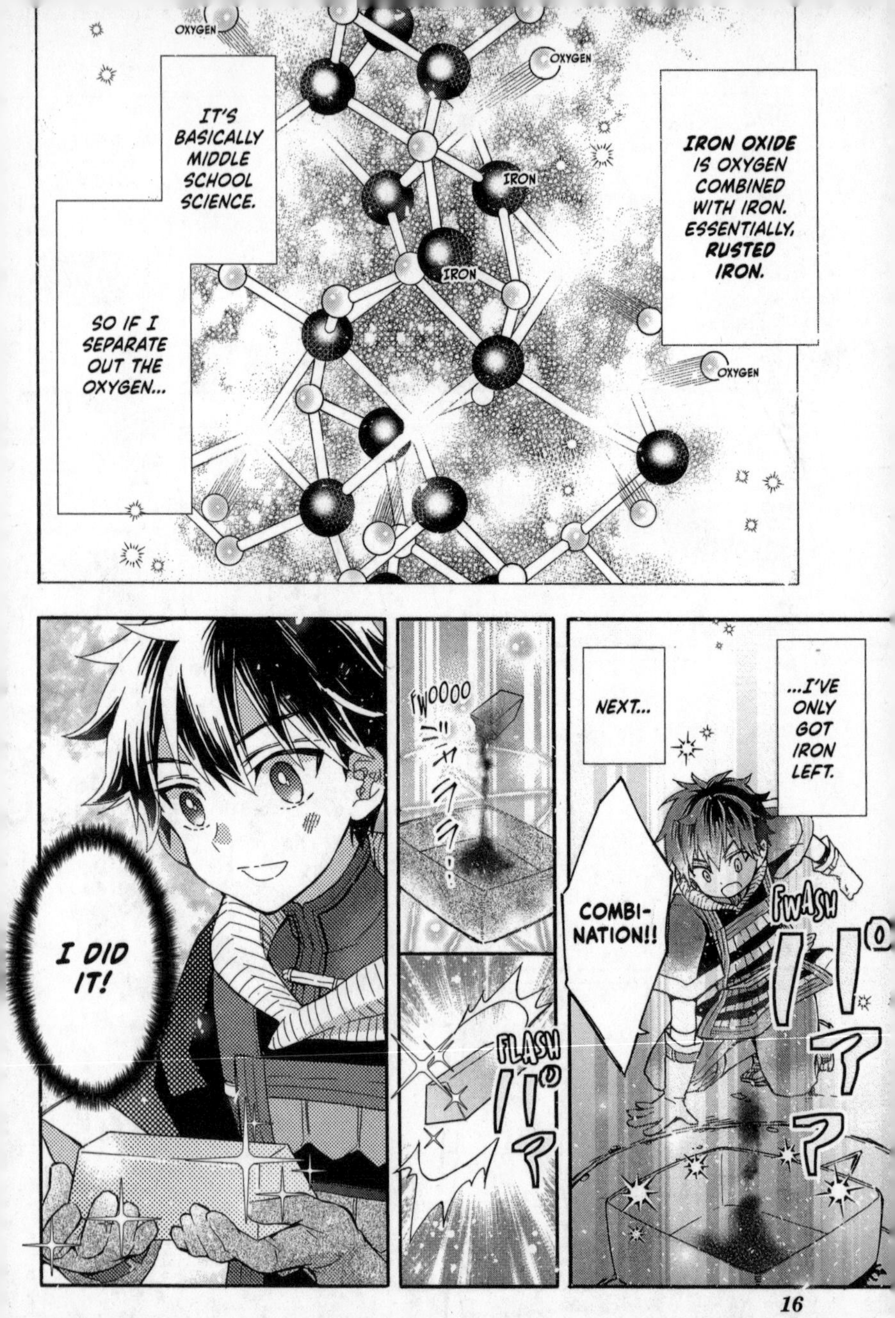
OXYGEN
OXYGEN
IRON OXIDE IS OXYGEN COMBINED WITH IRON. ESSENTIALLY, RUSTED IRON.
IRON
IRON
OXYGEN
IT'S BASICALLY MIDDLE SCHOOL SCIENCE.
SO IF I SEPARATE OUT THE OXYGEN...
...I'VE ONLY GOT IRON LEFT.
NEXT...
COMBI-NATION!!
FWASH
FWOOOO
FLASH
I DID IT!

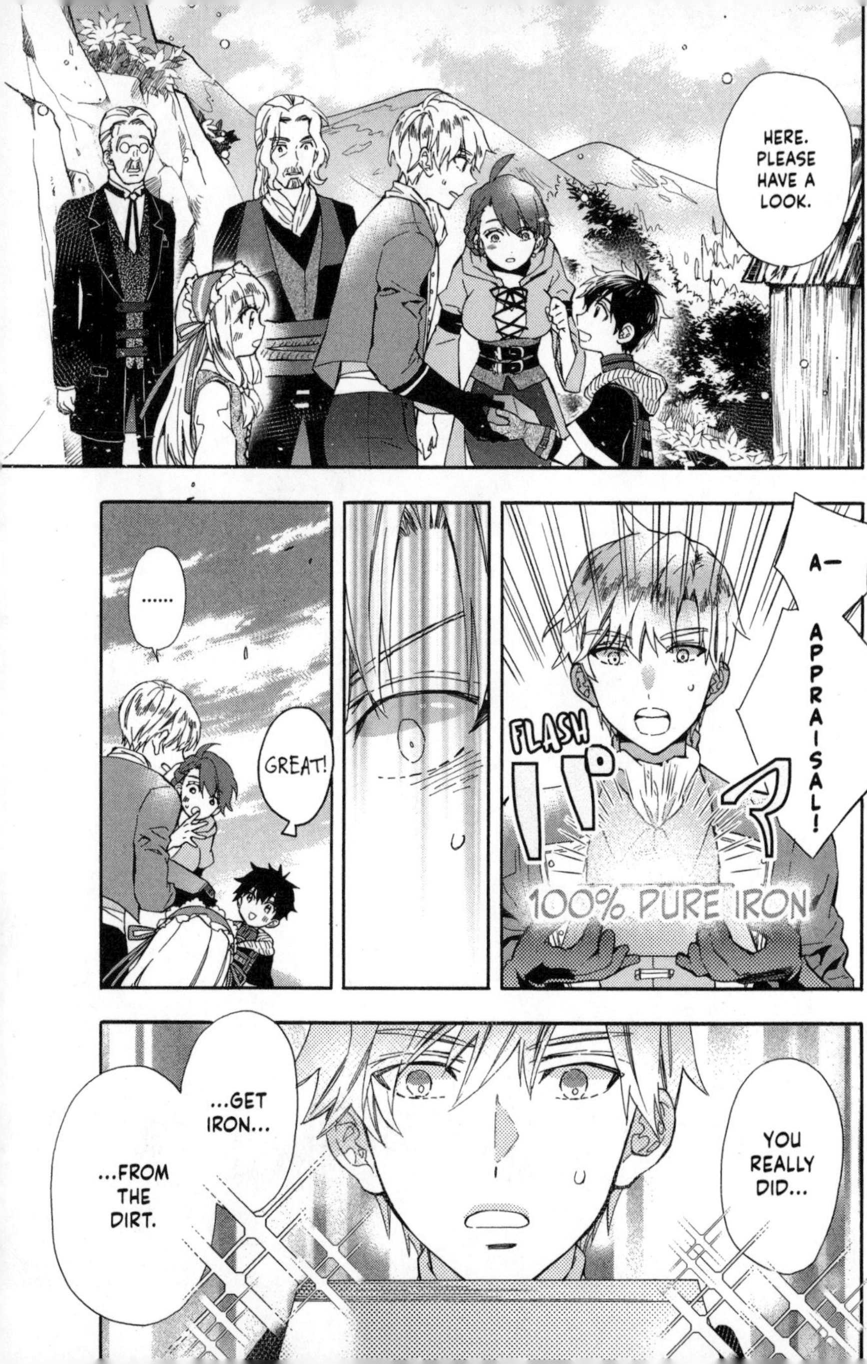
HERE. PLEASE HAVE A LOOK.
A— APPRAISAL!
FLASH
!?
100% PURE IRON
......
GREAT!
YOU REALLY DID...
...GET IRON...
...FROM THE DIRT.

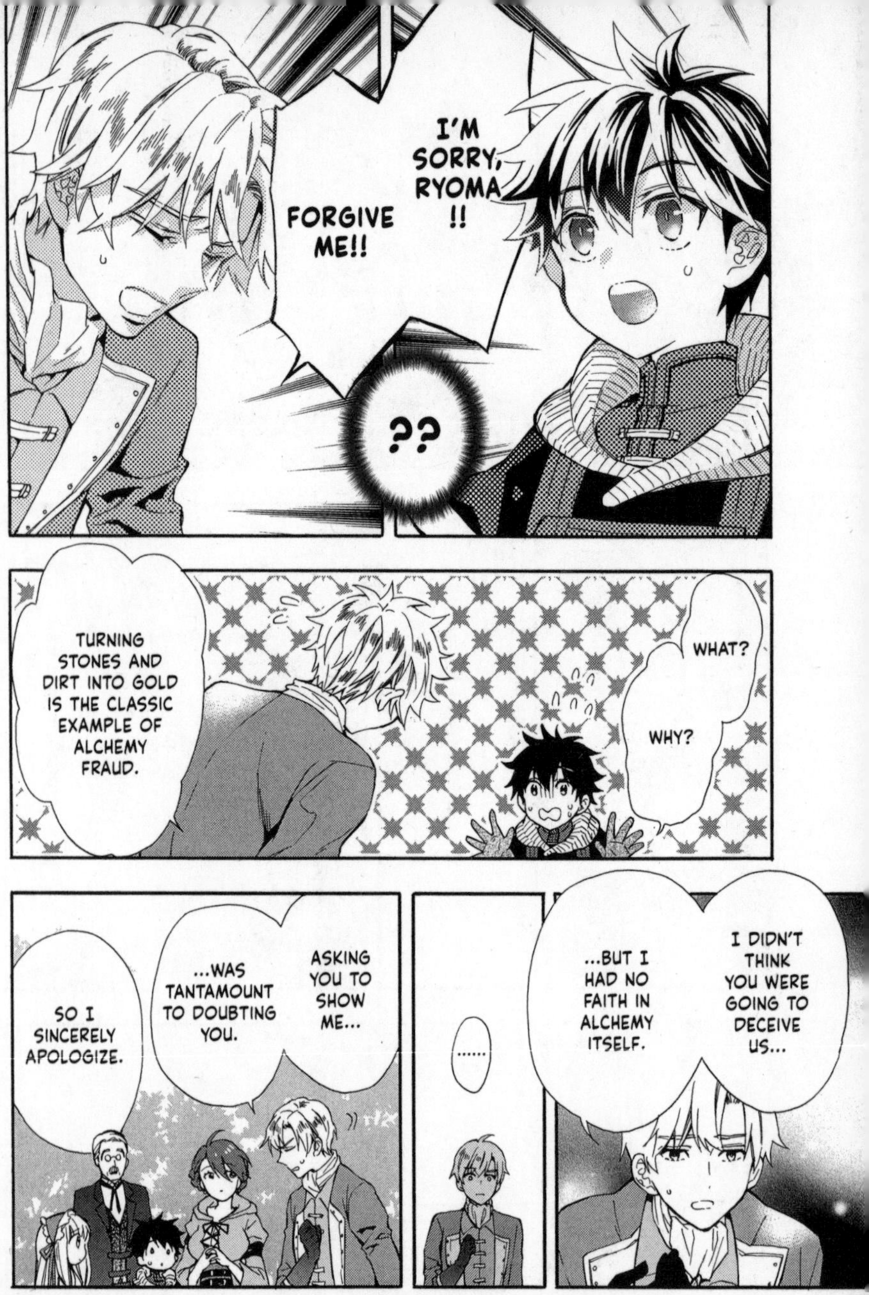
I'M SORRY, RYOMA!!
FORGIVE ME!!
??
WHAT?
WHY?
TURNING STONES AND DIRT INTO GOLD IS THE CLASSIC EXAMPLE OF ALCHEMY FRAUD.
I DIDN'T THINK YOU WERE GOING TO DECEIVE US...
...BUT I HAD NO FAITH IN ALCHEMY ITSELF.
......
ASKING YOU TO SHOW ME...
...WAS TANTAMOUNT TO DOUBTING YOU.
SO I SINCERELY APOLOGIZE.

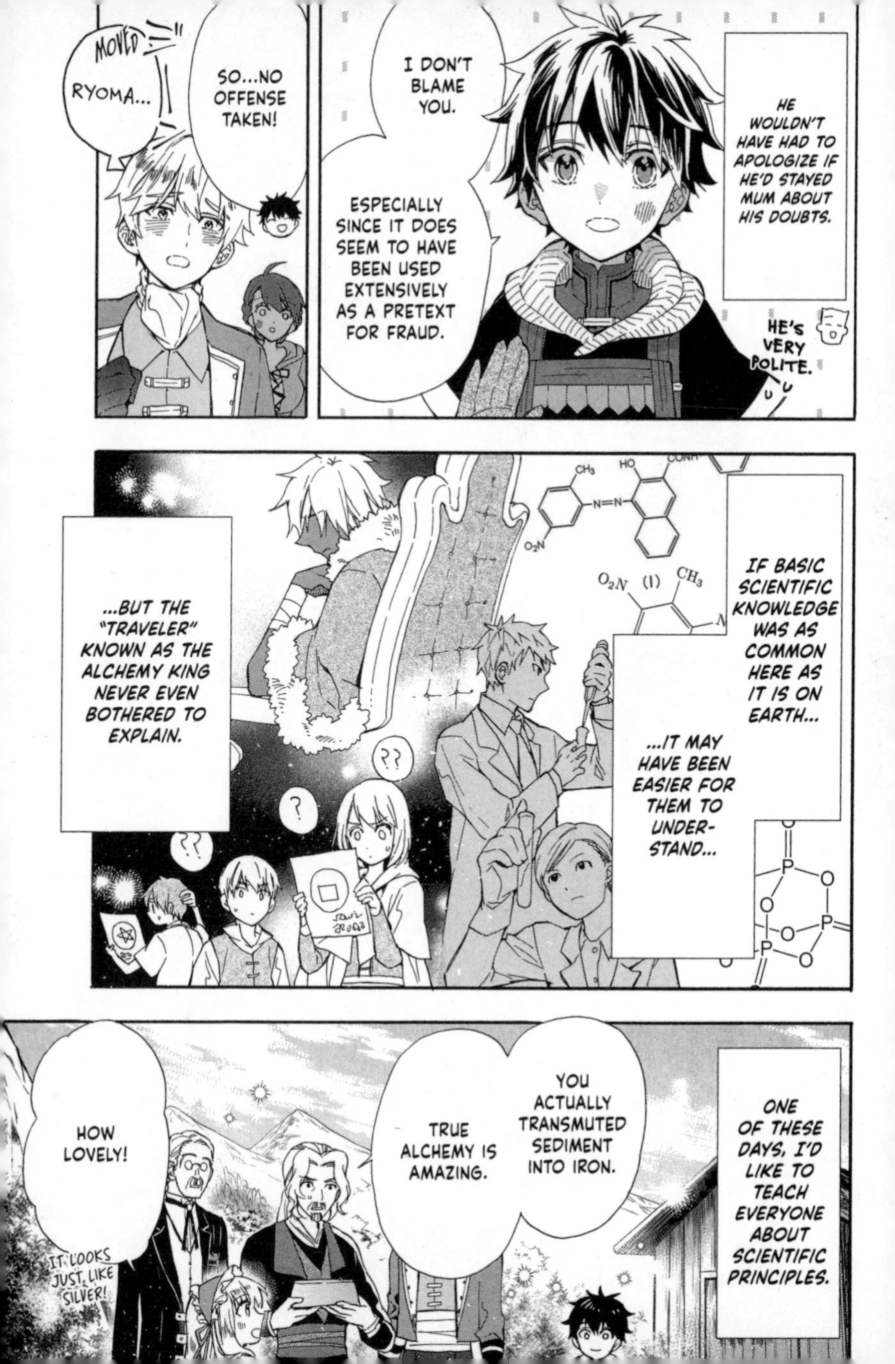
HE WOULDN'T HAVE HAD TO APOLOGIZE IF HE'D STAYED MUM ABOUT HIS DOUBTS.
HE'S VERY POLITE.
I DON'T BLAME YOU.
ESPECIALLY SINCE IT DOES SEEM TO HAVE BEEN USED EXTENSIVELY AS A PRETEXT FOR FRAUD.
SO...NO OFFENSE TAKEN!
MOVED
RYOMA...
IF BASIC SCIENTIFIC KNOWLEDGE WAS AS COMMON HERE AS IT IS ON EARTH...
...IT MAY HAVE BEEN EASIER FOR THEM TO UNDERSTAND...
...BUT THE "TRAVELER" KNOWN AS THE ALCHEMY KING NEVER EVEN BOTHERED TO EXPLAIN.
ONE OF THESE DAYS, I'D LIKE TO TEACH EVERYONE ABOUT SCIENTIFIC PRINCIPLES.
YOU ACTUALLY TRANSMUTED SEDIMENT INTO IRON.
TRUE ALCHEMY IS AMAZING.
HOW LOVELY!
IT LOOKS JUST LIKE SILVER!

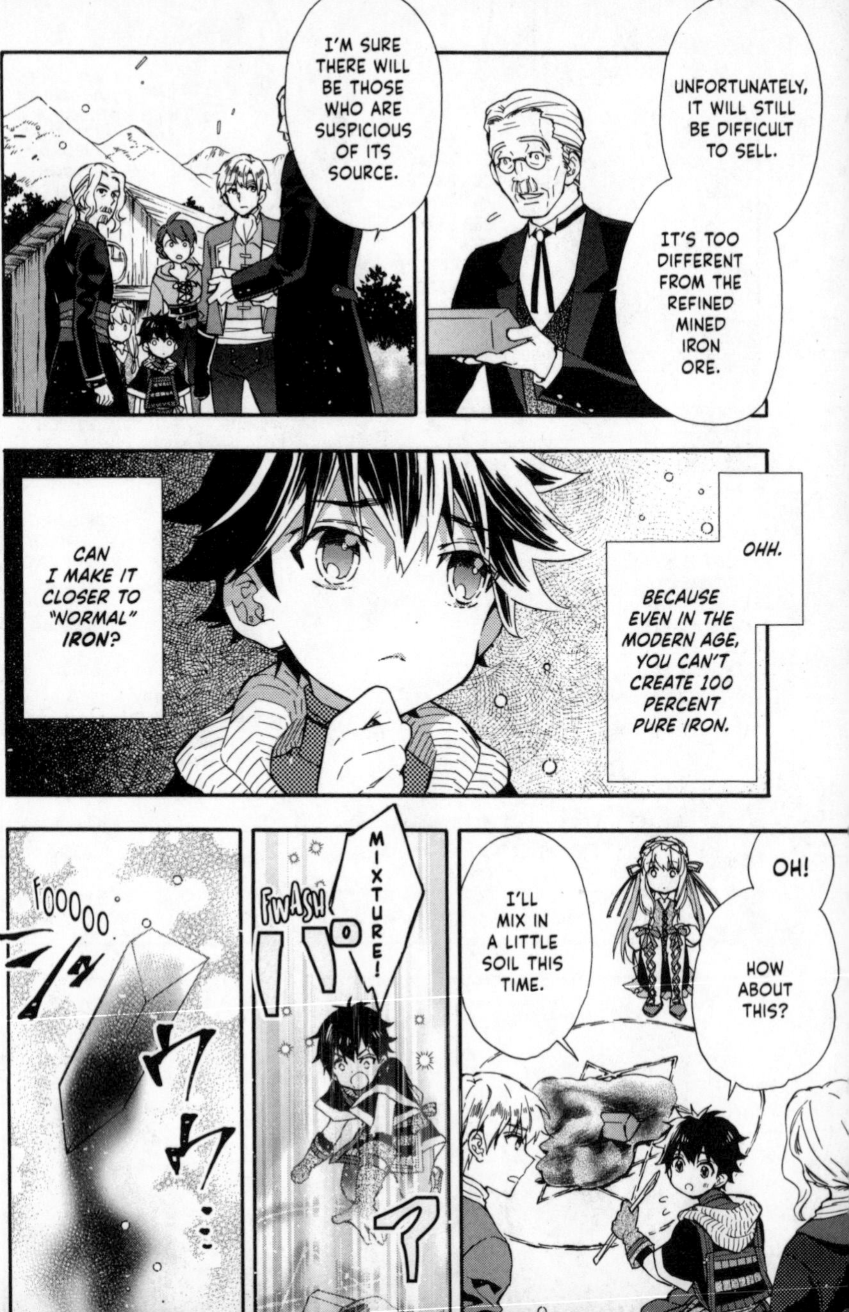
UNFORTUNATELY, IT WILL STILL BE DIFFICULT TO SELL.
IT'S TOO DIFFERENT FROM THE REFINED MINED IRON ORE.
I'M SURE THERE WILL BE THOSE WHO ARE SUSPICIOUS OF ITS SOURCE.
OHH.
BECAUSE EVEN IN THE MODERN AGE, YOU CAN'T CREATE 100 PERCENT PURE IRON.
CAN I MAKE IT CLOSER TO "NORMAL" IRON?
OH!
HOW ABOUT THIS?
I'LL MIX IN A LITTLE SOIL THIS TIME.
MIXTURE!
FWASH
FOOOOO

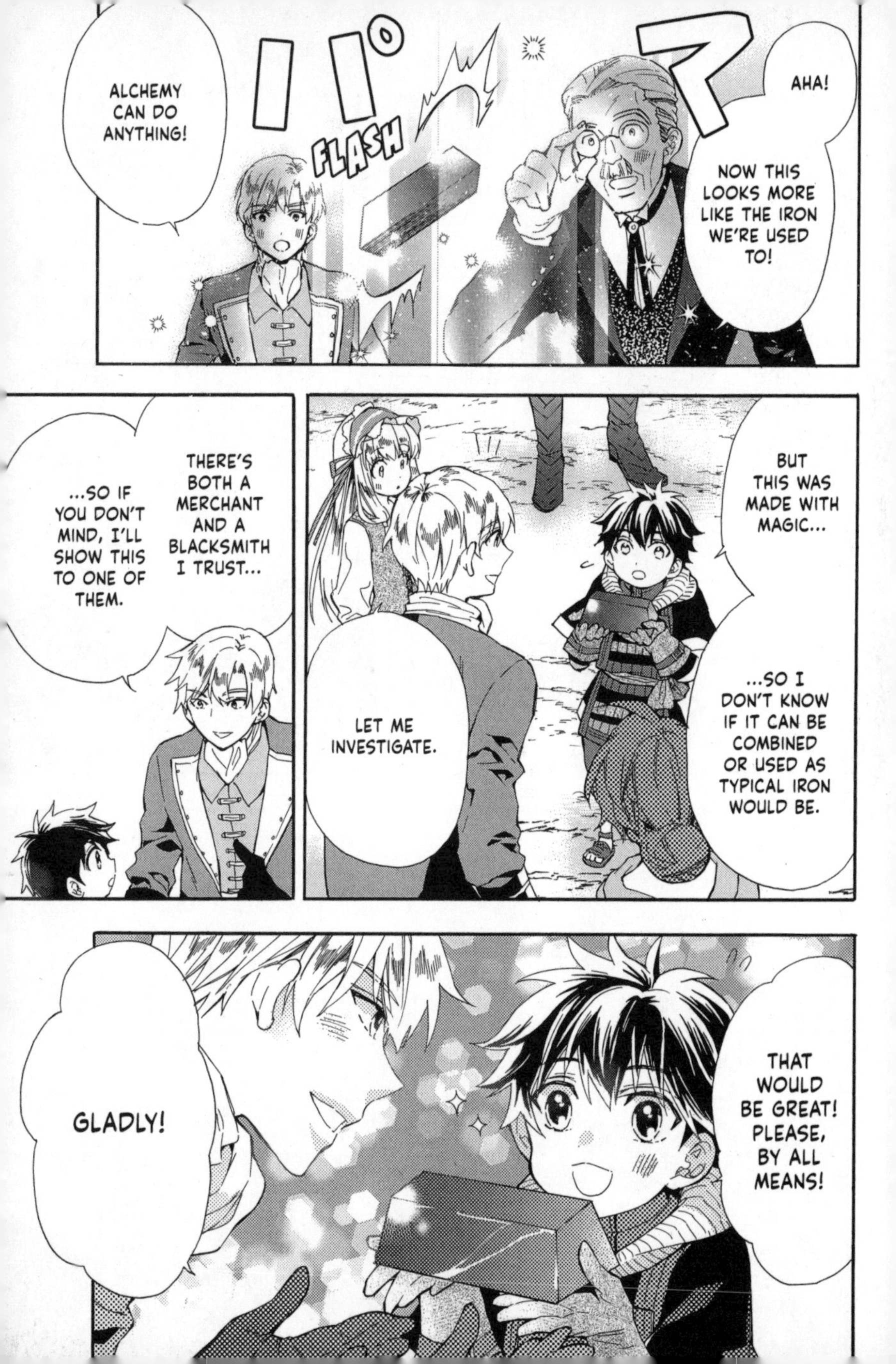
AHA!
NOW THIS LOOKS MORE LIKE THE IRON WE'RE USED TO!
FLASH
ALCHEMY CAN DO ANYTHING!
BUT THIS WAS MADE WITH MAGIC...
...SO I DON'T KNOW IF IT CAN BE COMBINED OR USED AS TYPICAL IRON WOULD BE.
LET ME INVESTIGATE.
THERE'S BOTH A MERCHANT AND A BLACKSMITH I TRUST...
...SO IF YOU DON'T MIND, I'LL SHOW THIS TO ONE OF THEM.
THAT WOULD BE GREAT! PLEASE, BY ALL MEANS!
GLADLY!

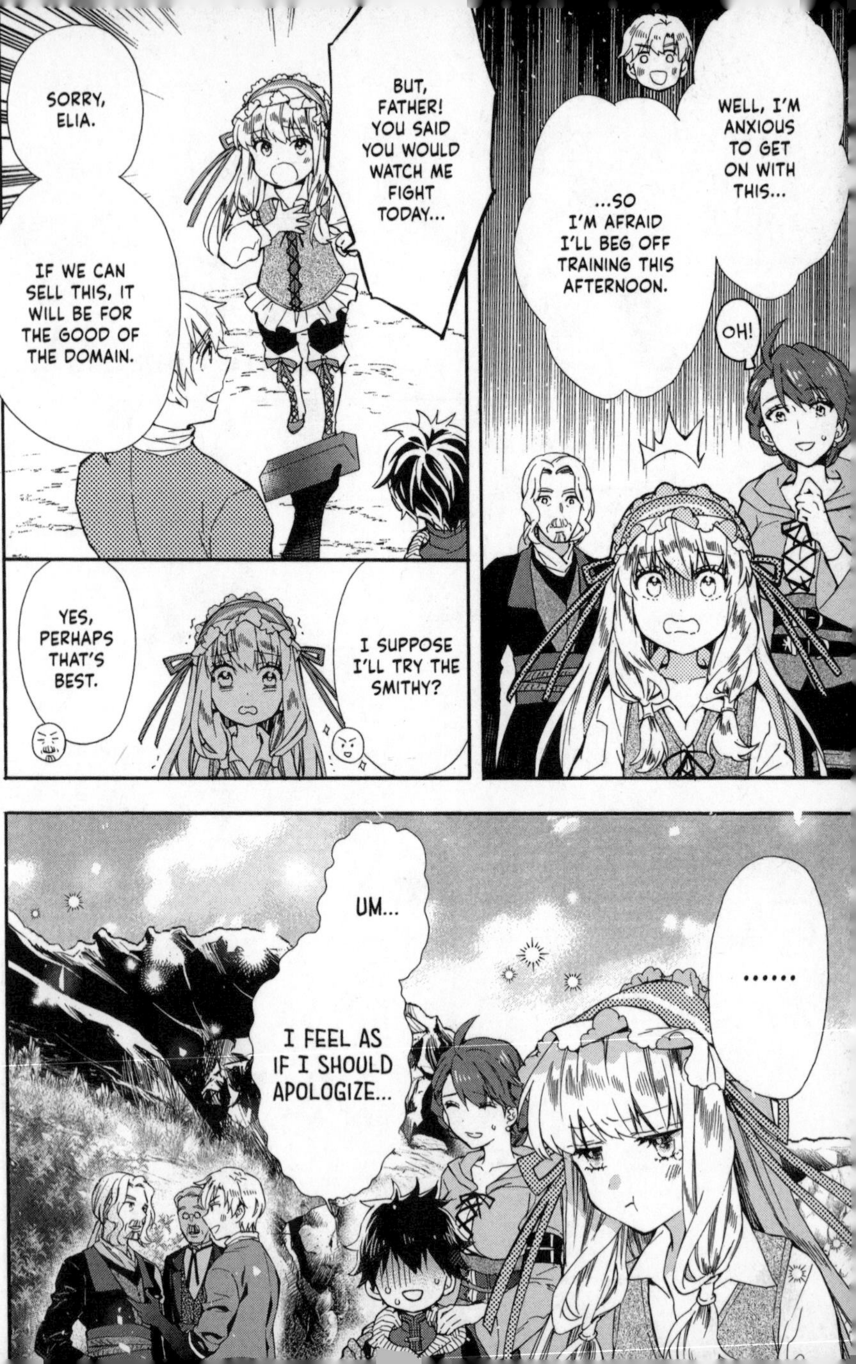
WELL, I'M ANXIOUS TO GET ON WITH THIS...
...SO I'M AFRAID I'LL BEG OFF TRAINING THIS AFTERNOON.
OH!
BUT, FATHER! YOU SAID YOU WOULD WATCH ME FIGHT TODAY...
SORRY, ELIA.
IF WE CAN SELL THIS, IT WILL BE FOR THE GOOD OF THE DOMAIN.
I SUPPOSE I'LL TRY THE SMITHY?
YES, PERHAPS THAT'S BEST.
......
UM...
I FEEL AS IF I SHOULD APOLOGIZE...

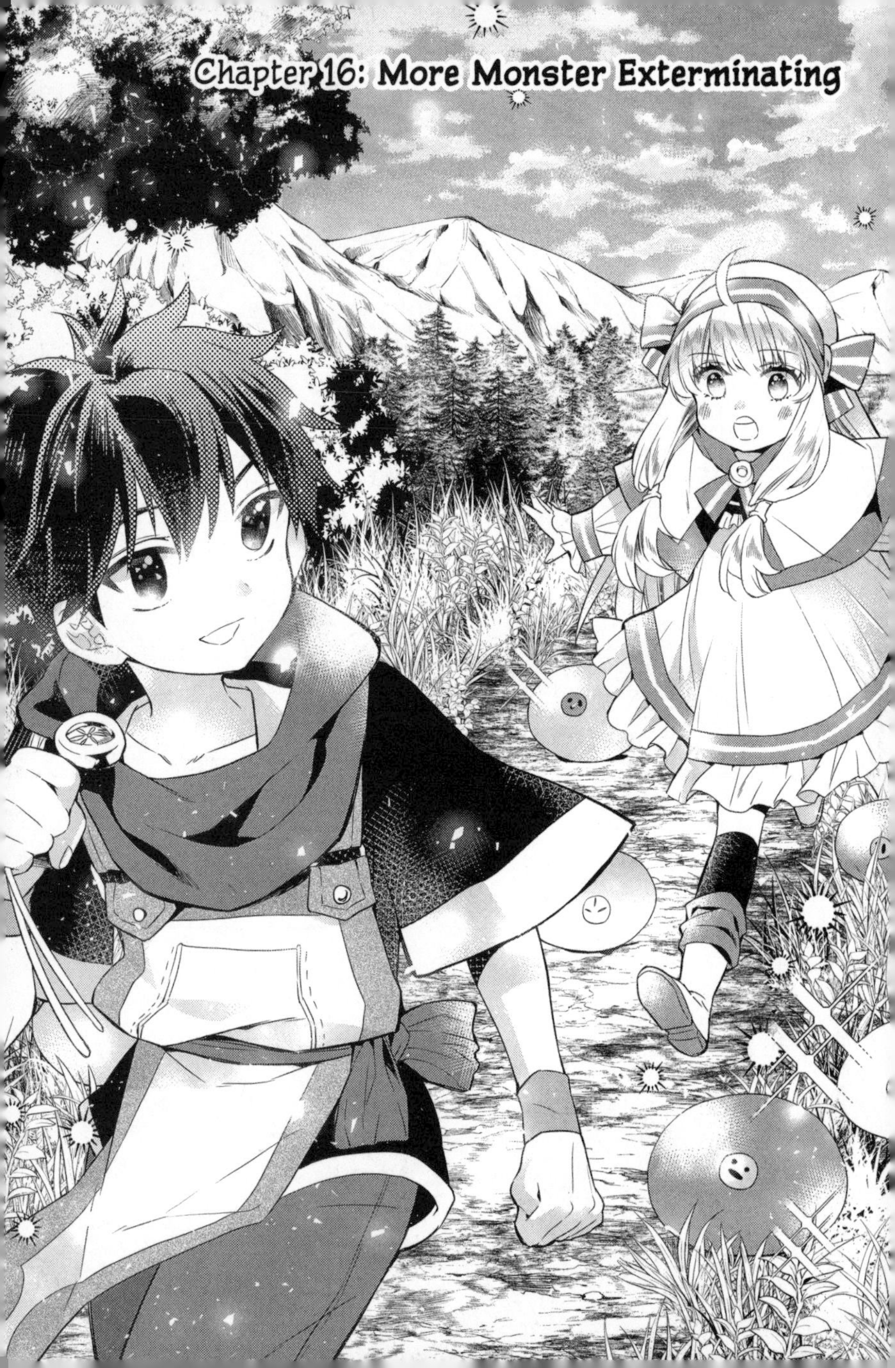
Chapter 16: More Monster Exterminating

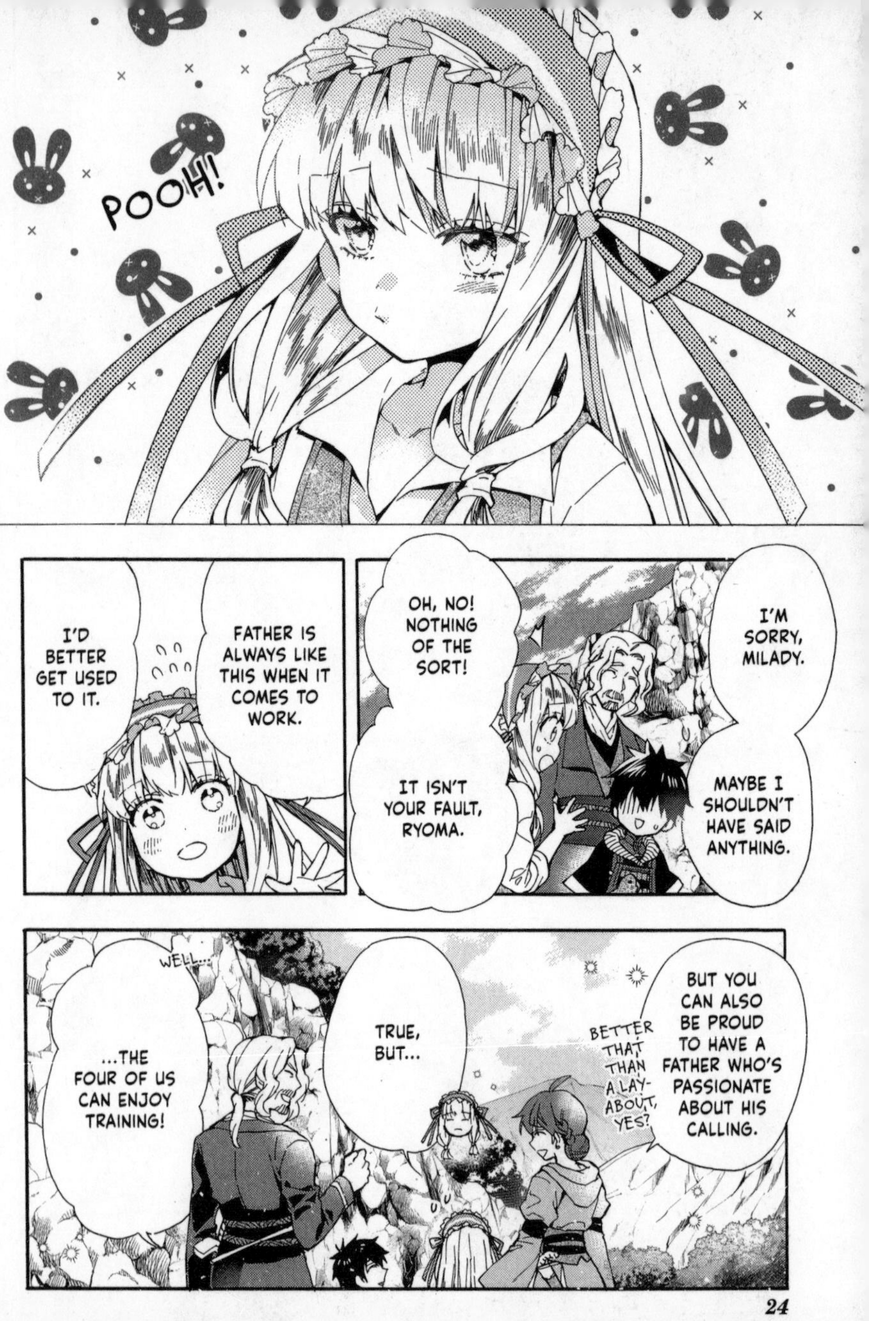
POOH!
I'M SORRY, MILADY.
MAYBE I SHOULDN'T HAVE SAID ANYTHING.
OH, NO! NOTHING OF THE SORT!
IT ISN'T YOUR FAULT, RYOMA.
FATHER IS ALWAYS LIKE THIS WHEN IT COMES TO WORK.
I'D BETTER GET USED TO IT.
BUT YOU CAN ALSO BE PROUD TO HAVE A FATHER WHO'S PASSIONATE ABOUT HIS CALLING.
BETTER THAT THAN A LAY-ABOUT, YES?
TRUE, BUT...
WELL...
...THE FOUR OF US CAN ENJOY TRAINING!

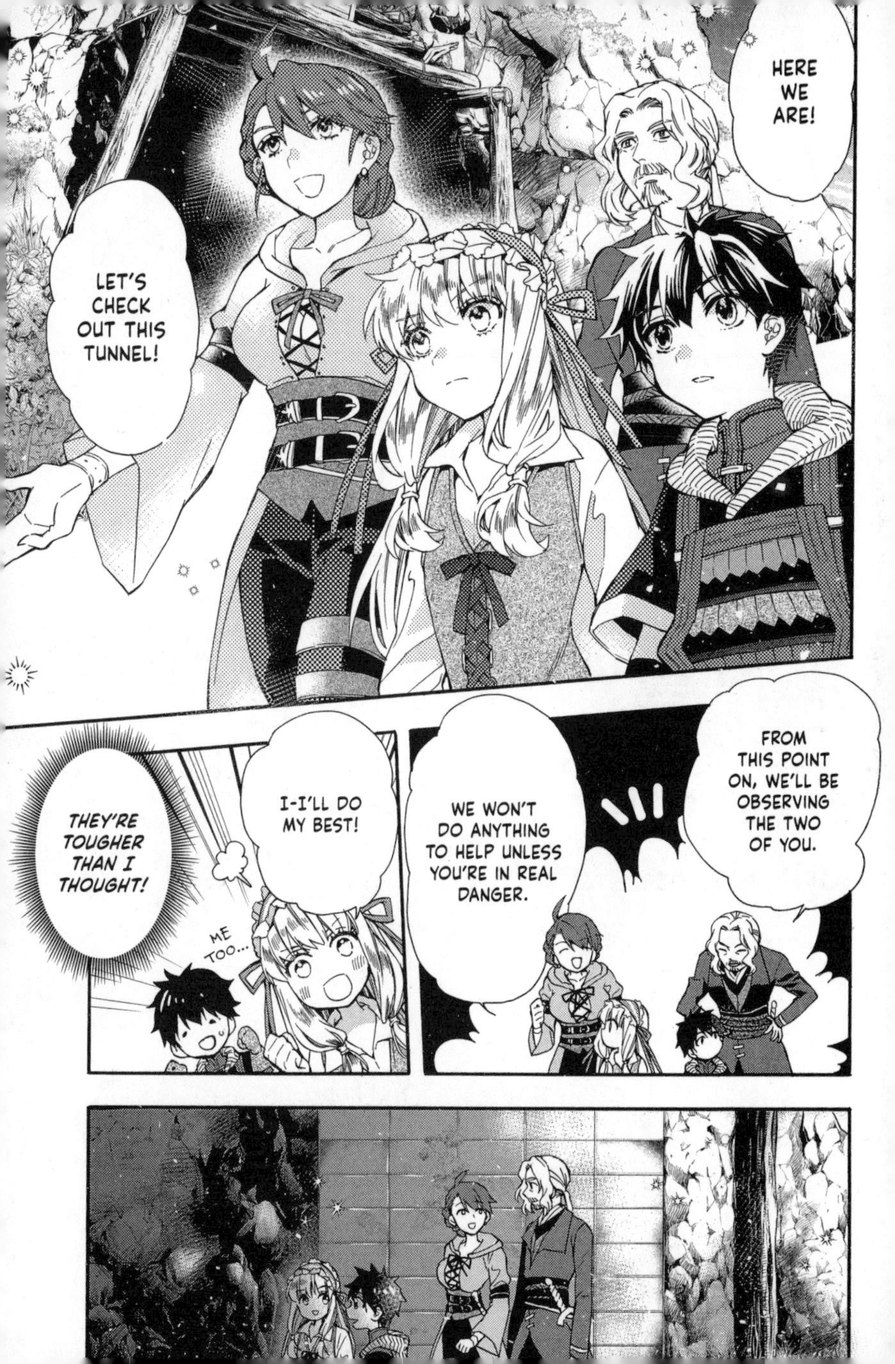
HERE WE ARE!
LET'S CHECK OUT THIS TUNNEL!
FROM THIS POINT ON, WE'LL BE OBSERVING THE TWO OF YOU.
WE WON'T DO ANYTHING TO HELP UNLESS YOU'RE IN REAL DANGER.
I-I'LL DO MY BEST!
ME TOO...
THEY'RE TOUGHER THAN I THOUGHT!

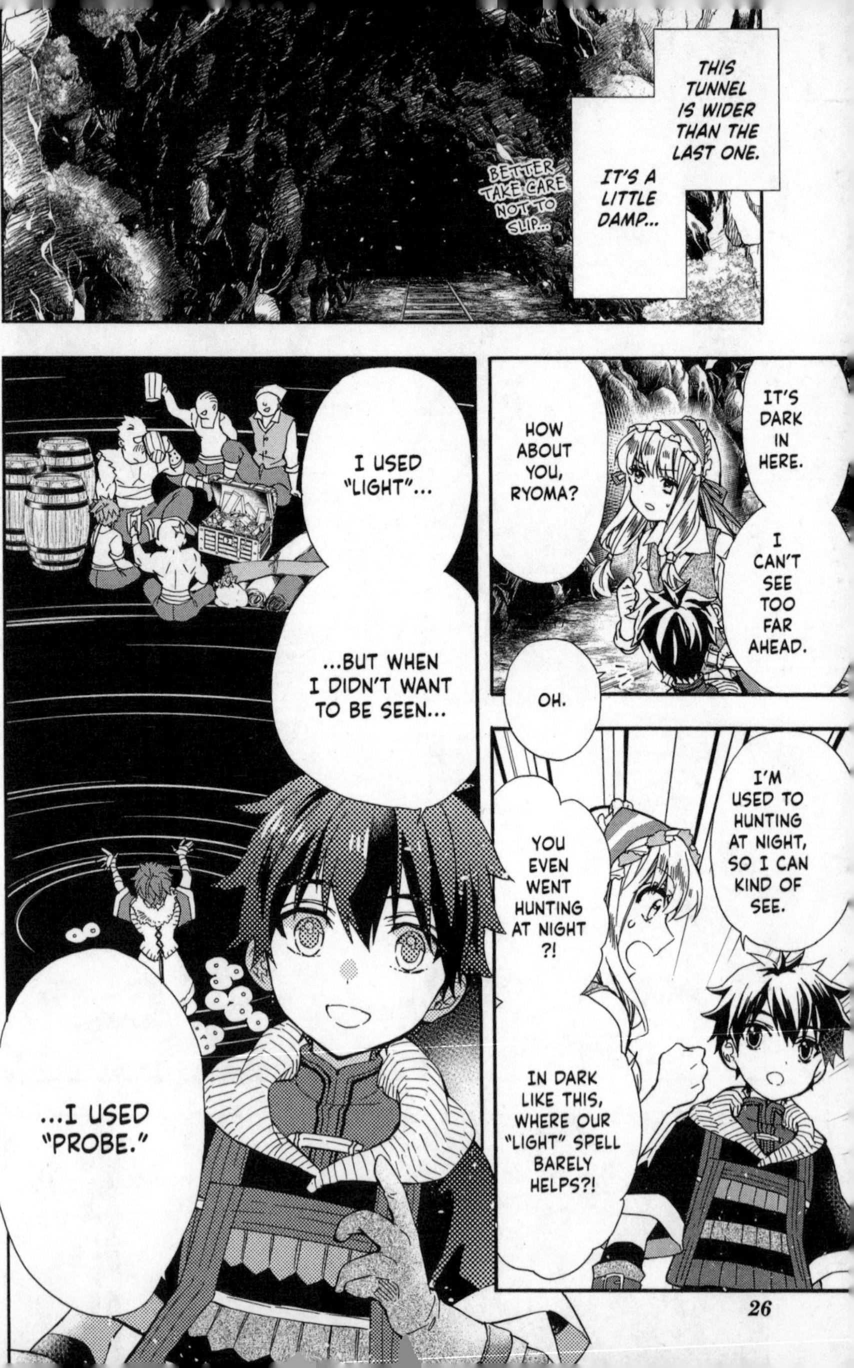
THIS TUNNEL IS WIDER THAN THE LAST ONE.
IT'S A LITTLE DAMP...
BETTER TAKE CARE NOT TO SLIP...
IT'S DARK IN HERE.
I CAN'T SEE TOO FAR AHEAD.
HOW ABOUT YOU, RYOMA?
OH.
I'M USED TO HUNTING AT NIGHT, SO I CAN KIND OF SEE.
YOU EVEN WENT HUNTING AT NIGHT?!
IN DARK LIKE THIS, WHERE OUR "LIGHT" SPELL BARELY HELPS?!
I USED "LIGHT"...
...BUT WHEN I DIDN'T WANT TO BE SEEN...
...I USED "PROBE."

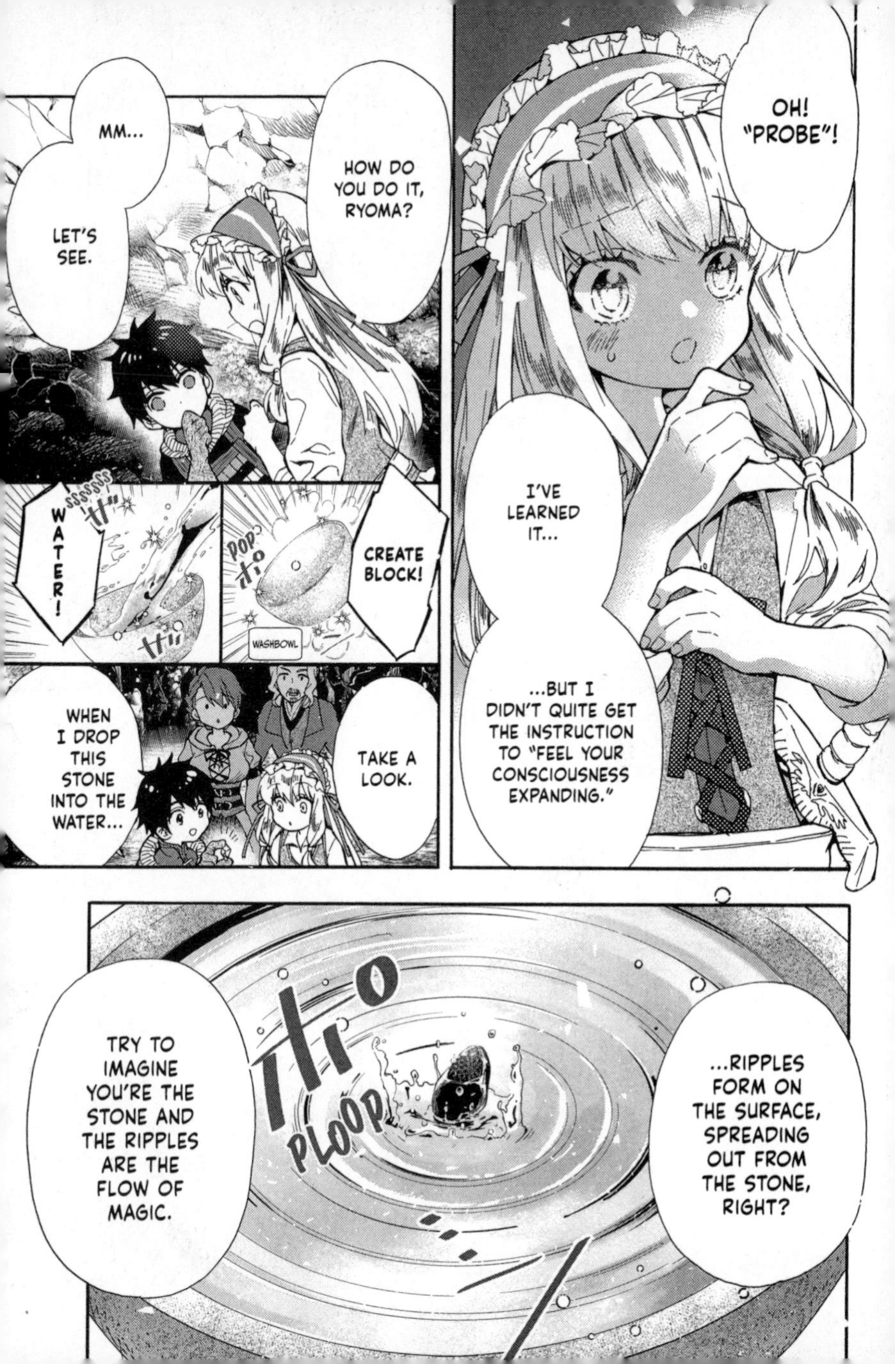
OH! "PROBE"!
I'VE LEARNED IT...
...BUT I DIDN'T QUITE GET THE INSTRUCTION TO "FEEL YOUR CONSCIOUSNESS EXPANDING."
HOW DO YOU DO IT, RYOMA?
MM...
LET'S SEE.
CREATE BLOCK!
POP
WASHBOWL
SSSSSS
WATER!
TAKE A LOOK.
WHEN I DROP THIS STONE INTO THE WATER...
...RIPPLES FORM ON THE SURFACE, SPREADING OUT FROM THE STONE, RIGHT?
PLOOP
TRY TO IMAGINE YOU'RE THE STONE AND THE RIPPLES ARE THE FLOW OF MAGIC.

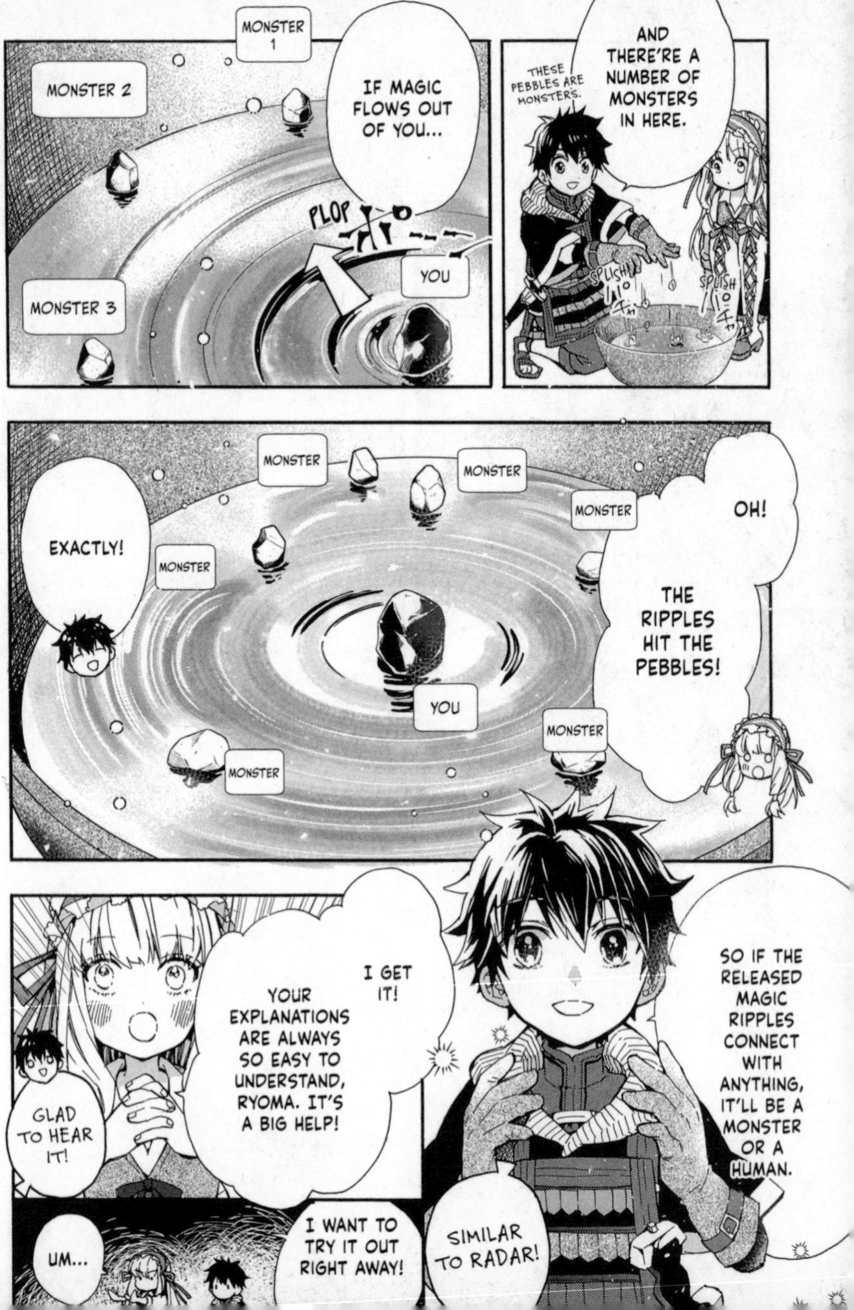
THESE PEBBLES ARE MONSTERS.
AND THERE'RE A NUMBER OF MONSTERS IN HERE.
SPLISH
SPLISH
MONSTER 1
IF MAGIC FLOWS OUT OF YOU...
MONSTER 2
PLOP
YOU
MONSTER 3
OH!
THE RIPPLES HIT THE PEBBLES!
MONSTER
MONSTER
MONSTER
MONSTER
YOU
MONSTER
MONSTER
EXACTLY!
SO IF THE RELEASED MAGIC RIPPLES CONNECT WITH ANYTHING, IT'LL BE A MONSTER OR A HUMAN.
SIMILAR TO RADAR!
I GET IT!
YOUR EXPLANATIONS ARE ALWAYS SO EASY TO UNDERSTAND, RYOMA. IT'S A BIG HELP!
GLAD TO HEAR IT!
I WANT TO TRY IT OUT RIGHT AWAY!
UM...

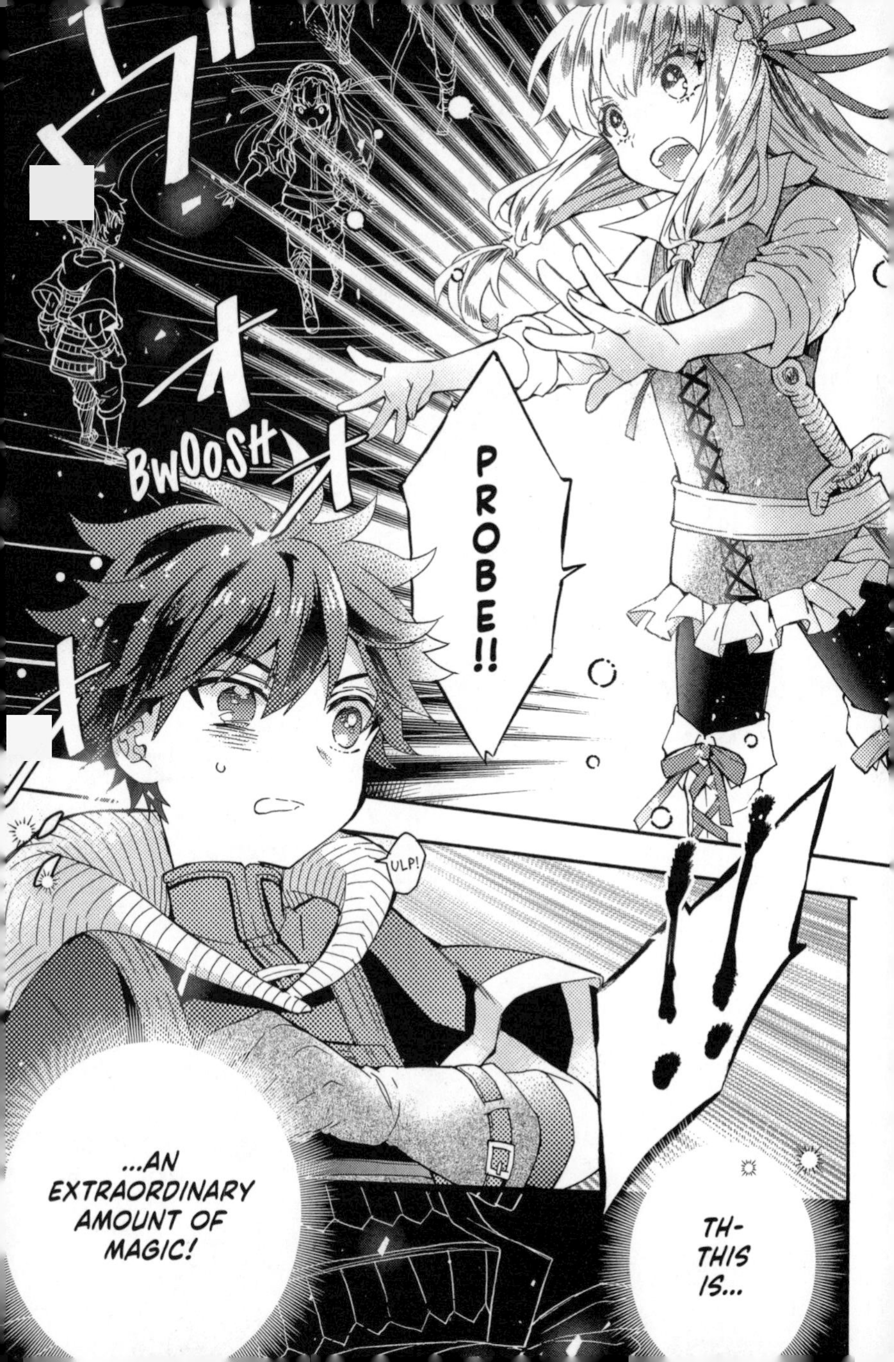
PROBE!!
BWOOSH
ULP!
TH-THIS IS...
...AN EXTRAORDINARY AMOUNT OF MAGIC!

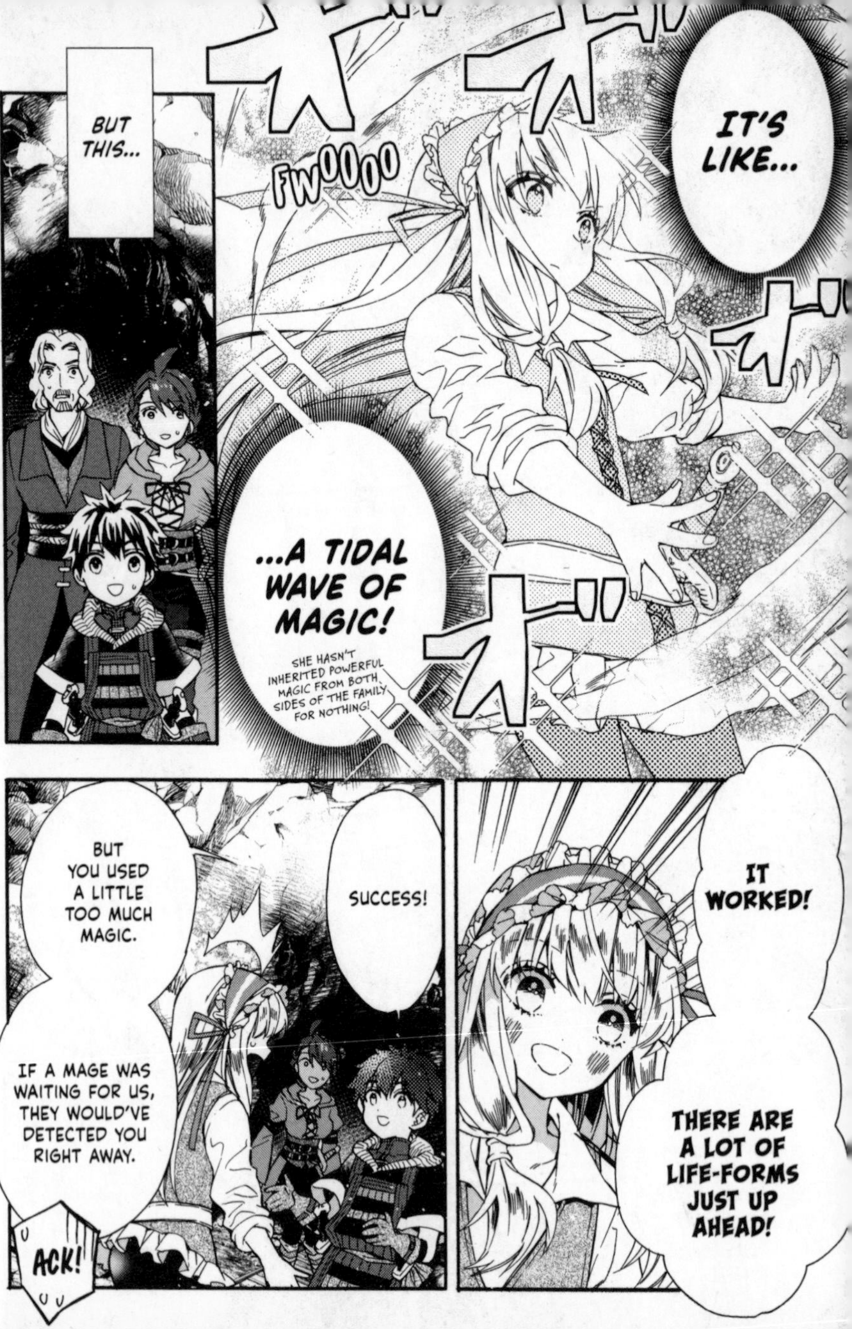
FWOOOO
IT'S LIKE...
...A TIDAL WAVE OF MAGIC!
SHE HASN'T INHERITED POWERFUL MAGIC FROM BOTH SIDES OF THE FAMILY FOR NOTHING!
BUT THIS...
IT WORKED!
THERE ARE A LOT OF LIFE-FORMS JUST UP AHEAD!
SUCCESS!
BUT YOU USED A LITTLE TOO MUCH MAGIC.
IF A MAGE WAS WAITING FOR US, THEY WOULD'VE DETECTED YOU RIGHT AWAY.
ACK!

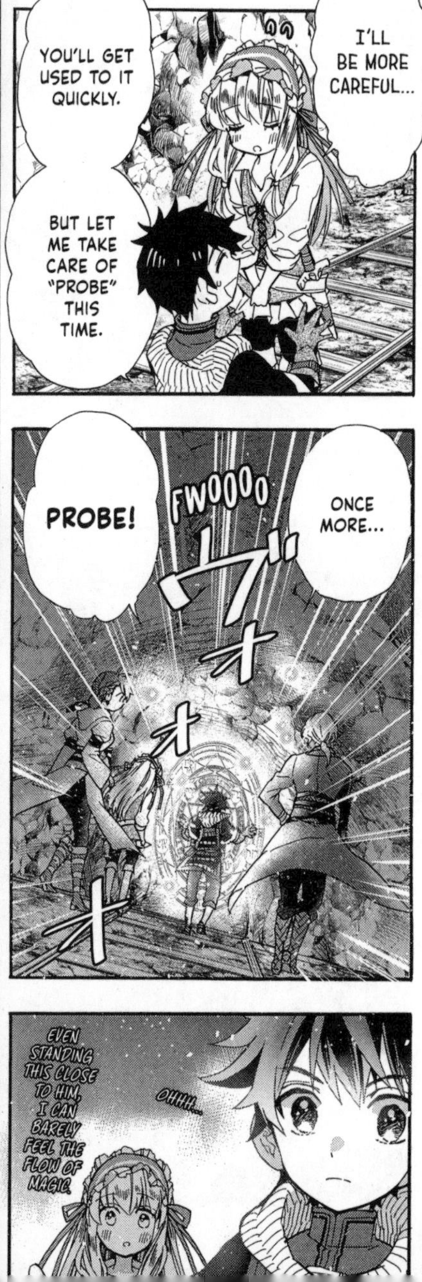
I'LL BE MORE CAREFUL...
YOU'LL GET USED TO IT QUICKLY.
BUT LET ME TAKE CARE OF "PROBE" THIS TIME.
ONCE MORE...
FWOOOO
PROBE!
OHHH...
EVEN STANDING THIS CLOSE TO HIM, I CAN BARELY FEEL THE FLOW OF MAGIC.
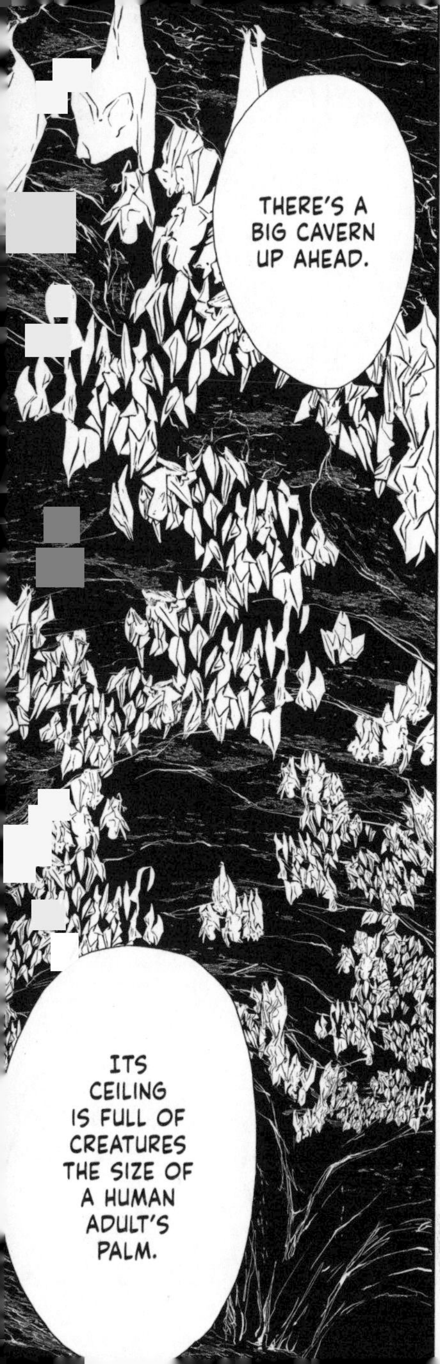
THERE'S A BIG CAVERN UP AHEAD.
ITS CEILING IS FULL OF CREATURES THE SIZE OF A HUMAN ADULT'S PALM.

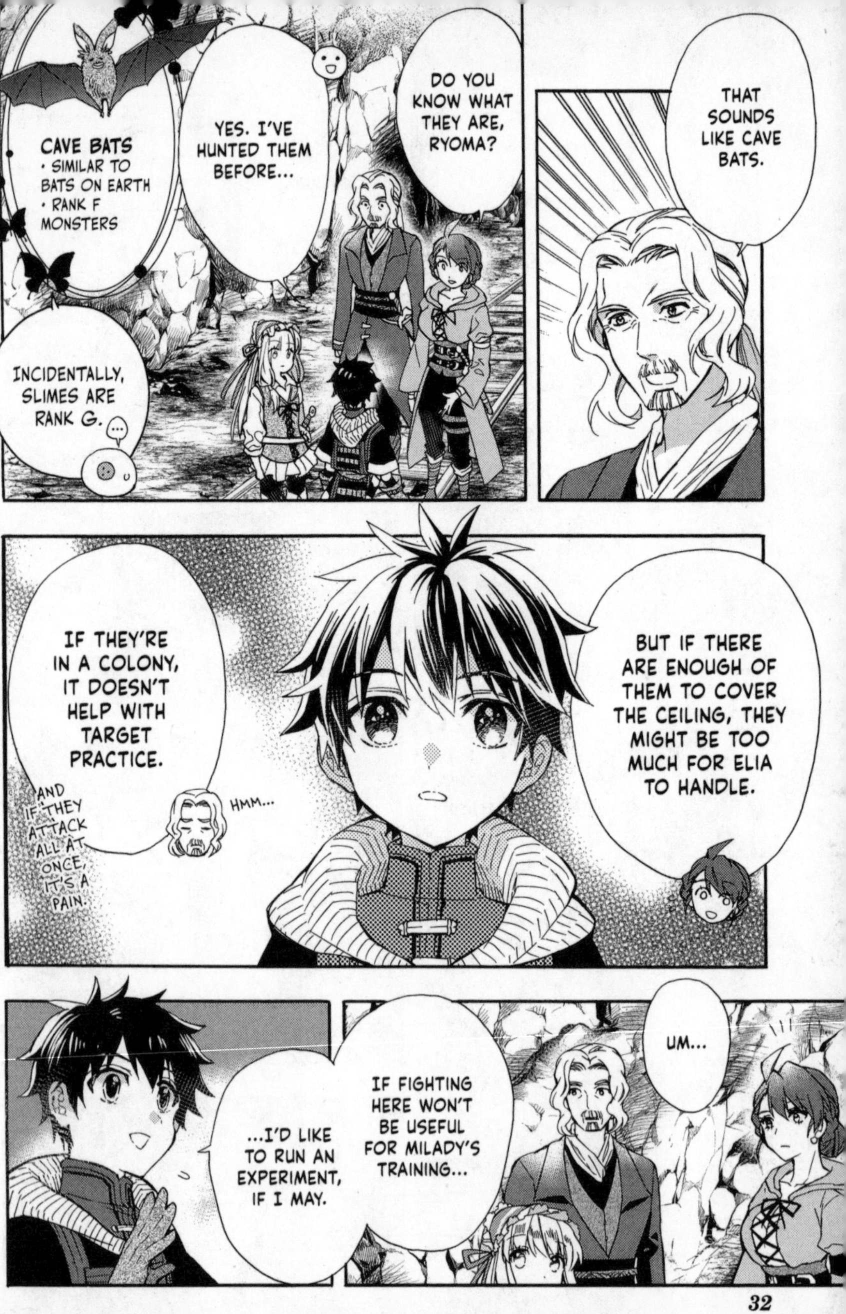
THAT SOUNDS LIKE CAVE BATS.
DO YOU KNOW WHAT THEY ARE, RYOMA?
YES. I'VE HUNTED THEM BEFORE...
CAVE BATS
• SIMILAR TO BATS ON EARTH
• RANK F MONSTERS
INCIDENTALLY, SLIMES ARE RANK G.
...
BUT IF THERE ARE ENOUGH OF THEM TO COVER THE CEILING, THEY MIGHT BE TOO MUCH FOR ELIA TO HANDLE.
IF THEY'RE IN A COLONY, IT DOESN'T HELP WITH TARGET PRACTICE.
HMM...
AND IF THEY ATTACK ALL AT ONCE, IT'S A PAIN.
UM...
IF FIGHTING HERE WON'T BE USEFUL FOR MILADY'S TRAINING...
...I'D LIKE TO RUN AN EXPERIMENT, IF I MAY.

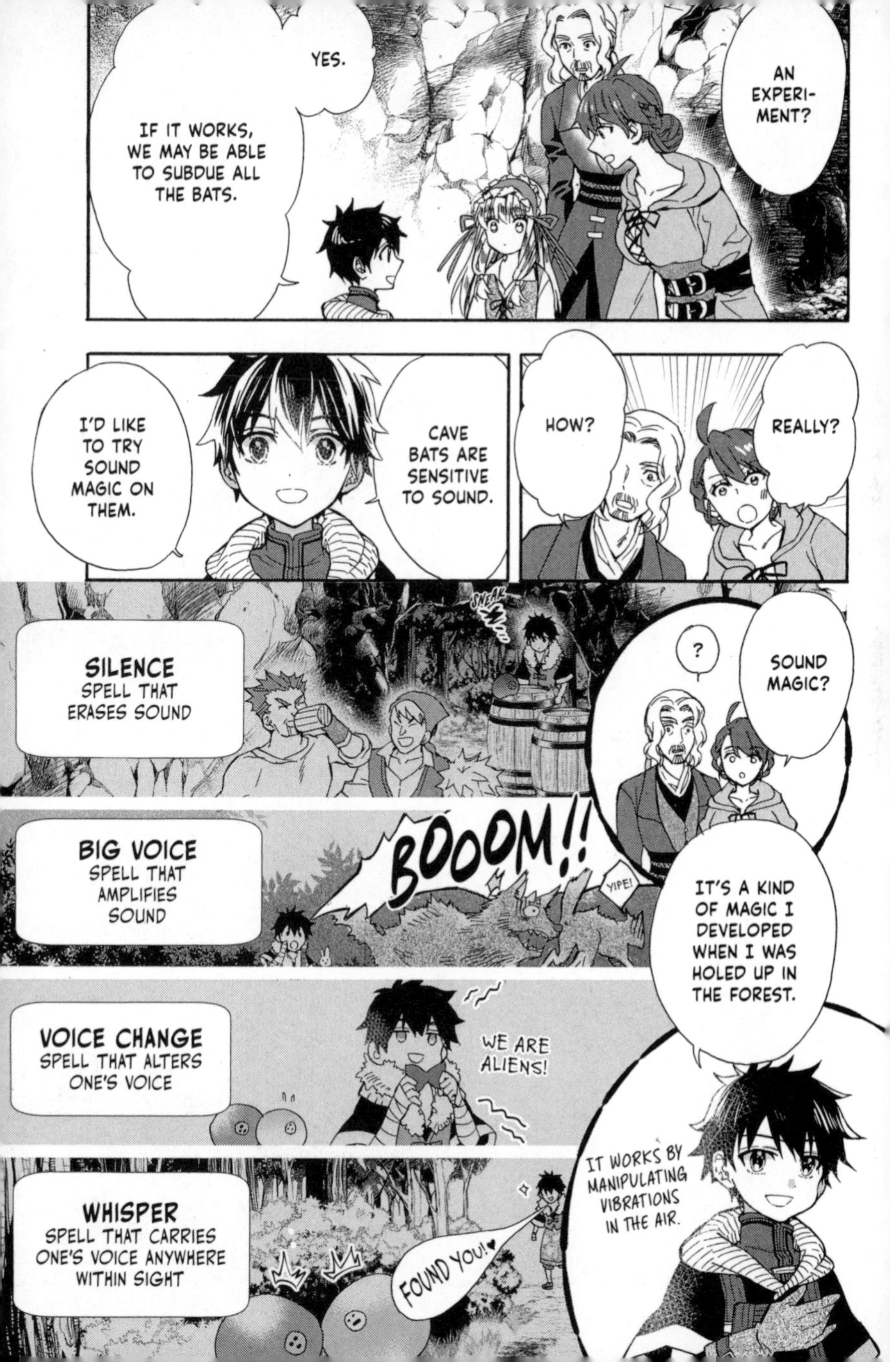

AN EXPERIMENT?
YES.
IF IT WORKS, WE MAY BE ABLE TO SUBDUE ALL THE BATS.
REALLY?
HOW?
CAVE BATS ARE SENSITIVE TO SOUND.
I'D LIKE TO TRY SOUND MAGIC ON THEM.
SOUND MAGIC?
?
IT'S A KIND OF MAGIC I DEVELOPED WHEN I WAS HOLED UP IN THE FOREST.
IT WORKS BY MANIPULATING VIBRATIONS IN THE AIR.
SNEAK
SILENCE
SPELL THAT ERASES SOUND
BOOOM!!
YIPE!
BIG VOICE
SPELL THAT AMPLIFIES SOUND
WE ARE ALIENS!
VOICE CHANGE
SPELL THAT ALTERS ONE'S VOICE
FOUND YOU!♥
WHISPER
SPELL THAT CARRIES ONE'S VOICE ANYWHERE WITHIN SIGHT

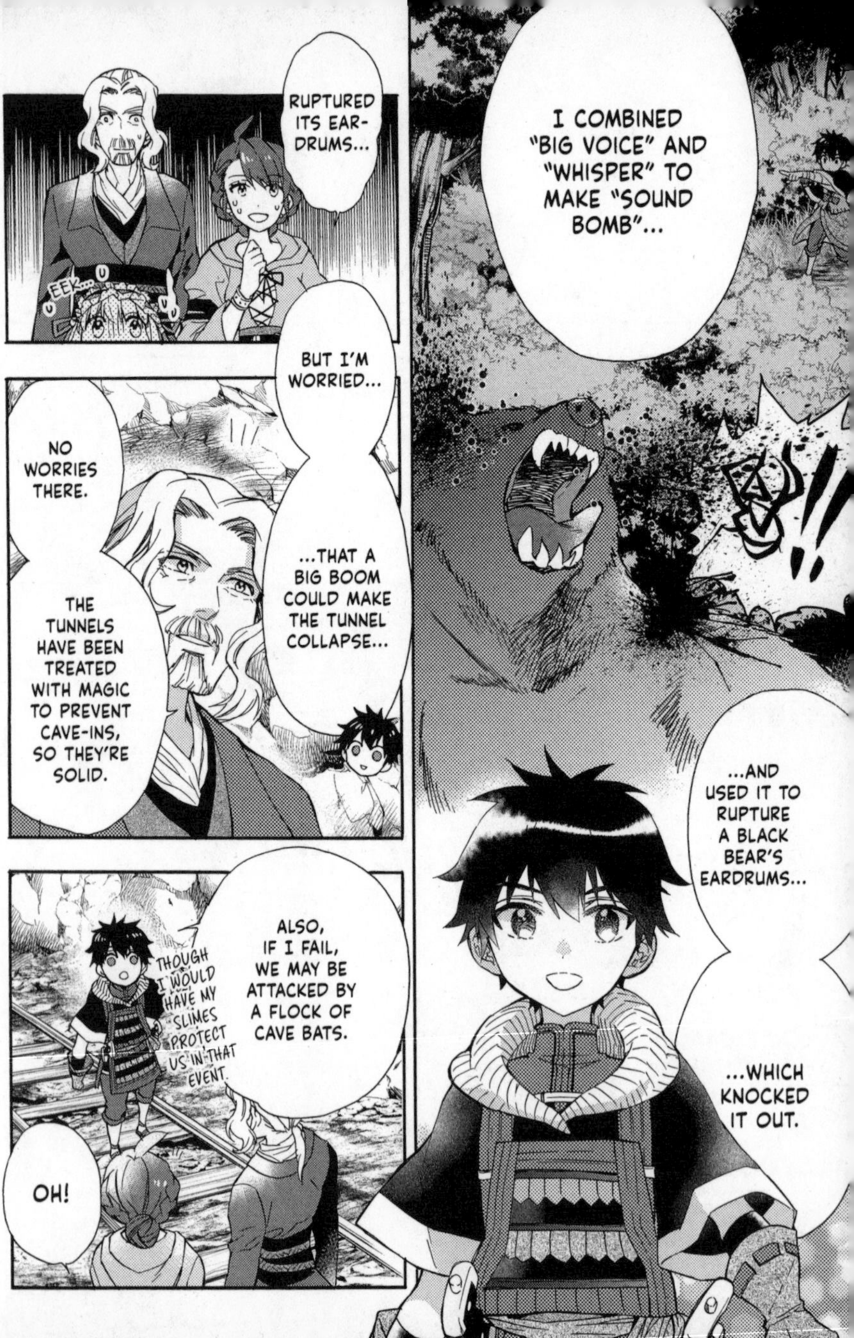
I COMBINED "BIG VOICE" AND "WHISPER" TO MAKE "SOUND BOMB"...
!!
...AND USED IT TO RUPTURE A BLACK BEAR'S EARDRUMS...
...WHICH KNOCKED IT OUT.
RUPTURED ITS EAR-DRUMS...
EEK...
BUT I'M WORRIED...
...THAT A BIG BOOM COULD MAKE THE TUNNEL COLLAPSE...
NO WORRIES THERE.
THE TUNNELS HAVE BEEN TREATED WITH MAGIC TO PREVENT CAVE-INS, SO THEY'RE SOLID.
ALSO, IF I FAIL, WE MAY BE ATTACKED BY A FLOCK OF CAVE BATS.
THOUGH I WOULD HAVE MY SLIMES PROTECT US IN THAT EVENT.
OH!

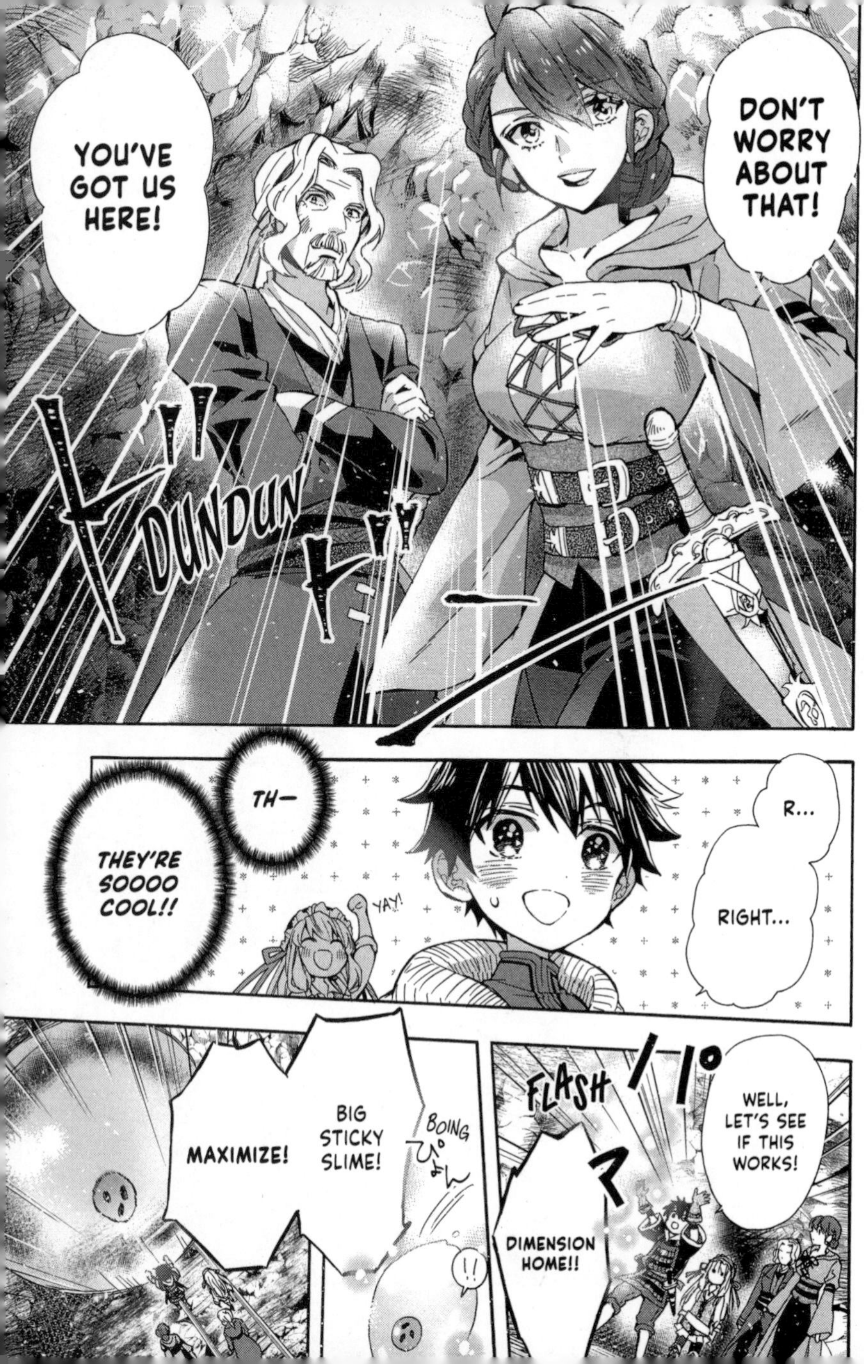
DON'T WORRY ABOUT THAT!
YOU'VE GOT US HERE!
DUNDUN
R...
RIGHT...
TH—
THEY'RE SOOOO COOL!!
YAY!
WELL, LET'S SEE IF THIS WORKS!
FLASH
DIMENSION HOME!!
BIG STICKY SLIME!
BOING
MAXIMIZE!
!!

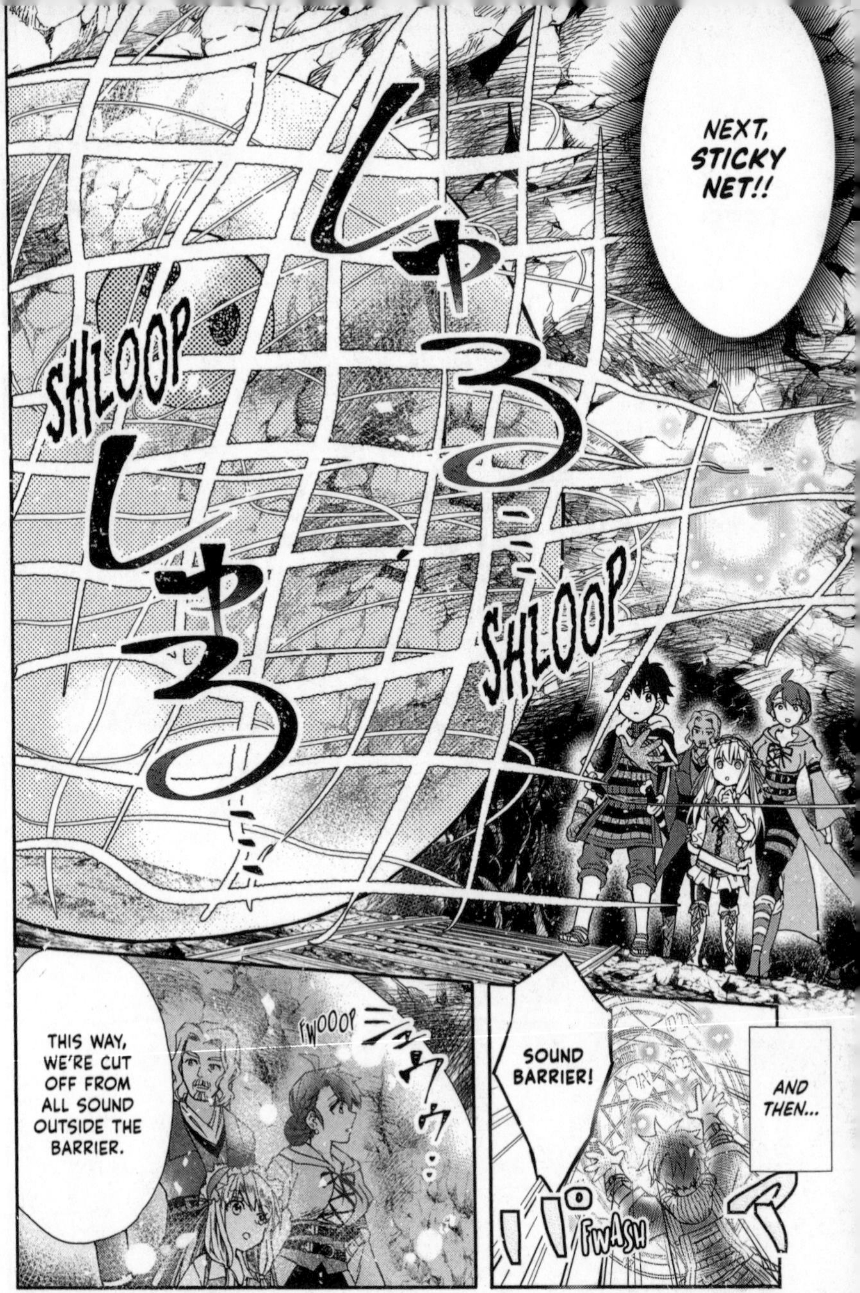
NEXT, STICKY NET!!
しゅるる
SHLOOP
しゅるる
SHLOOP
AND THEN...
SOUND BARRIER!
FWASH
FWOOOP
THIS WAY, WE'RE CUT OFF FROM ALL SOUND OUTSIDE THE BARRIER.

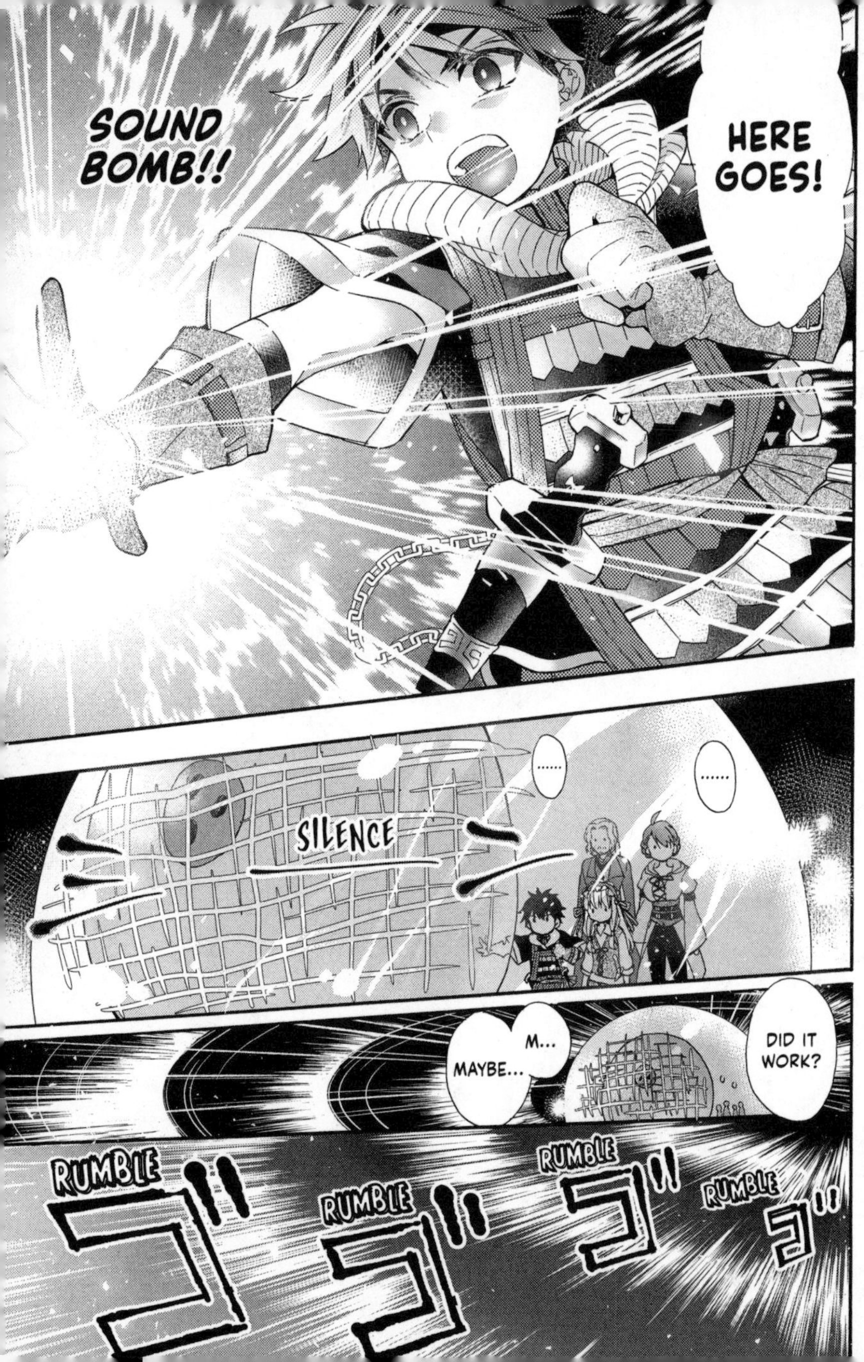
HERE GOES!
SOUND BOMB!!
......
......
SILENCE
DID IT WORK?
M... MAYBE...
RUMBLE
RUMBLE
RUMBLE
RUMBLE
ゴゴゴゴ

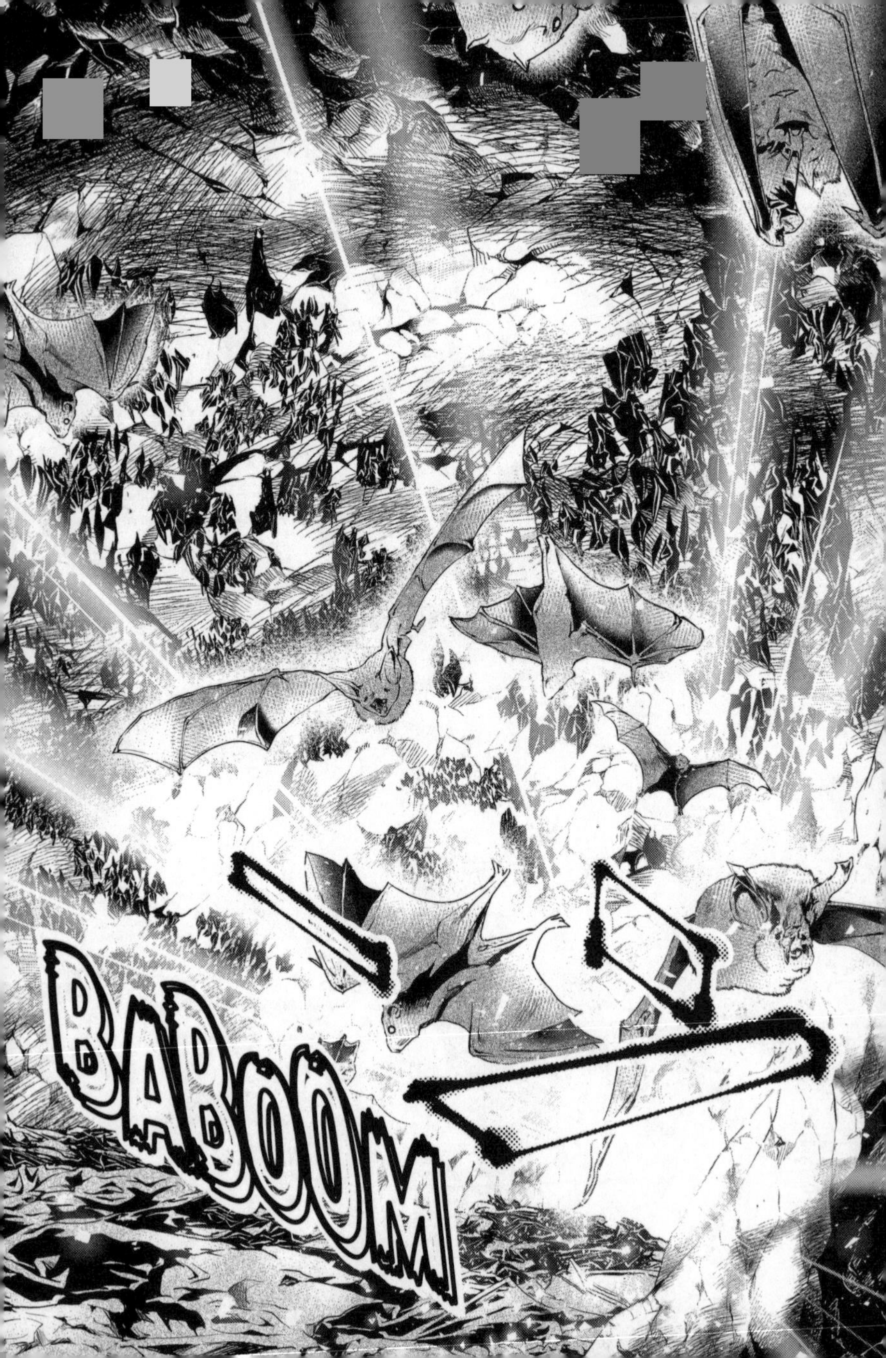
BABOOM

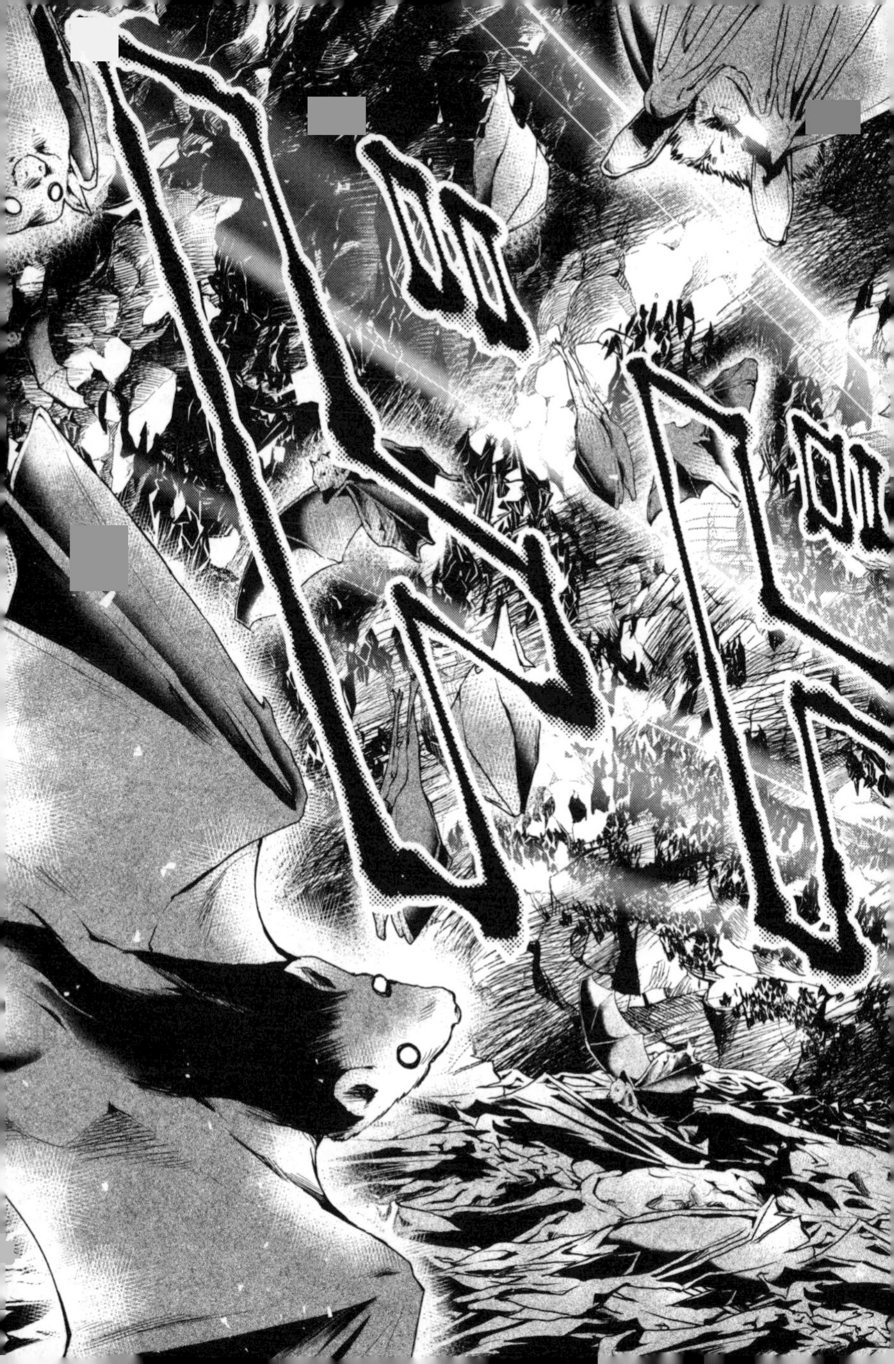

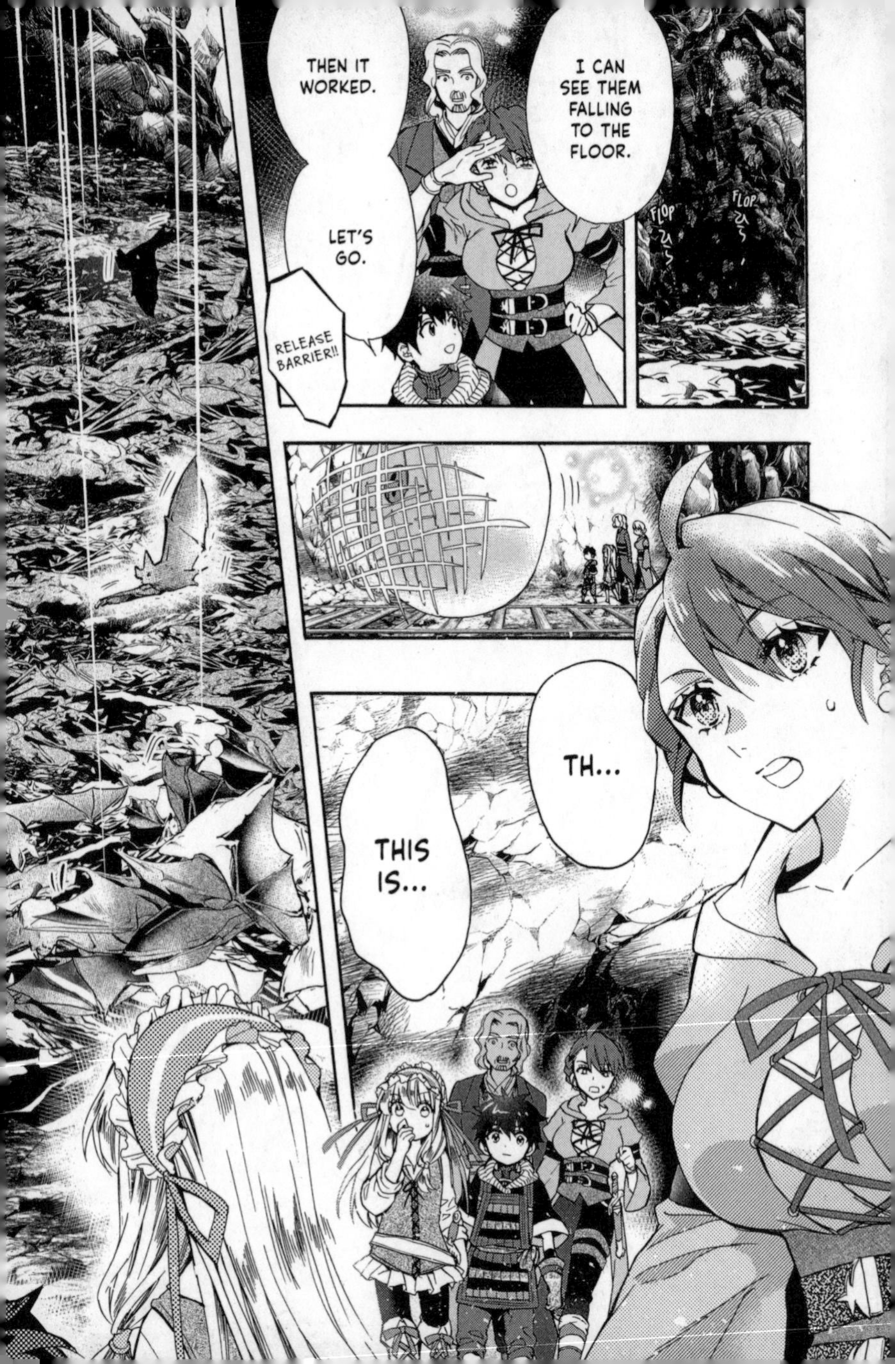
FLOP
FLOP
I CAN SEE THEM FALLING TO THE FLOOR.
THEN IT WORKED.
LET'S GO.
RELEASE BARRIER!!
TH...
THIS IS...

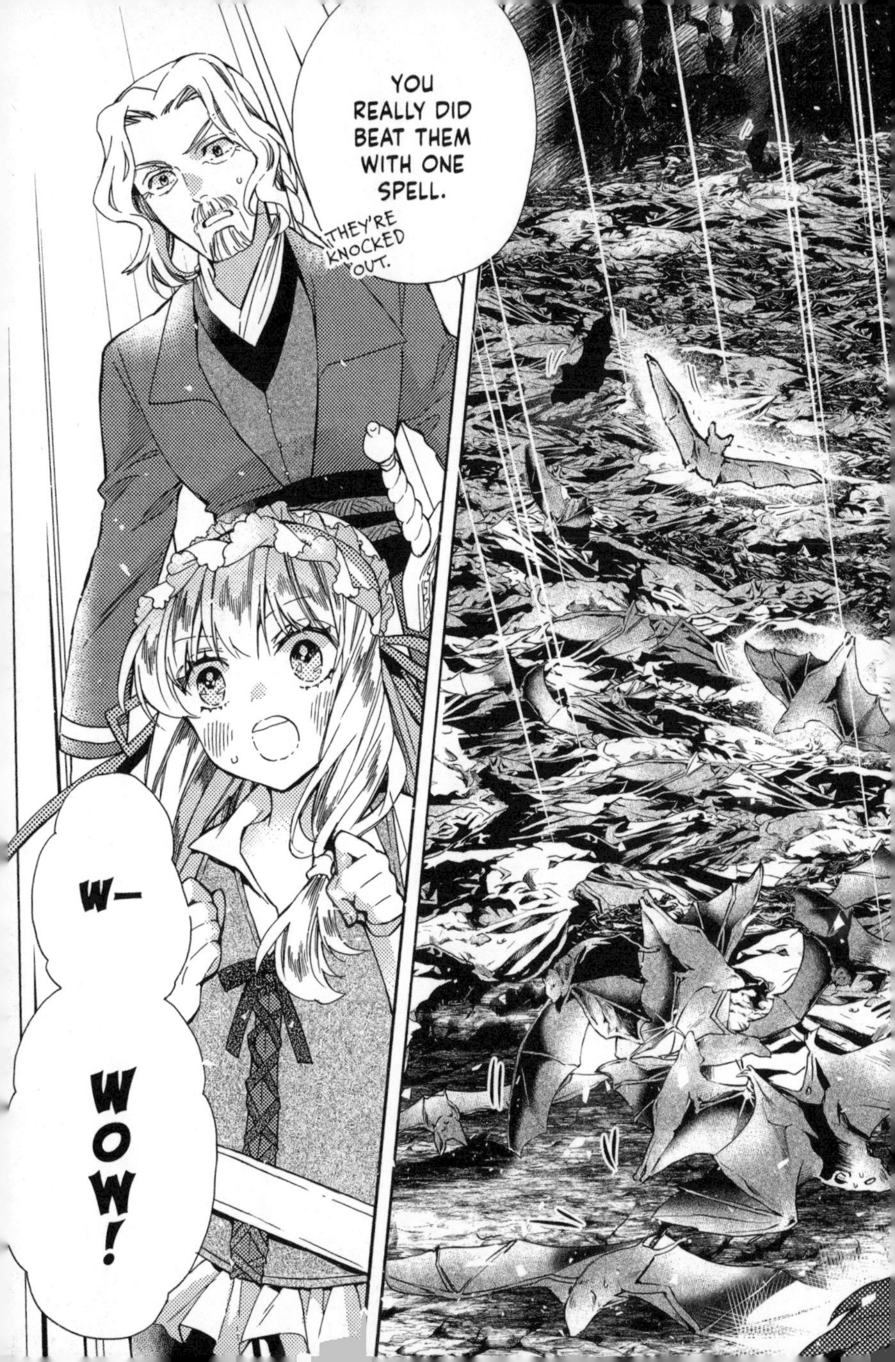
YOU REALLY DID BEAT THEM WITH ONE SPELL.
THEY'RE KNOCKED OUT.
W—
WOW!

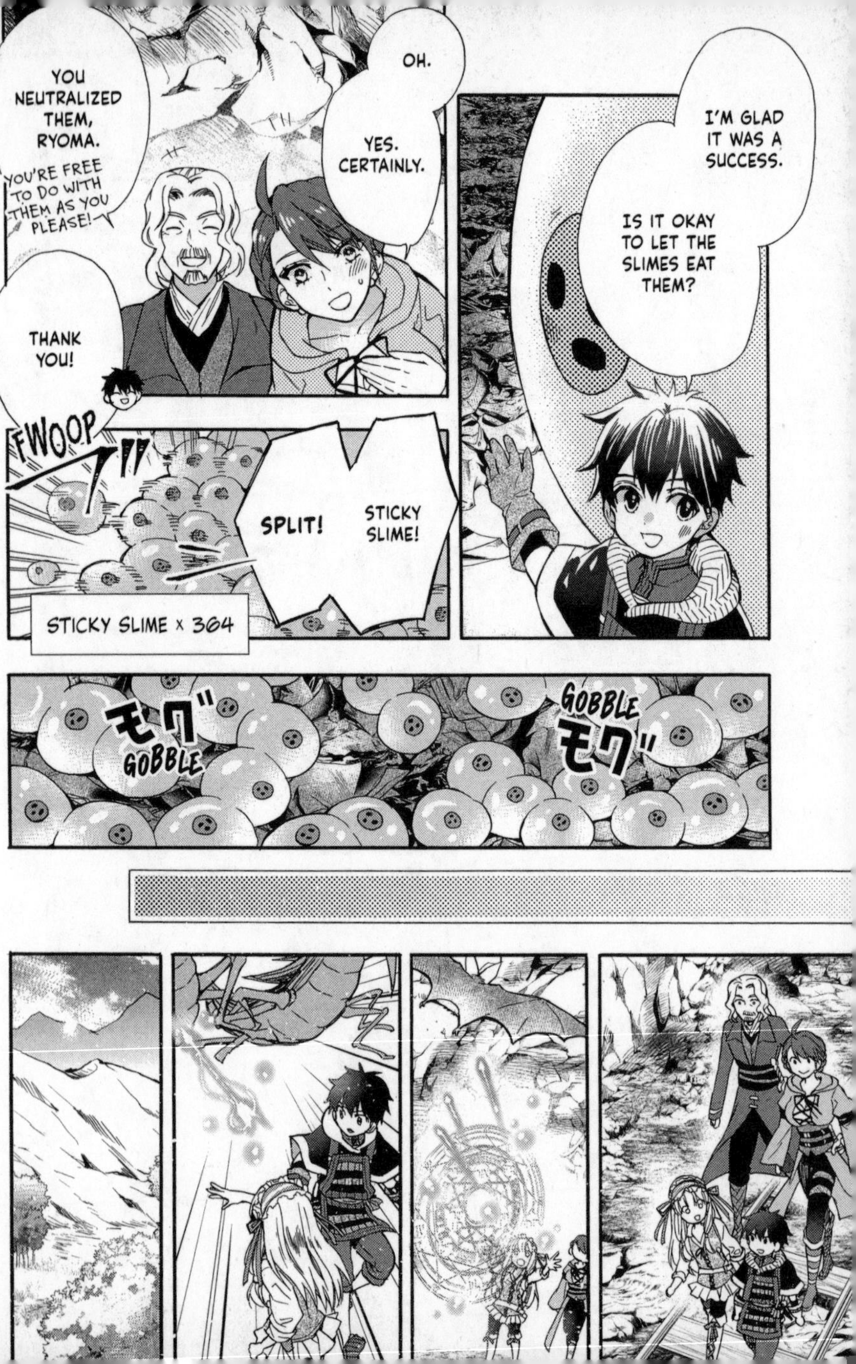

I'M GLAD IT WAS A SUCCESS.
IS IT OKAY TO LET THE SLIMES EAT THEM?
OH.
YES. CERTAINLY.
YOU NEUTRALIZED THEM, RYOMA.
YOU'RE FREE TO DO WITH THEM AS YOU PLEASE!
THANK YOU!
STICKY SLIME!
SPLIT!
FWOOP
STICKY SLIME x 364
GOBBLE
モグ
モグ
GOBBLE

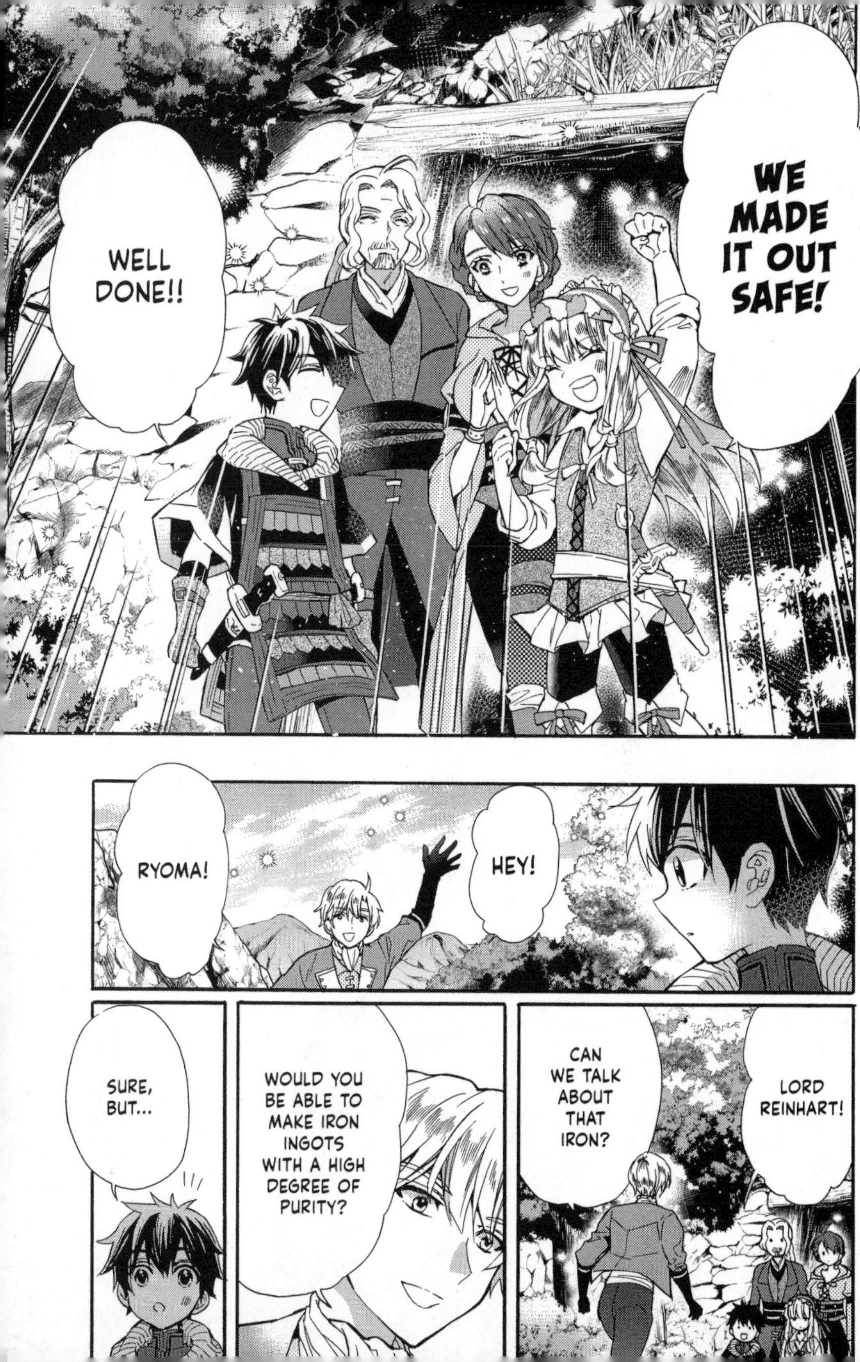
WE MADE IT OUT SAFE!
WELL DONE!!
HEY!
RYOMA!
LORD REINHART!
CAN WE TALK ABOUT THAT IRON?
WOULD YOU BE ABLE TO MAKE IRON INGOTS WITH A HIGH DEGREE OF PURITY?
SURE, BUT...

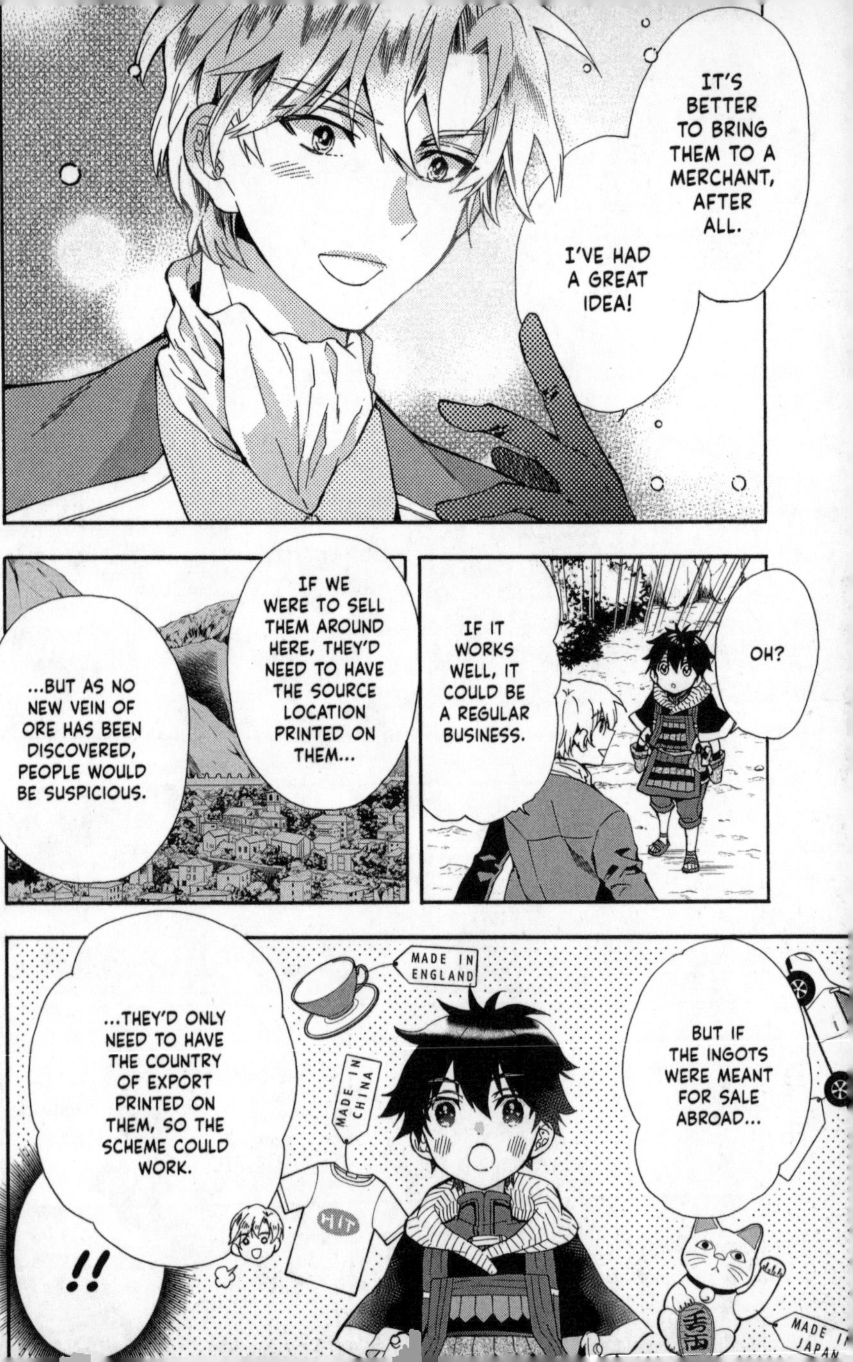
IT'S BETTER TO BRING THEM TO A MERCHANT, AFTER ALL.
I'VE HAD A GREAT IDEA!
OH?
IF IT WORKS WELL, IT COULD BE A REGULAR BUSINESS.
IF WE WERE TO SELL THEM AROUND HERE, THEY'D NEED TO HAVE THE SOURCE LOCATION PRINTED ON THEM...
...BUT AS NO NEW VEIN OF ORE HAS BEEN DISCOVERED, PEOPLE WOULD BE SUSPICIOUS.
BUT IF THE INGOTS WERE MEANT FOR SALE ABROAD...
MADE IN ENGLAND
...THEY'D ONLY NEED TO HAVE THE COUNTRY OF EXPORT PRINTED ON THEM, SO THE SCHEME COULD WORK.
MADE IN CHINA
!!
MADE IN JAPAN

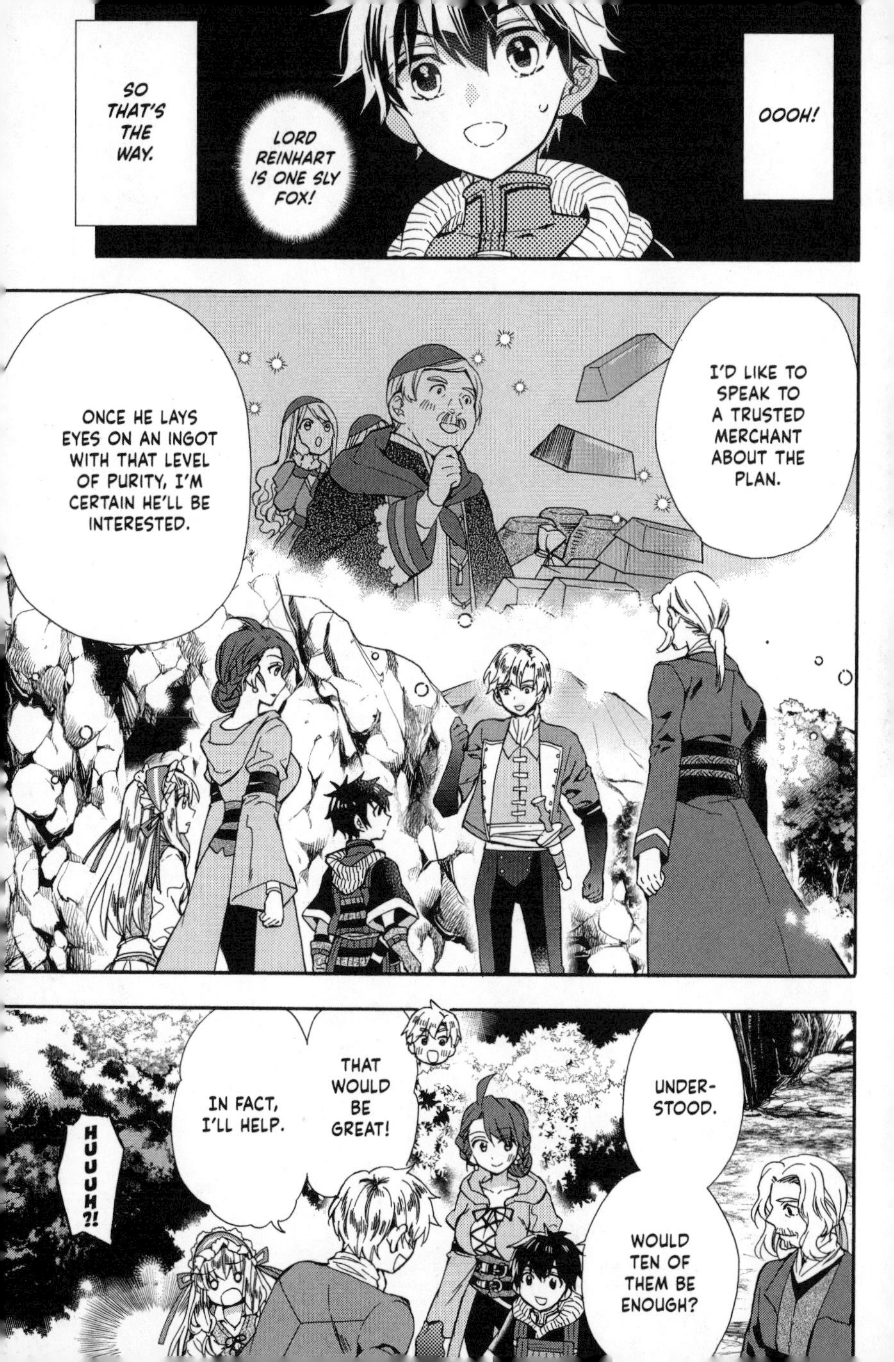
OOOH!
LORD REINHART IS ONE SLY FOX!
SO THAT'S THE WAY.
I'D LIKE TO SPEAK TO A TRUSTED MERCHANT ABOUT THE PLAN.
ONCE HE LAYS EYES ON AN INGOT WITH THAT LEVEL OF PURITY, I'M CERTAIN HE'LL BE INTERESTED.
UNDER-STOOD.
WOULD TEN OF THEM BE ENOUGH?
THAT WOULD BE GREAT!
IN FACT, I'LL HELP.
HUUUUH?!

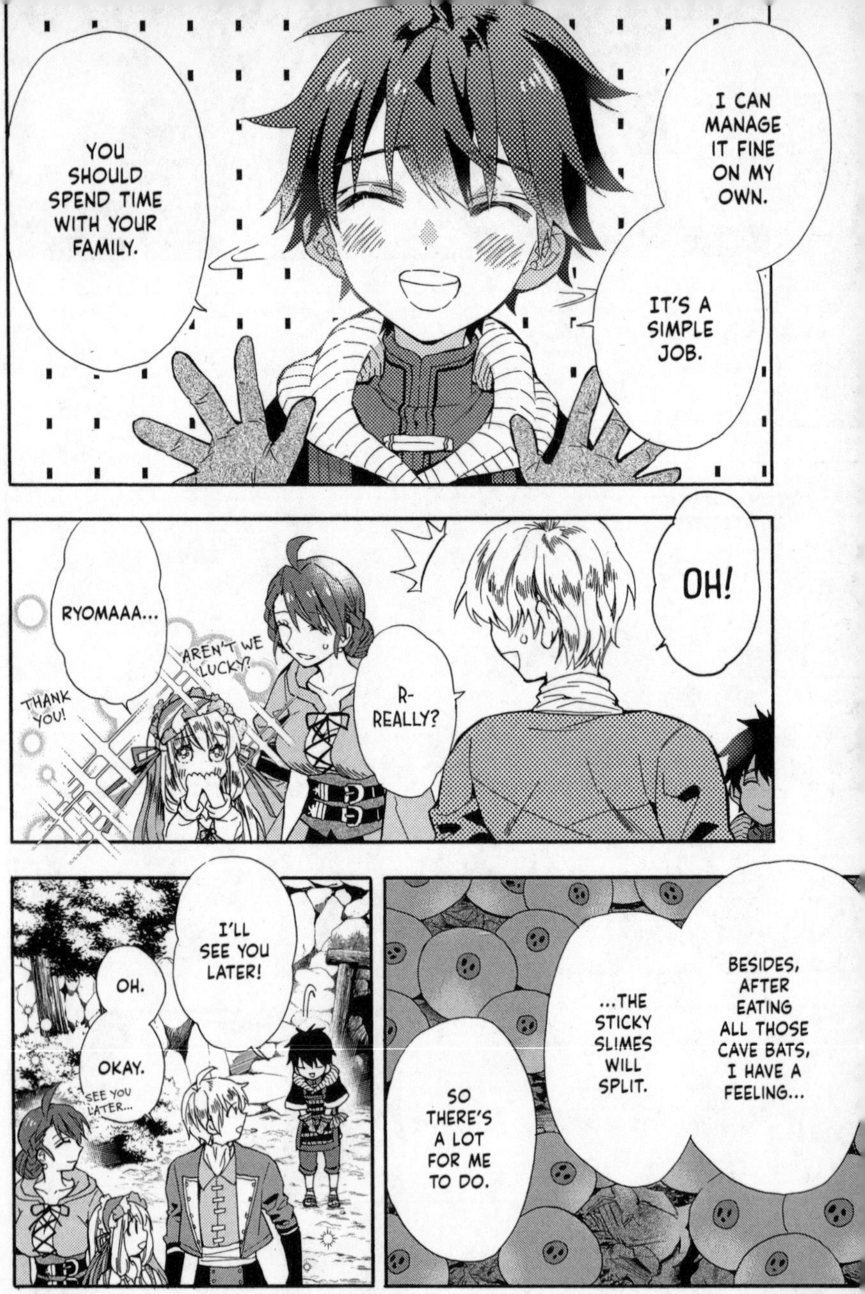
I CAN MANAGE IT FINE ON MY OWN.
IT'S A SIMPLE JOB.
YOU SHOULD SPEND TIME WITH YOUR FAMILY.
OH!
R- REALLY?
AREN'T WE LUCKY?
RYOMAAA...
THANK YOU!
BESIDES, AFTER EATING ALL THOSE CAVE BATS, I HAVE A FEELING...
...THE STICKY SLIMES WILL SPLIT.
SO THERE'S A LOT FOR ME TO DO.
I'LL SEE YOU LATER!
OH.
OKAY.
SEE YOU LATER...

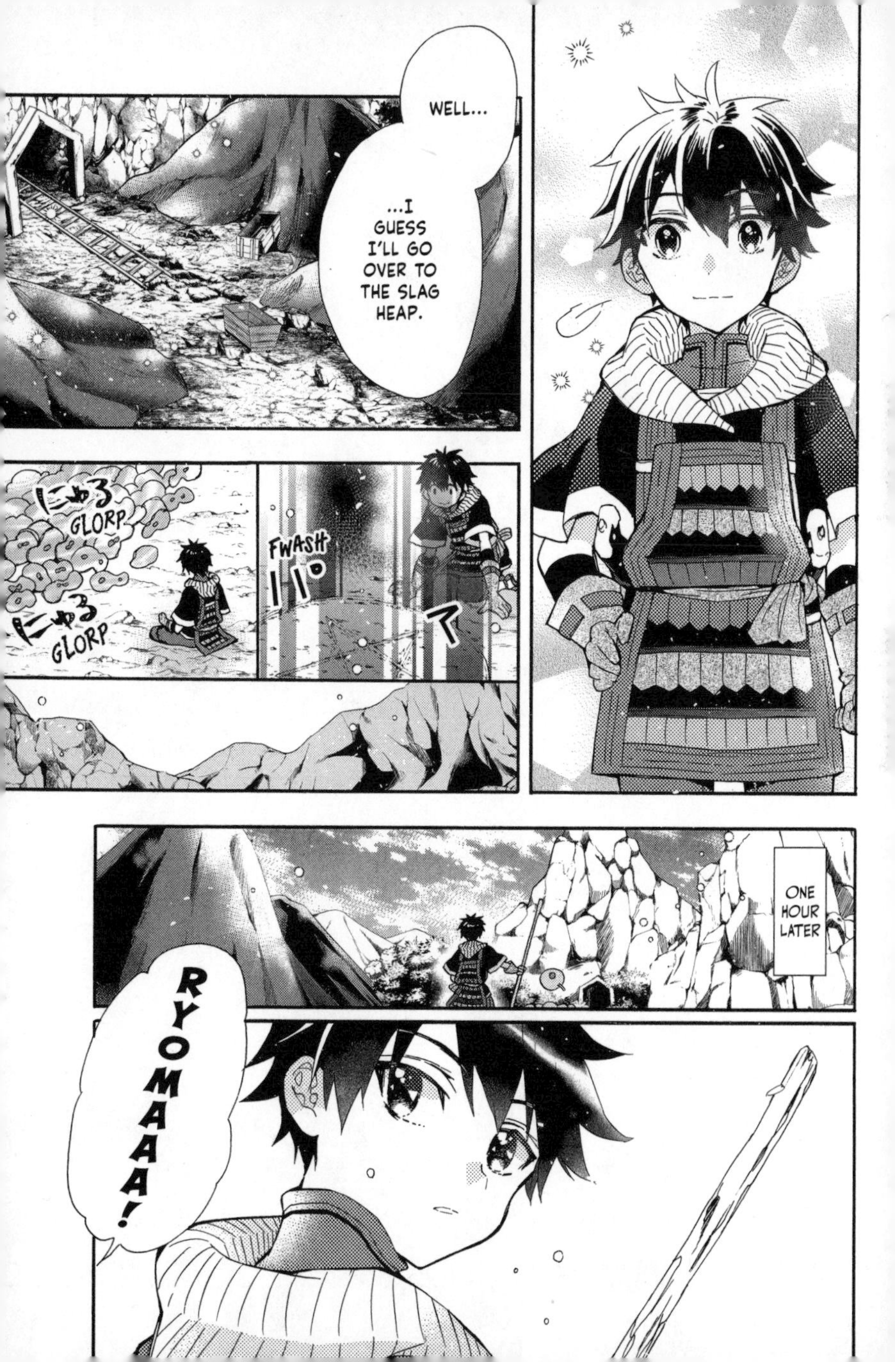
WELL...
...I GUESS I'LL GO OVER TO THE SLAG HEAP.
FWASH
パァ
にゅる GLORP
にゅる GLORP
ONE HOUR LATER
RYOMAAA!

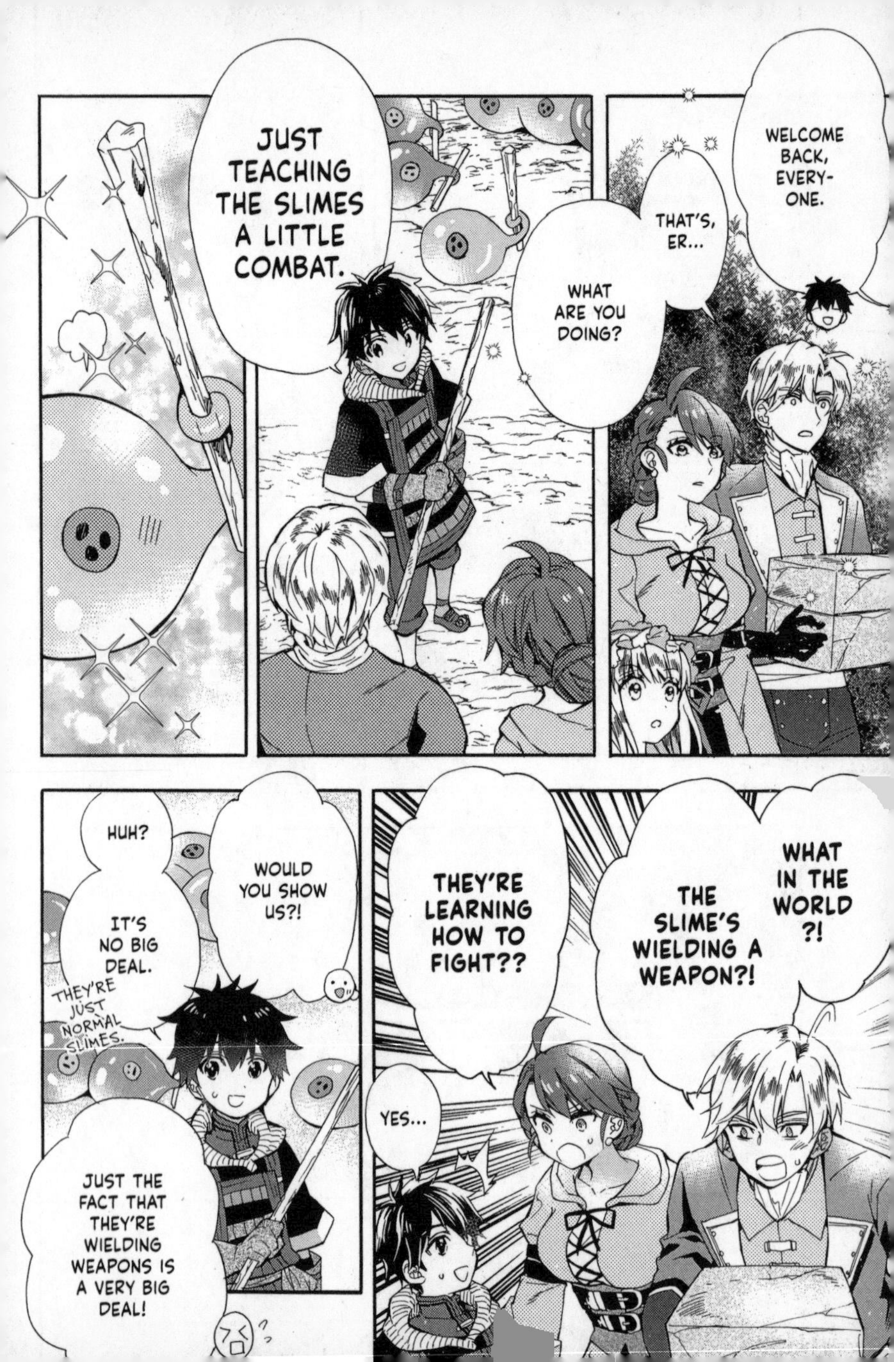

WELCOME BACK, EVERY-ONE.
THAT'S, ER...
WHAT ARE YOU DOING?
JUST TEACHING THE SLIMES A LITTLE COMBAT.
WHAT IN THE WORLD?!
THE SLIME'S WIELDING A WEAPON?!
THEY'RE LEARNING HOW TO FIGHT??
YES...
WOULD YOU SHOW US?!
HUH?
IT'S NO BIG DEAL.
THEY'RE JUST NORMAL SLIMES.
JUST THE FACT THAT THEY'RE WIELDING WEAPONS IS A VERY BIG DEAL!

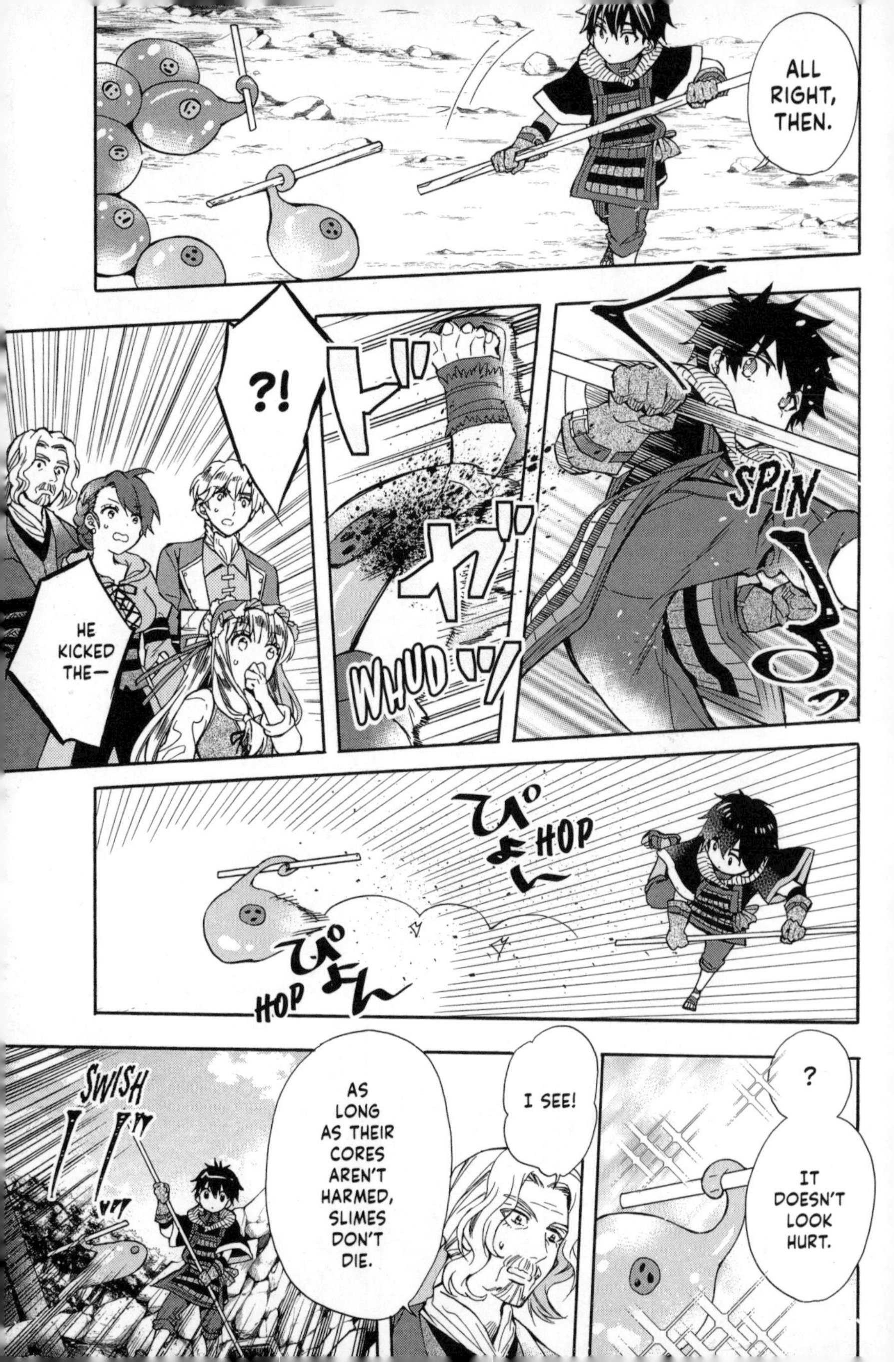
ALL RIGHT, THEN.
SPIN
WHUD
?!
HE KICKED THE—
ぴょん HOP
ぴょん HOP
?
IT DOESN'T LOOK HURT.
I SEE!
AS LONG AS THEIR CORES AREN'T HARMED, SLIMES DON'T DIE.
SWISH

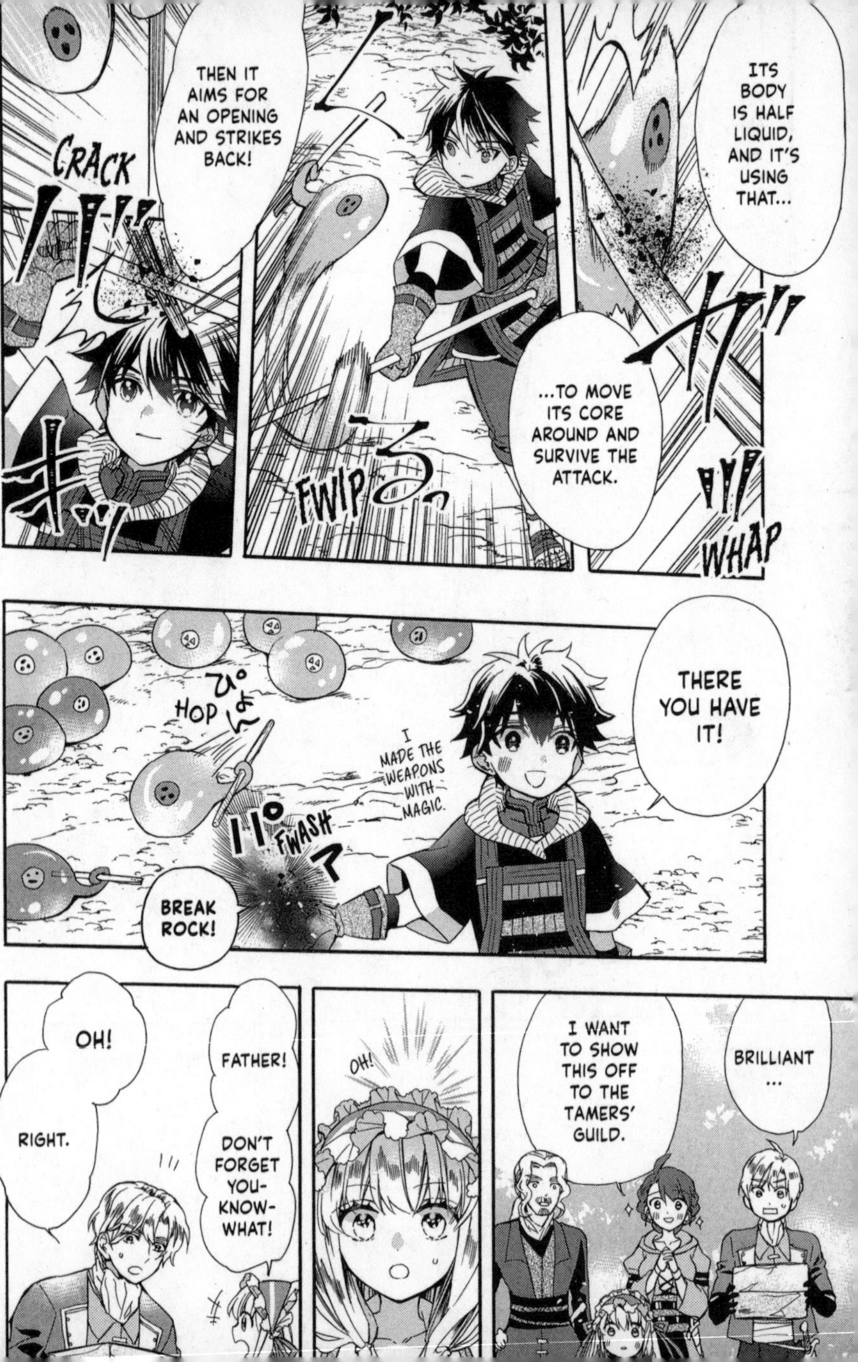
ITS BODY IS HALF LIQUID, AND IT'S USING THAT...
...TO MOVE ITS CORE AROUND AND SURVIVE THE ATTACK.
WHAP
FWIP
THEN IT AIMS FOR AN OPENING AND STRIKES BACK!
CRACK
THERE YOU HAVE IT!
I MADE THE WEAPONS WITH MAGIC.
HOP
FWASH
BREAK ROCK!
BRILLIANT ...
I WANT TO SHOW THIS OFF TO THE TAMERS' GUILD.
OH!
FATHER!
DON'T FORGET YOU-KNOW-WHAT!
OH!
RIGHT.

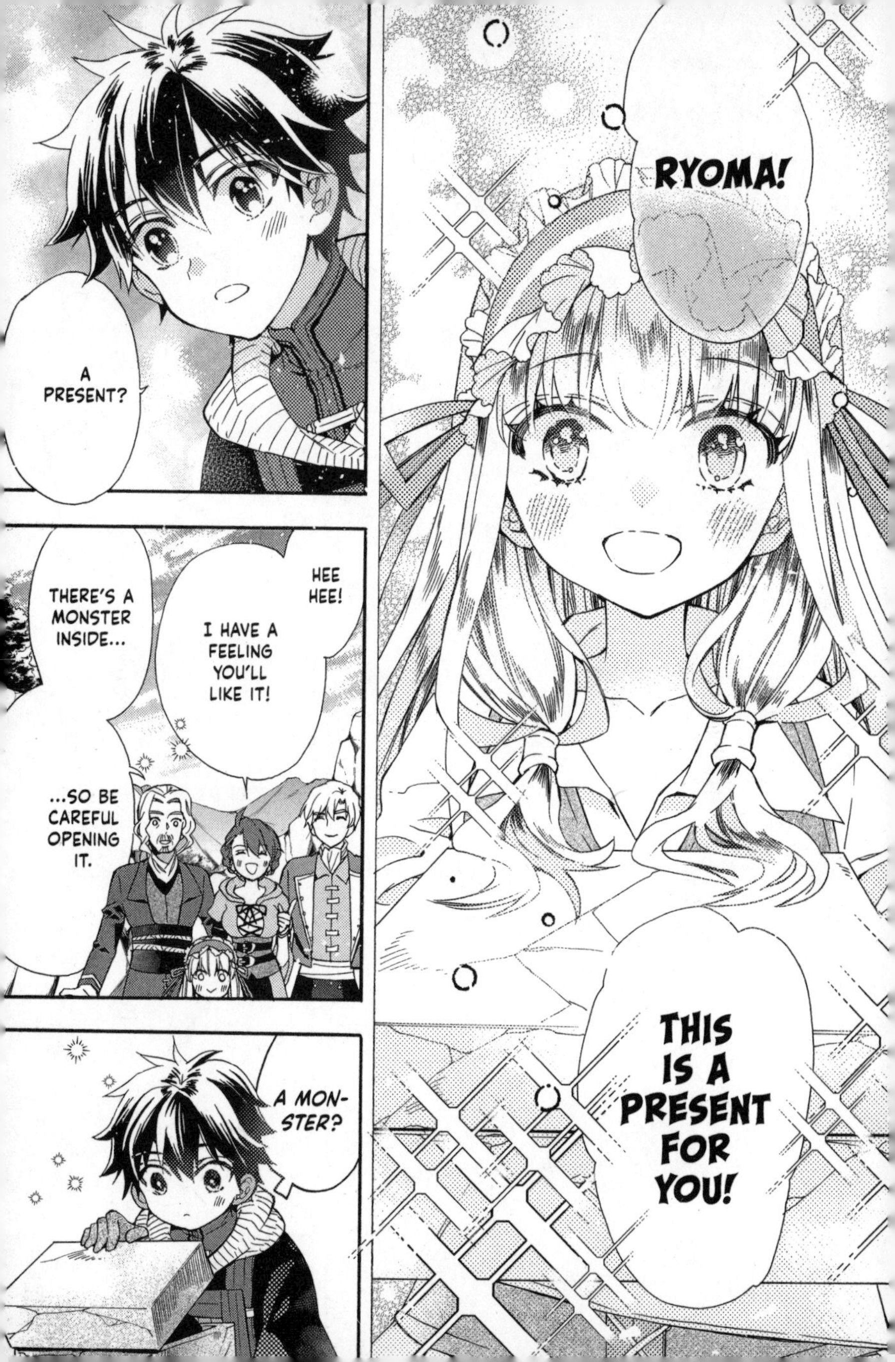
RYOMA!
THIS IS A PRESENT FOR YOU!
A PRESENT?
HEE HEE!
I HAVE A FEELING YOU'LL LIKE IT!
THERE'S A MONSTER INSIDE...
...SO BE CAREFUL OPENING IT.
A MON-STER?

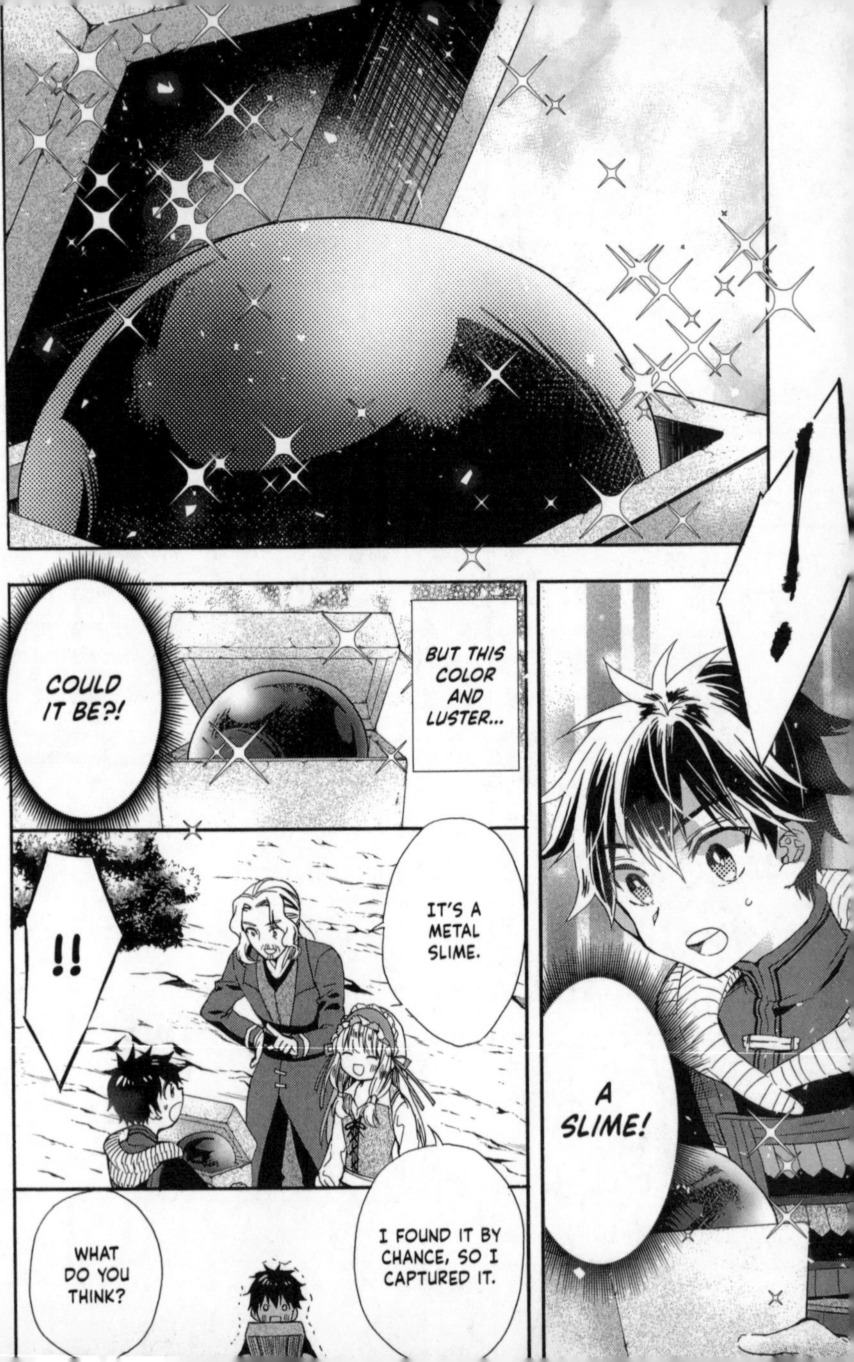
!
A SLIME!
BUT THIS COLOR AND LUSTER...
COULD IT BE?!
IT'S A METAL SLIME.
!!
I FOUND IT BY CHANCE, SO I CAPTURED IT.
WHAT DO YOU THINK?

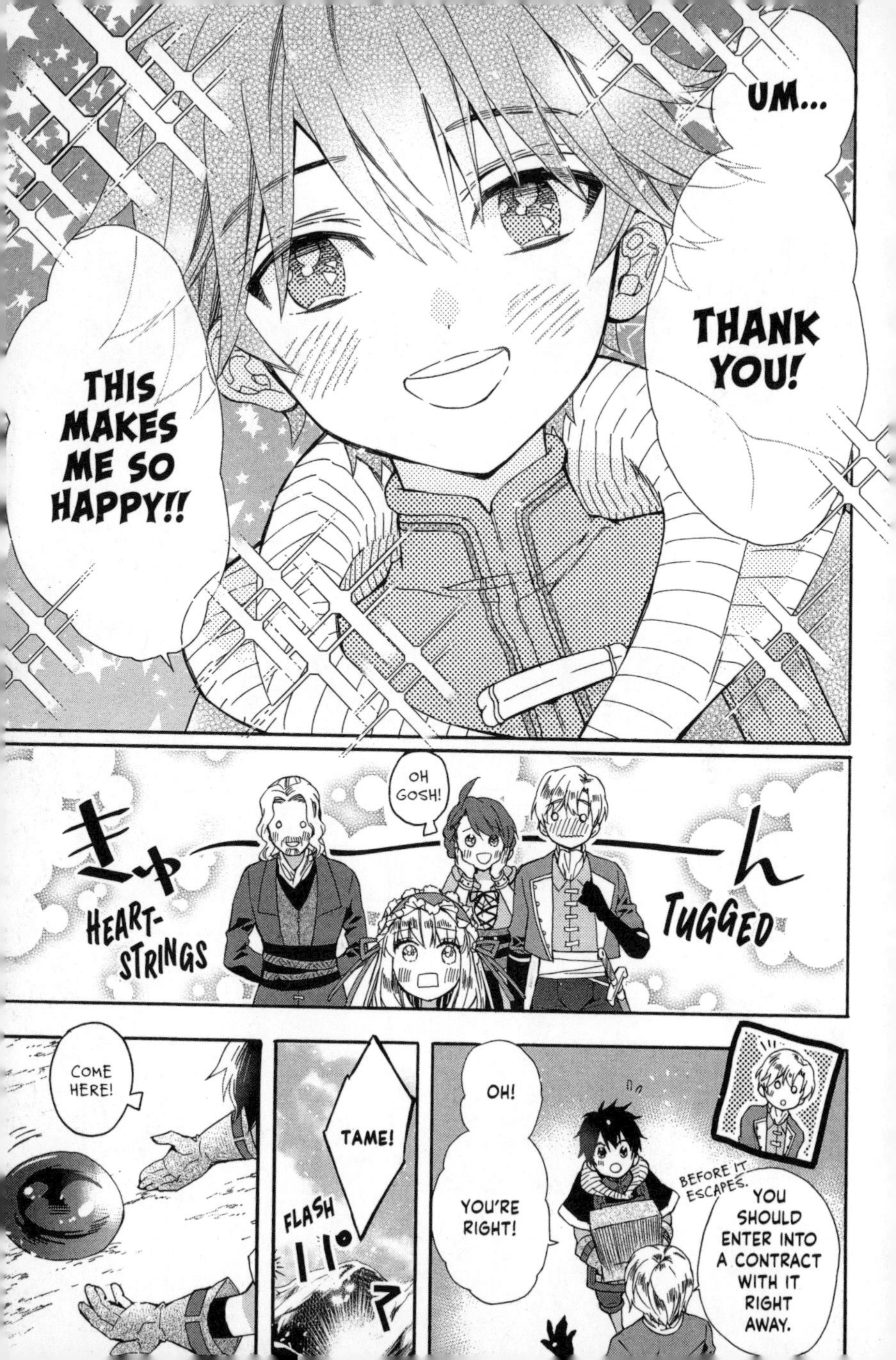
UM...
THANK YOU!
THIS MAKES ME SO HAPPY!!
OH GOSH!
きゅーーん
HEART-STRINGS TUGGED
BEFORE IT ESCAPES.
YOU SHOULD ENTER INTO A CONTRACT WITH IT RIGHT AWAY.
OH!
YOU'RE RIGHT!
TAME!
FLASH
COME HERE!

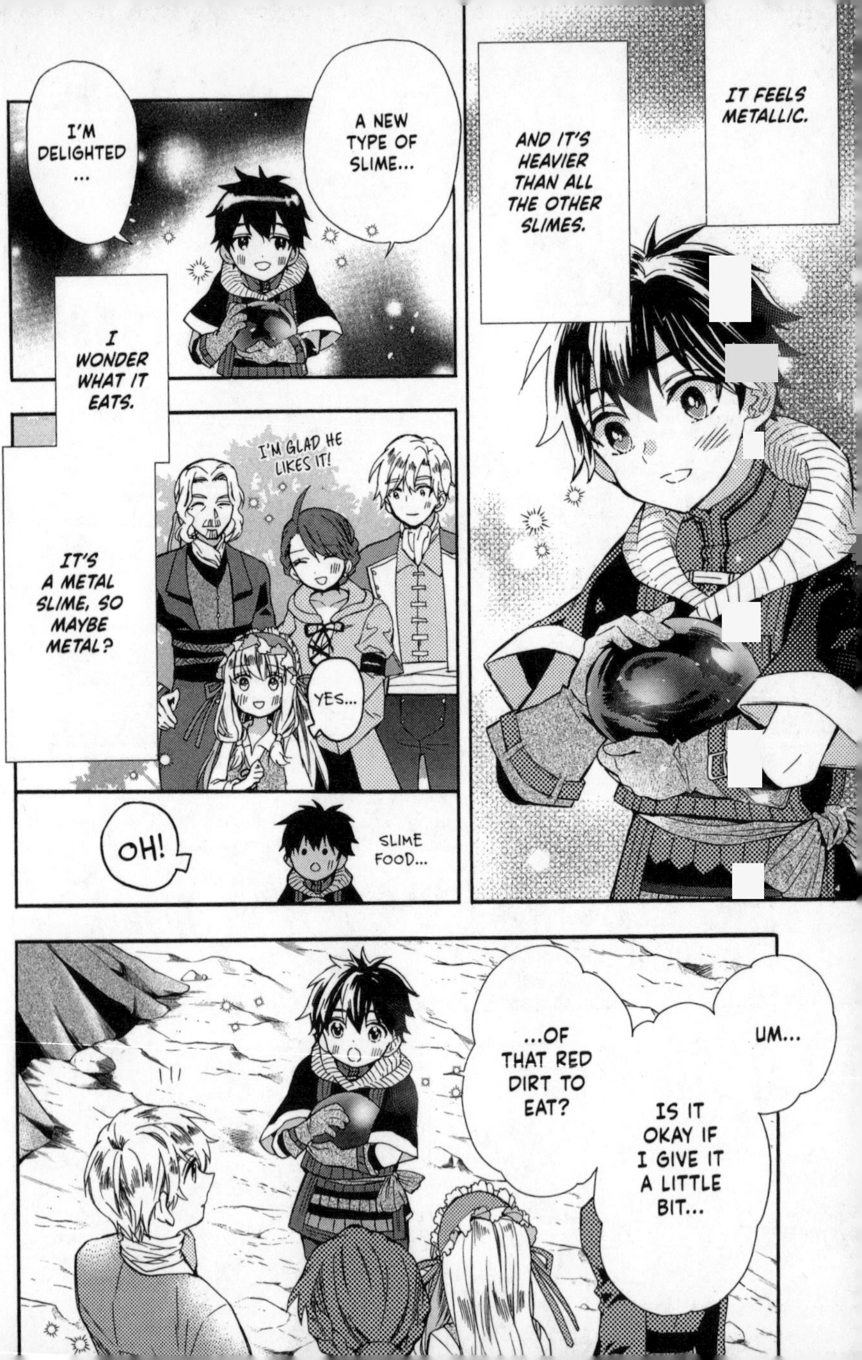
IT FEELS METALLIC.
AND IT'S HEAVIER THAN ALL THE OTHER SLIMES.
A NEW TYPE OF SLIME...
I'M DELIGHTED...
I WONDER WHAT IT EATS.
I'M GLAD HE LIKES IT!
YES...
IT'S A METAL SLIME, SO MAYBE METAL?
SLIME FOOD...
OH!
UM...
IS IT OKAY IF I GIVE IT A LITTLE BIT...
...OF THAT RED DIRT TO EAT?

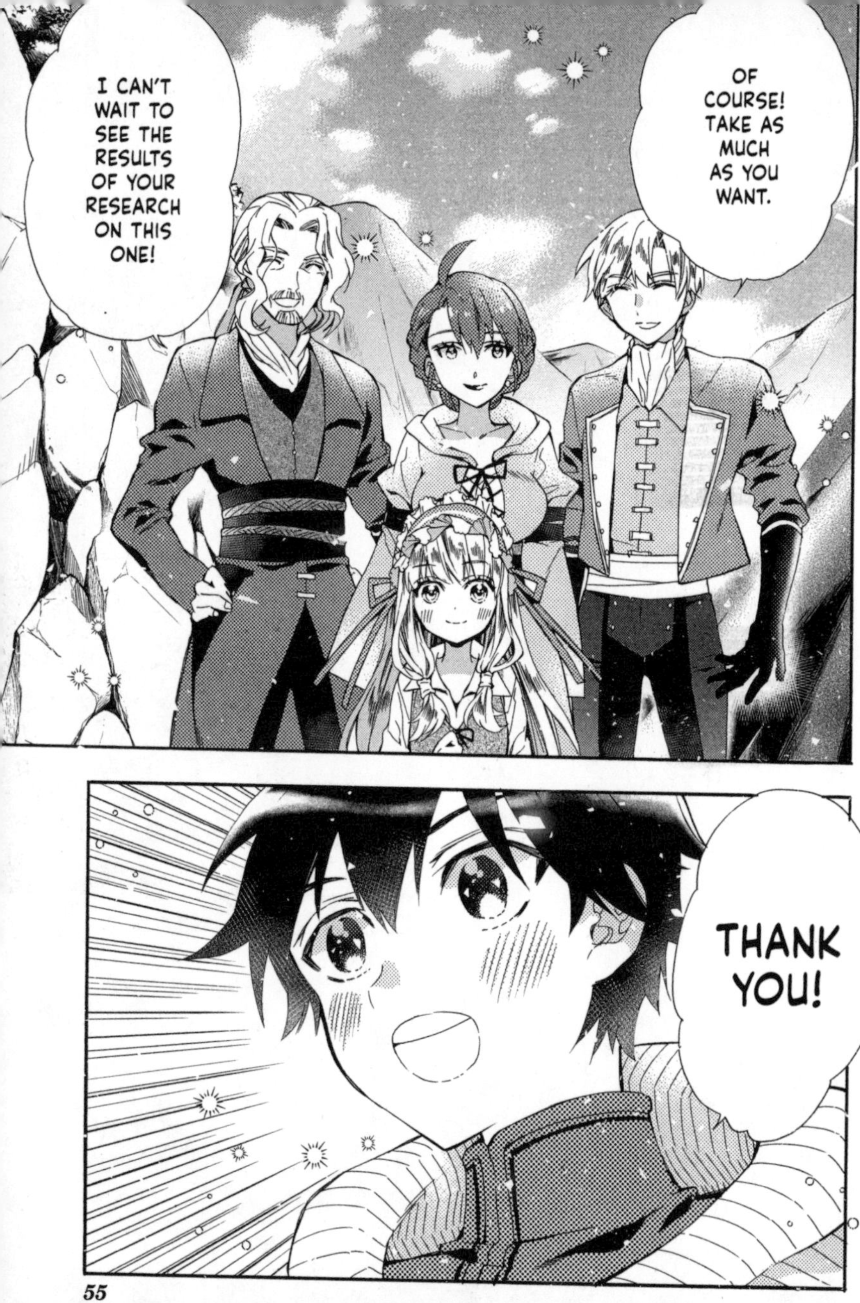
OF COURSE! TAKE AS MUCH AS YOU WANT.
I CAN'T WAIT TO SEE THE RESULTS OF YOUR RESEARCH ON THIS ONE!
THANK YOU!

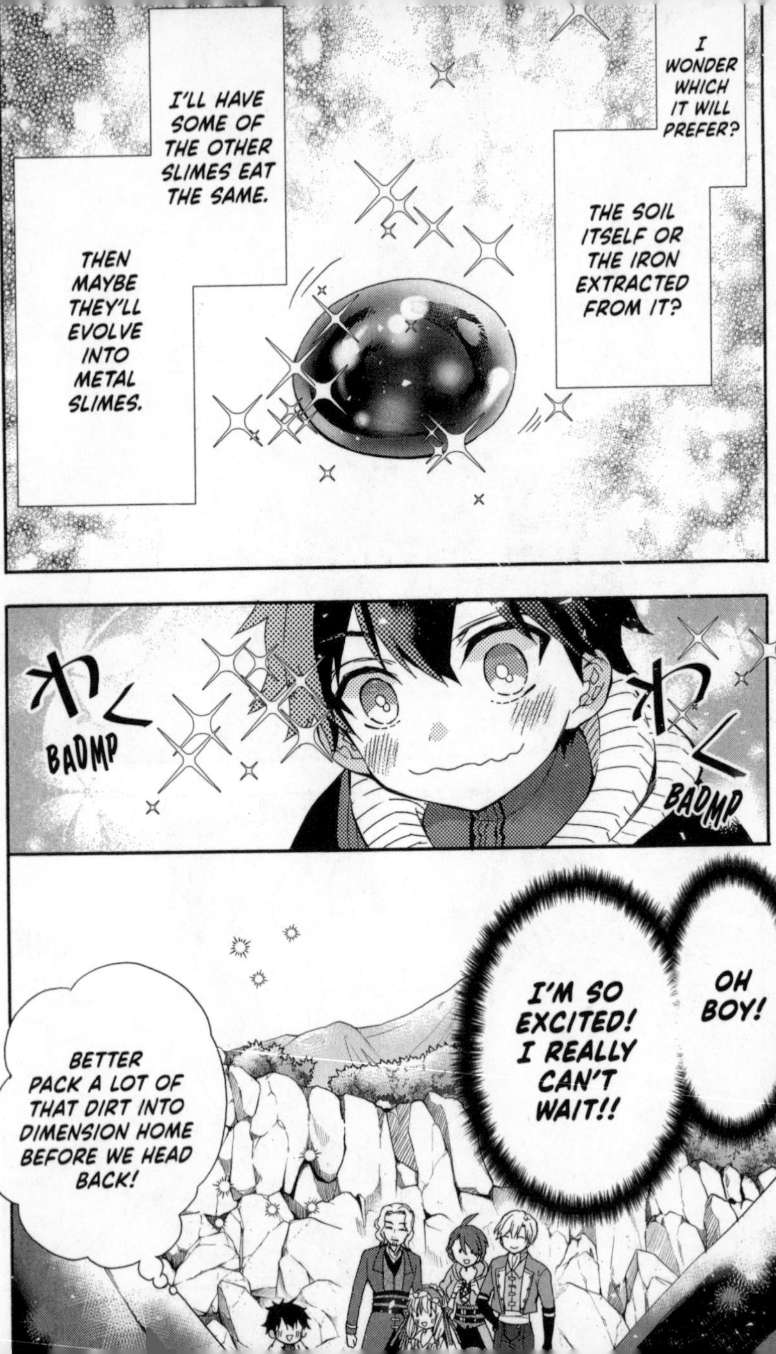

I WONDER WHICH IT WILL PREFER?
THE SOIL ITSELF OR THE IRON EXTRACTED FROM IT?
I'LL HAVE SOME OF THE OTHER SLIMES EAT THE SAME.
THEN MAYBE THEY'LL EVOLVE INTO METAL SLIMES.
わく
BADMP
わく
BADMP
OH BOY!
I'M SO EXCITED! I REALLY CAN'T WAIT!!
BETTER PACK A LOT OF THAT DIRT INTO DIMENSION HOME BEFORE WE HEAD BACK!

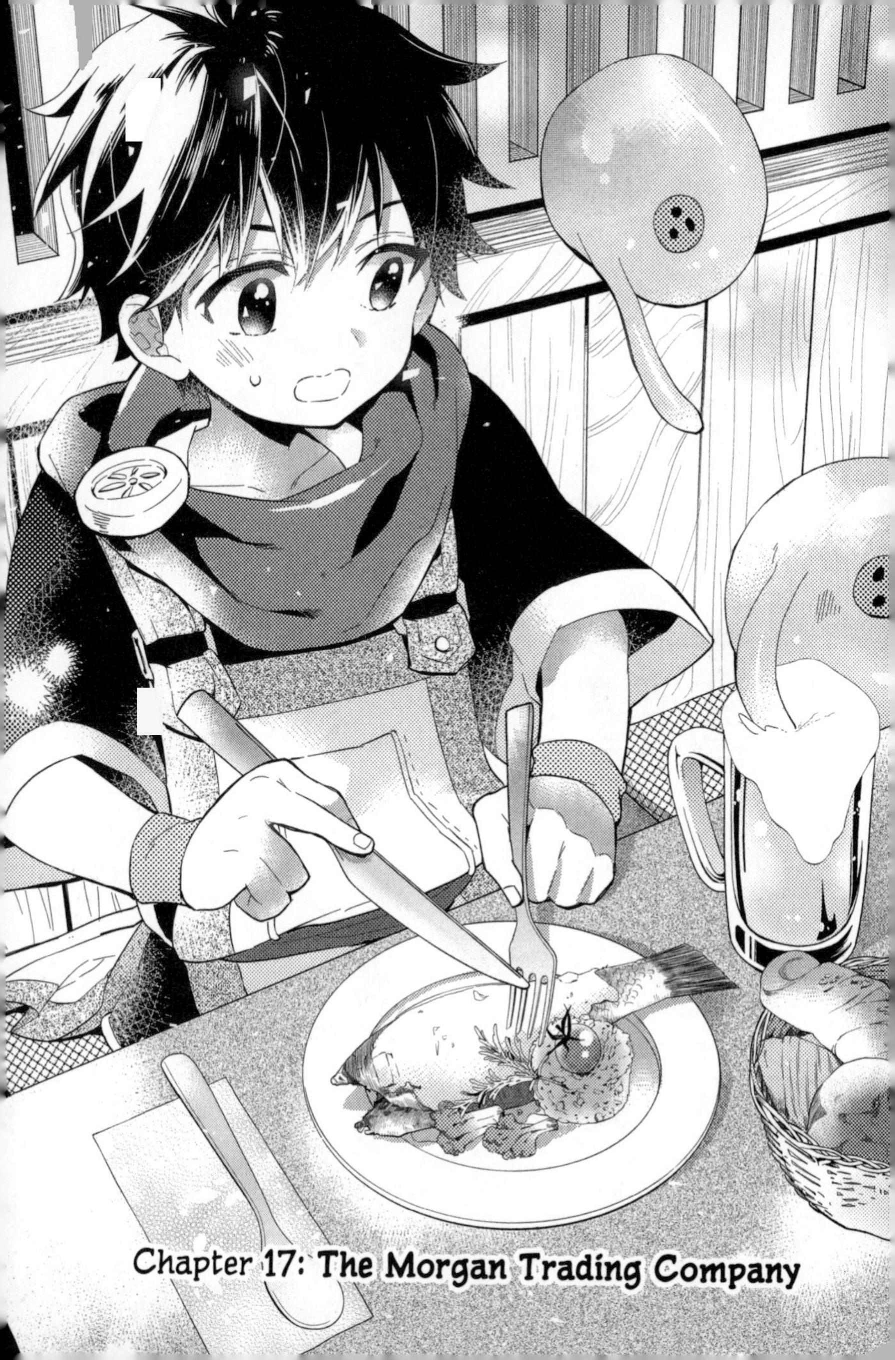

Chapter 17: The Morgan Trading Company

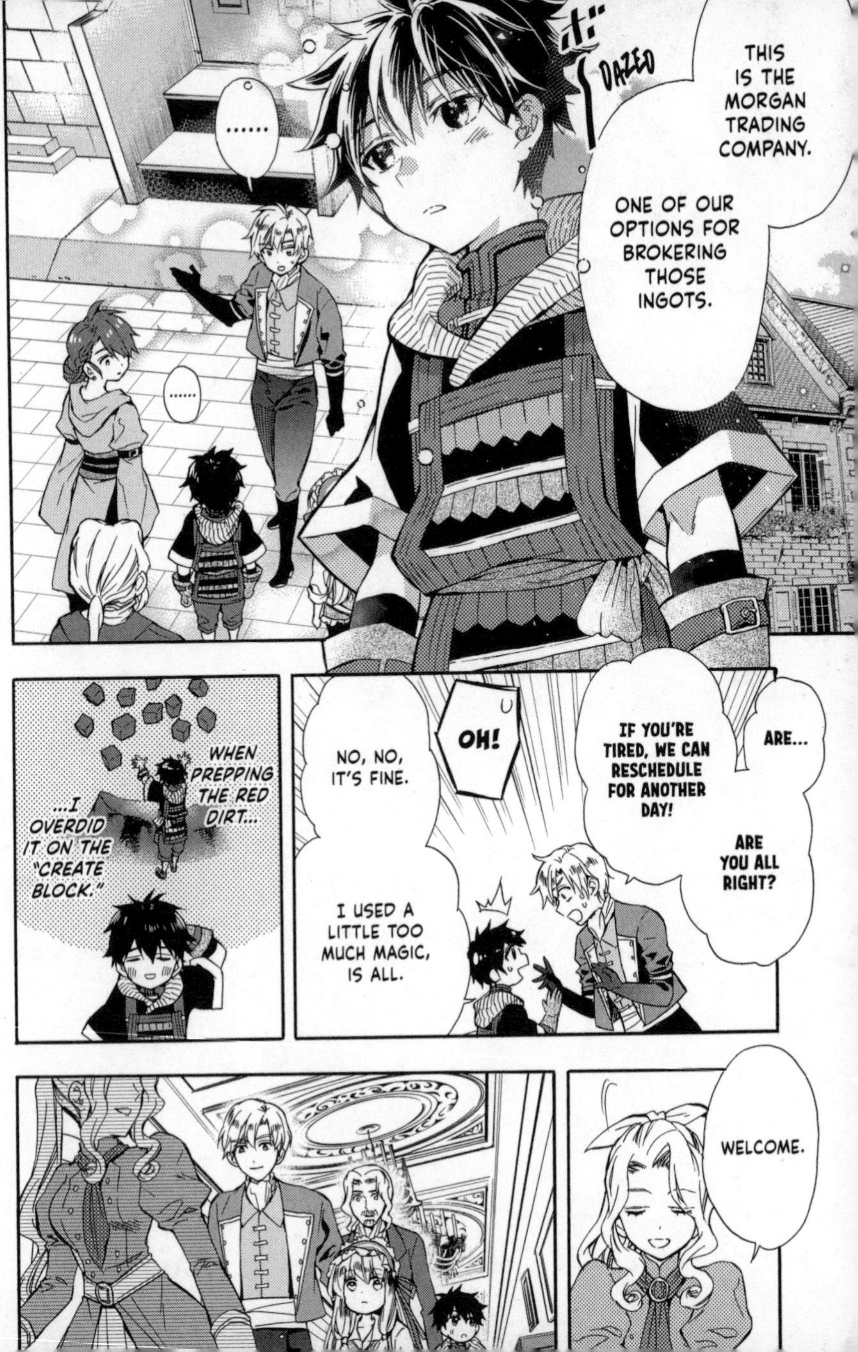
THIS IS THE MORGAN TRADING COMPANY.
ONE OF OUR OPTIONS FOR BROKERING THOSE INGOTS.
DAZED
....
......
ARE...
ARE YOU ALL RIGHT?
IF YOU'RE TIRED, WE CAN RESCHEDULE FOR ANOTHER DAY!
OH!
NO, NO, IT'S FINE.
I USED A LITTLE TOO MUCH MAGIC, IS ALL.
WHEN PREPPING THE RED DIRT...
...I OVERDID IT ON THE "CREATE BLOCK."
WELCOME.

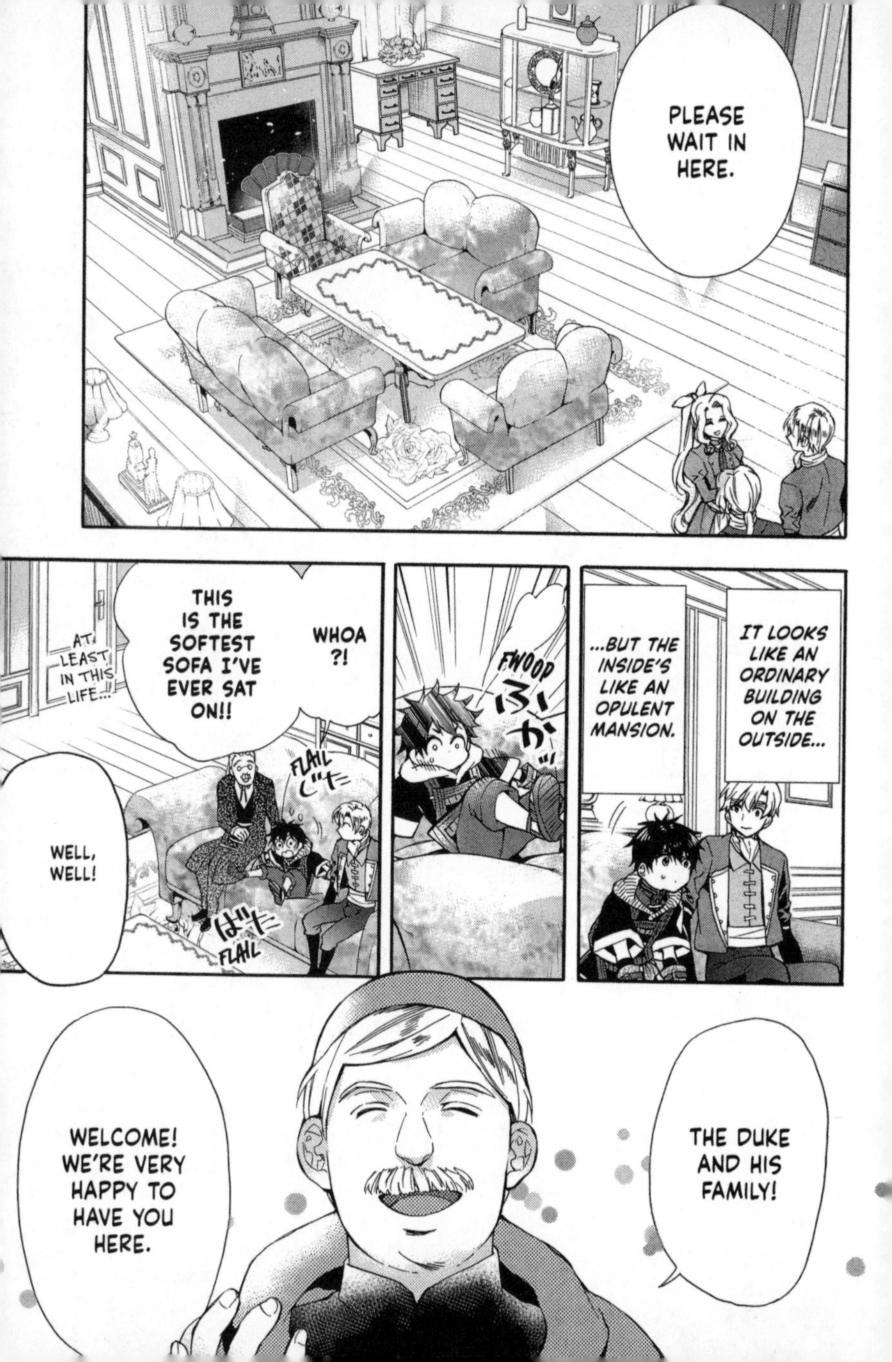
PLEASE WAIT IN HERE.
IT LOOKS LIKE AN ORDINARY BUILDING ON THE OUTSIDE...
...BUT THE INSIDE'S LIKE AN OPULENT MANSION.
FWOOP
WHOA ?!
THIS IS THE SOFTEST SOFA I'VE EVER SAT ON!!
AT LEAST IN THIS LIFE...
FLAIL
FLAIL
WELL, WELL!
THE DUKE AND HIS FAMILY!
WELCOME! WE'RE VERY HAPPY TO HAVE YOU HERE.

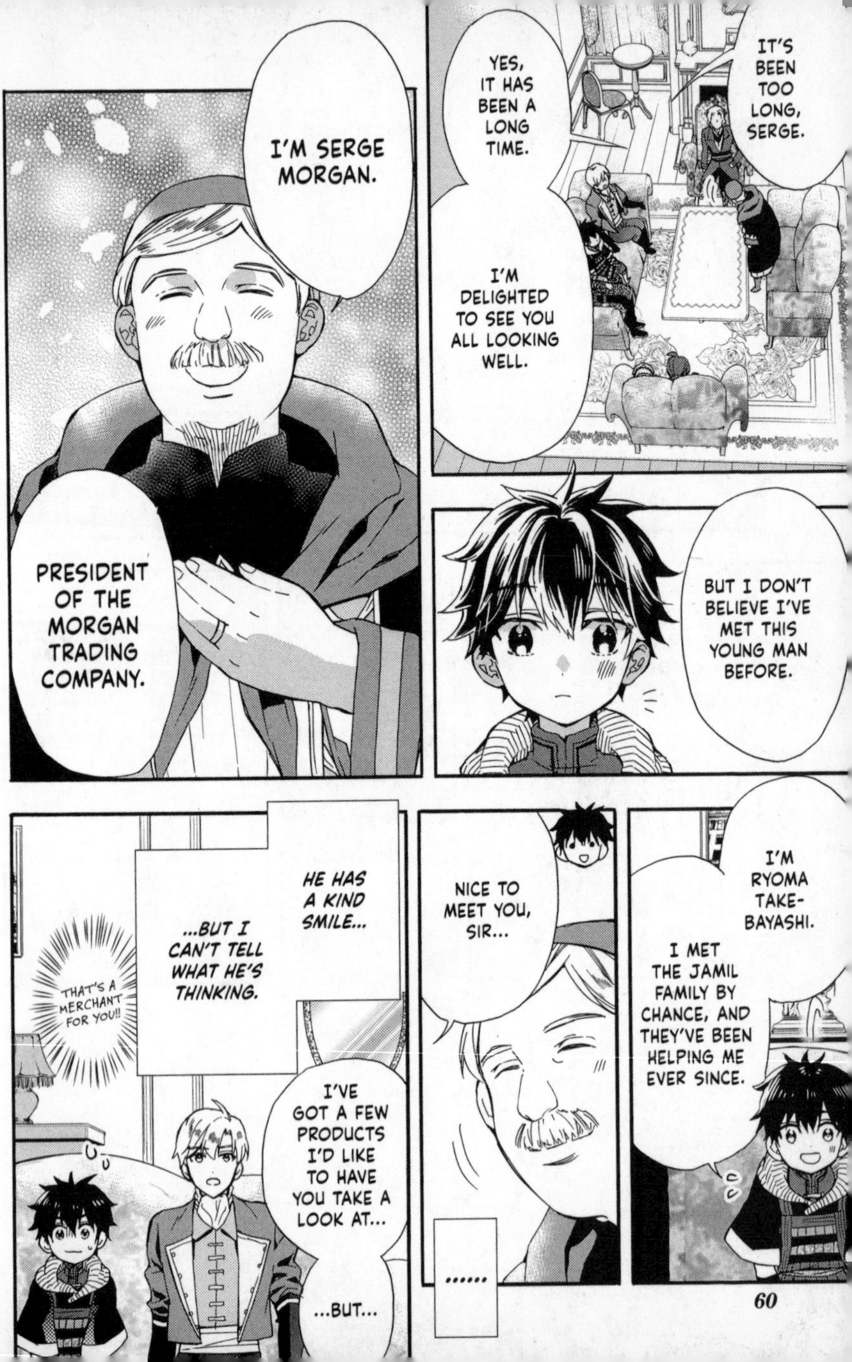
IT'S BEEN TOO LONG, SERGE.
YES, IT HAS BEEN A LONG TIME.
I'M DELIGHTED TO SEE YOU ALL LOOKING WELL.
BUT I DON'T BELIEVE I'VE MET THIS YOUNG MAN BEFORE.
I'M SERGE MORGAN.
PRESIDENT OF THE MORGAN TRADING COMPANY.
I'M RYOMA TAKE-BAYASHI.
I MET THE JAMIL FAMILY BY CHANCE, AND THEY'VE BEEN HELPING ME EVER SINCE.
NICE TO MEET YOU, SIR...
......
HE HAS A KIND SMILE...
...BUT I CAN'T TELL WHAT HE'S THINKING.
THAT'S A MERCHANT FOR YOU!!
I'VE GOT A FEW PRODUCTS I'D LIKE TO HAVE YOU TAKE A LOOK AT...
...BUT...

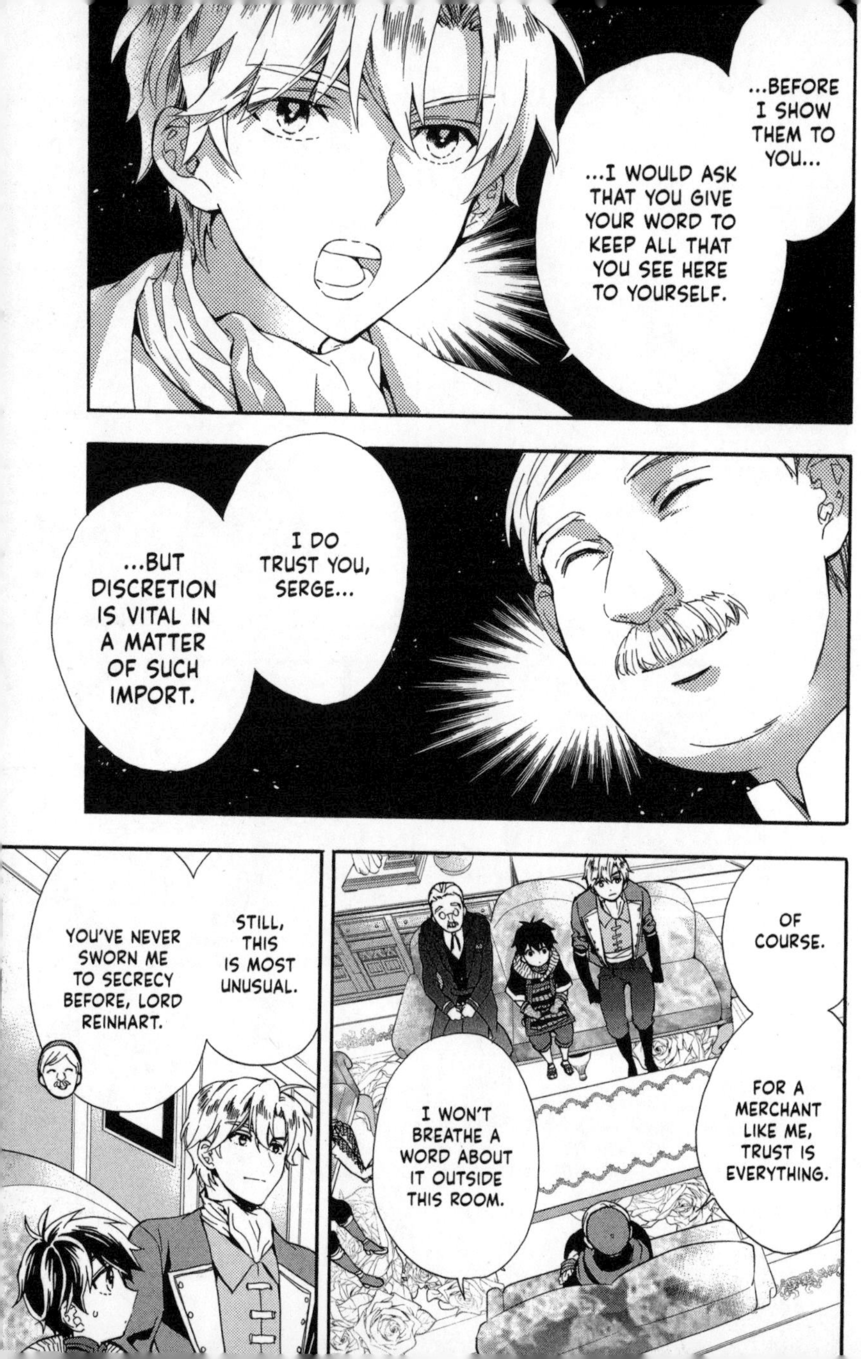
...BEFORE I SHOW THEM TO YOU...
...I WOULD ASK THAT YOU GIVE YOUR WORD TO KEEP ALL THAT YOU SEE HERE TO YOURSELF.
I DO TRUST YOU, SERGE...
...BUT DISCRETION IS VITAL IN A MATTER OF SUCH IMPORT.
OF COURSE.
FOR A MERCHANT LIKE ME, TRUST IS EVERYTHING.
I WON'T BREATHE A WORD ABOUT IT OUTSIDE THIS ROOM.
STILL, THIS IS MOST UNUSUAL.
YOU'VE NEVER SWORN ME TO SECRECY BEFORE, LORD REINHART.

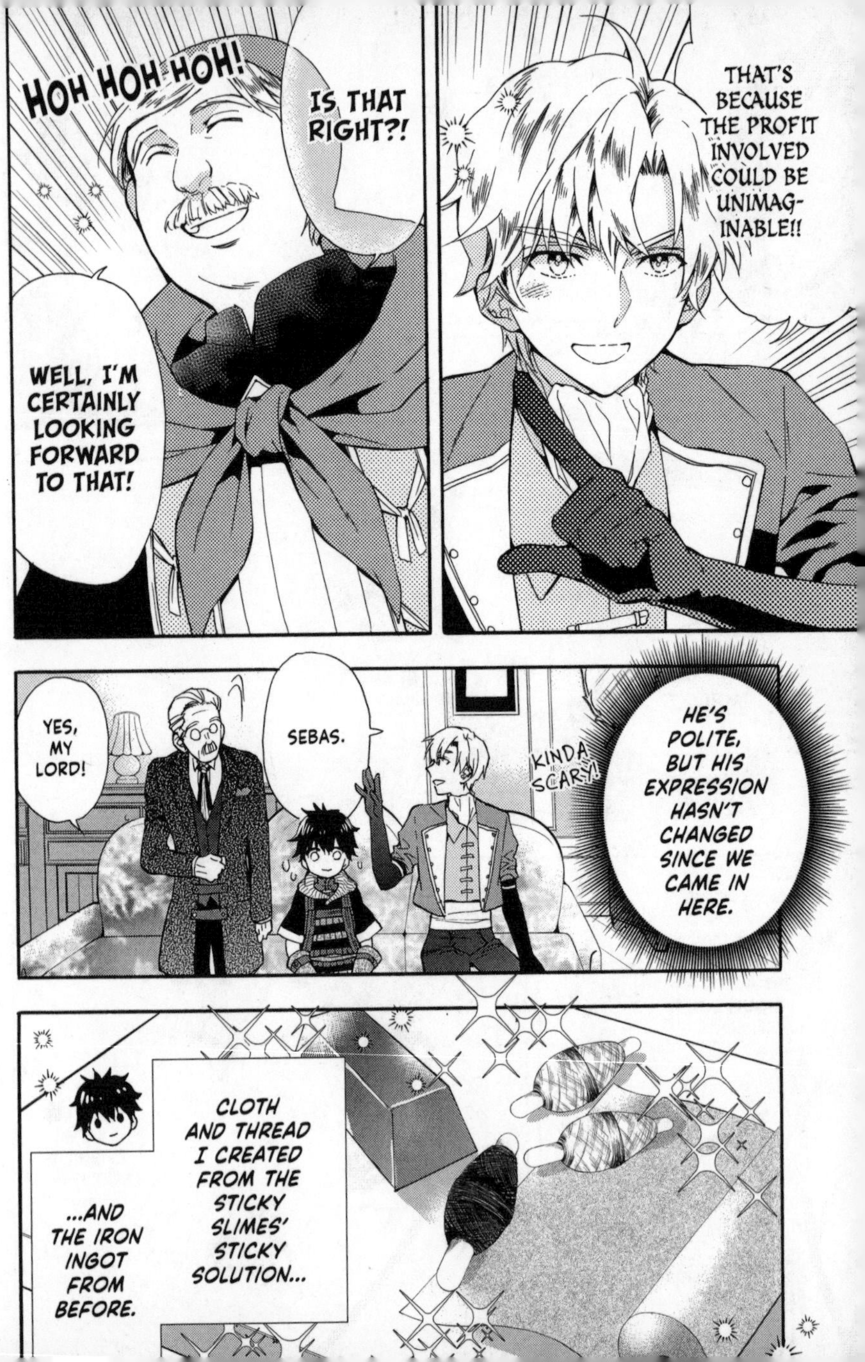
THAT'S BECAUSE THE PROFIT INVOLVED COULD BE UNIMAG-INABLE!!
IS THAT RIGHT?!
HOH HOH HOH!
WELL, I'M CERTAINLY LOOKING FORWARD TO THAT!
HE'S POLITE, BUT HIS EXPRESSION HASN'T CHANGED SINCE WE CAME IN HERE.
KINDA SCARY!
SEBAS.
YES, MY LORD!
CLOTH AND THREAD I CREATED FROM THE STICKY SLIMES' STICKY SOLUTION...
...AND THE IRON INGOT FROM BEFORE.

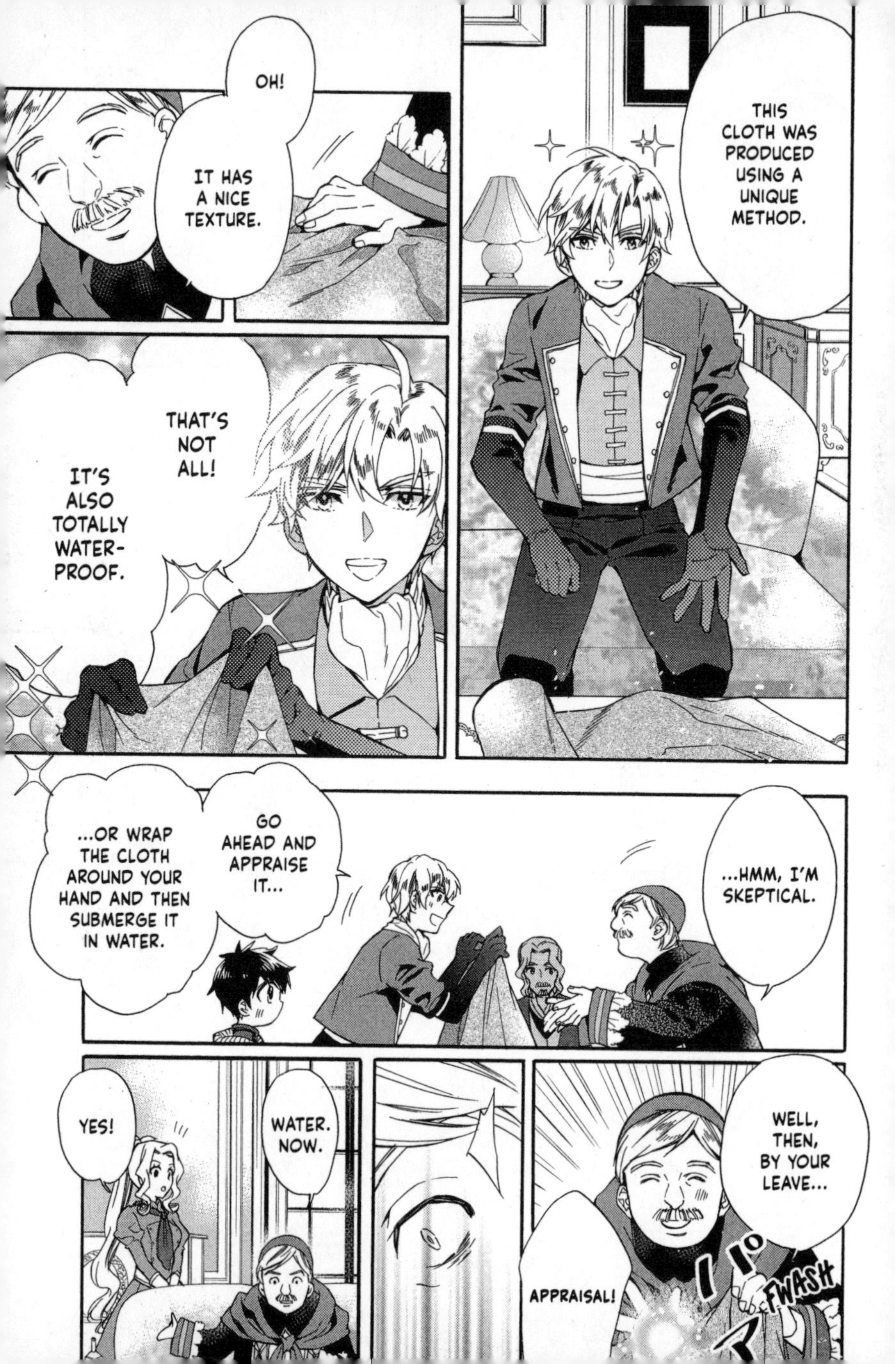
THIS CLOTH WAS PRODUCED USING A UNIQUE METHOD.
OH!
IT HAS A NICE TEXTURE.
THAT'S NOT ALL!
IT'S ALSO TOTALLY WATER-PROOF.
...HMM, I'M SKEPTICAL.
GO AHEAD AND APPRAISE IT...
...OR WRAP THE CLOTH AROUND YOUR HAND AND THEN SUBMERGE IT IN WATER.
WELL, THEN, BY YOUR LEAVE...
APPRAISAL!
FWASH
WATER. NOW.
YES!

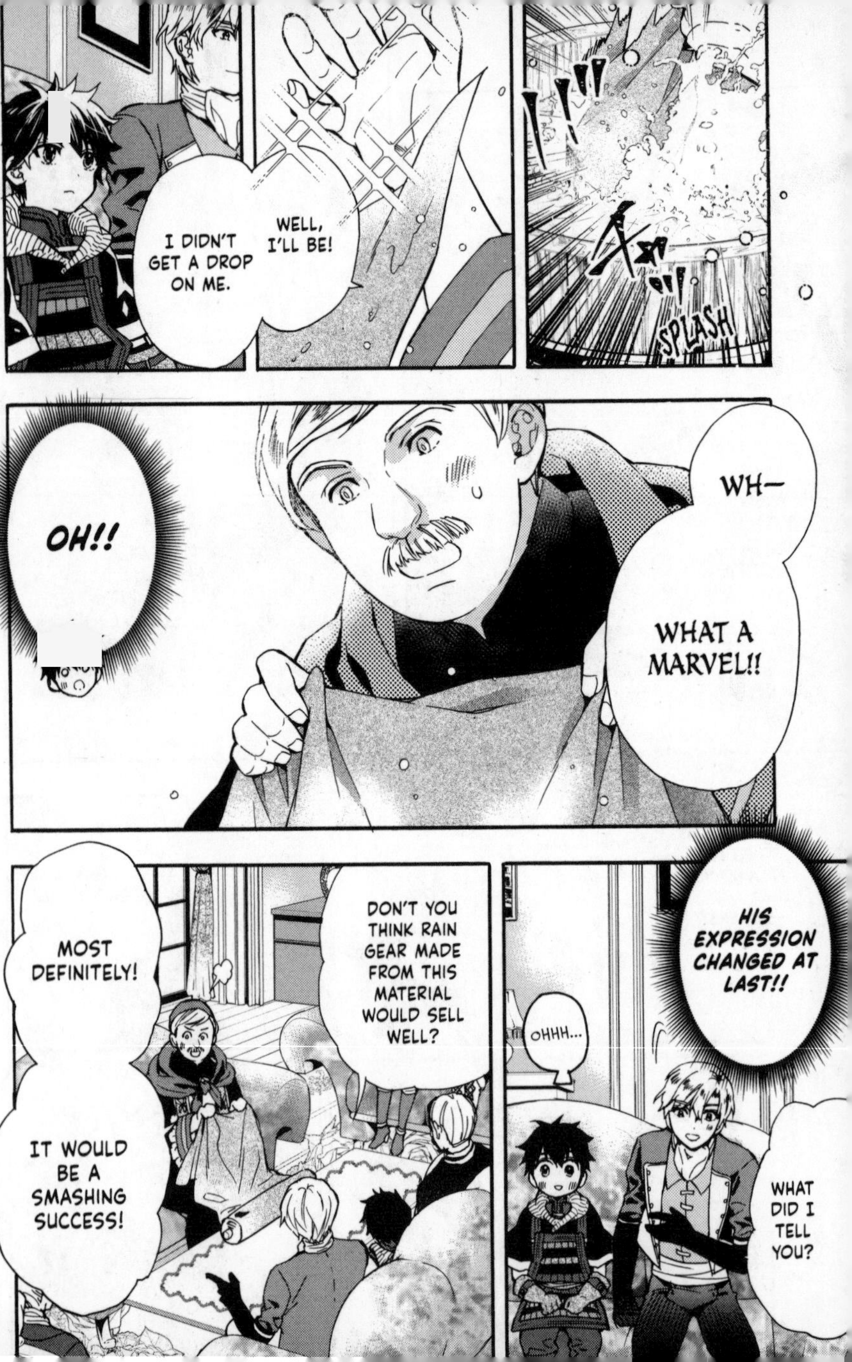
SPLASH
WELL, I'LL BE!
I DIDN'T GET A DROP ON ME.
WH—
WHAT A MARVEL!!
OH!!
HIS EXPRESSION CHANGED AT LAST!!
OHHH...
WHAT DID I TELL YOU?
DON'T YOU THINK RAIN GEAR MADE FROM THIS MATERIAL WOULD SELL WELL?
MOST DEFINITELY!
IT WOULD BE A SMASHING SUCCESS!

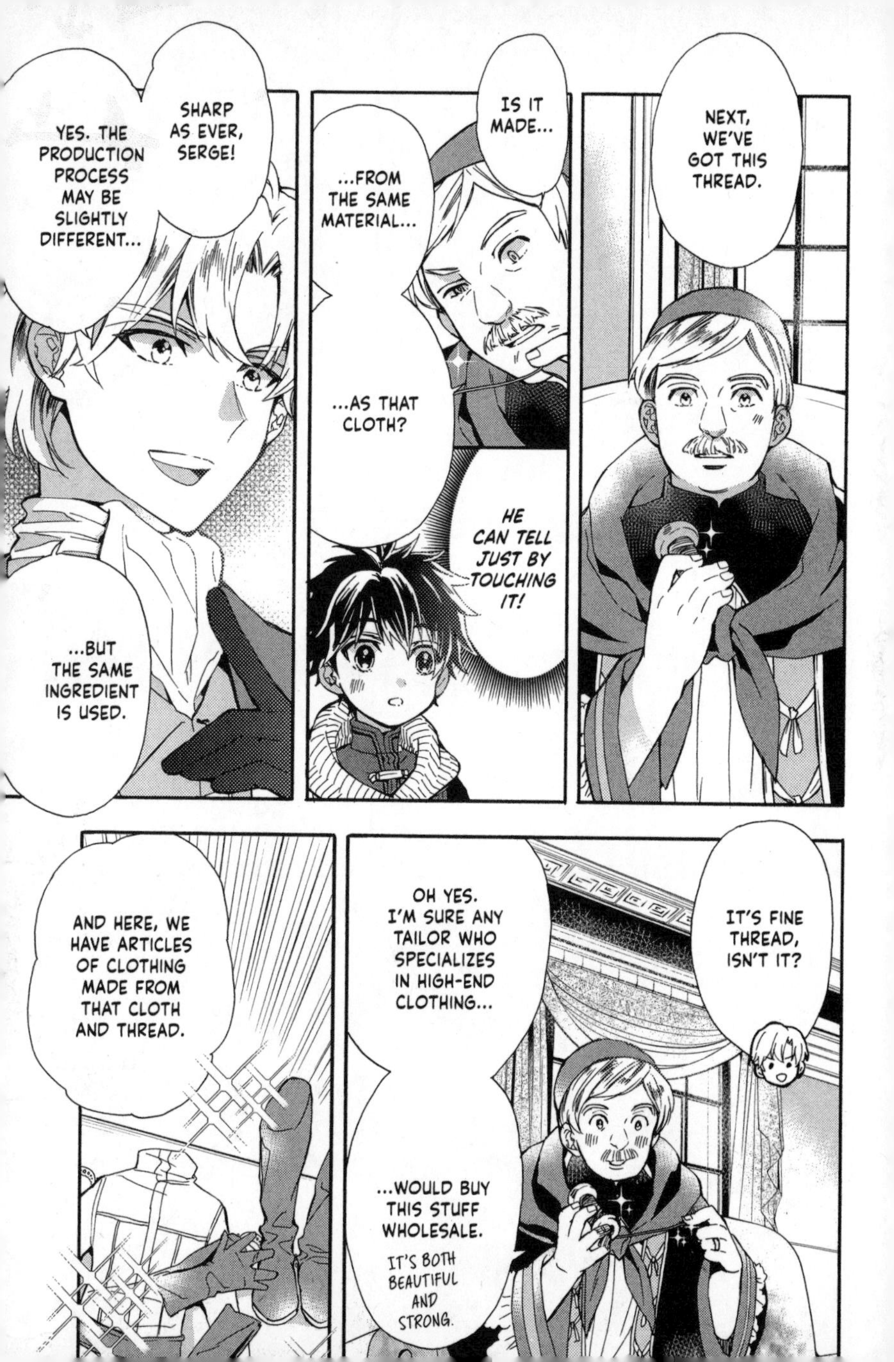
NEXT, WE'VE GOT THIS THREAD.
IS IT MADE...
...FROM THE SAME MATERIAL...
...AS THAT CLOTH?
HE CAN TELL JUST BY TOUCHING IT!
SHARP AS EVER, SERGE!
YES. THE PRODUCTION PROCESS MAY BE SLIGHTLY DIFFERENT...
...BUT THE SAME INGREDIENT IS USED.
IT'S FINE THREAD, ISN'T IT?
OH YES. I'M SURE ANY TAILOR WHO SPECIALIZES IN HIGH-END CLOTHING...
...WOULD BUY THIS STUFF WHOLESALE.
IT'S BOTH BEAUTIFUL AND STRONG.
AND HERE, WE HAVE ARTICLES OF CLOTHING MADE FROM THAT CLOTH AND THREAD.

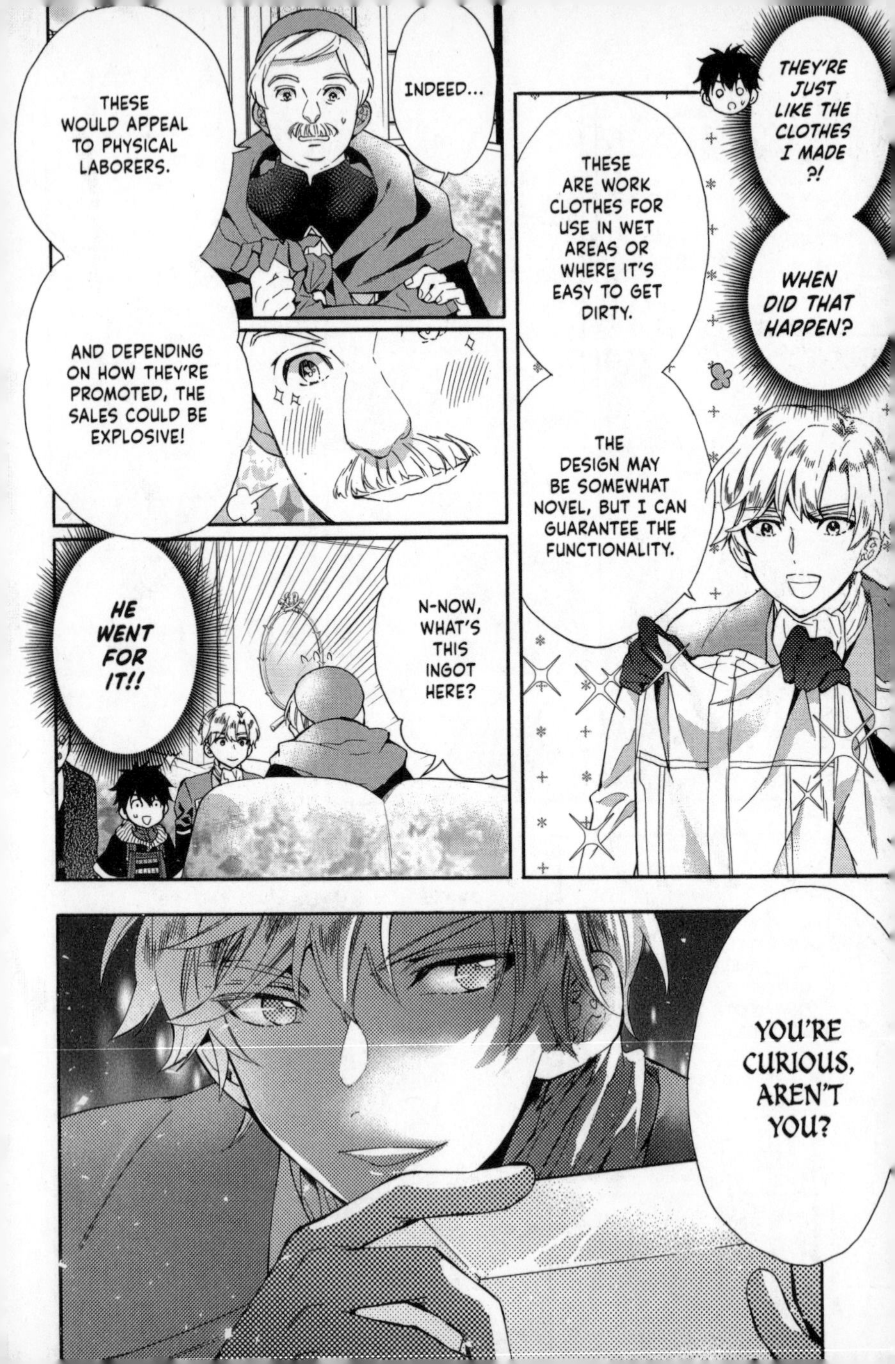
THEY'RE JUST LIKE THE CLOTHES I MADE?!
WHEN DID THAT HAPPEN?
THESE ARE WORK CLOTHES FOR USE IN WET AREAS OR WHERE IT'S EASY TO GET DIRTY.
THE DESIGN MAY BE SOMEWHAT NOVEL, BUT I CAN GUARANTEE THE FUNCTIONALITY.
INDEED...
THESE WOULD APPEAL TO PHYSICAL LABORERS.
AND DEPENDING ON HOW THEY'RE PROMOTED, THE SALES COULD BE EXPLOSIVE!
N-NOW, WHAT'S THIS INGOT HERE?
HE WENT FOR IT!!
YOU'RE CURIOUS, AREN'T YOU?

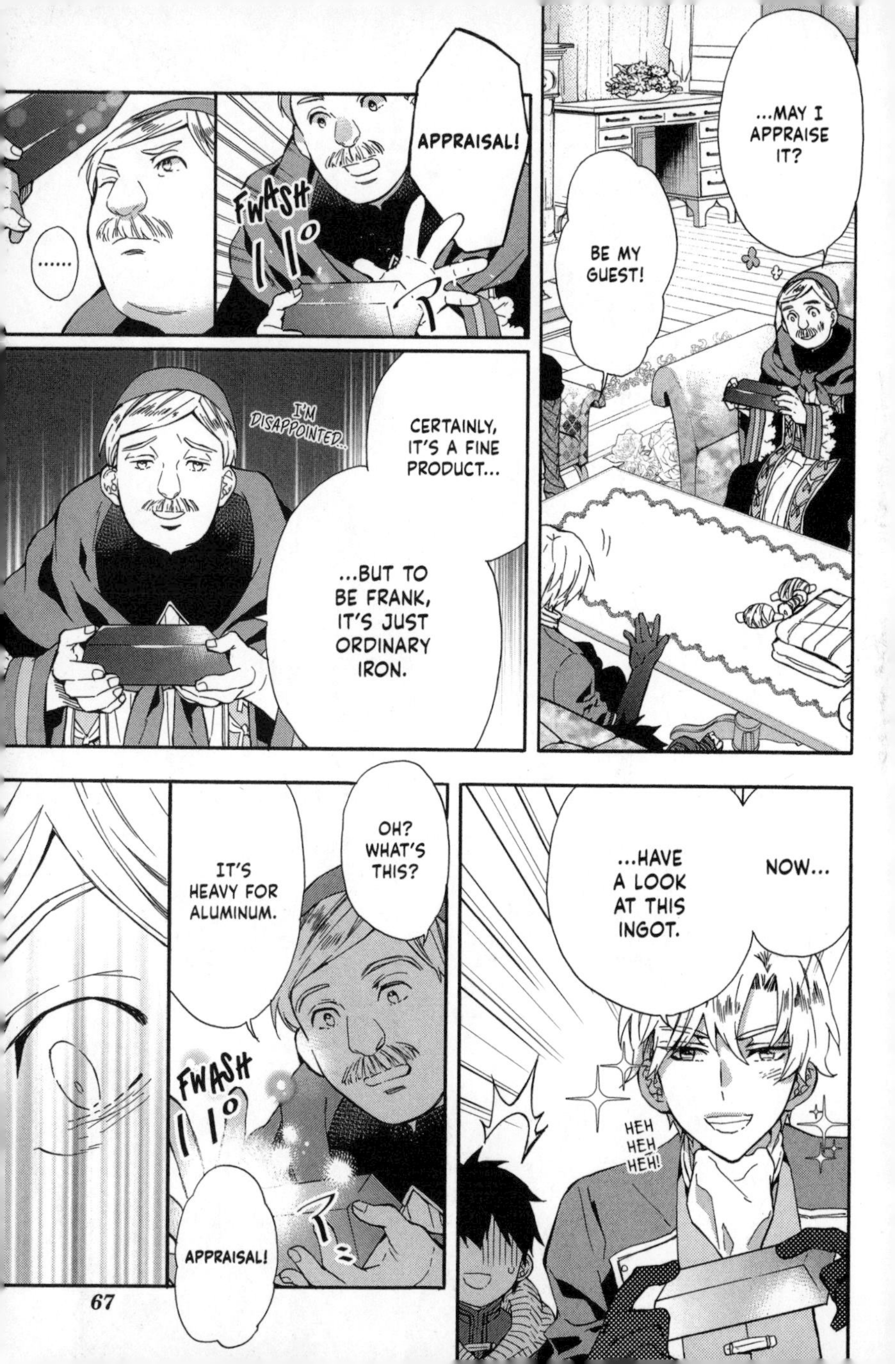
...MAY I APPRAISE IT?
BE MY GUEST!
APPRAISAL!
FWASH
......
CERTAINLY, IT'S A FINE PRODUCT...
I'M DISAPPOINTED...
...BUT TO BE FRANK, IT'S JUST ORDINARY IRON.
NOW...
...HAVE A LOOK AT THIS INGOT.
HEH HEH HEH!
OH? WHAT'S THIS?
IT'S HEAVY FOR ALUMINUM.
FWASH
APPRAISAL!

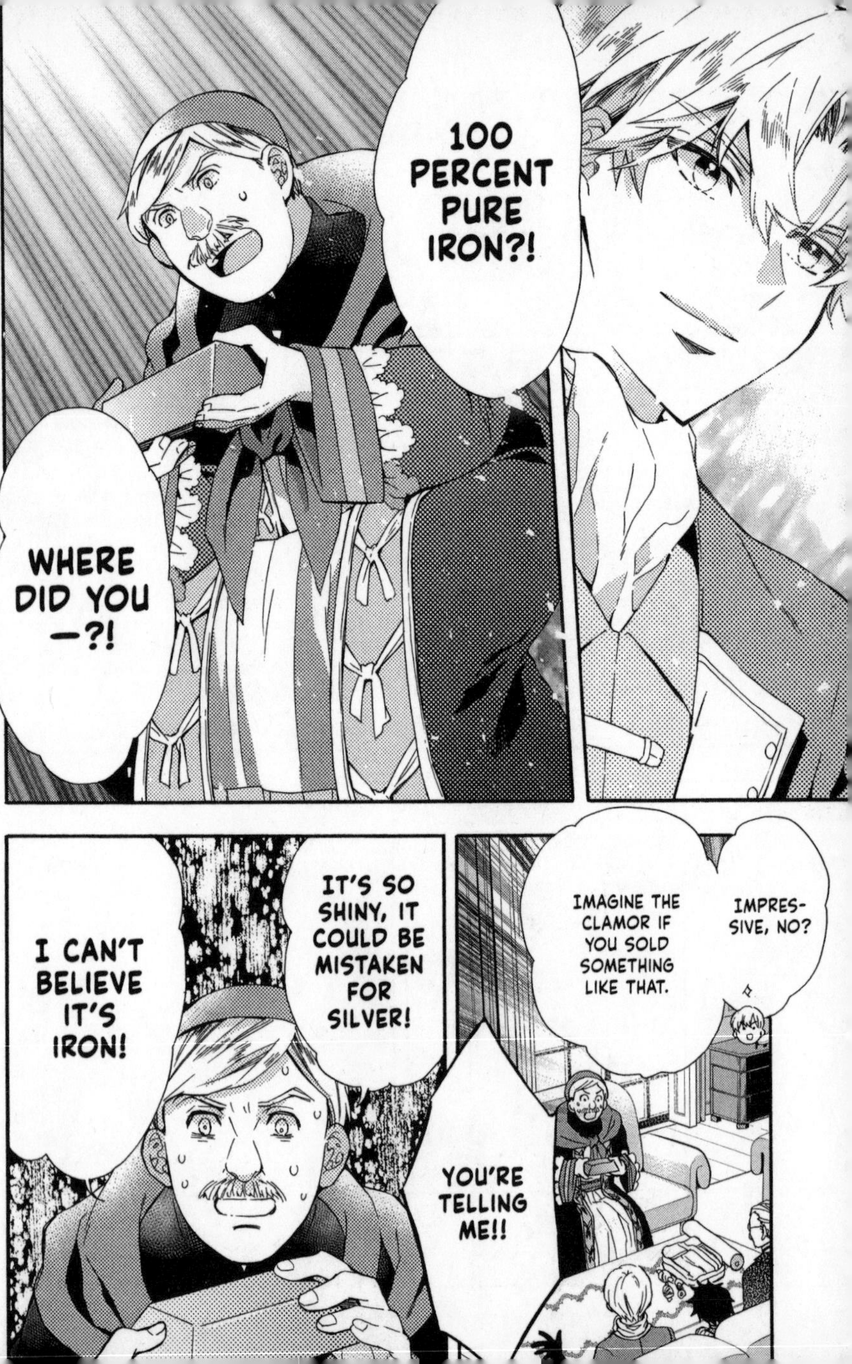
100 PERCENT PURE IRON?!
WHERE DID YOU —?!
IMPRES-SIVE, NO?
IMAGINE THE CLAMOR IF YOU SOLD SOMETHING LIKE THAT.
YOU'RE TELLING ME!!
IT'S SO SHINY, IT COULD BE MISTAKEN FOR SILVER!
I CAN'T BELIEVE IT'S IRON!

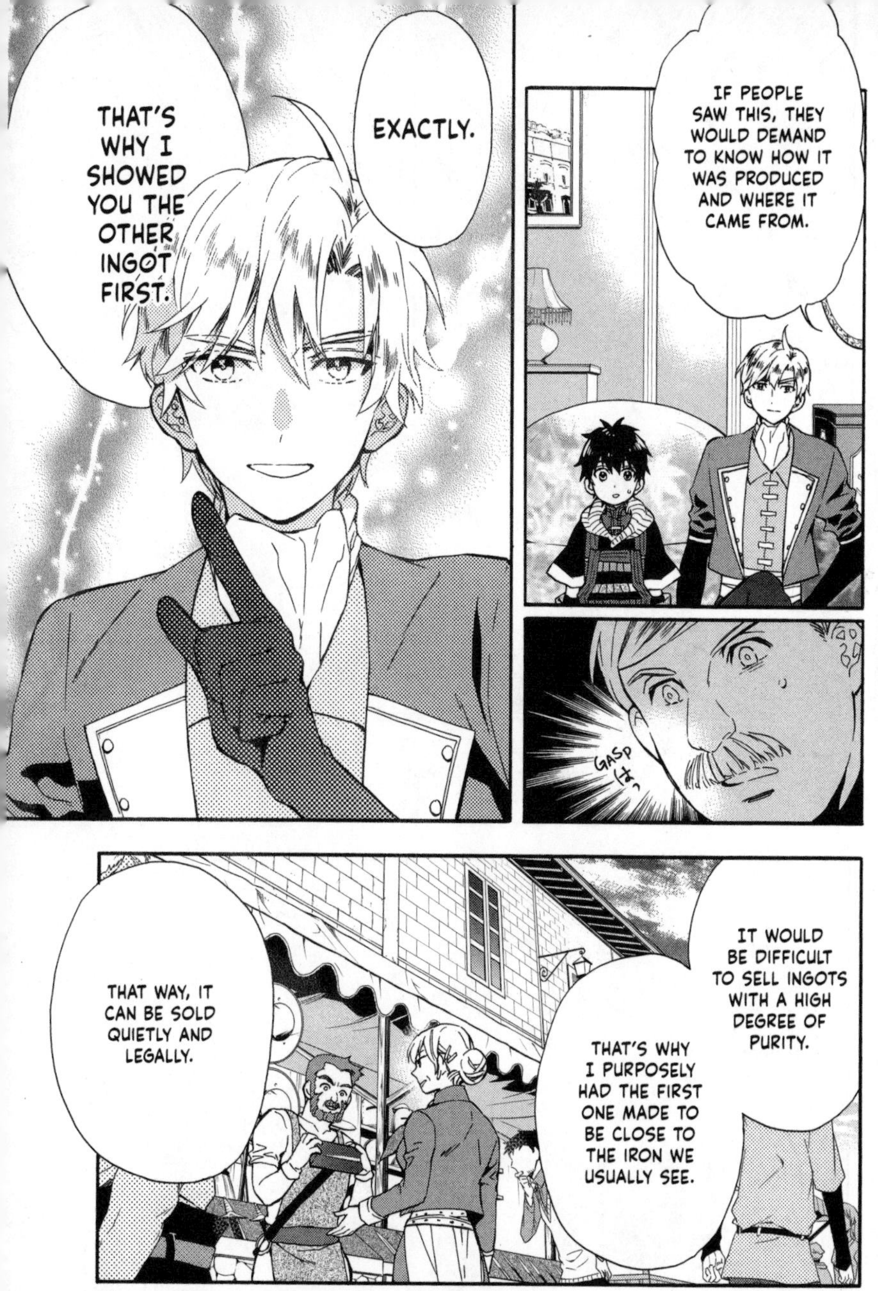
IF PEOPLE SAW THIS, THEY WOULD DEMAND TO KNOW HOW IT WAS PRODUCED AND WHERE IT CAME FROM.
GASP は、
EXACTLY.
THAT'S WHY I SHOWED YOU THE OTHER INGOT FIRST.
IT WOULD BE DIFFICULT TO SELL INGOTS WITH A HIGH DEGREE OF PURITY.
THAT'S WHY I PURPOSELY HAD THE FIRST ONE MADE TO BE CLOSE TO THE IRON WE USUALLY SEE.
THAT WAY, IT CAN BE SOLD QUIETLY AND LEGALLY.

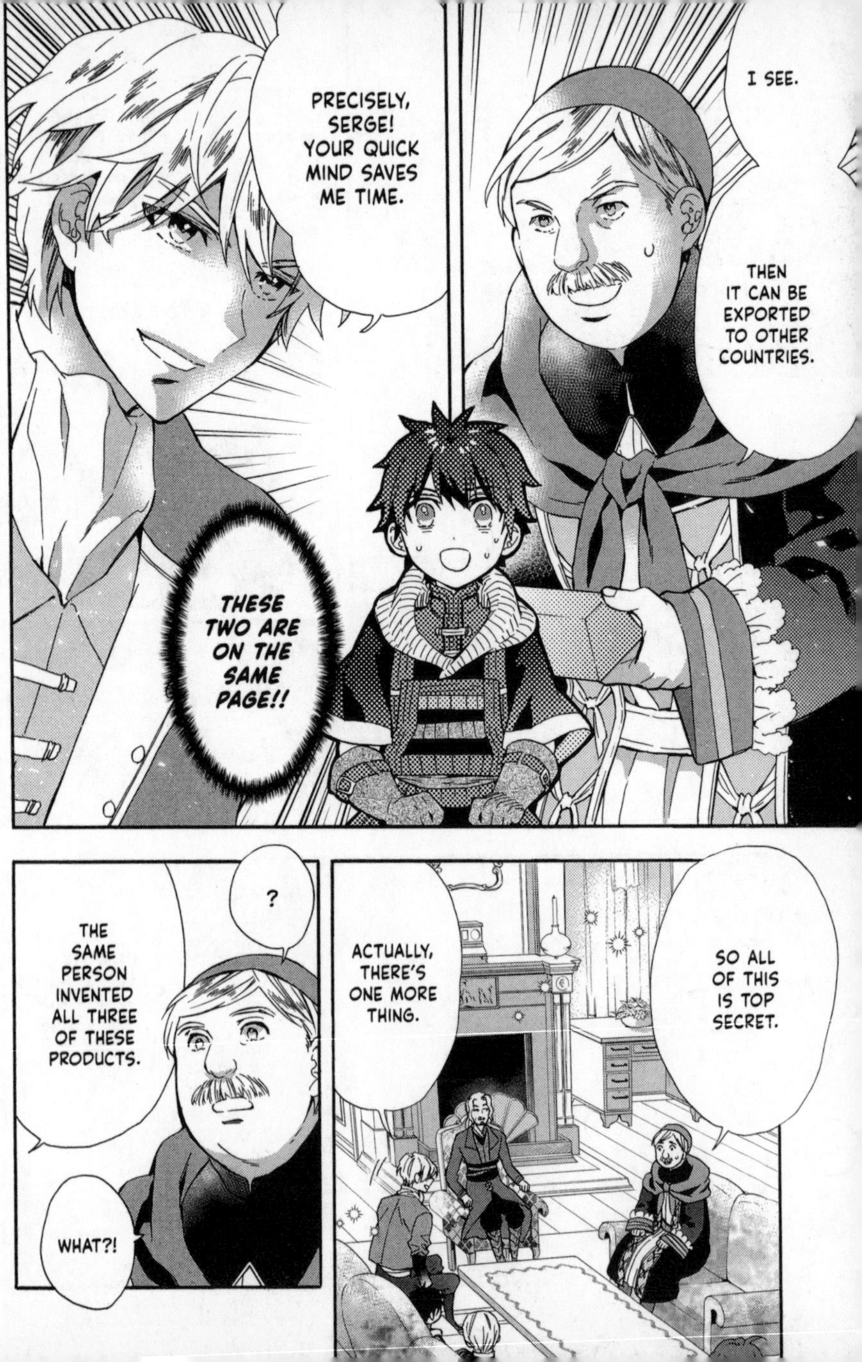
I SEE.
THEN IT CAN BE EXPORTED TO OTHER COUNTRIES.
PRECISELY, SERGE! YOUR QUICK MIND SAVES ME TIME.
THESE TWO ARE ON THE SAME PAGE!!
SO ALL OF THIS IS TOP SECRET.
ACTUALLY, THERE'S ONE MORE THING.
?
THE SAME PERSON INVENTED ALL THREE OF THESE PRODUCTS.
WHAT?!

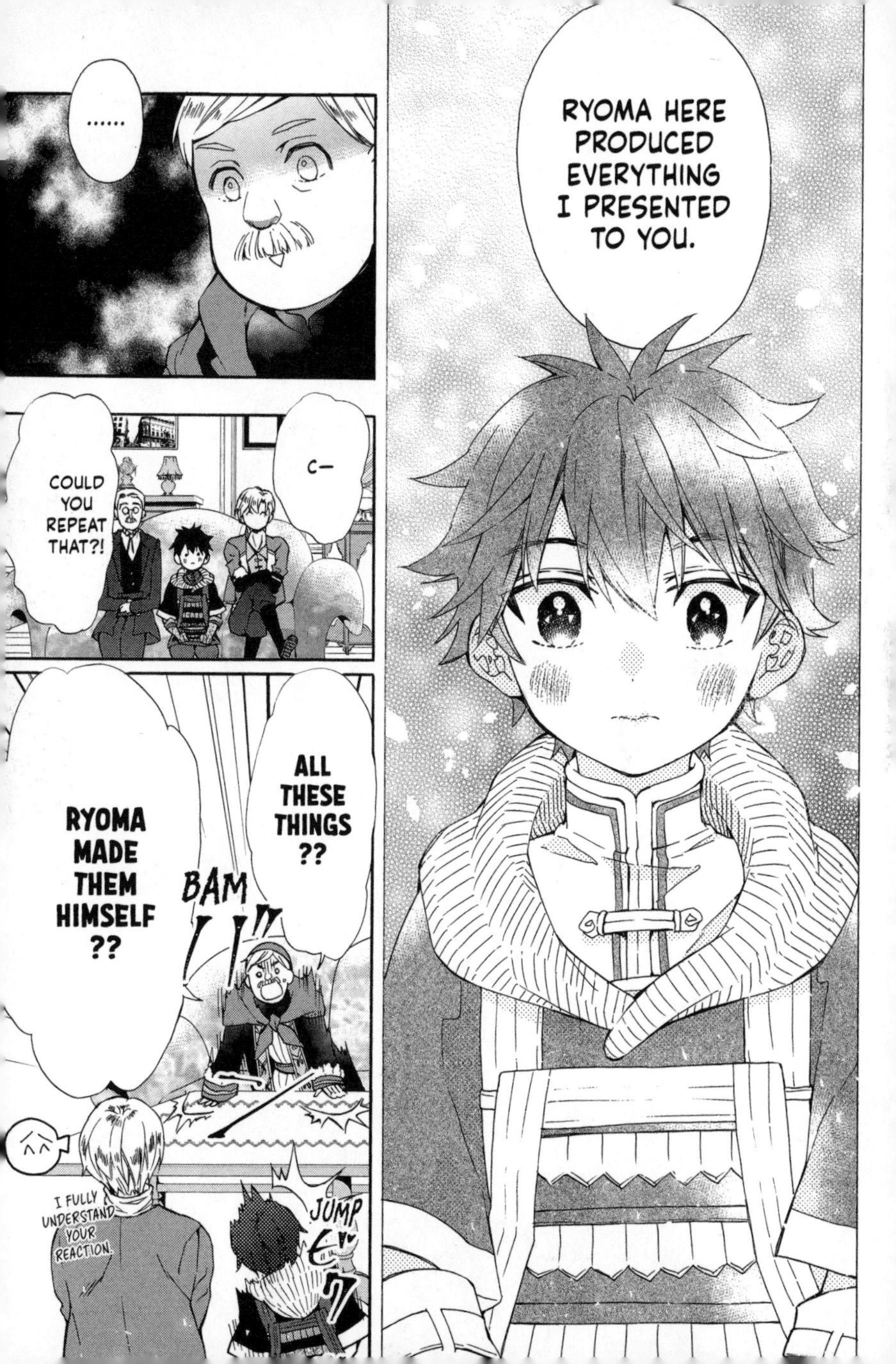
RYOMA HERE PRODUCED EVERYTHING I PRESENTED TO YOU.
......
C—
COULD YOU REPEAT THAT?!
ALL THESE THINGS ??
RYOMA MADE THEM HIMSELF ??
BAM
I FULLY UNDERSTAND YOUR REACTION.
JUMP

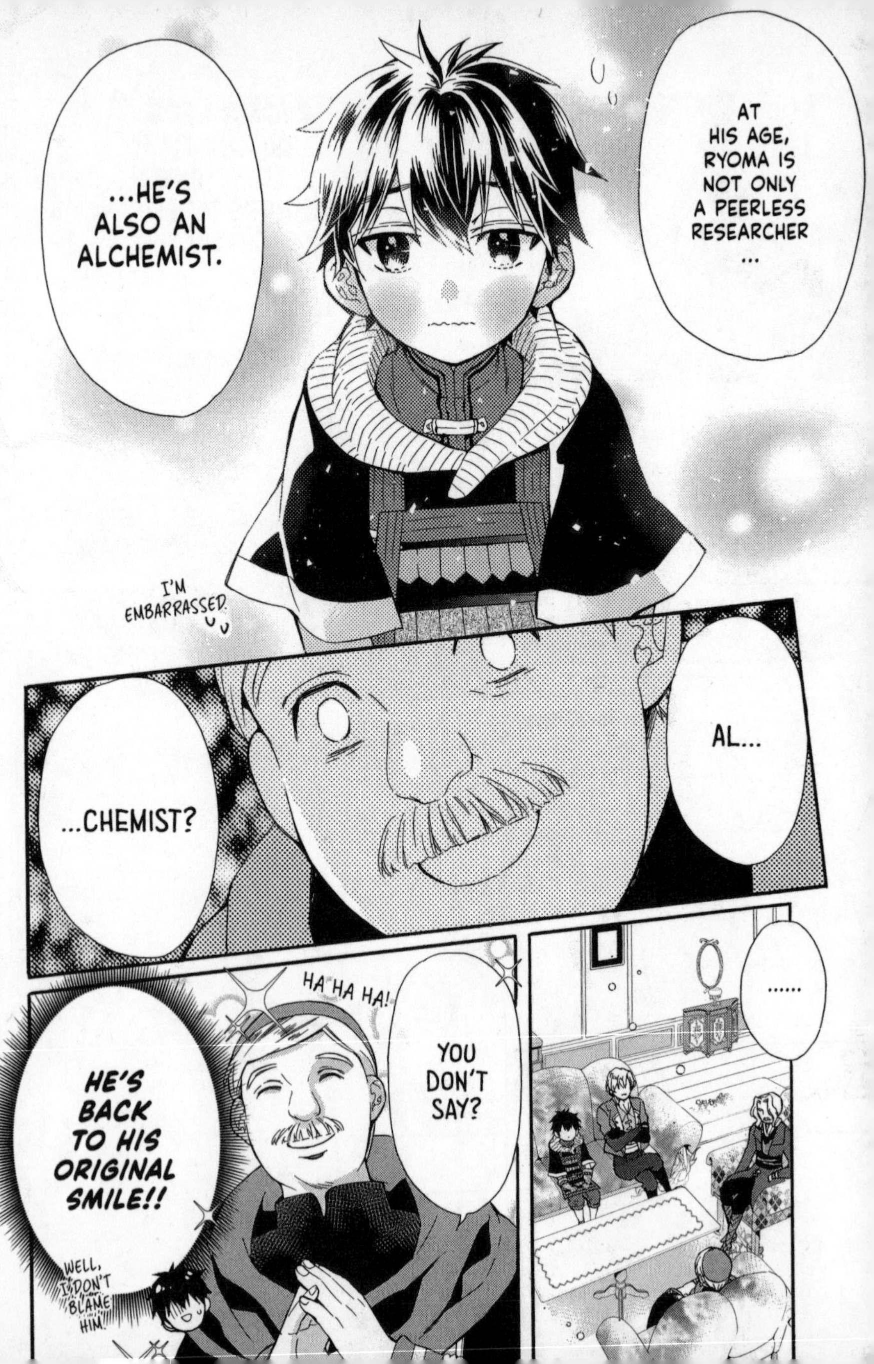
AT HIS AGE, RYOMA IS NOT ONLY A PEERLESS RESEARCHER ...
...HE'S ALSO AN ALCHEMIST.
I'M EMBARRASSED.
AL...
...CHEMIST?
......
HA HA HA!
YOU DON'T SAY?
HE'S BACK TO HIS ORIGINAL SMILE!!
WELL, I DON'T BLAME HIM.

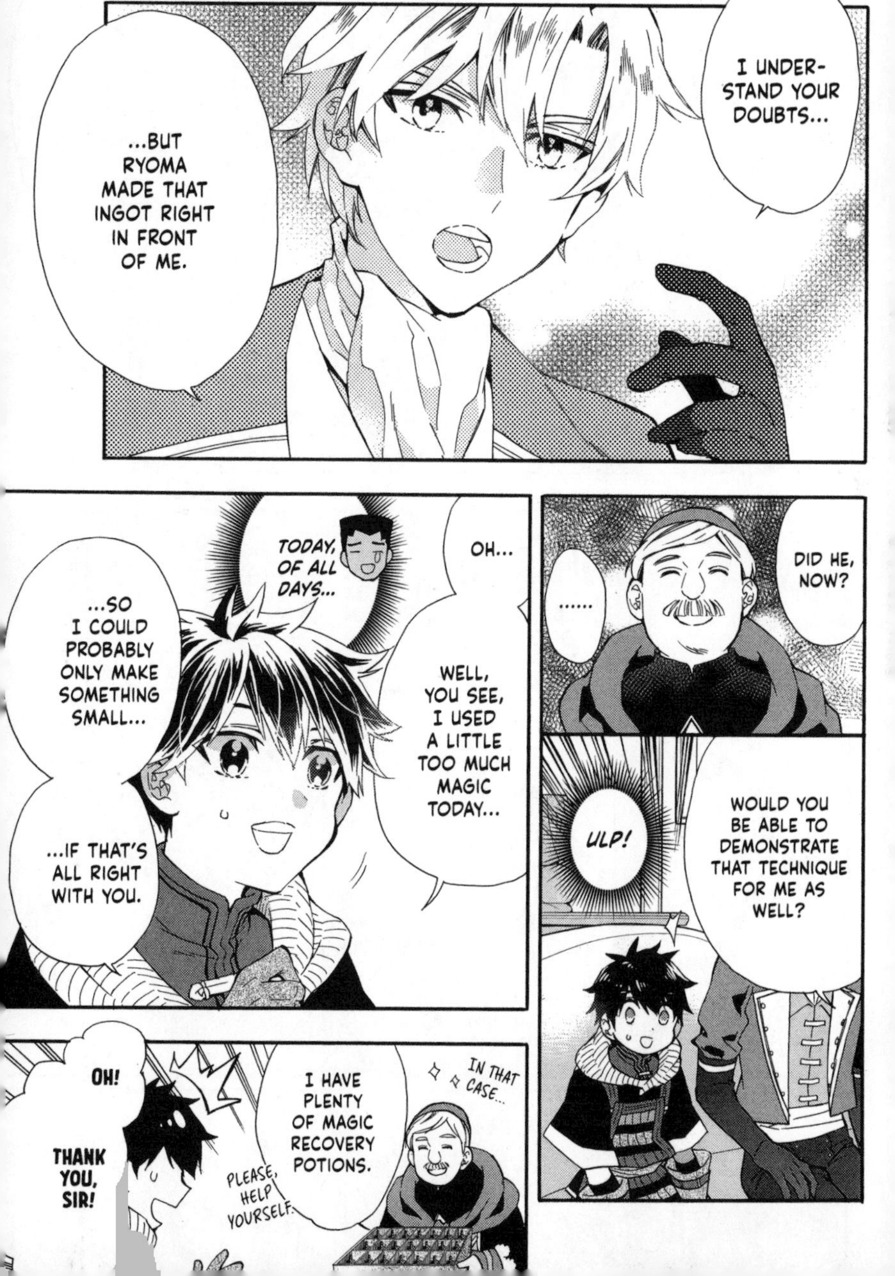
I UNDER-STAND YOUR DOUBTS...
...BUT RYOMA MADE THAT INGOT RIGHT IN FRONT OF ME.
DID HE, NOW?
......
WOULD YOU BE ABLE TO DEMONSTRATE THAT TECHNIQUE FOR ME AS WELL?
ULP!
OH...
TODAY, OF ALL DAYS...
WELL, YOU SEE, I USED A LITTLE TOO MUCH MAGIC TODAY...
...SO I COULD PROBABLY ONLY MAKE SOMETHING SMALL...
...IF THAT'S ALL RIGHT WITH YOU.
IN THAT CASE...
I HAVE PLENTY OF MAGIC RECOVERY POTIONS.
PLEASE, HELP YOURSELF.
OH!
THANK YOU, SIR!

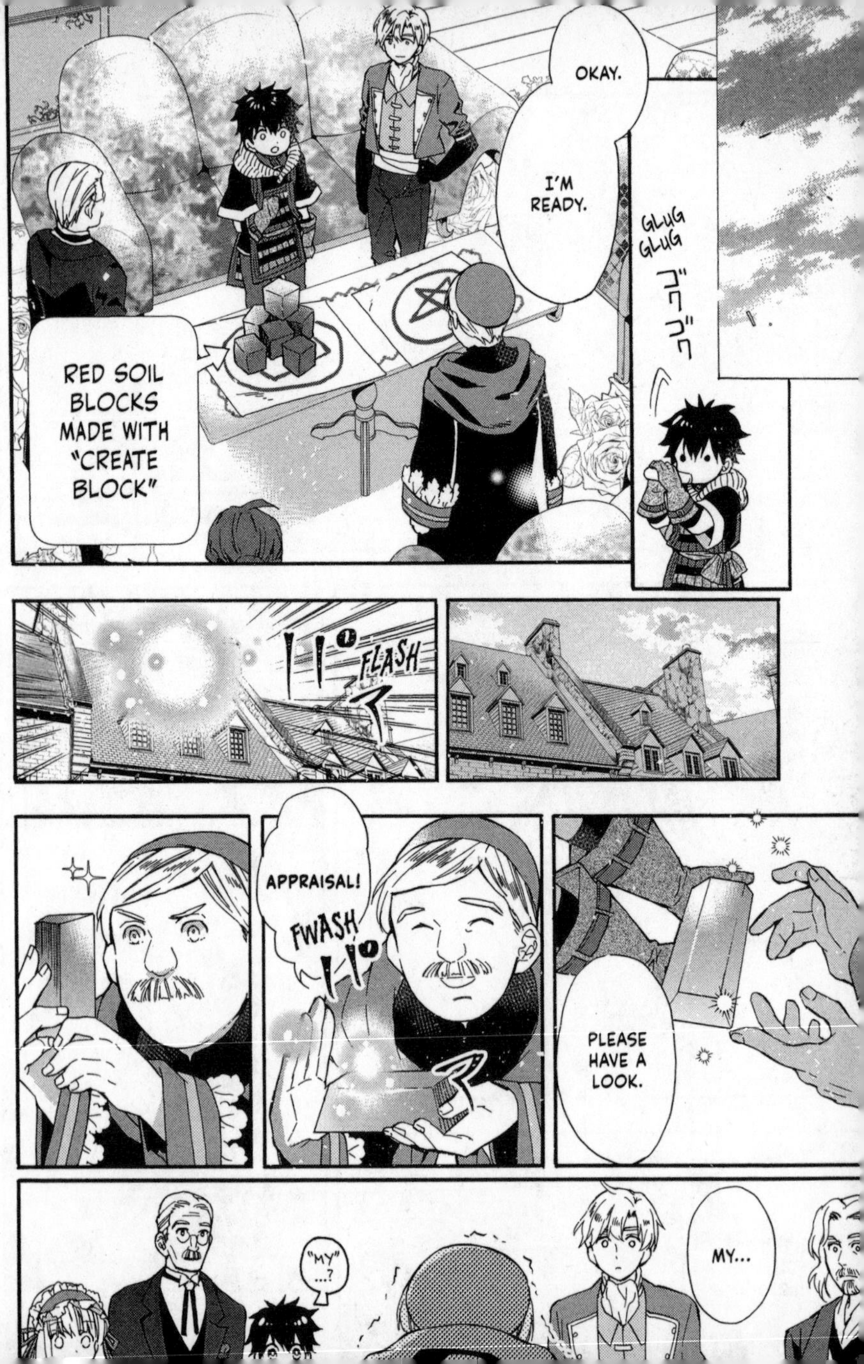
GLUG GLUG
ゴクゴク
OKAY.
I'M READY.
RED SOIL BLOCKS MADE WITH "CREATE BLOCK"
FLASH
PLEASE HAVE A LOOK.
APPRAISAL!
FWASH
MY...
"MY" ...?

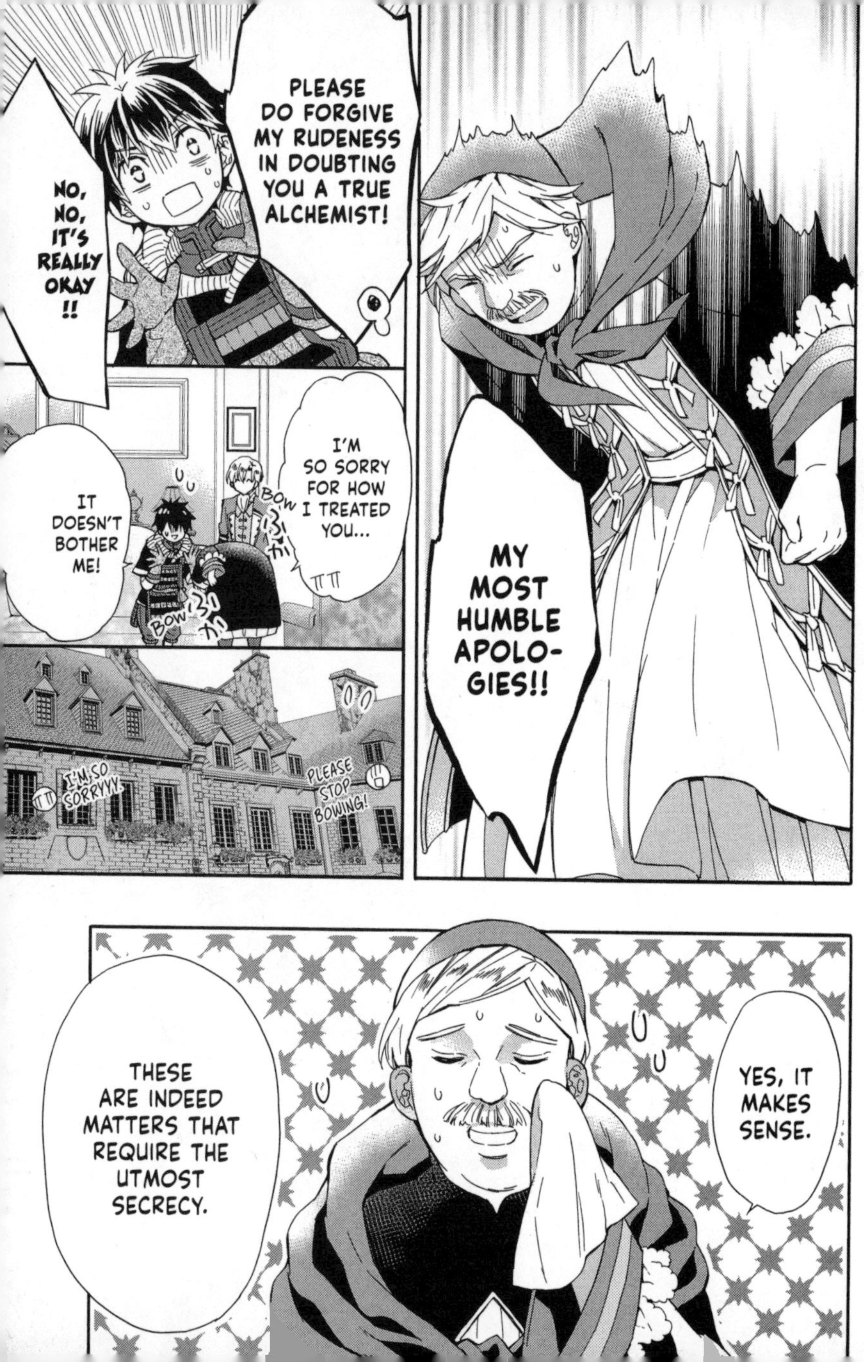
MY MOST HUMBLE APOLOGIES!!
PLEASE DO FORGIVE MY RUDENESS IN DOUBTING YOU A TRUE ALCHEMIST!
NO, NO, IT'S REALLY OKAY!!
I'M SO SORRY FOR HOW I TREATED YOU...
BOW
BOW
IT DOESN'T BOTHER ME!
PLEASE STOP BOWING!
I'M SO SORRYYY.
YES, IT MAKES SENSE.
THESE ARE INDEED MATTERS THAT REQUIRE THE UTMOST SECRECY.

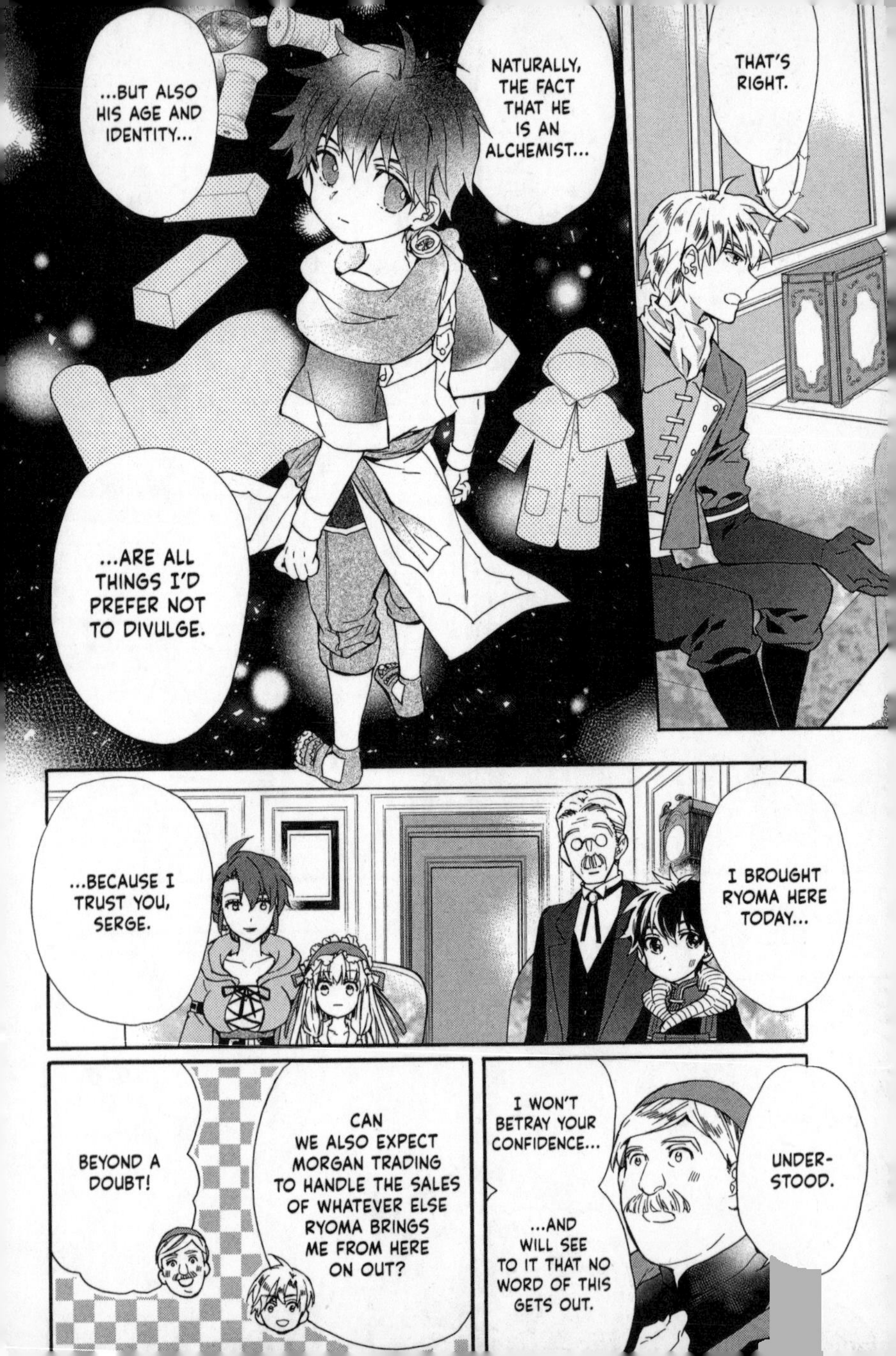
THAT'S RIGHT.
NATURALLY, THE FACT THAT HE IS AN ALCHEMIST...
...BUT ALSO HIS AGE AND IDENTITY...
...ARE ALL THINGS I'D PREFER NOT TO DIVULGE.
I BROUGHT RYOMA HERE TODAY...
...BECAUSE I TRUST YOU, SERGE.
UNDER-STOOD.
I WON'T BETRAY YOUR CONFIDENCE...
...AND WILL SEE TO IT THAT NO WORD OF THIS GETS OUT.
CAN WE ALSO EXPECT MORGAN TRADING TO HANDLE THE SALES OF WHATEVER ELSE RYOMA BRINGS ME FROM HERE ON OUT?
BEYOND A DOUBT!

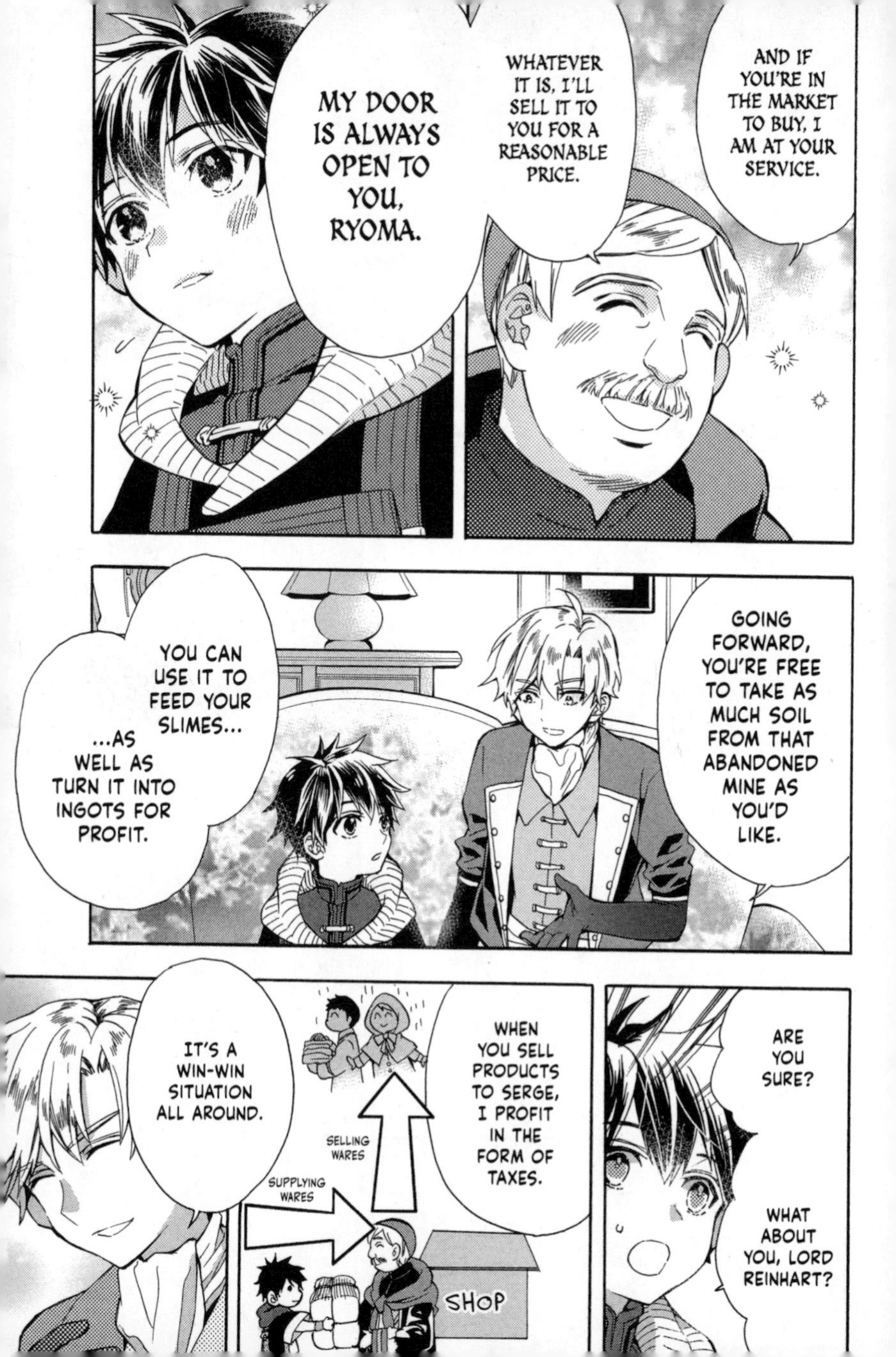
AND IF YOU'RE IN THE MARKET TO BUY, I AM AT YOUR SERVICE.
WHATEVER IT IS, I'LL SELL IT TO YOU FOR A REASONABLE PRICE.
MY DOOR IS ALWAYS OPEN TO YOU, RYOMA.
GOING FORWARD, YOU'RE FREE TO TAKE AS MUCH SOIL FROM THAT ABANDONED MINE AS YOU'D LIKE.
YOU CAN USE IT TO FEED YOUR SLIMES...
...AS WELL AS TURN IT INTO INGOTS FOR PROFIT.
ARE YOU SURE?
WHAT ABOUT YOU, LORD REINHART?
WHEN YOU SELL PRODUCTS TO SERGE, I PROFIT IN THE FORM OF TAXES.
SELLING WARES
SUPPLYING WARES
SHOP
IT'S A WIN-WIN SITUATION ALL AROUND.

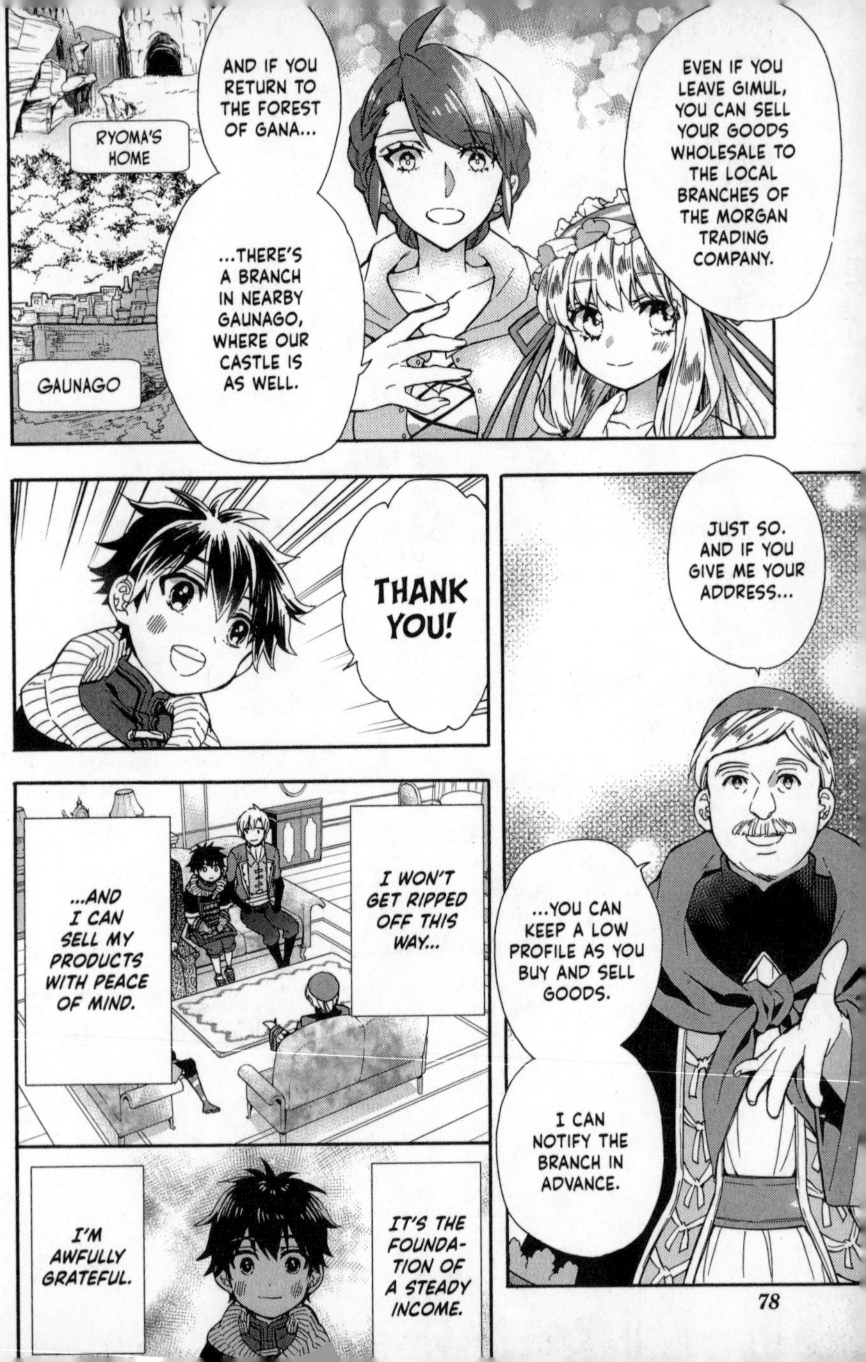
EVEN IF YOU LEAVE GIMUL, YOU CAN SELL YOUR GOODS WHOLESALE TO THE LOCAL BRANCHES OF THE MORGAN TRADING COMPANY.
AND IF YOU RETURN TO THE FOREST OF GANA...
RYOMA'S HOME
...THERE'S A BRANCH IN NEARBY GAUNAGO, WHERE OUR CASTLE IS AS WELL.
GAUNAGO
JUST SO. AND IF YOU GIVE ME YOUR ADDRESS...
...YOU CAN KEEP A LOW PROFILE AS YOU BUY AND SELL GOODS.
I CAN NOTIFY THE BRANCH IN ADVANCE.
THANK YOU!
I WON'T GET RIPPED OFF THIS WAY...
...AND I CAN SELL MY PRODUCTS WITH PEACE OF MIND.
IT'S THE FOUNDATION OF A STEADY INCOME.
I'M AWFULLY GRATEFUL.

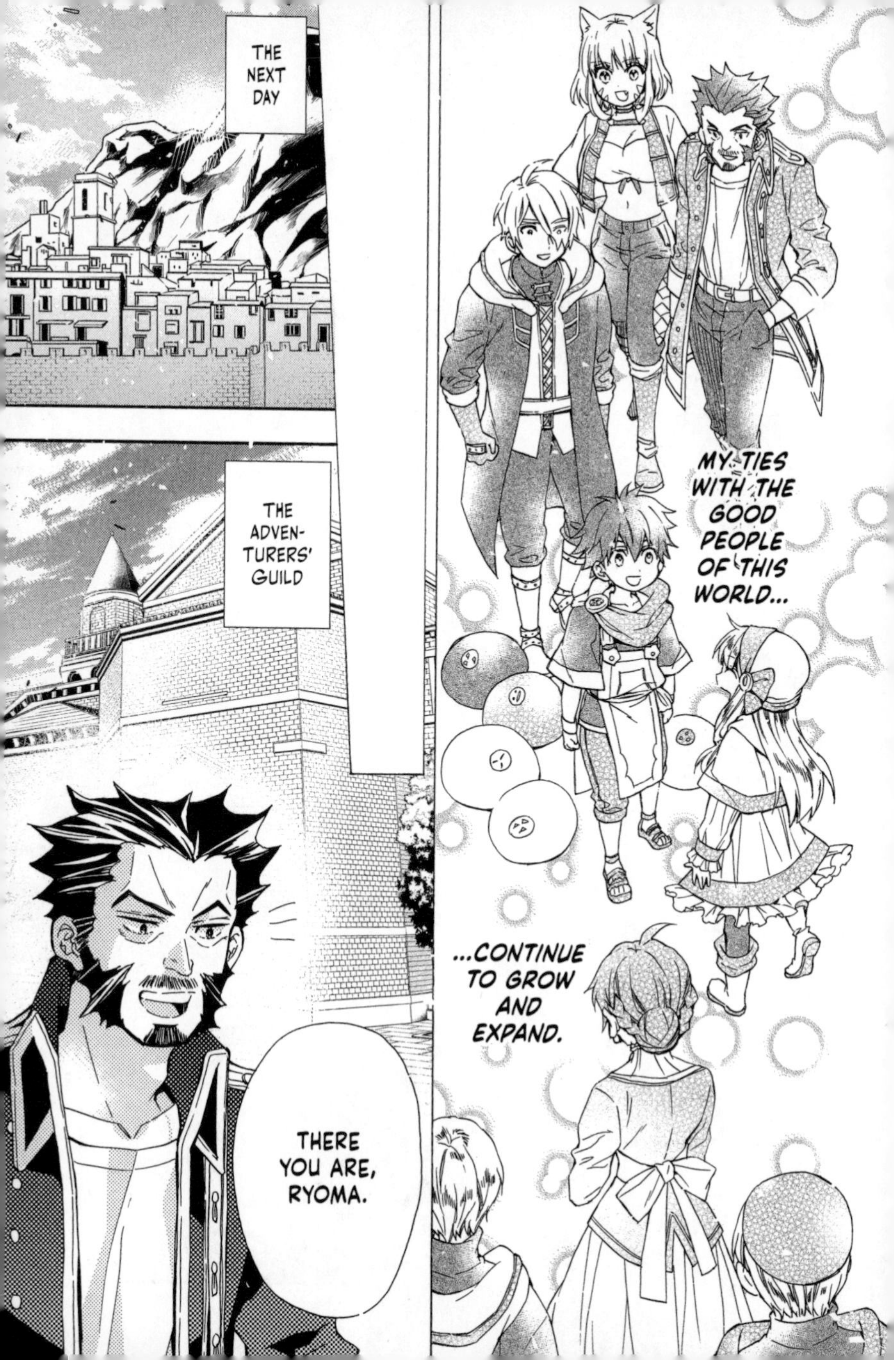
MY TIES WITH THE GOOD PEOPLE OF THIS WORLD...
...CONTINUE TO GROW AND EXPAND.
THE NEXT DAY
THE ADVEN-TURERS' GUILD
THERE YOU ARE, RYOMA.

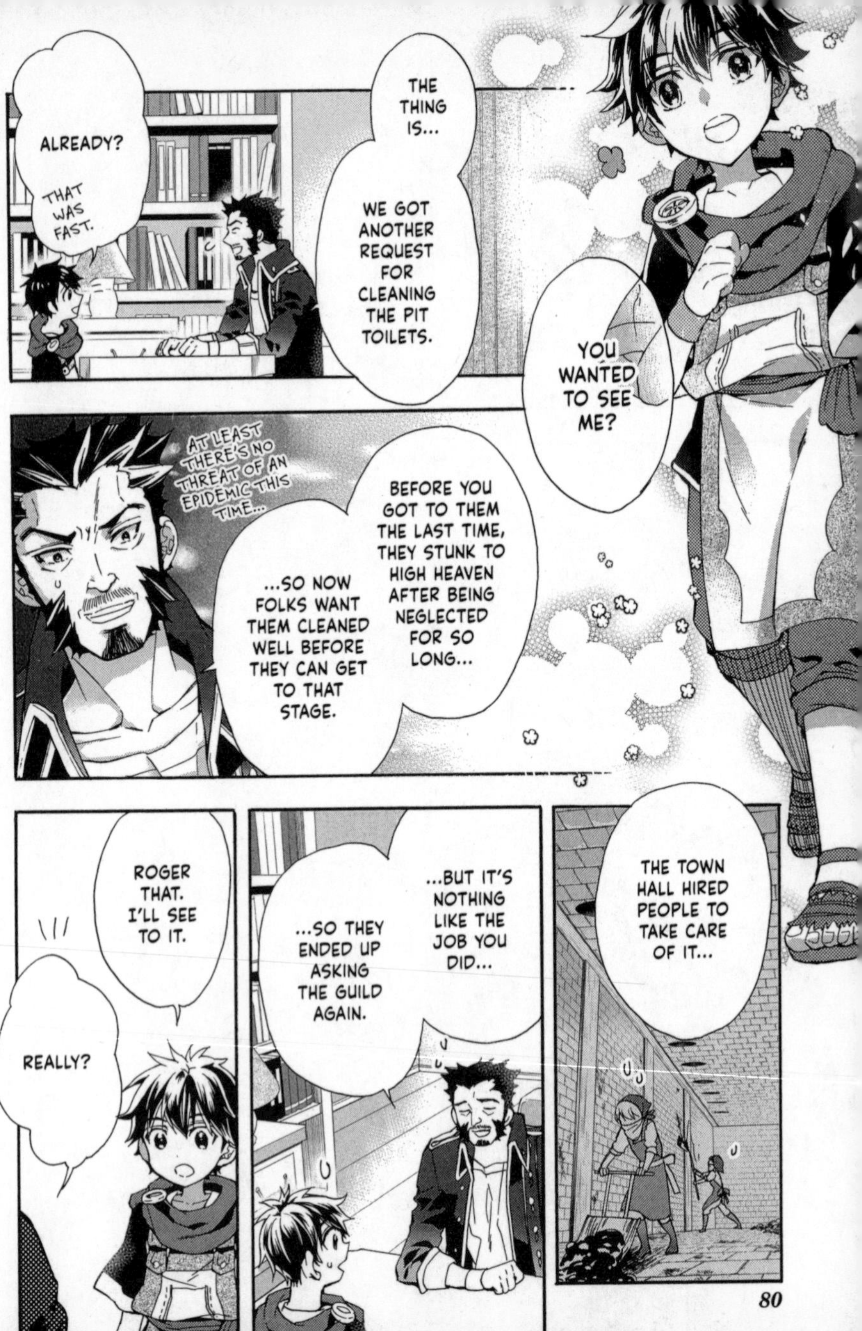

YOU WANTED TO SEE ME?
THE THING IS...
WE GOT ANOTHER REQUEST FOR CLEANING THE PIT TOILETS.
ALREADY?
THAT WAS FAST.
BEFORE YOU GOT TO THEM THE LAST TIME, THEY STUNK TO HIGH HEAVEN AFTER BEING NEGLECTED FOR SO LONG...
...SO NOW FOLKS WANT THEM CLEANED WELL BEFORE THEY CAN GET TO THAT STAGE.
AT LEAST THERE'S NO THREAT OF AN EPIDEMIC THIS TIME...
THE TOWN HALL HIRED PEOPLE TO TAKE CARE OF IT...
...BUT IT'S NOTHING LIKE THE JOB YOU DID...
...SO THEY ENDED UP ASKING THE GUILD AGAIN.
ROGER THAT. I'LL SEE TO IT.
REALLY?

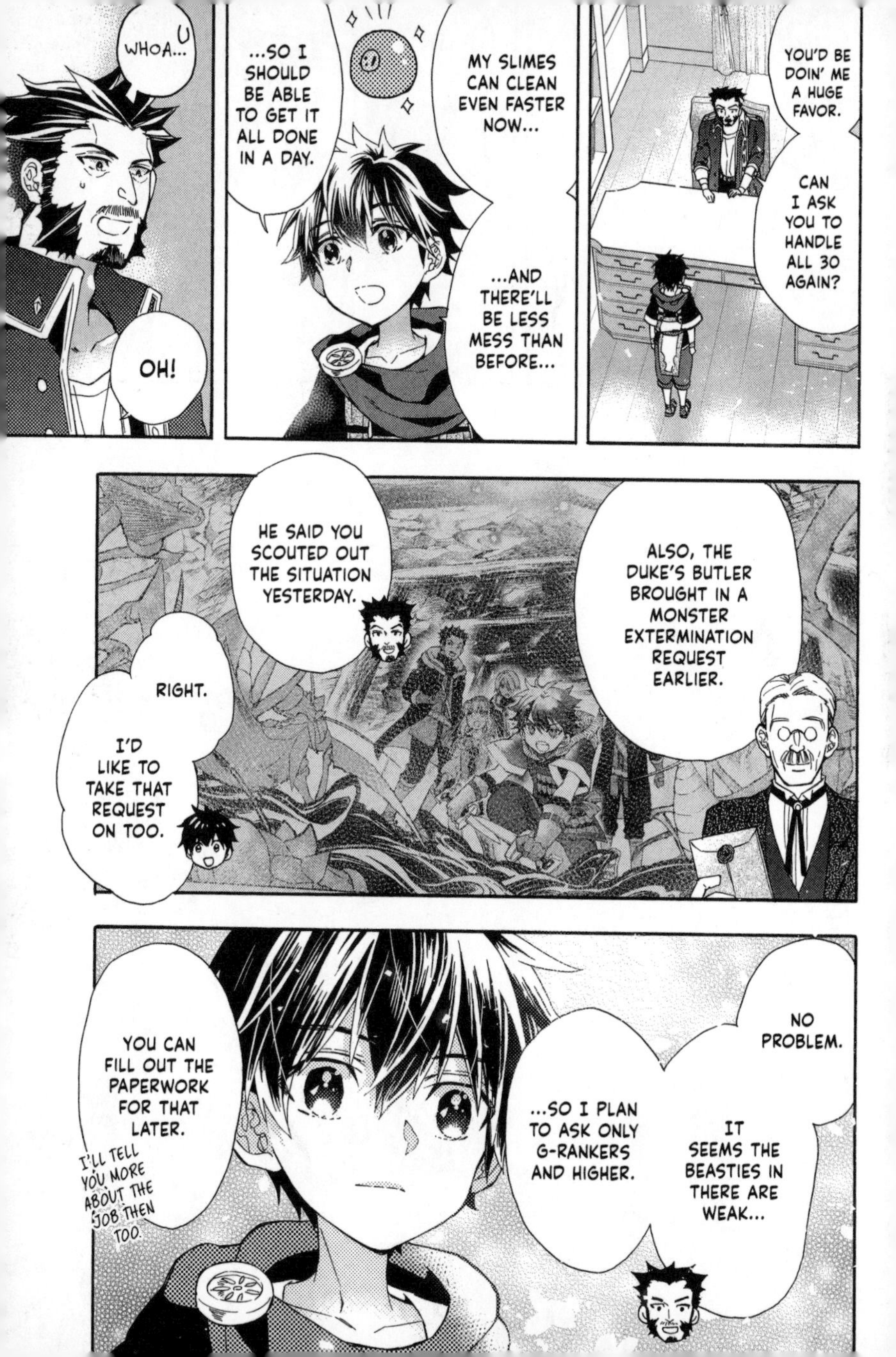
YOU'D BE DOIN' ME A HUGE FAVOR.
CAN I ASK YOU TO HANDLE ALL 30 AGAIN?
MY SLIMES CAN CLEAN EVEN FASTER NOW...
...AND THERE'LL BE LESS MESS THAN BEFORE...
...SO I SHOULD BE ABLE TO GET IT ALL DONE IN A DAY.
WHOA...
OH!
ALSO, THE DUKE'S BUTLER BROUGHT IN A MONSTER EXTERMINATION REQUEST EARLIER.
HE SAID YOU SCOUTED OUT THE SITUATION YESTERDAY.
RIGHT.
I'D LIKE TO TAKE THAT REQUEST ON TOO.
NO PROBLEM.
IT SEEMS THE BEASTIES IN THERE ARE WEAK...
...SO I PLAN TO ASK ONLY G-RANKERS AND HIGHER.
YOU CAN FILL OUT THE PAPERWORK FOR THAT LATER.
I'LL TELL YOU MORE ABOUT THE JOB THEN TOO.

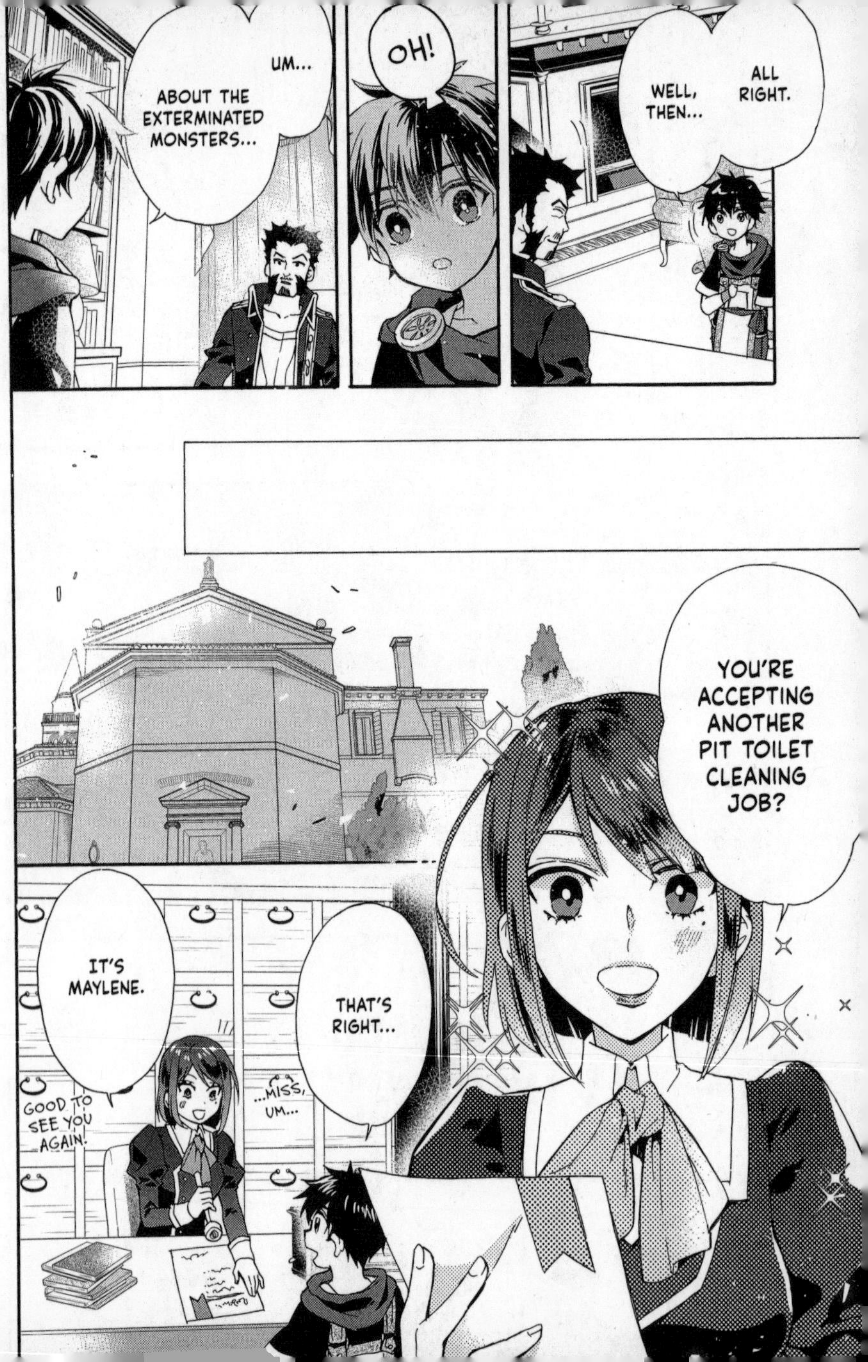
WELL, THEN... ALL RIGHT.
OH!
UM... ABOUT THE EXTERMINATED MONSTERS...
YOU'RE ACCEPTING ANOTHER PIT TOILET CLEANING JOB?
THAT'S RIGHT...
...MISS, UM...
IT'S MAYLENE.
GOOD TO SEE YOU AGAIN!

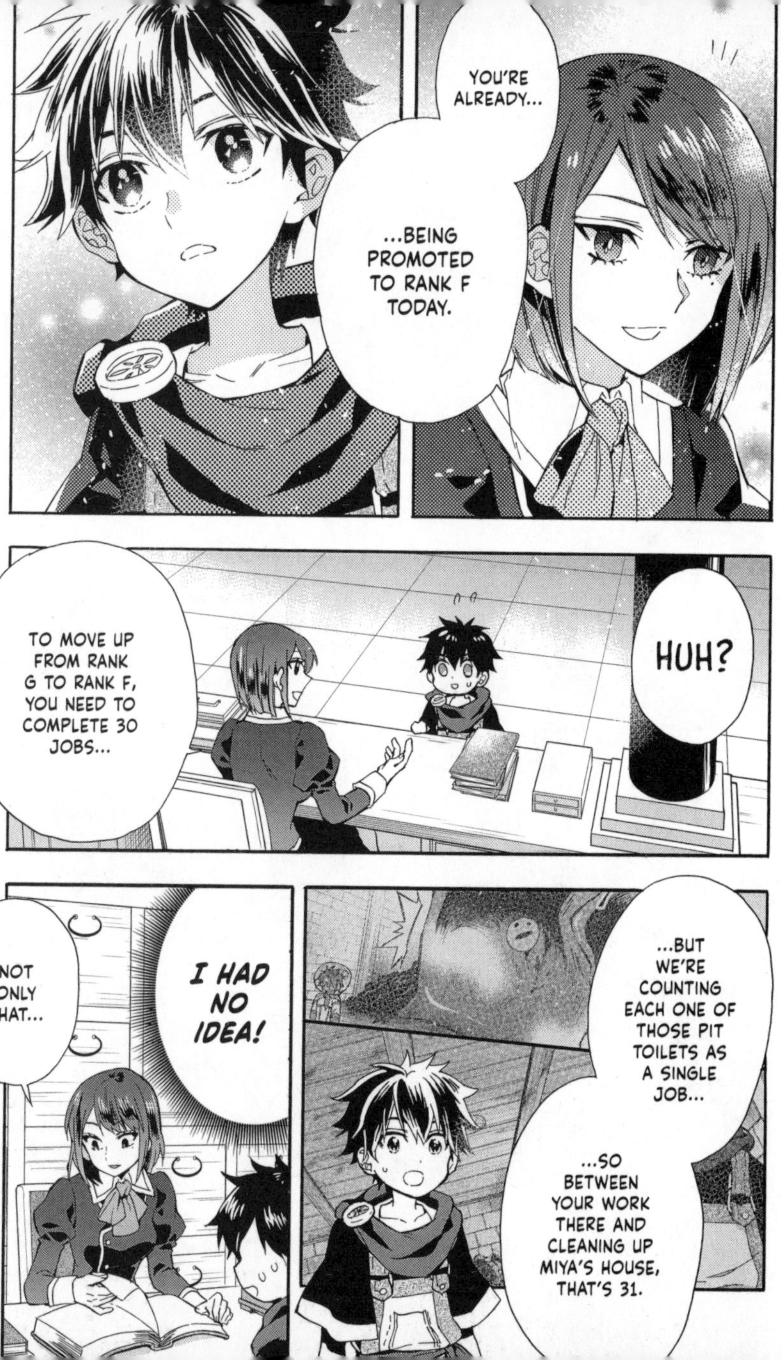
YOU'RE ALREADY...
...BEING PROMOTED TO RANK F TODAY.
HUH?
TO MOVE UP FROM RANK G TO RANK F, YOU NEED TO COMPLETE 30 JOBS...
...BUT WE'RE COUNTING EACH ONE OF THOSE PIT TOILETS AS A SINGLE JOB...
...SO BETWEEN YOUR WORK THERE AND CLEANING UP MIYA'S HOUSE, THAT'S 31.
I HAD NO IDEA!
NOT ONLY THAT...

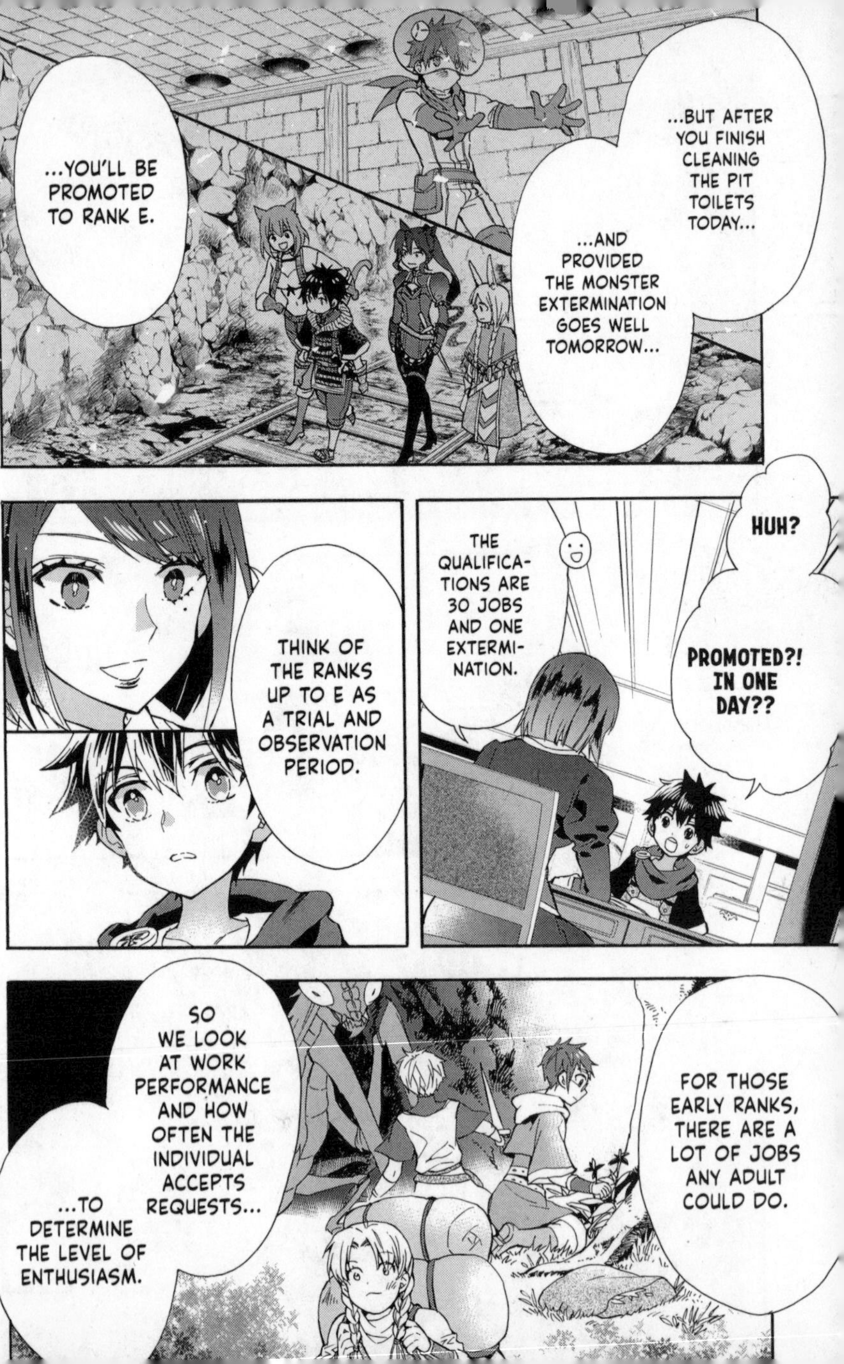
...BUT AFTER YOU FINISH CLEANING THE PIT TOILETS TODAY...
...AND PROVIDED THE MONSTER EXTERMINATION GOES WELL TOMORROW...
...YOU'LL BE PROMOTED TO RANK E.
HUH?
PROMOTED?! IN ONE DAY??
THE QUALIFICATIONS ARE 30 JOBS AND ONE EXTERMINATION.
THINK OF THE RANKS UP TO E AS A TRIAL AND OBSERVATION PERIOD.
FOR THOSE EARLY RANKS, THERE ARE A LOT OF JOBS ANY ADULT COULD DO.
SO WE LOOK AT WORK PERFORMANCE AND HOW OFTEN THE INDIVIDUAL ACCEPTS REQUESTS...
...TO DETERMINE THE LEVEL OF ENTHUSIASM.

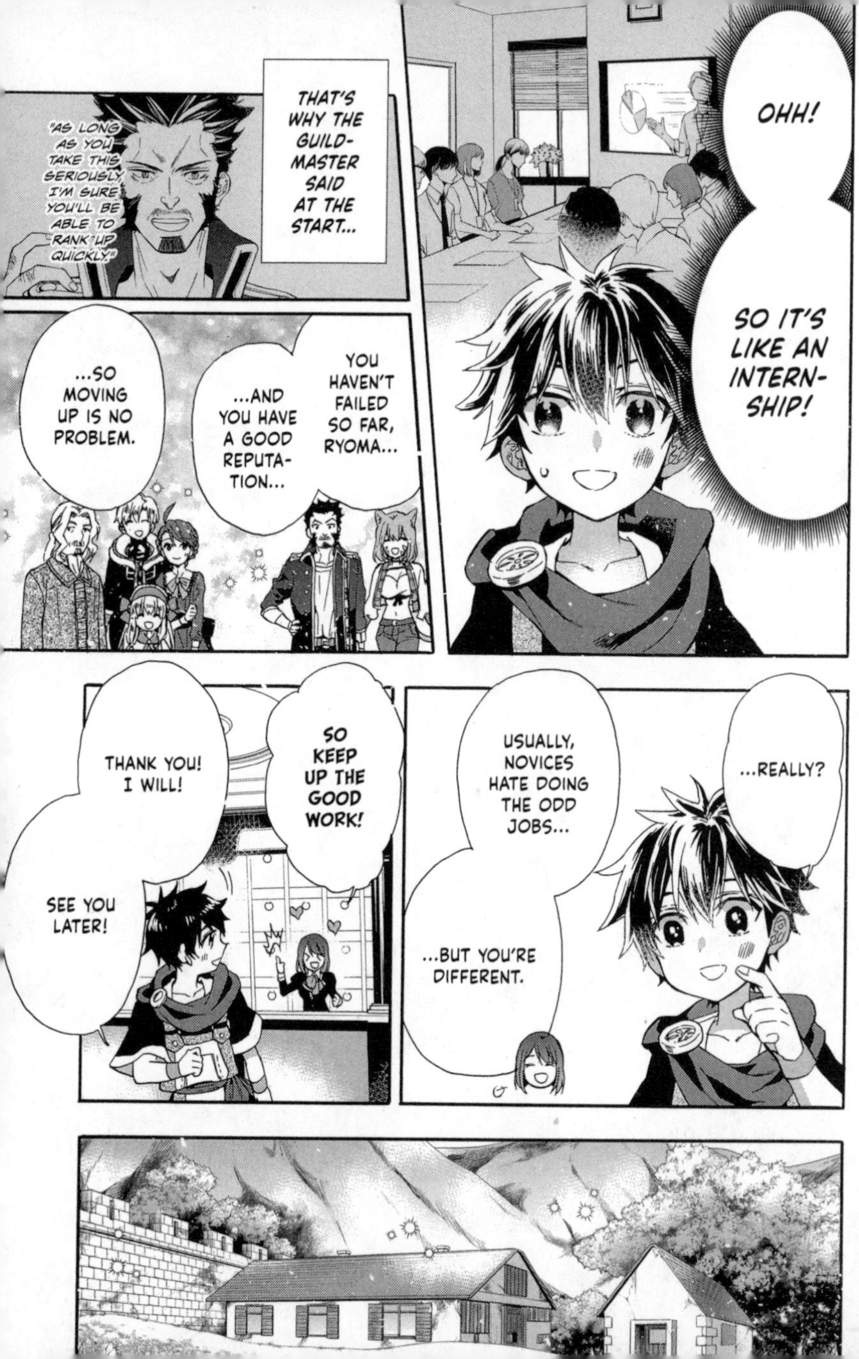
OHH!
SO IT'S LIKE AN INTERN-SHIP!
THAT'S WHY THE GUILD-MASTER SAID AT THE START...
"AS LONG AS YOU TAKE THIS SERIOUSLY, I'M SURE YOU'LL BE ABLE TO RANK UP QUICKLY."
YOU HAVEN'T FAILED SO FAR, RYOMA...
...AND YOU HAVE A GOOD REPUTA-TION...
...SO MOVING UP IS NO PROBLEM.
...REALLY?
USUALLY, NOVICES HATE DOING THE ODD JOBS...
...BUT YOU'RE DIFFERENT.
SO KEEP UP THE GOOD WORK!
THANK YOU! I WILL!
SEE YOU LATER!

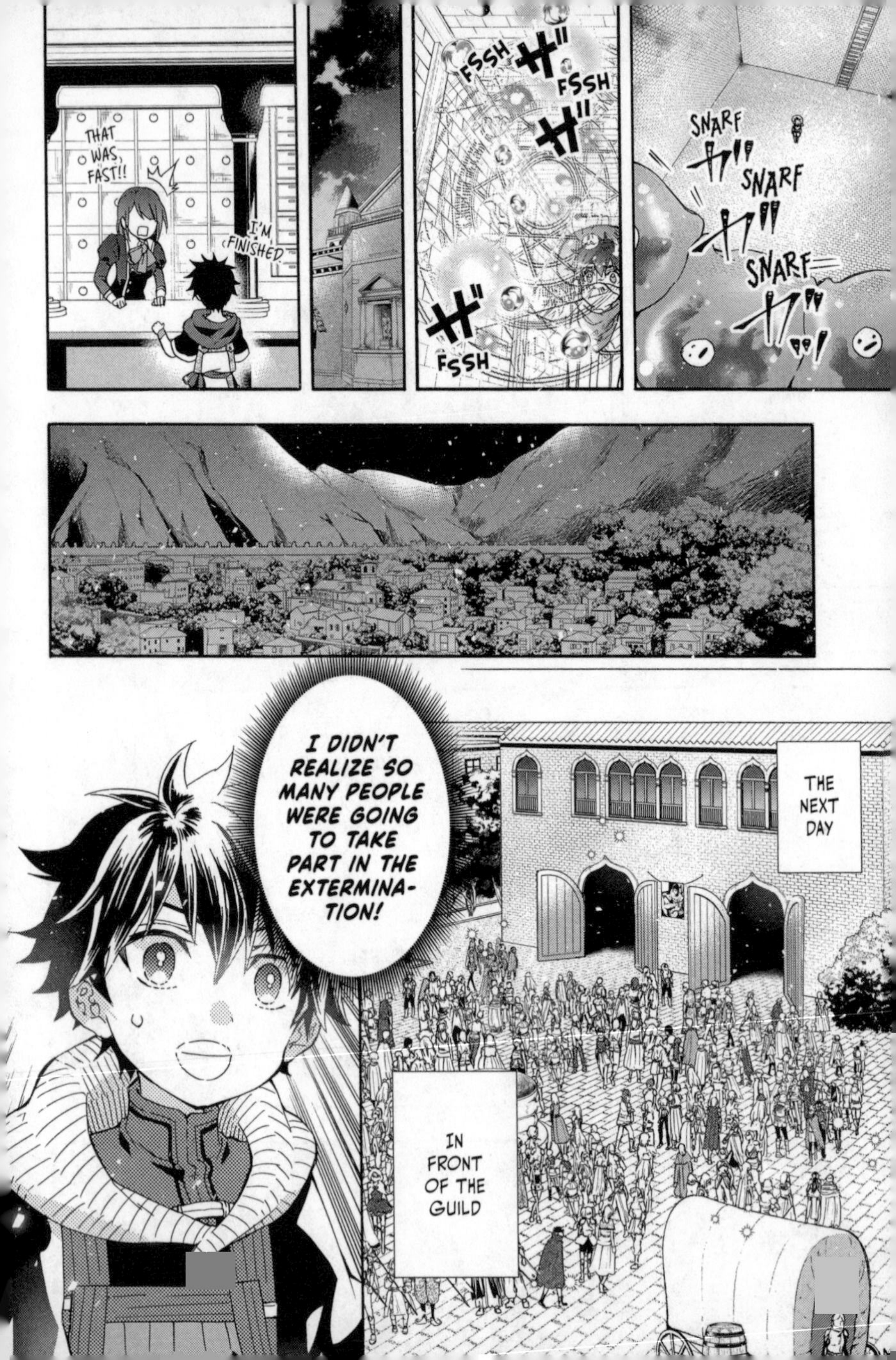
SNARF
SNARF
SNARF
FSSH
FSSH
FSSH
I'M FINISHED
THAT WAS, FAST!!
THE NEXT DAY
IN FRONT OF THE GUILD
I DIDN'T REALIZE SO MANY PEOPLE WERE GOING TO TAKE PART IN THE EXTERMINA-TION!

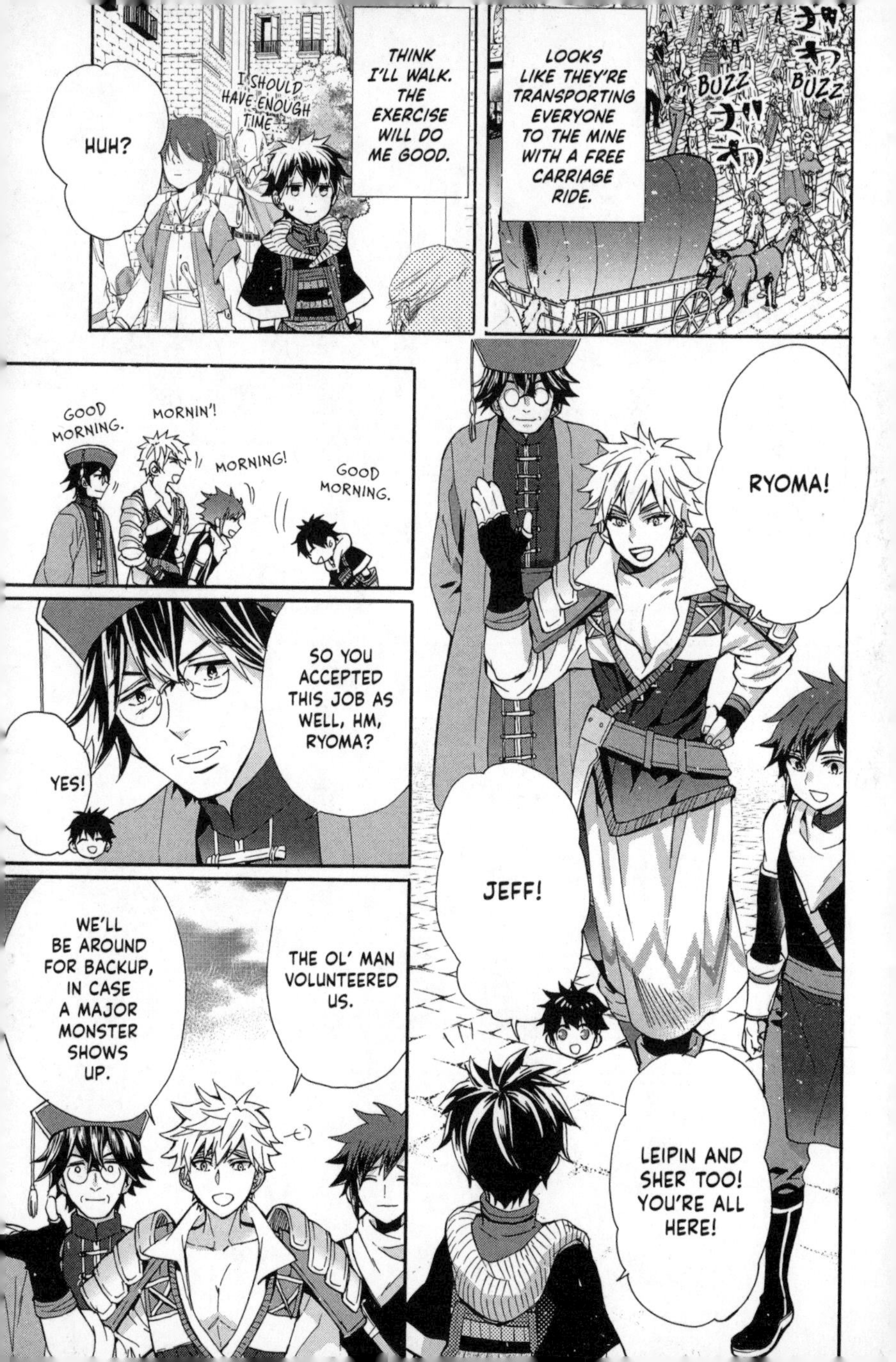
LOOKS LIKE THEY'RE TRANSPORTING EVERYONE TO THE MINE WITH A FREE CARRIAGE RIDE.
BUZZ BUZZ
THINK I'LL WALK. THE EXERCISE WILL DO ME GOOD.
I SHOULD HAVE ENOUGH TIME
HUH?
RYOMA!
JEFF!
LEIPIN AND SHER TOO! YOU'RE ALL HERE!
GOOD MORNING.
MORNING!
MORNIN'!
GOOD MORNING.
SO YOU ACCEPTED THIS JOB AS WELL, HM, RYOMA?
YES!
THE OL' MAN VOLUNTEERED US.
WE'LL BE AROUND FOR BACKUP, IN CASE A MAJOR MONSTER SHOWS UP.

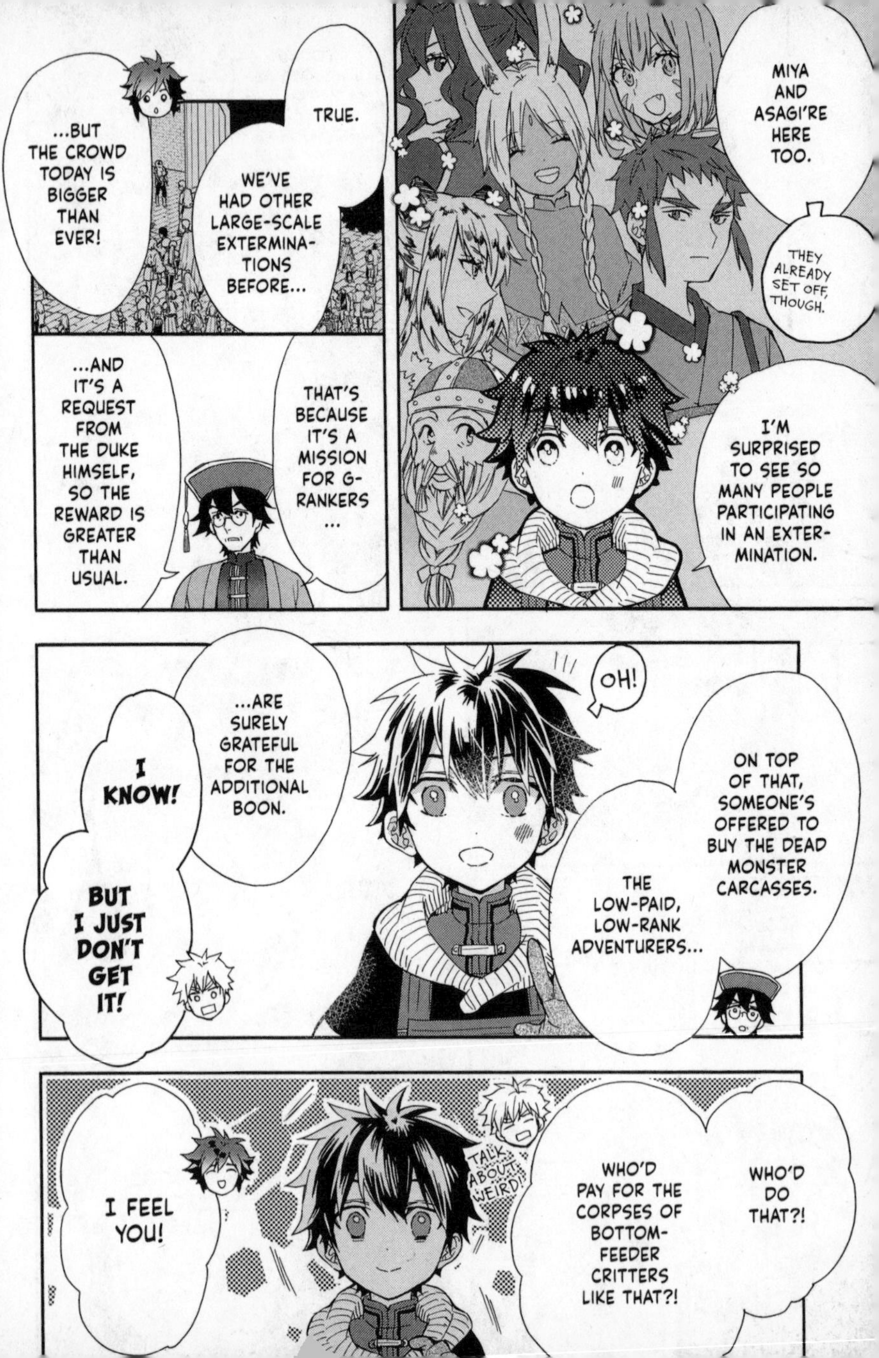
MIYA AND ASAGI'RE HERE TOO.
THEY ALREADY SET OFF, THOUGH.
I'M SURPRISED TO SEE SO MANY PEOPLE PARTICIPATING IN AN EXTERMINATION.
TRUE.
WE'VE HAD OTHER LARGE-SCALE EXTERMINATIONS BEFORE...
...BUT THE CROWD TODAY IS BIGGER THAN EVER!
THAT'S BECAUSE IT'S A MISSION FOR G-RANKERS...
...AND IT'S A REQUEST FROM THE DUKE HIMSELF, SO THE REWARD IS GREATER THAN USUAL.
ON TOP OF THAT, SOMEONE'S OFFERED TO BUY THE DEAD MONSTER CARCASSES.
OH!
THE LOW-PAID, LOW-RANK ADVENTURERS...
...ARE SURELY GRATEFUL FOR THE ADDITIONAL BOON.
I KNOW!
BUT I JUST DON'T GET IT!
WHO'D DO THAT?!
WHO'D PAY FOR THE CORPSES OF BOTTOM-FEEDER CRITTERS LIKE THAT?!
TALK ABOUT WEIRD!
I FEEL YOU!

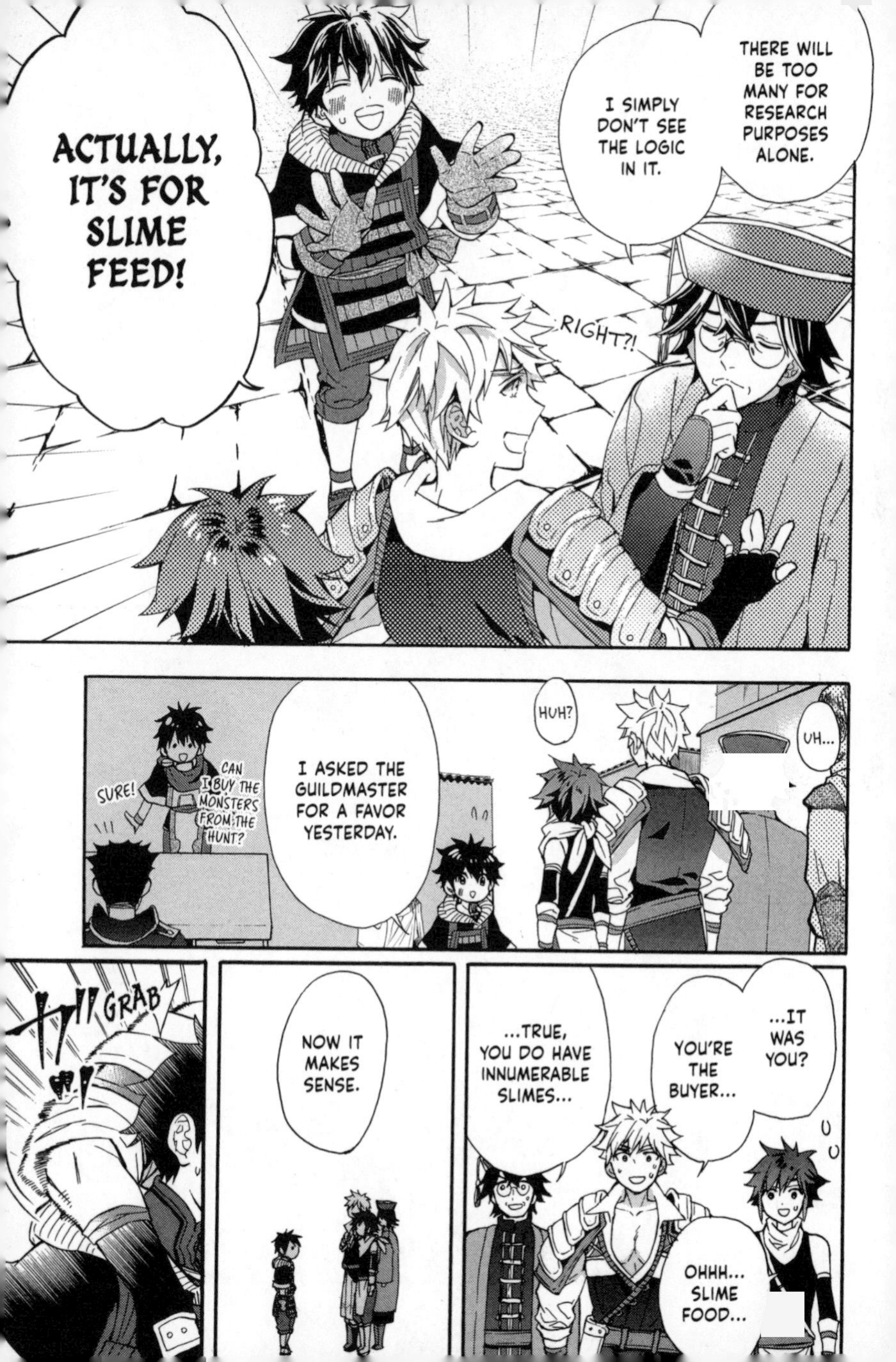
THERE WILL BE TOO MANY FOR RESEARCH PURPOSES ALONE.
I SIMPLY DON'T SEE THE LOGIC IN IT.
RIGHT?!
ACTUALLY, IT'S FOR SLIME FEED!
UH...
HUH?
I ASKED THE GUILDMASTER FOR A FAVOR YESTERDAY.
CAN I BUY THE MONSTERS FROM THE HUNT?
SURE!
...IT WAS YOU?
YOU'RE THE BUYER...
...TRUE, YOU DO HAVE INNUMERABLE SLIMES...
OHHH... SLIME FOOD...
NOW IT MAKES SENSE.
GRAB

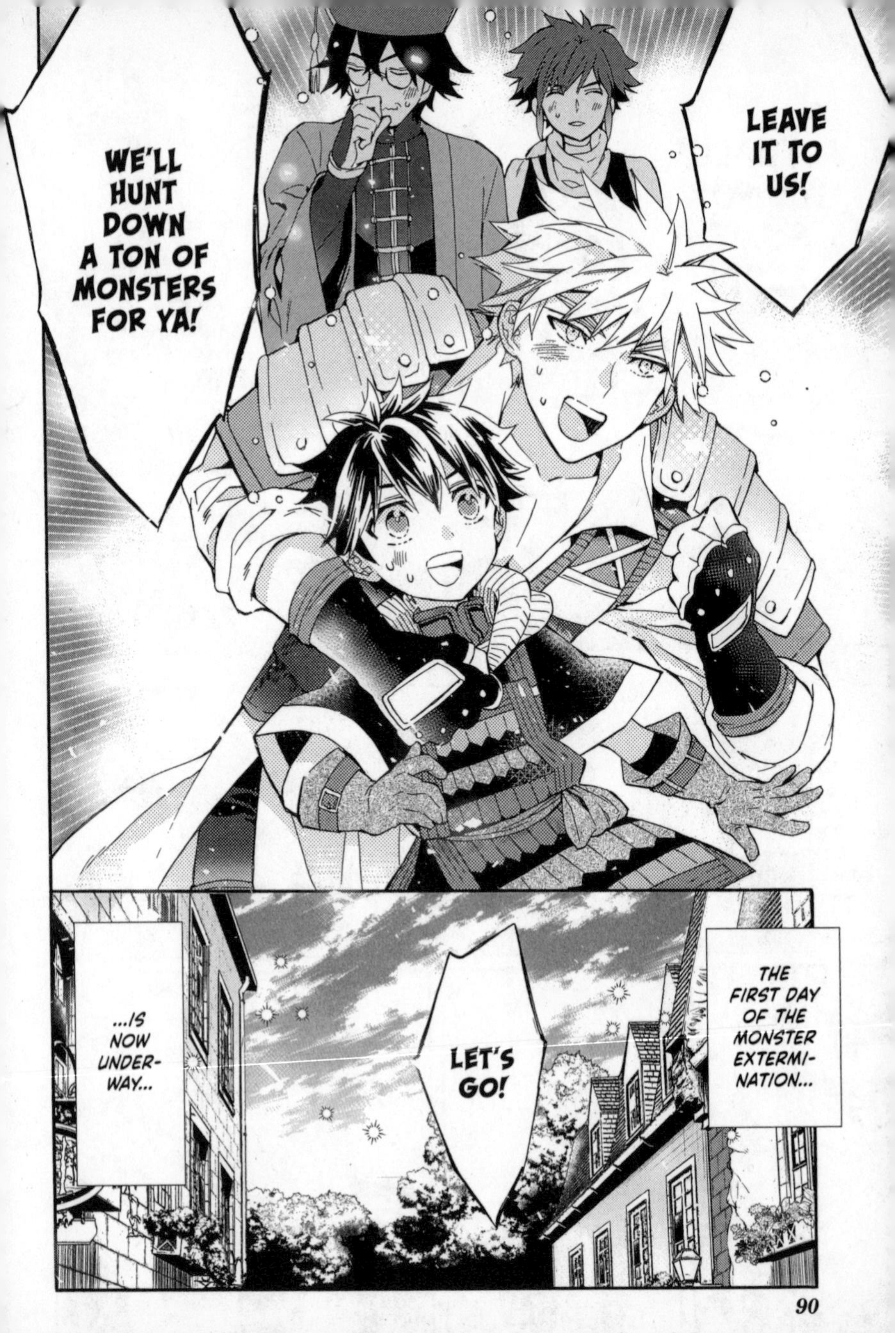
LEAVE IT TO US!
WE'LL HUNT DOWN A TON OF MONSTERS FOR YA!
THE FIRST DAY OF THE MONSTER EXTERMINATION...
LET'S GO!
...IS NOW UNDERWAY...

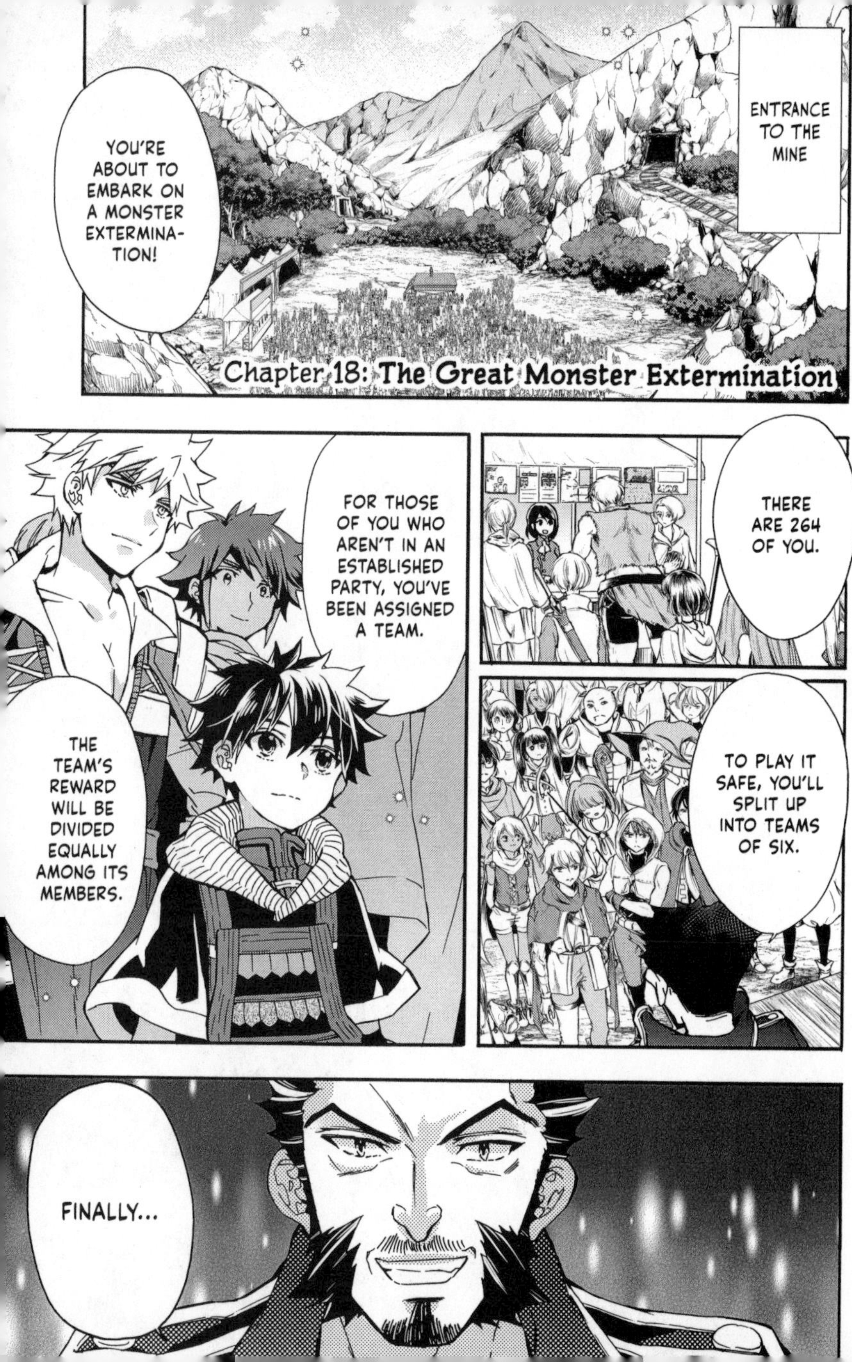
ENTRANCE TO THE MINE
YOU'RE ABOUT TO EMBARK ON A MONSTER EXTERMINATION!
Chapter 18: The Great Monster Extermination
THERE ARE 264 OF YOU.
TO PLAY IT SAFE, YOU'LL SPLIT UP INTO TEAMS OF SIX.
FOR THOSE OF YOU WHO AREN'T IN AN ESTABLISHED PARTY, YOU'VE BEEN ASSIGNED A TEAM.
THE TEAM'S REWARD WILL BE DIVIDED EQUALLY AMONG ITS MEMBERS.
FINALLY...

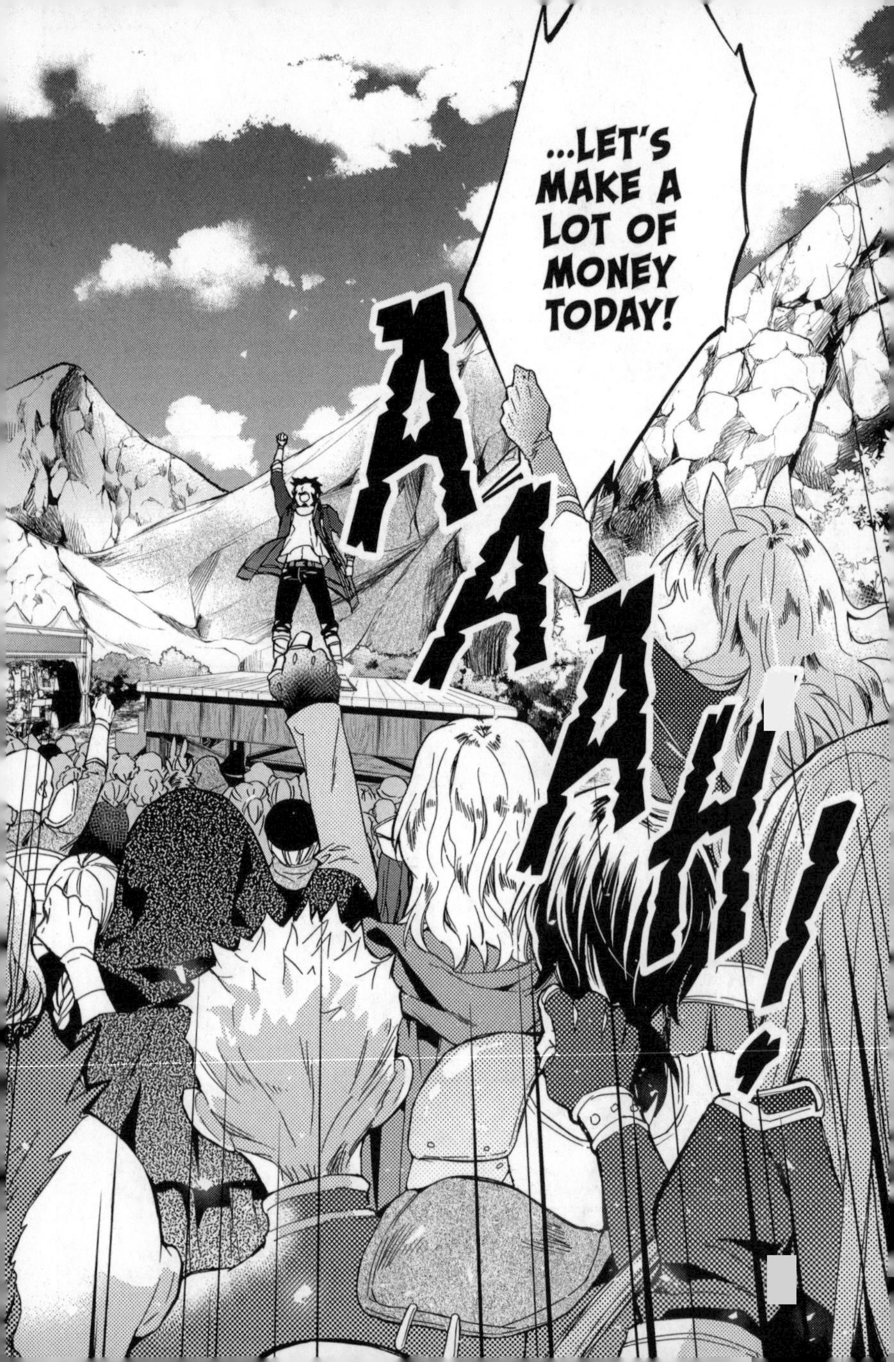
...LET'S MAKE A LOT OF MONEY TODAY!
AAAH!!

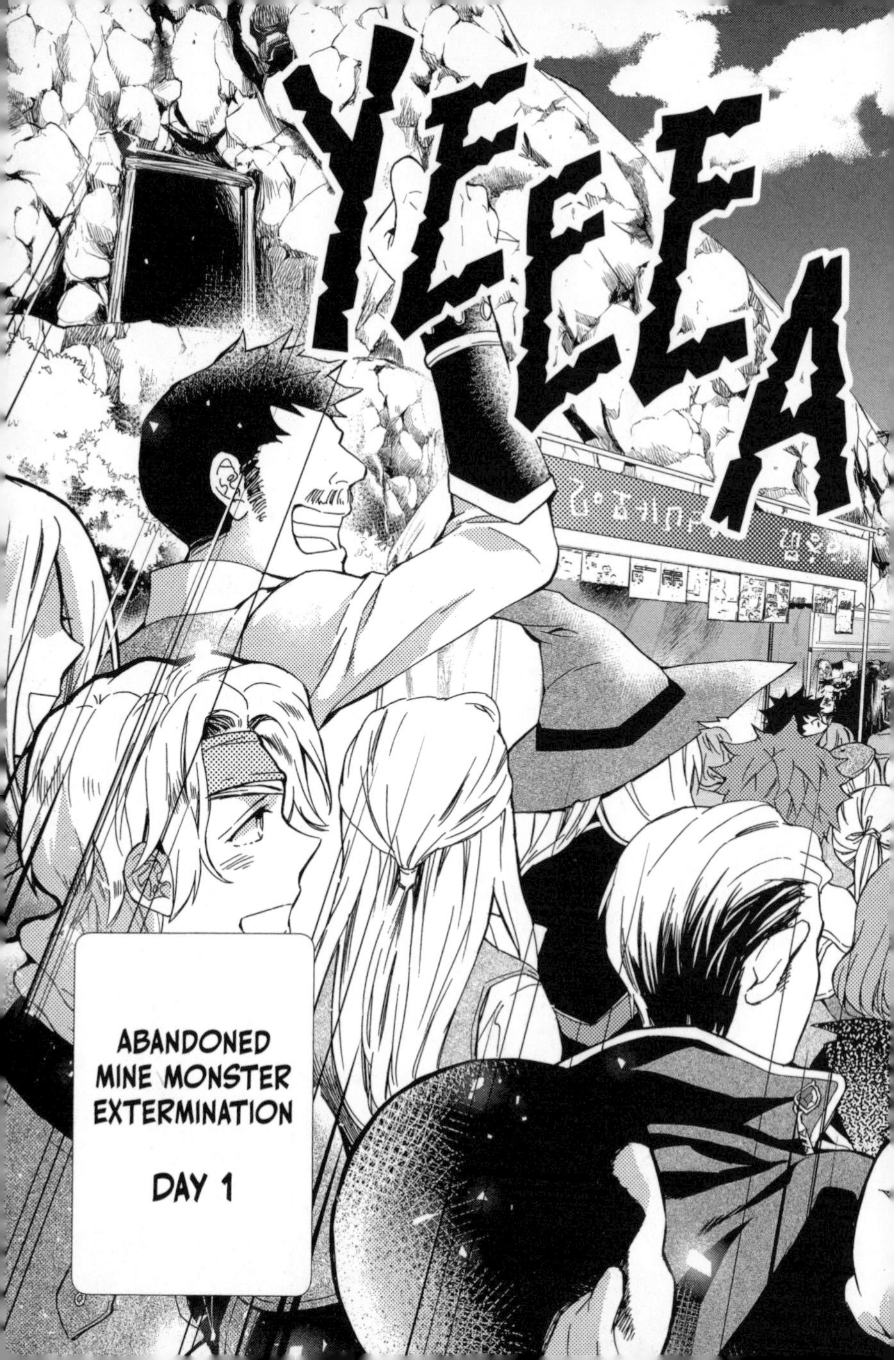
YEEEA
ABANDONED MINE MONSTER EXTERMINATION
DAY 1

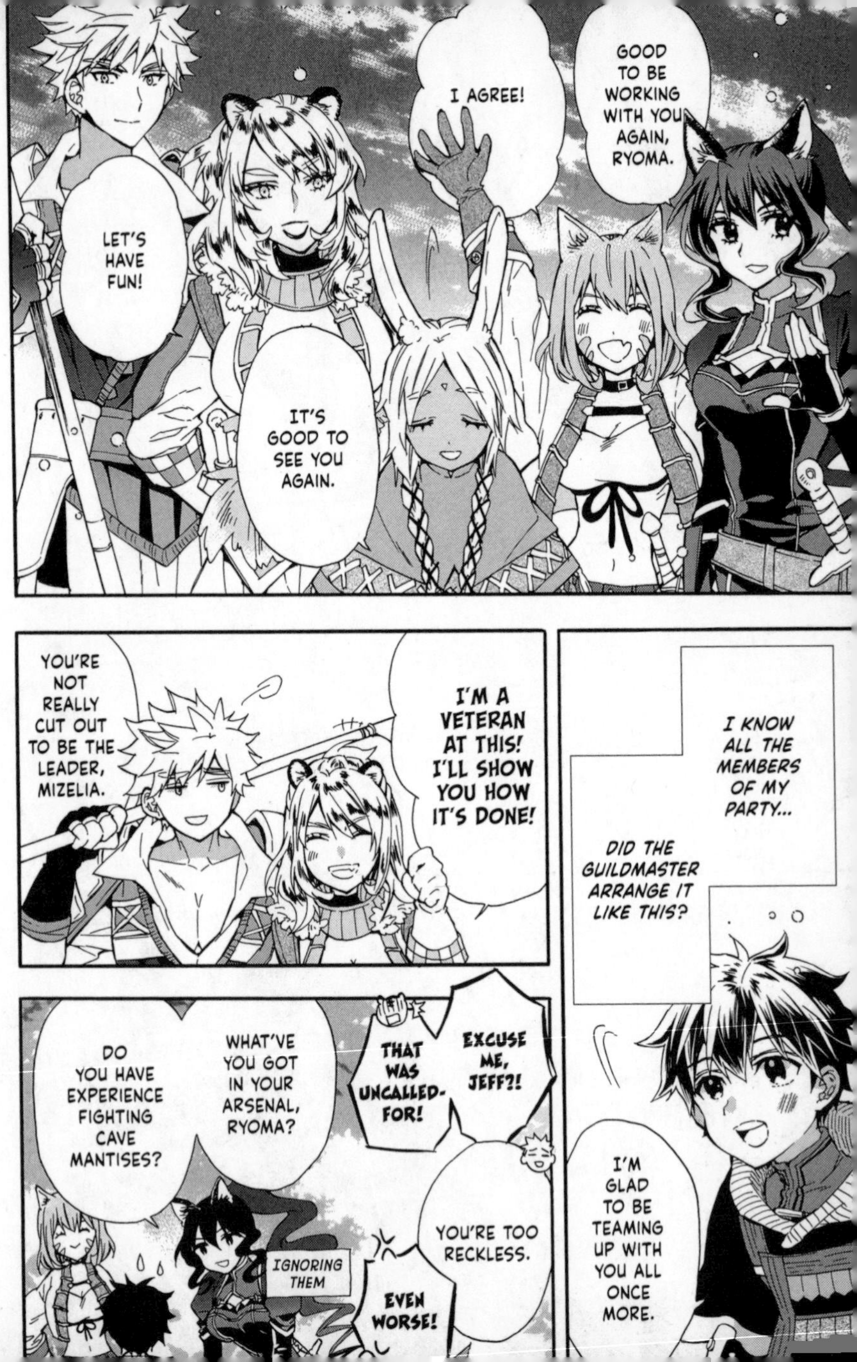

GOOD TO BE WORKING WITH YOU AGAIN, RYOMA.
I AGREE!
IT'S GOOD TO SEE YOU AGAIN.
LET'S HAVE FUN!
I KNOW ALL THE MEMBERS OF MY PARTY...
DID THE GUILDMASTER ARRANGE IT LIKE THIS?
I'M GLAD TO BE TEAMING UP WITH YOU ALL ONCE MORE.
I'M A VETERAN AT THIS! I'LL SHOW YOU HOW IT'S DONE!
YOU'RE NOT REALLY CUT OUT TO BE THE LEADER, MIZELIA.
EXCUSE ME, JEFF?!
THAT WAS UNCALLED-FOR!
WHAT'VE YOU GOT IN YOUR ARSENAL, RYOMA?
DO YOU HAVE EXPERIENCE FIGHTING CAVE MANTISES?
YOU'RE TOO RECKLESS.
EVEN WORSE!
IGNORING THEM

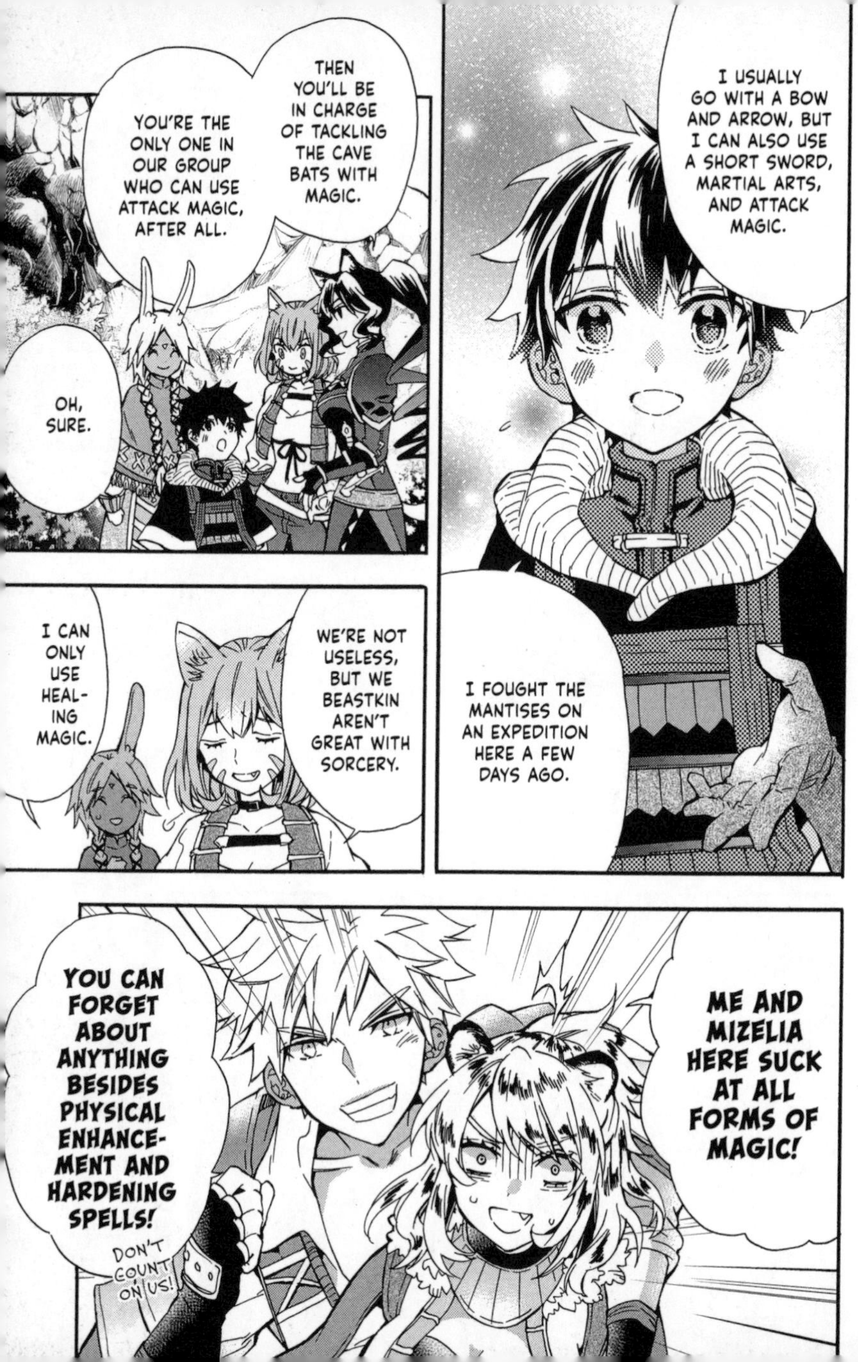
I USUALLY GO WITH A BOW AND ARROW, BUT I CAN ALSO USE A SHORT SWORD, MARTIAL ARTS, AND ATTACK MAGIC.
I FOUGHT THE MANTISES ON AN EXPEDITION HERE A FEW DAYS AGO.
THEN YOU'LL BE IN CHARGE OF TACKLING THE CAVE BATS WITH MAGIC.
YOU'RE THE ONLY ONE IN OUR GROUP WHO CAN USE ATTACK MAGIC, AFTER ALL.
OH, SURE.
WE'RE NOT USELESS, BUT WE BEASTKIN AREN'T GREAT WITH SORCERY.
I CAN ONLY USE HEAL-ING MAGIC.
ME AND MIZELIA HERE SUCK AT ALL FORMS OF MAGIC!
YOU CAN FORGET ABOUT ANYTHING BESIDES PHYSICAL ENHANCE-MENT AND HARDENING SPELLS!
DON'T COUNT ON US!

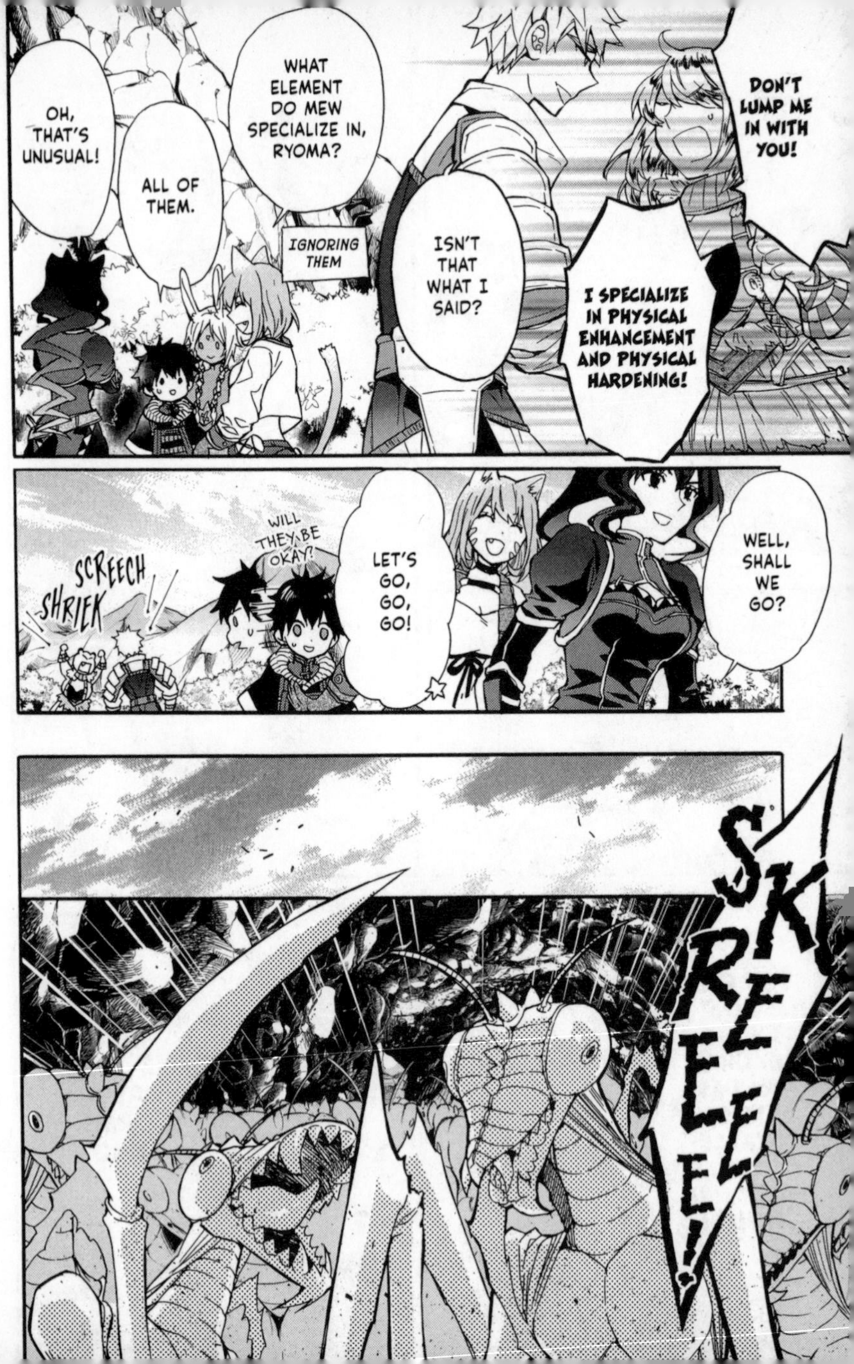
DON'T LUMP ME IN WITH YOU!
I SPECIALIZE IN PHYSICAL ENHANCEMENT AND PHYSICAL HARDENING!
ISN'T THAT WHAT I SAID?
WHAT ELEMENT DO MEW SPECIALIZE IN, RYOMA?
IGNORING THEM
ALL OF THEM.
OH, THAT'S UNUSUAL!
WELL, SHALL WE GO?
LET'S GO, GO, GO!
WILL THEY BE OKAY?
SCREECH
SHRIEK
SKREEEEE!

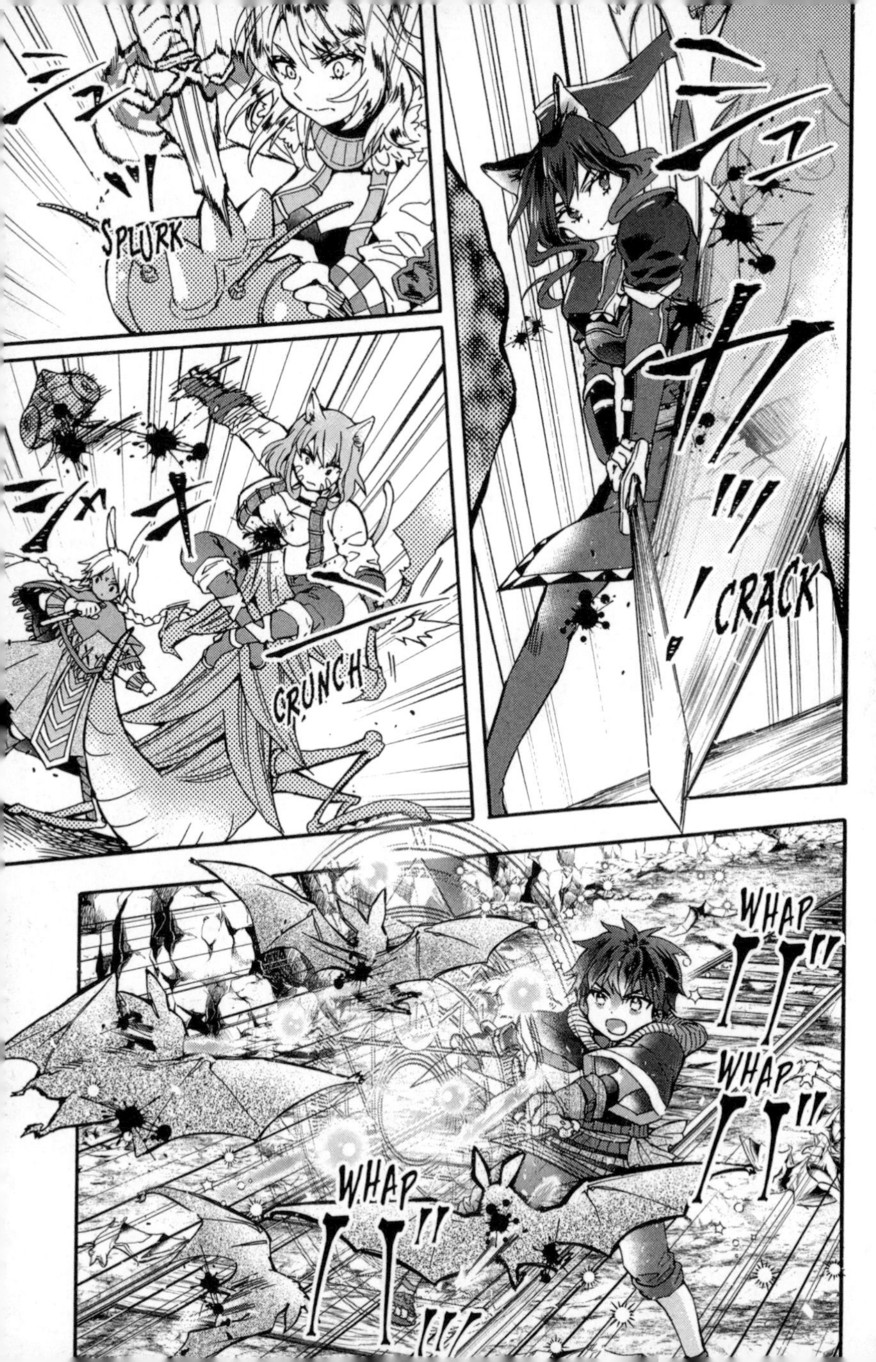
CRACK
SPLURK
CRUNCH
WHAP
WHAP
WHAP

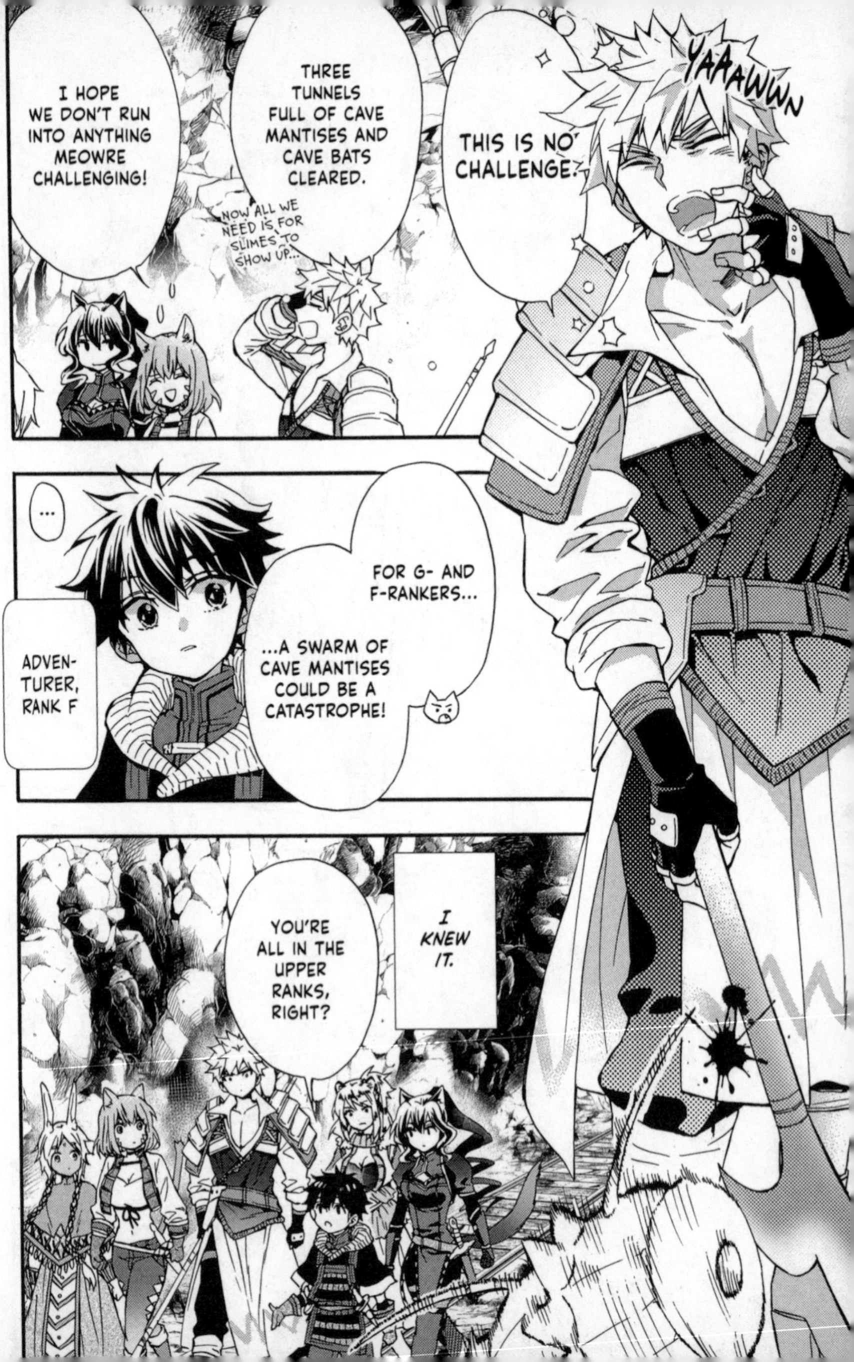
YAAAWWN
THIS IS NO CHALLENGE?
THREE TUNNELS FULL OF CAVE MANTISES AND CAVE BATS CLEARED.
I HOPE WE DON'T RUN INTO ANYTHING MEOWRE CHALLENGING!
NOW ALL WE NEED IS FOR SLIMES TO SHOW UP...
FOR G- AND F-RANKERS...
...A SWARM OF CAVE MANTISES COULD BE A CATASTROPHE!
...
ADVEN-TURER, RANK F
I KNEW IT.
YOU'RE ALL IN THE UPPER RANKS, RIGHT?

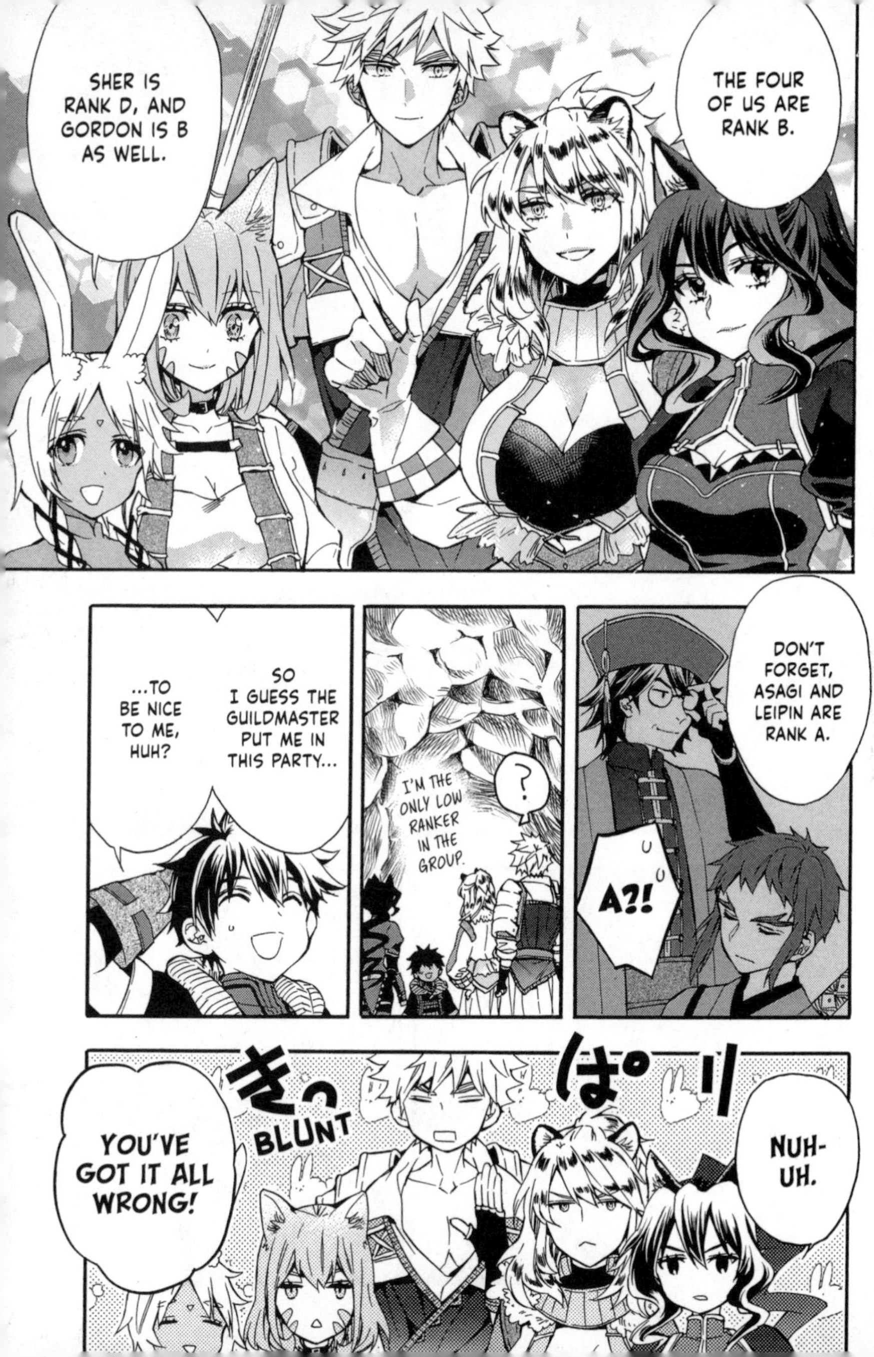
THE FOUR OF US ARE RANK B.
SHER IS RANK D, AND GORDON IS B AS WELL.
DON'T FORGET, ASAGI AND LEIPIN ARE RANK A.
A?!
?
I'M THE ONLY LOW RANKER IN THE GROUP.
SO I GUESS THE GUILDMASTER PUT ME IN THIS PARTY...
...TO BE NICE TO ME, HUH?
NUH-UH.
ぱ!
きっ
BLUNT
YOU'VE GOT IT ALL WRONG!

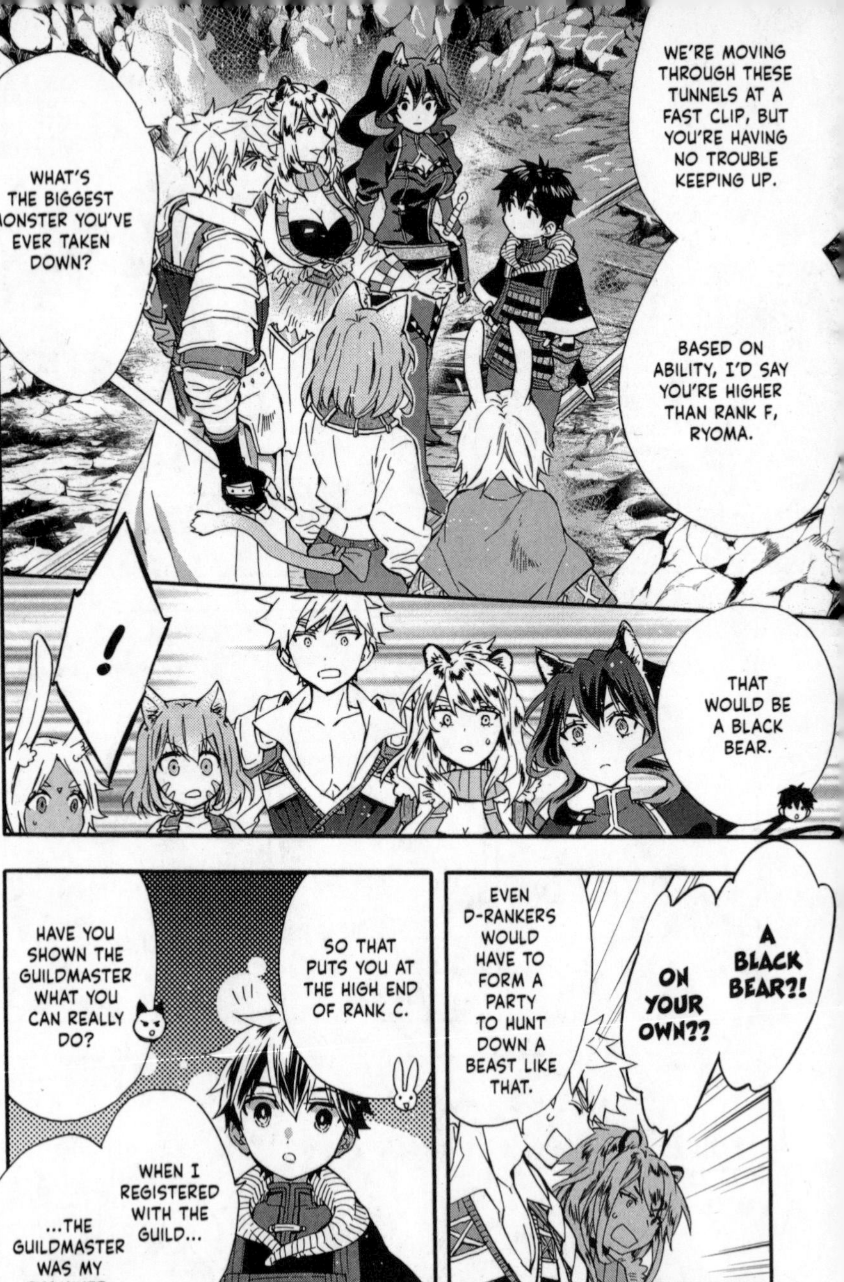
WE'RE MOVING THROUGH THESE TUNNELS AT A FAST CLIP, BUT YOU'RE HAVING NO TROUBLE KEEPING UP.
BASED ON ABILITY, I'D SAY YOU'RE HIGHER THAN RANK F, RYOMA.
WHAT'S THE BIGGEST MONSTER YOU'VE EVER TAKEN DOWN?
THAT WOULD BE A BLACK BEAR.
!
A BLACK BEAR?!
ON YOUR OWN??
EVEN D-RANKERS WOULD HAVE TO FORM A PARTY TO HUNT DOWN A BEAST LIKE THAT.
SO THAT PUTS YOU AT THE HIGH END OF RANK C.
HAVE YOU SHOWN THE GUILDMASTER WHAT YOU CAN REALLY DO?
WHEN I REGISTERED WITH THE GUILD...
...THE GUILDMASTER WAS MY EXAMINER.

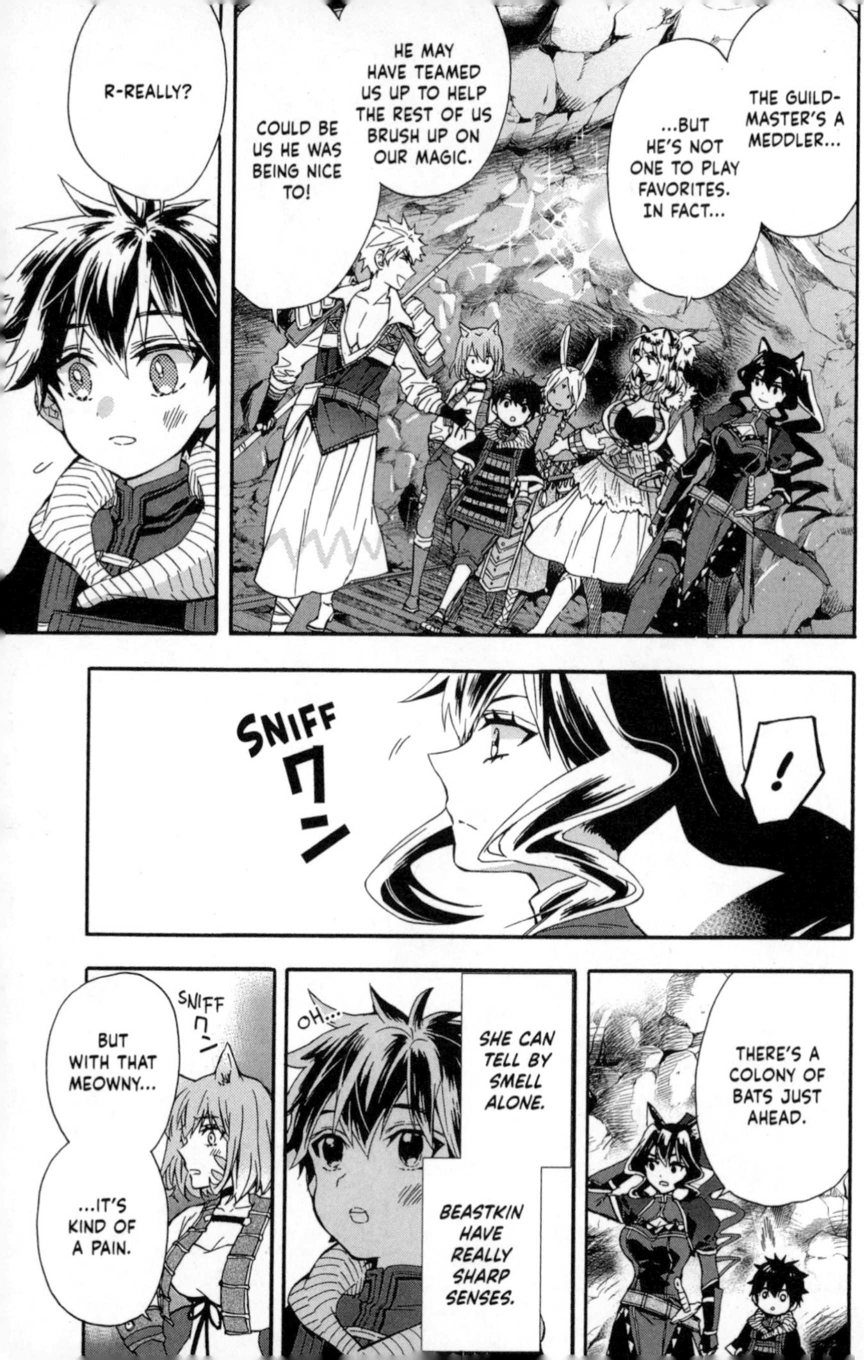
THE GUILD-MASTER'S A MEDDLER...
...BUT HE'S NOT ONE TO PLAY FAVORITES. IN FACT...
HE MAY HAVE TEAMED US UP TO HELP THE REST OF US BRUSH UP ON OUR MAGIC.
COULD BE US HE WAS BEING NICE TO!
R-REALLY?
!
SNIFF
THERE'S A COLONY OF BATS JUST AHEAD.
SHE CAN TELL BY SMELL ALONE.
OH...
BEASTKIN HAVE REALLY SHARP SENSES.
SNIFF
BUT WITH THAT MEOWNY...
...IT'S KIND OF A PAIN.

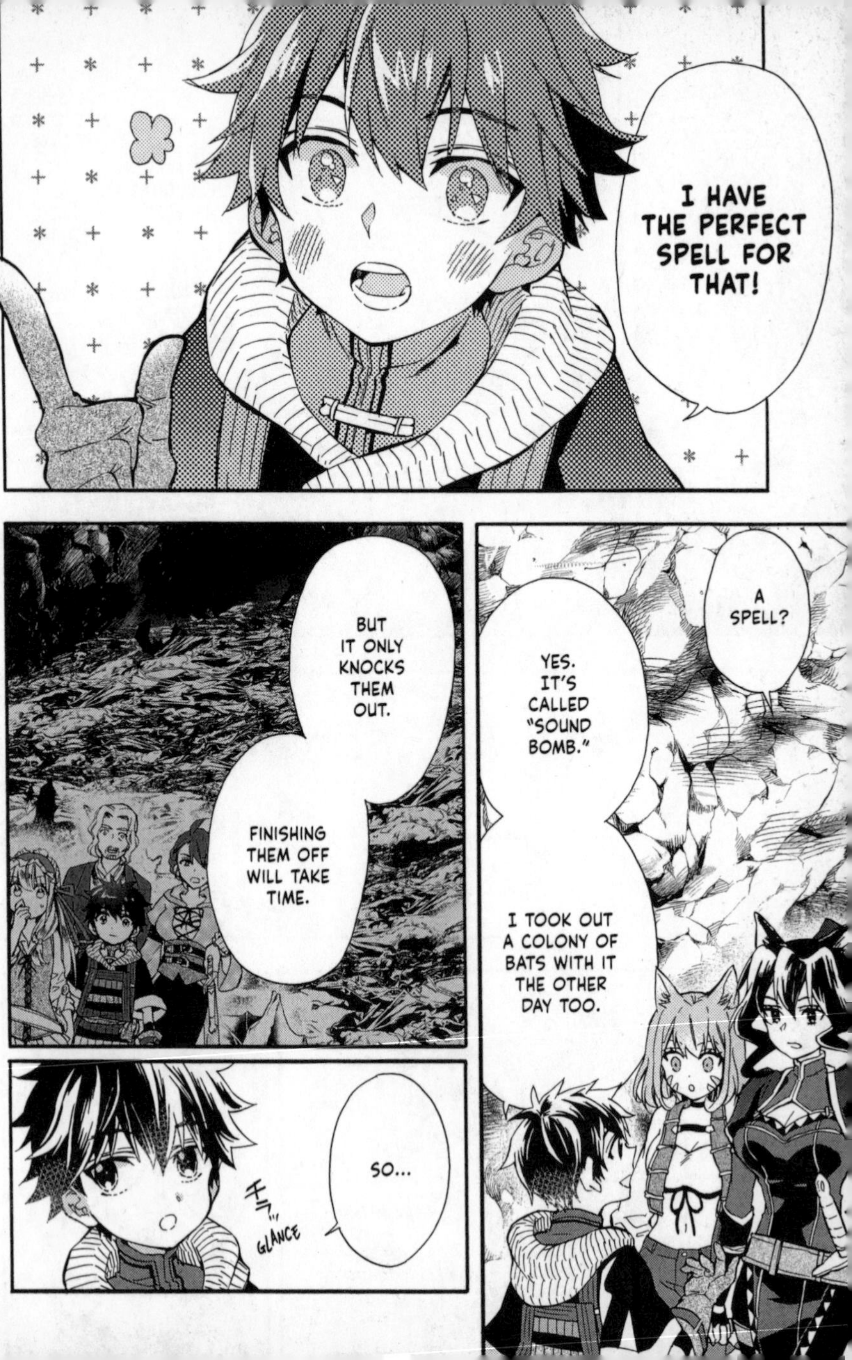
I HAVE THE PERFECT SPELL FOR THAT!
A SPELL?
YES. IT'S CALLED "SOUND BOMB."
I TOOK OUT A COLONY OF BATS WITH IT THE OTHER DAY TOO.
BUT IT ONLY KNOCKS THEM OUT.
FINISHING THEM OFF WILL TAKE TIME.
SO...
GLANCE

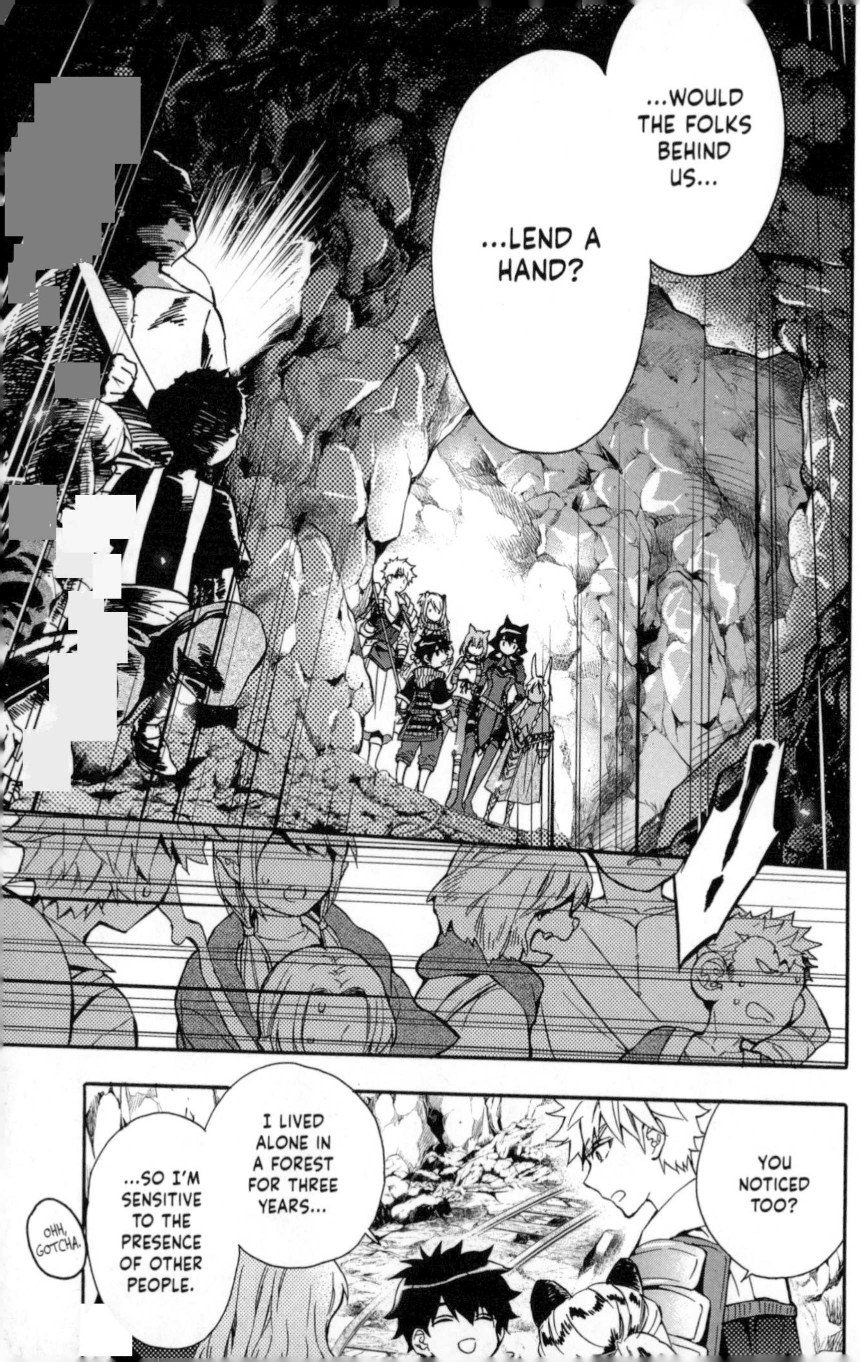
...WOULD THE FOLKS BEHIND US...
...LEND A HAND?
YOU NOTICED TOO?
I LIVED ALONE IN A FOREST FOR THREE YEARS...
...SO I'M SENSITIVE TO THE PRESENCE OF OTHER PEOPLE.
OHH, GOTCHA.

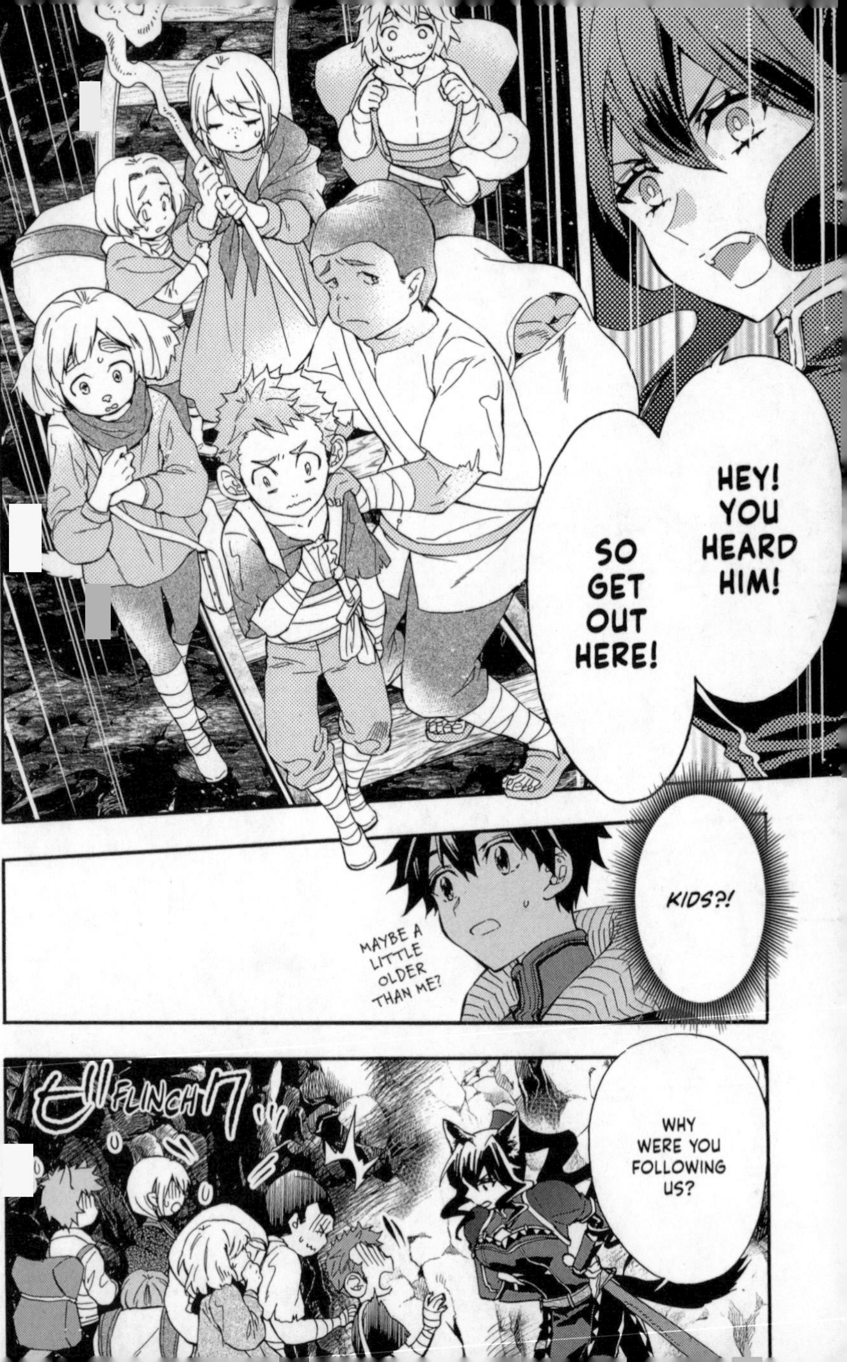
HEY! YOU HEARD HIM!
SO GET OUT HERE!
KIDS?!
MAYBE A LITTLE OLDER THAN ME?
WHY WERE YOU FOLLOWING US?
FLINCH

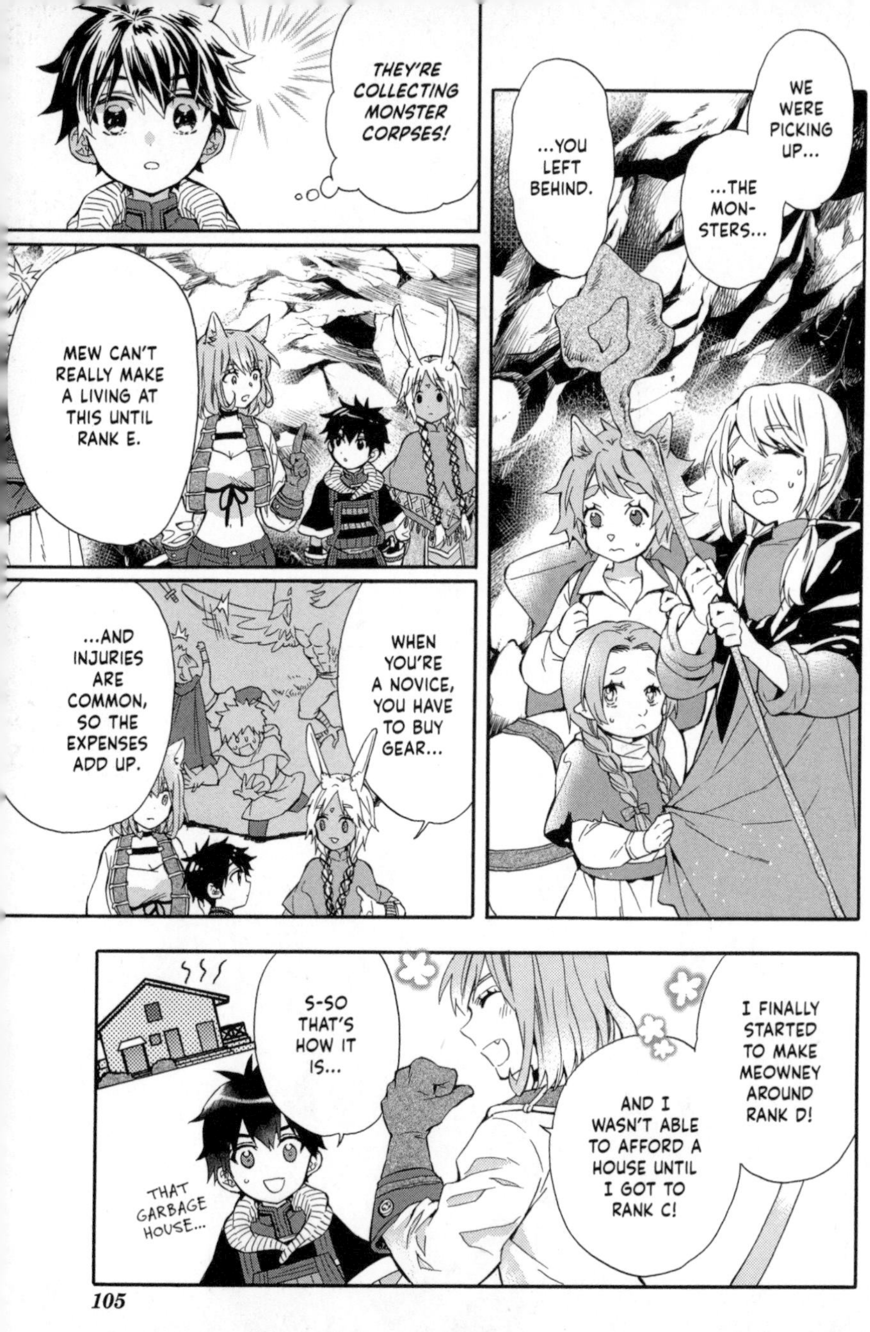
WE WERE PICKING UP...
...THE MONSTERS...
...YOU LEFT BEHIND.
THEY'RE COLLECTING MONSTER CORPSES!
MEW CAN'T REALLY MAKE A LIVING AT THIS UNTIL RANK E.
WHEN YOU'RE A NOVICE, YOU HAVE TO BUY GEAR...
...AND INJURIES ARE COMMON, SO THE EXPENSES ADD UP.
I FINALLY STARTED TO MAKE MEOWNEY AROUND RANK D!
AND I WASN'T ABLE TO AFFORD A HOUSE UNTIL I GOT TO RANK C!
S-SO THAT'S HOW IT IS...
THAT GARBAGE HOUSE...

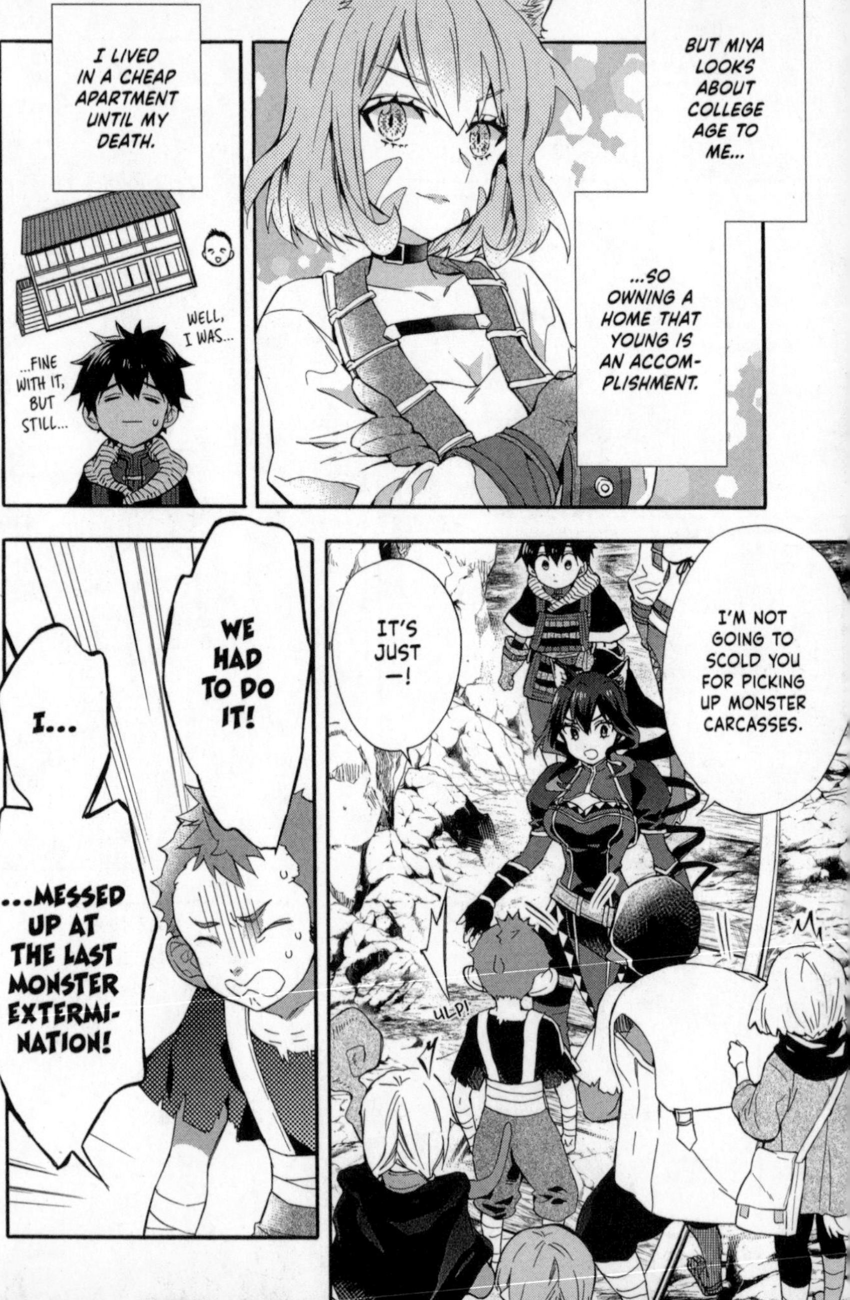
BUT MIYA LOOKS ABOUT COLLEGE AGE TO ME...
...SO OWNING A HOME THAT YOUNG IS AN ACCOMPLISHMENT.
I LIVED IN A CHEAP APARTMENT UNTIL MY DEATH.
WELL, I WAS...
...FINE WITH IT, BUT STILL...
I'M NOT GOING TO SCOLD YOU FOR PICKING UP MONSTER CARCASSES.
IT'S JUST—!
ULP!
WE HAD TO DO IT!
I...
...MESSED UP AT THE LAST MONSTER EXTERMINATION!

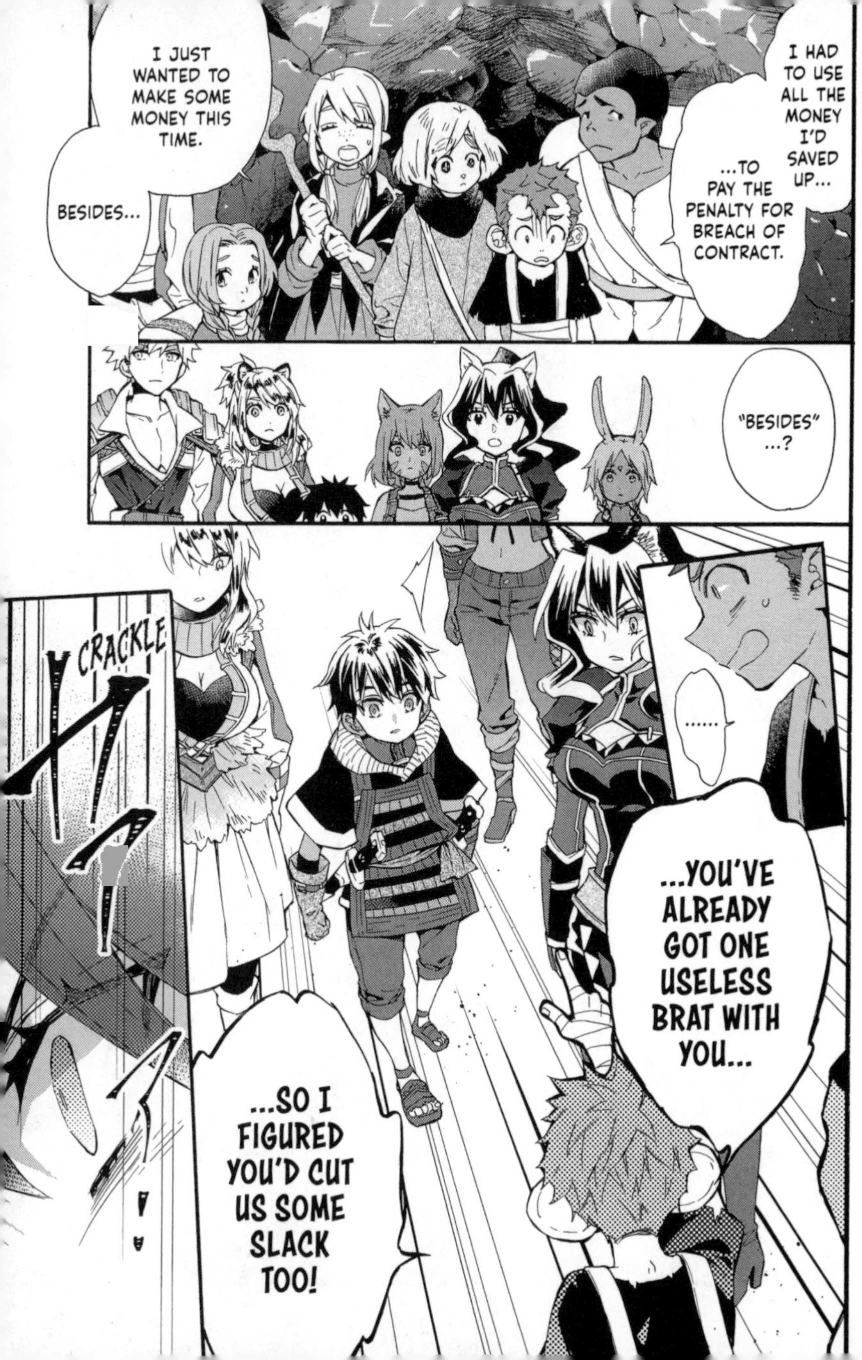
I HAD TO USE ALL THE MONEY I'D SAVED UP...
...TO PAY THE PENALTY FOR BREACH OF CONTRACT.
I JUST WANTED TO MAKE SOME MONEY THIS TIME.
BESIDES...
"BESIDES" ...?
......
...YOU'VE ALREADY GOT ONE USELESS BRAT WITH YOU...
...SO I FIGURED YOU'D CUT US SOME SLACK TOO!
CRACKLE

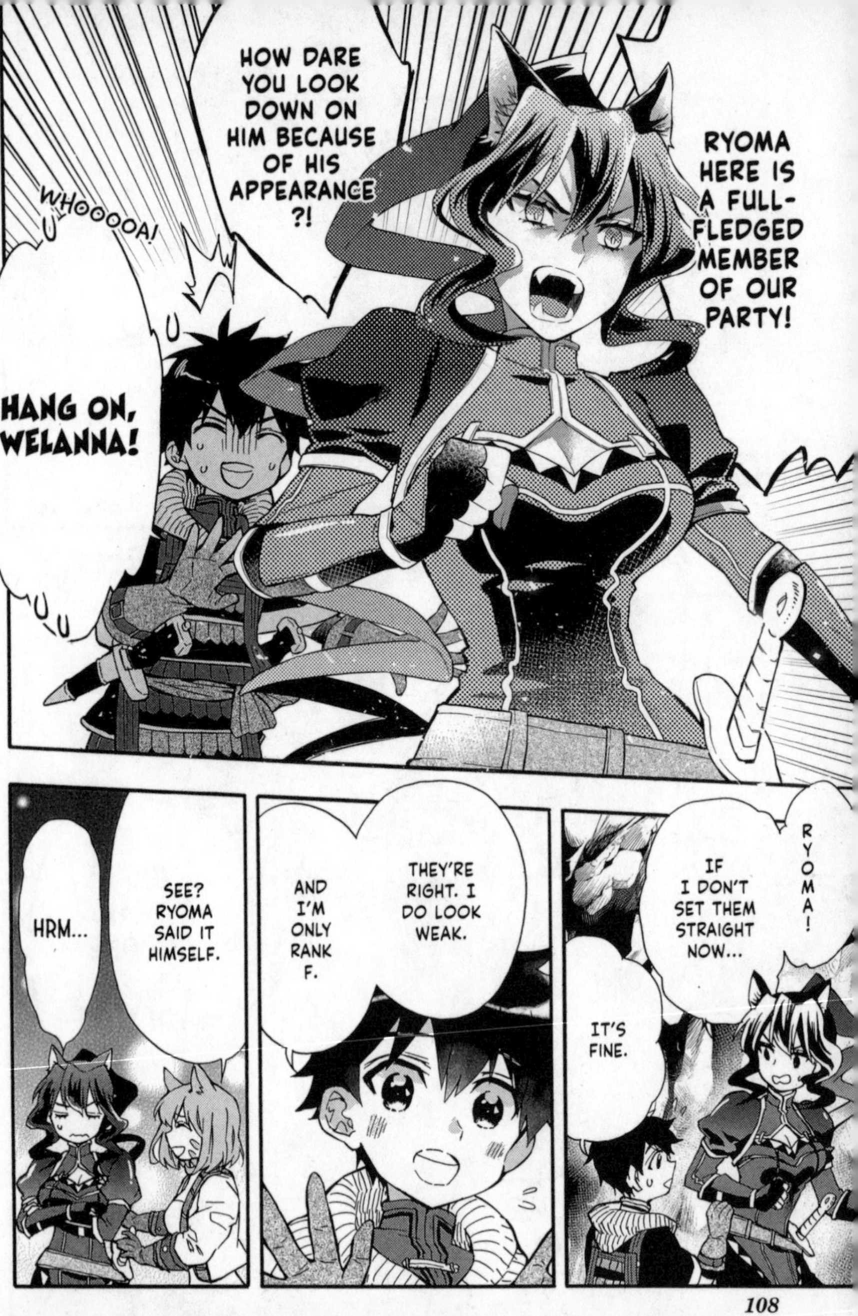
RYOMA HERE IS A FULL-FLEDGED MEMBER OF OUR PARTY!
HOW DARE YOU LOOK DOWN ON HIM BECAUSE OF HIS APPEARANCE?!
WHOOOOOA!
HANG ON, WELANNA!
RYOMA!
IF I DON'T SET THEM STRAIGHT NOW...
IT'S FINE.
THEY'RE RIGHT. I DO LOOK WEAK.
AND I'M ONLY RANK F.
SEE? RYOMA SAID IT HIMSELF.
HRM...

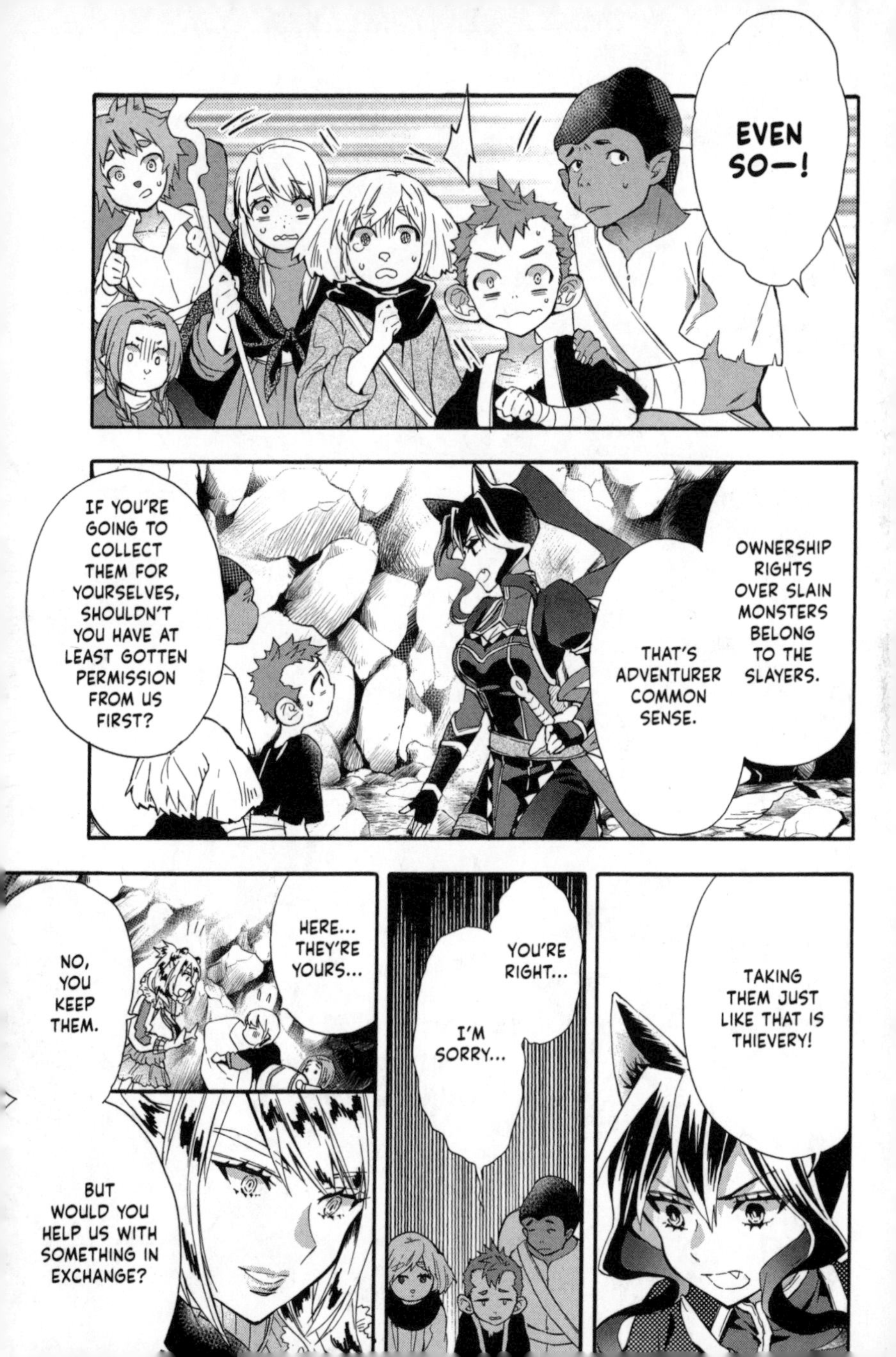
EVEN SO—!
OWNERSHIP RIGHTS OVER SLAIN MONSTERS BELONG TO THE SLAYERS.
THAT'S ADVENTURER COMMON SENSE.
IF YOU'RE GOING TO COLLECT THEM FOR YOURSELVES, SHOULDN'T YOU HAVE AT LEAST GOTTEN PERMISSION FROM US FIRST?
TAKING THEM JUST LIKE THAT IS THIEVERY!
YOU'RE RIGHT...
I'M SORRY...
HERE... THEY'RE YOURS...
NO, YOU KEEP THEM.
BUT WOULD YOU HELP US WITH SOMETHING IN EXCHANGE?

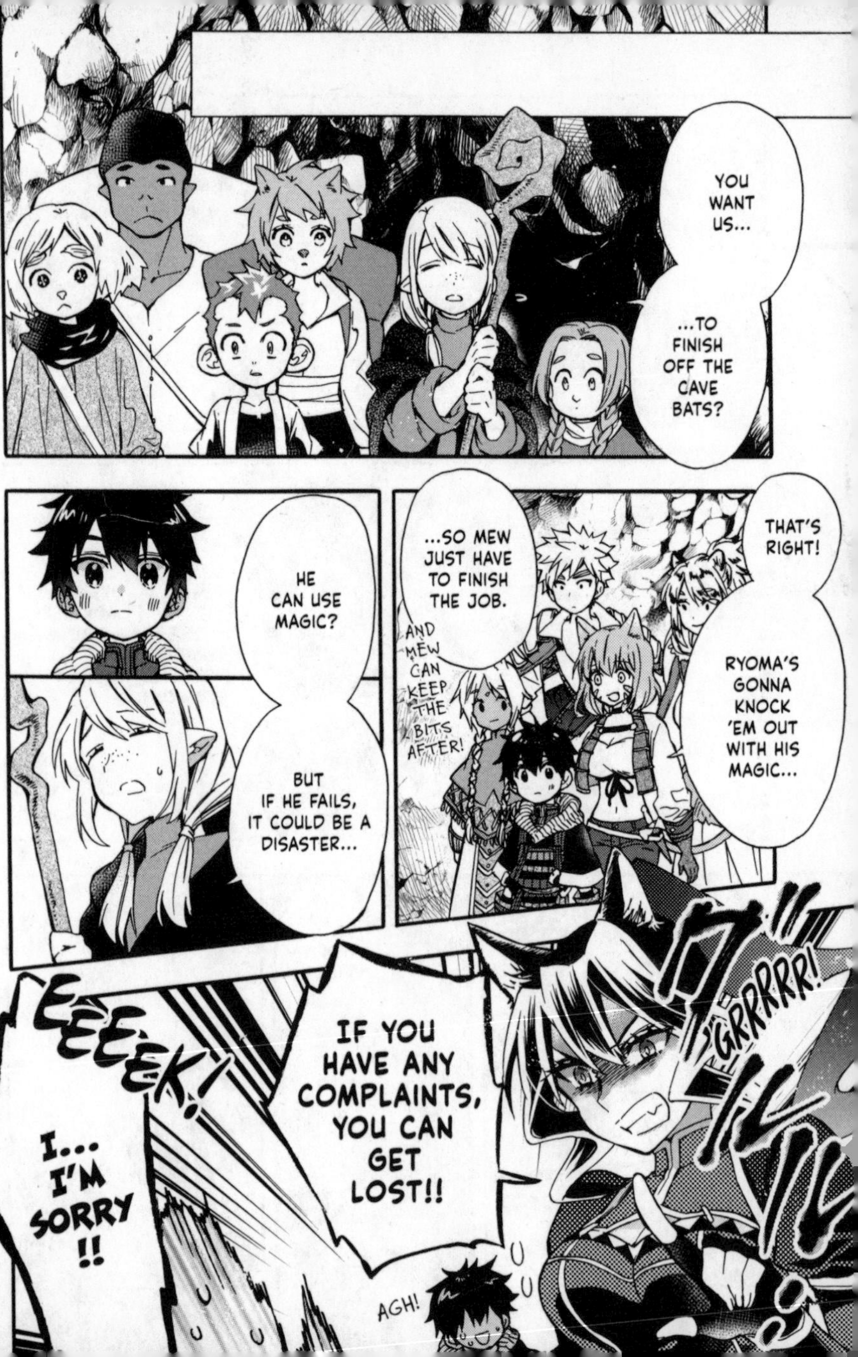
YOU WANT US...
...TO FINISH OFF THE CAVE BATS?
THAT'S RIGHT!
RYOMA'S GONNA KNOCK 'EM OUT WITH HIS MAGIC...
...SO MEW JUST HAVE TO FINISH THE JOB.
AND MEW CAN KEEP THE BITS AFTER!
HE CAN USE MAGIC?
BUT IF HE FAILS, IT COULD BE A DISASTER...
GRRRRR!
IF YOU HAVE ANY COMPLAINTS, YOU CAN GET LOST!!
EEEEEK!
I... I'M SORRY!!
AGH!

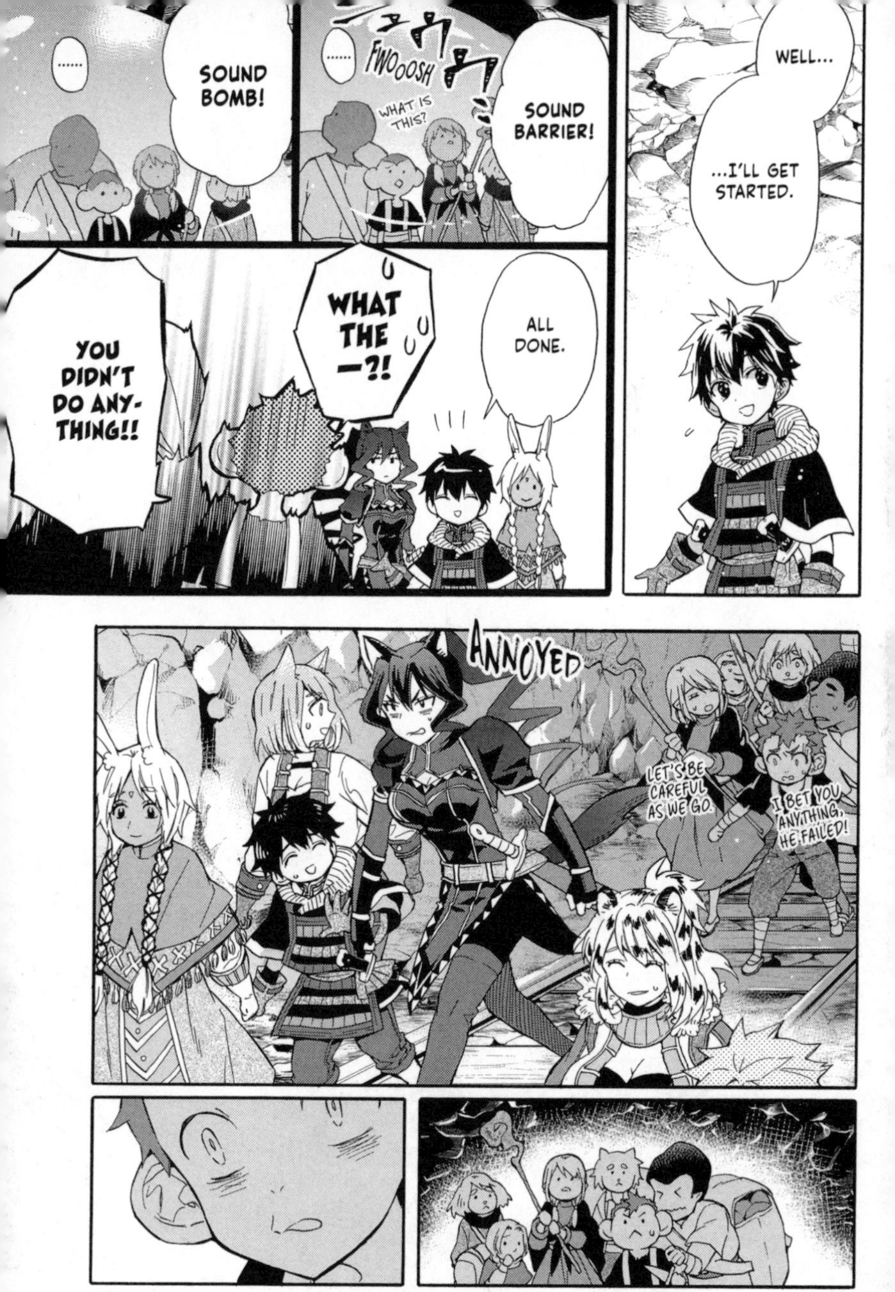
WELL...
...I'LL GET STARTED.
SOUND BARRIER!
FWOOOSH
WHAT IS THIS?
......
SOUND BOMB!
......
ALL DONE.
WHAT THE—?!
YOU DIDN'T DO ANY-THING!!
ANNOYED
I BET YOU ANYTHING, HE FAILED!
LET'S BE CAREFUL AS WE GO.

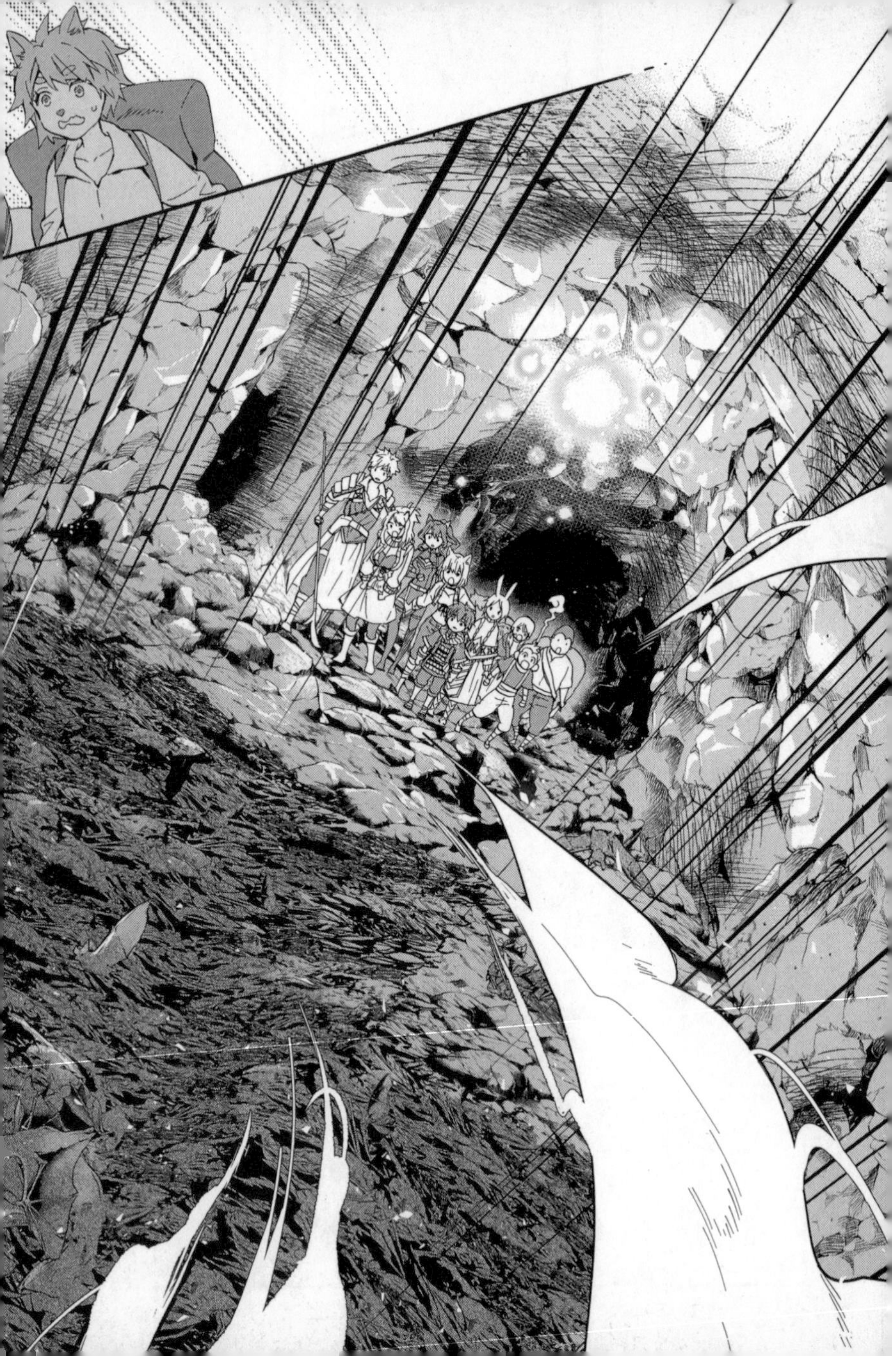

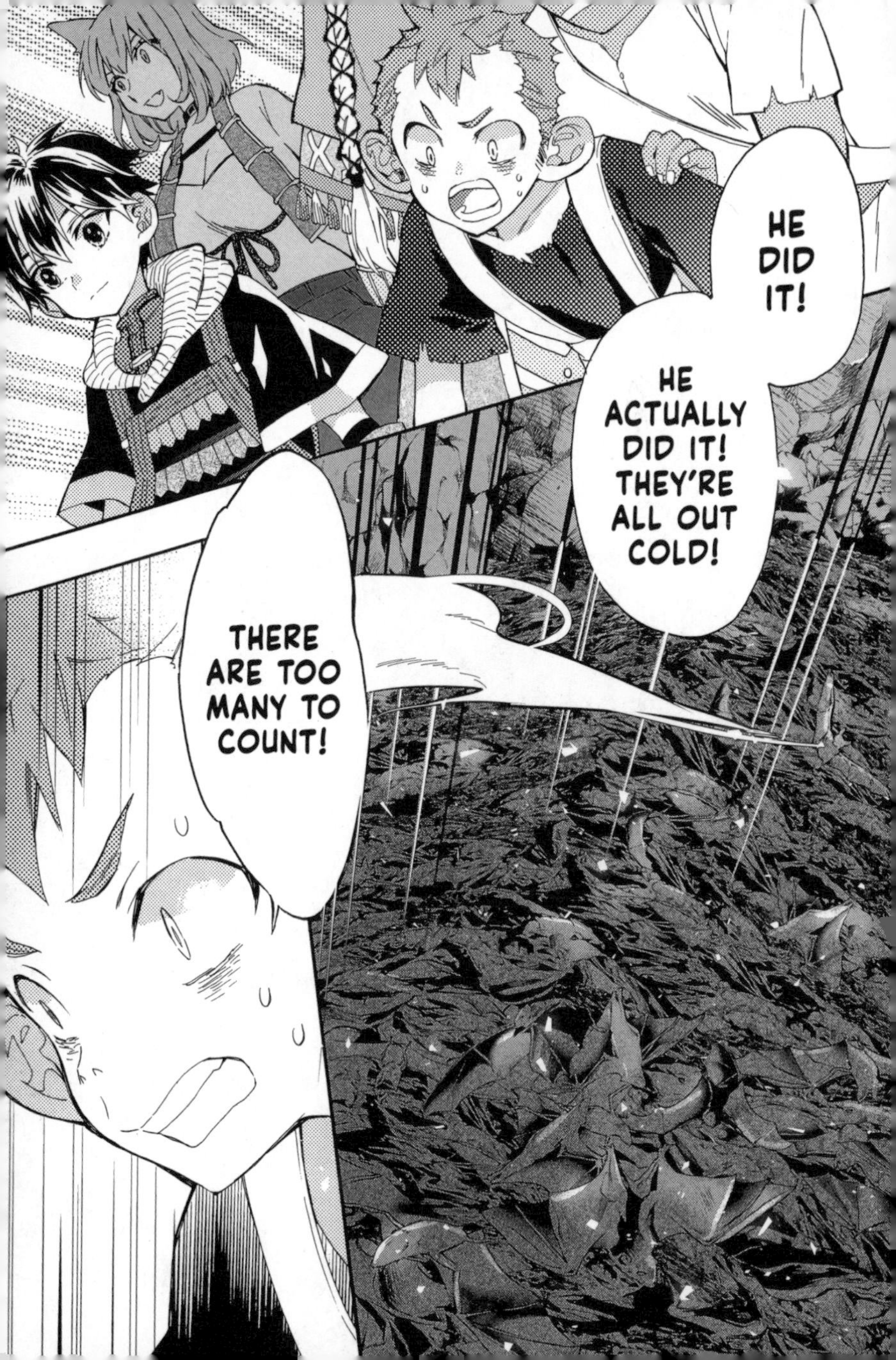
HE DID IT!
HE ACTUALLY DID IT! THEY'RE ALL OUT COLD!
THERE ARE TOO MANY TO COUNT!

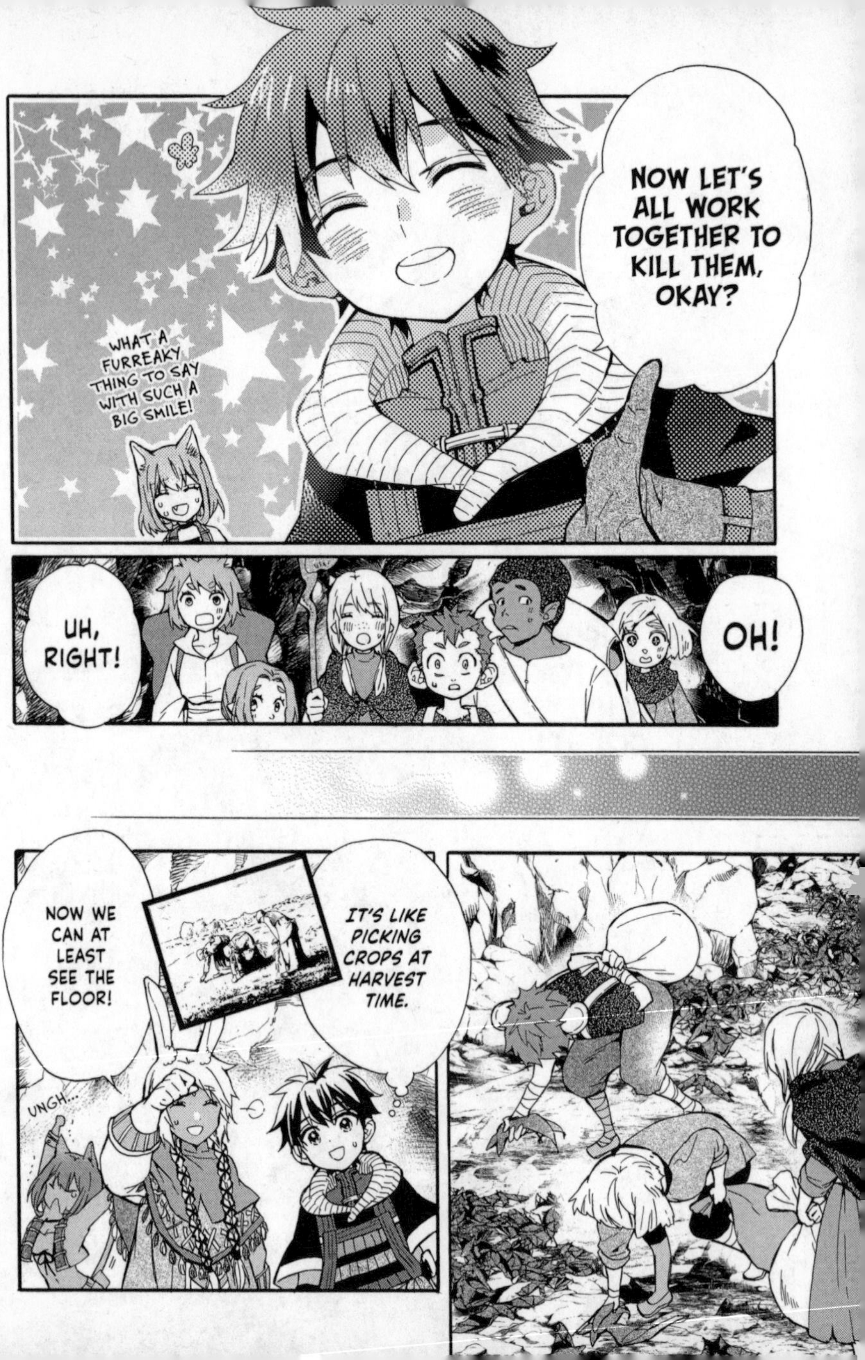
NOW LET'S ALL WORK TOGETHER TO KILL THEM, OKAY?
WHAT A FURREAKY THING TO SAY WITH SUCH A BIG SMILE!
OH!
UH, RIGHT!
IT'S LIKE PICKING CROPS AT HARVEST TIME.
NOW WE CAN AT LEAST SEE THE FLOOR!
UNGH...

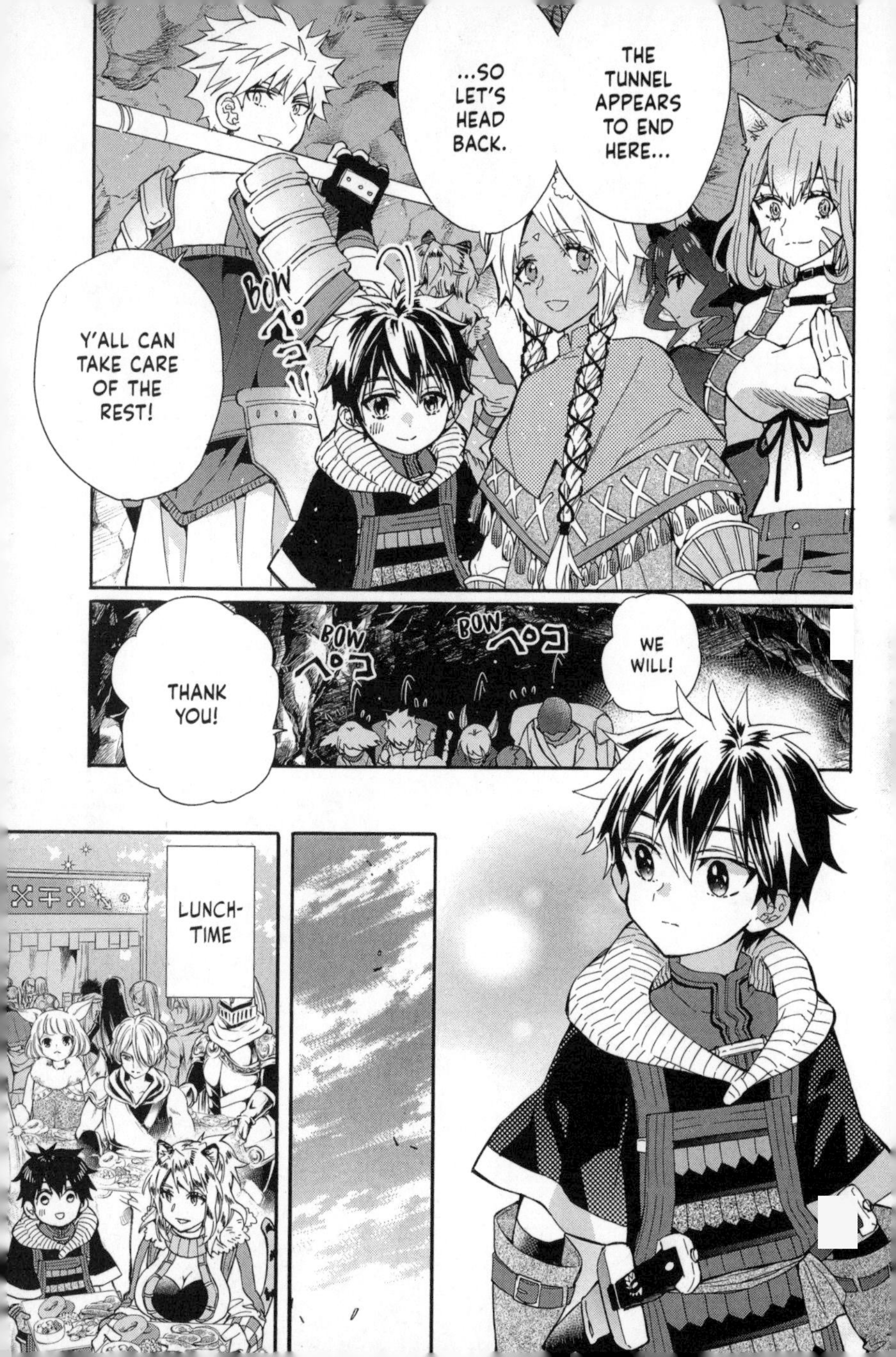

THE TUNNEL APPEARS TO END HERE...
...SO LET'S HEAD BACK.
BOW
ペコ
Y'ALL CAN TAKE CARE OF THE REST!
WE WILL!
BOW
ペコ
BOW
ペコ
THANK YOU!
LUNCH-TIME

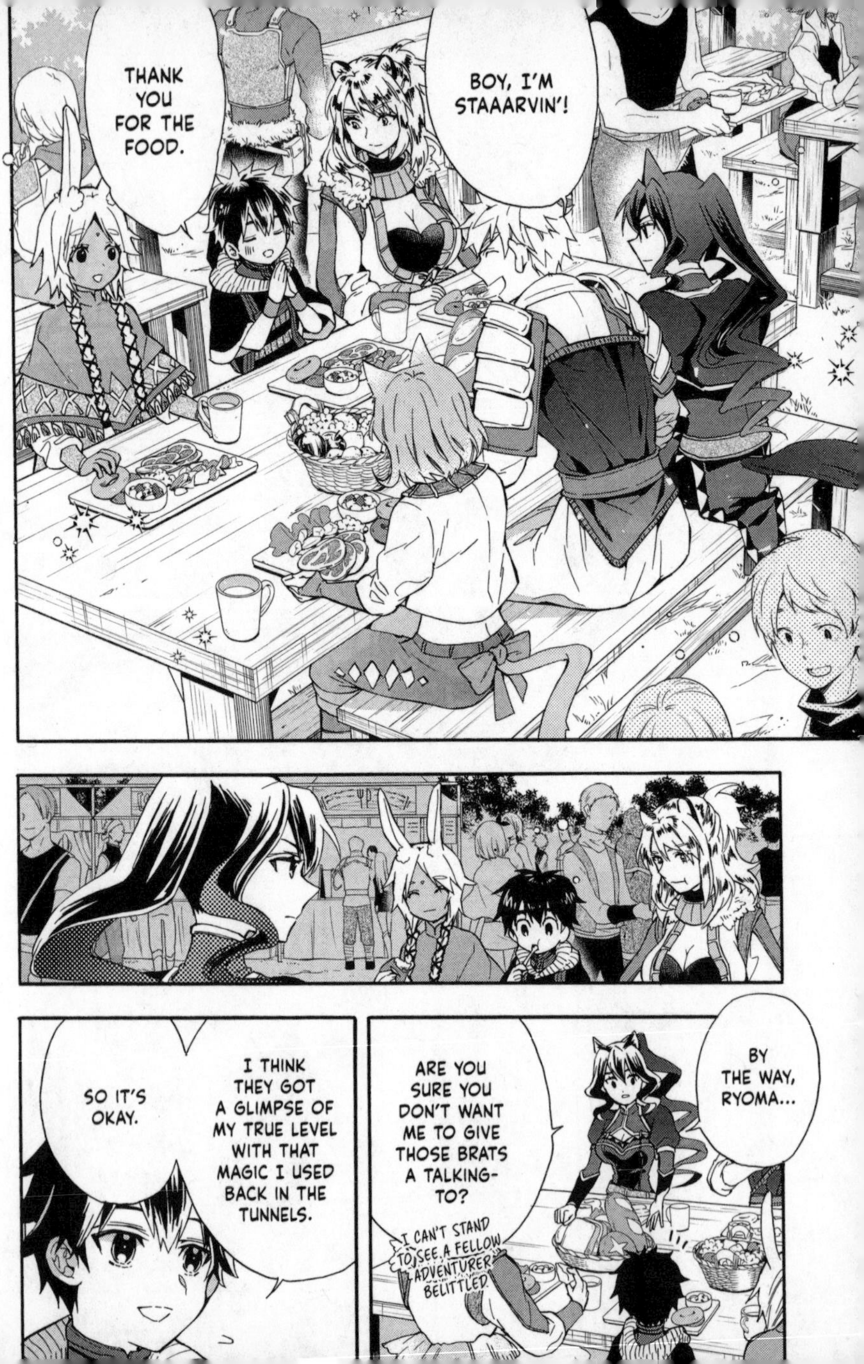
BOY, I'M STAAARVIN'!
THANK YOU FOR THE FOOD.
BY THE WAY, RYOMA...
ARE YOU SURE YOU DON'T WANT ME TO GIVE THOSE BRATS A TALKING-TO?
I CAN'T STAND TO SEE A FELLOW ADVENTURER BELITTLED.
I THINK THEY GOT A GLIMPSE OF MY TRUE LEVEL WITH THAT MAGIC I USED BACK IN THE TUNNELS.
SO IT'S OKAY.

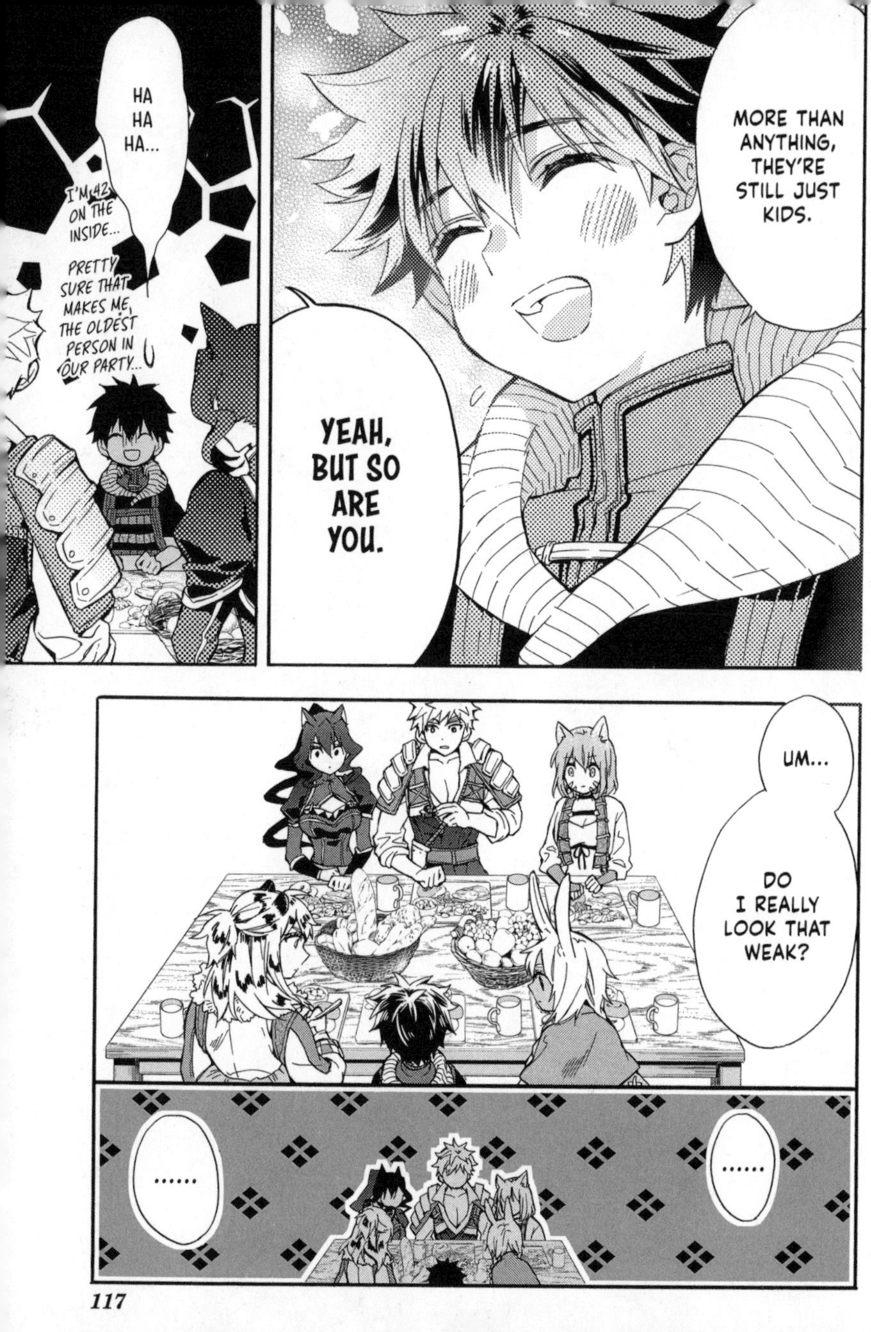
MORE THAN ANYTHING, THEY'RE STILL JUST KIDS.
YEAH, BUT SO ARE YOU.
HA HA HA...
I'M 42 ON THE INSIDE...
PRETTY SURE THAT MAKES ME, THE OLDEST PERSON IN OUR PARTY...
UM...
DO I REALLY LOOK THAT WEAK?
......
......

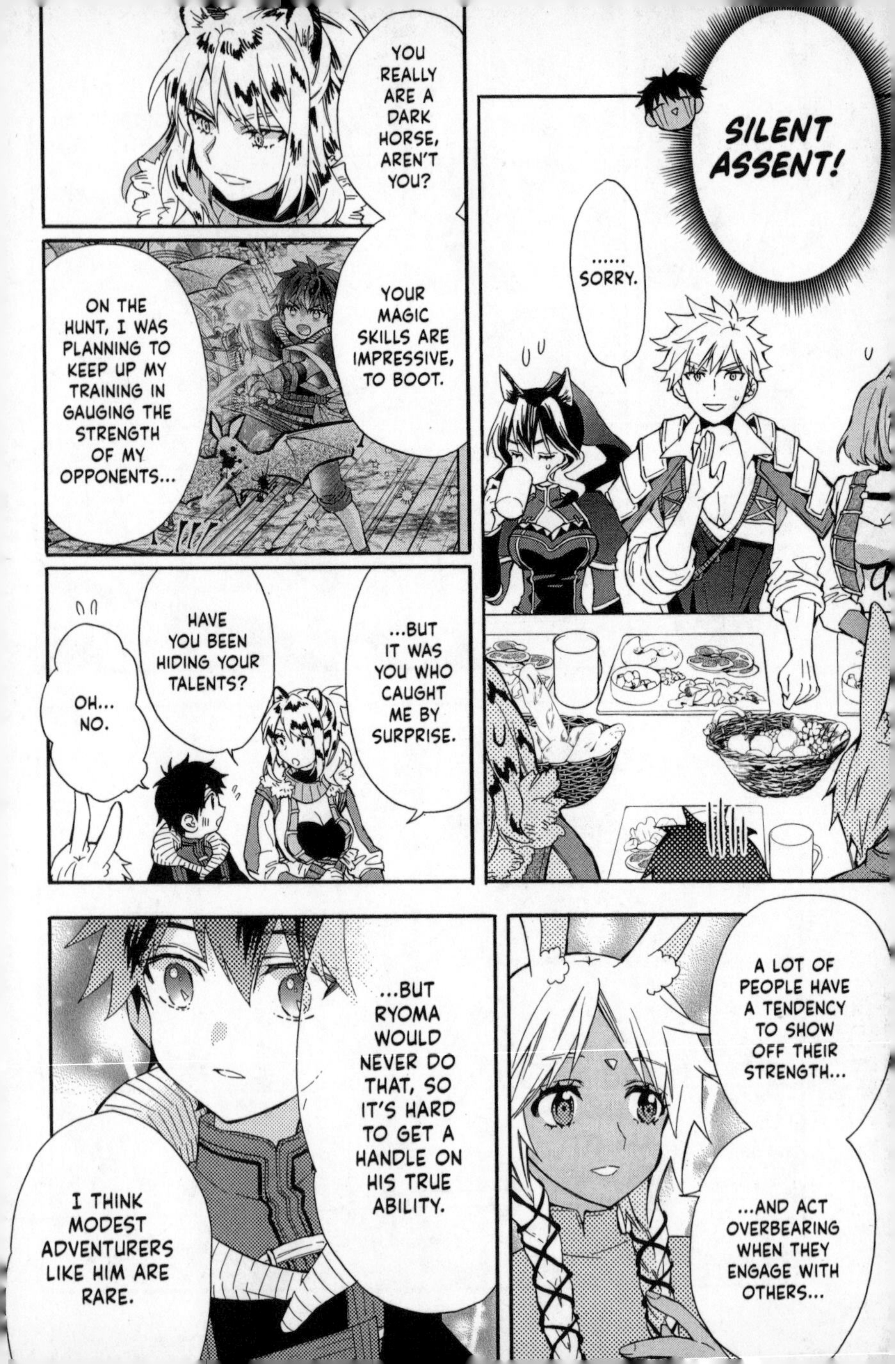
SILENT ASSENT!
......SORRY.
YOU REALLY ARE A DARK HORSE, AREN'T YOU?
YOUR MAGIC SKILLS ARE IMPRESSIVE, TO BOOT.
ON THE HUNT, I WAS PLANNING TO KEEP UP MY TRAINING IN GAUGING THE STRENGTH OF MY OPPONENTS...
...BUT IT WAS YOU WHO CAUGHT ME BY SURPRISE.
HAVE YOU BEEN HIDING YOUR TALENTS?
OH... NO.
A LOT OF PEOPLE HAVE A TENDENCY TO SHOW OFF THEIR STRENGTH...
...AND ACT OVERBEARING WHEN THEY ENGAGE WITH OTHERS...
...BUT RYOMA WOULD NEVER DO THAT, SO IT'S HARD TO GET A HANDLE ON HIS TRUE ABILITY.
I THINK MODEST ADVENTURERS LIKE HIM ARE RARE.

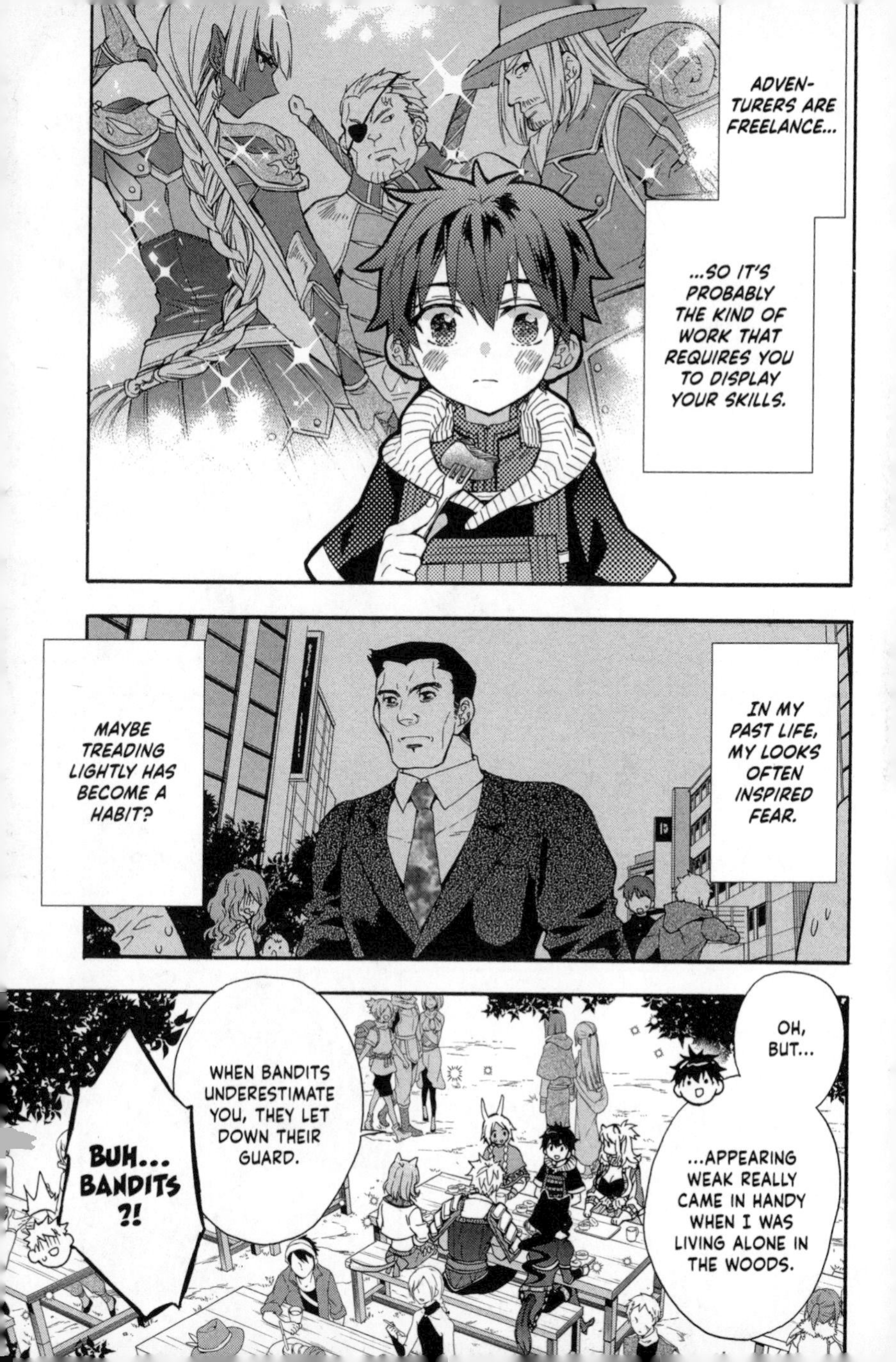
ADVENTURERS ARE FREELANCE...
...SO IT'S PROBABLY THE KIND OF WORK THAT REQUIRES YOU TO DISPLAY YOUR SKILLS.
IN MY PAST LIFE, MY LOOKS OFTEN INSPIRED FEAR.
MAYBE TREADING LIGHTLY HAS BECOME A HABIT?
OH, BUT...
...APPEARING WEAK REALLY CAME IN HANDY WHEN I WAS LIVING ALONE IN THE WOODS.
WHEN BANDITS UNDERESTIMATE YOU, THEY LET DOWN THEIR GUARD.
BUH... BANDITS?!

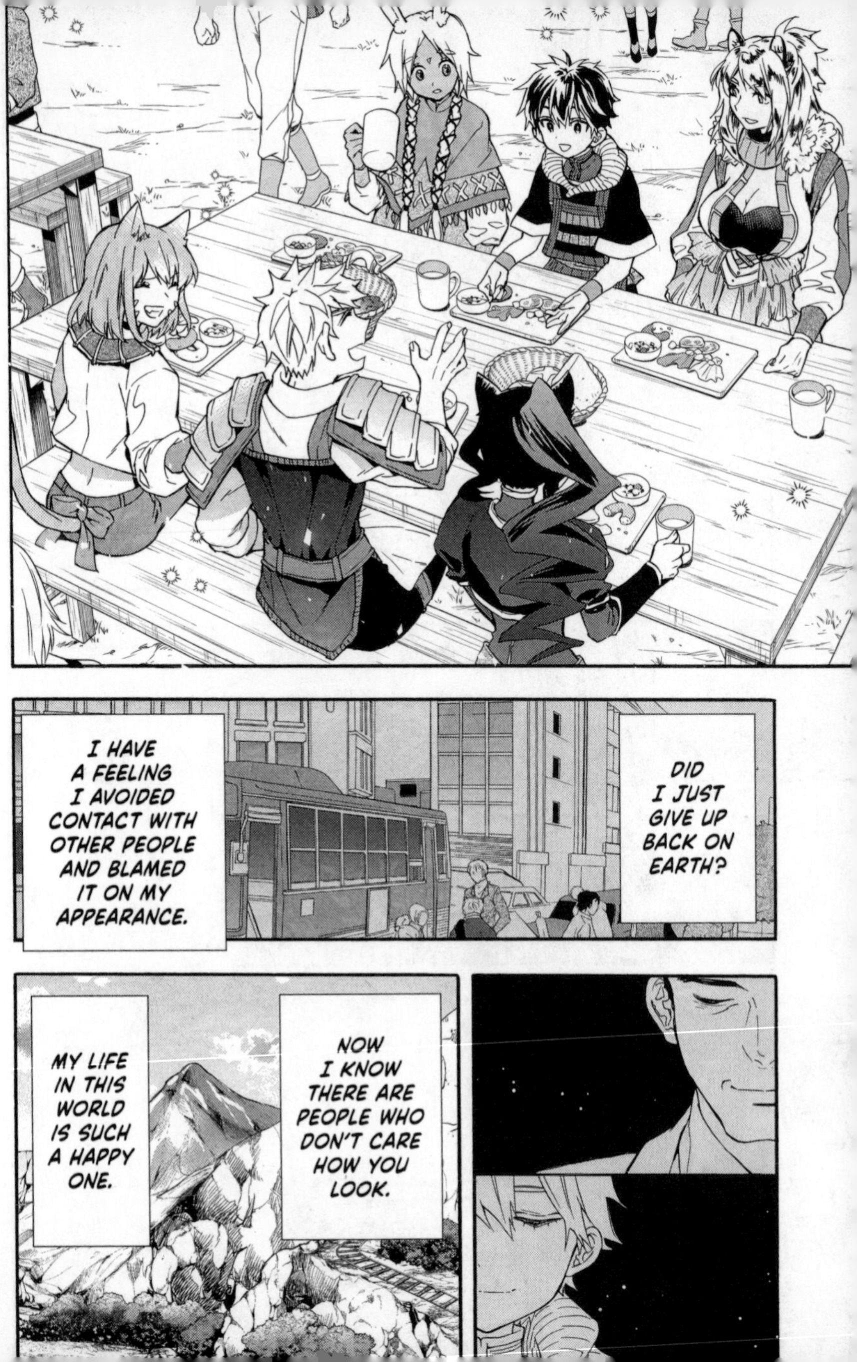
DID I JUST GIVE UP BACK ON EARTH?
I HAVE A FEELING I AVOIDED CONTACT WITH OTHER PEOPLE AND BLAMED IT ON MY APPEARANCE.
NOW I KNOW THERE ARE PEOPLE WHO DON'T CARE HOW YOU LOOK.
MY LIFE IN THIS WORLD IS SUCH A HAPPY ONE.

Chapter 19

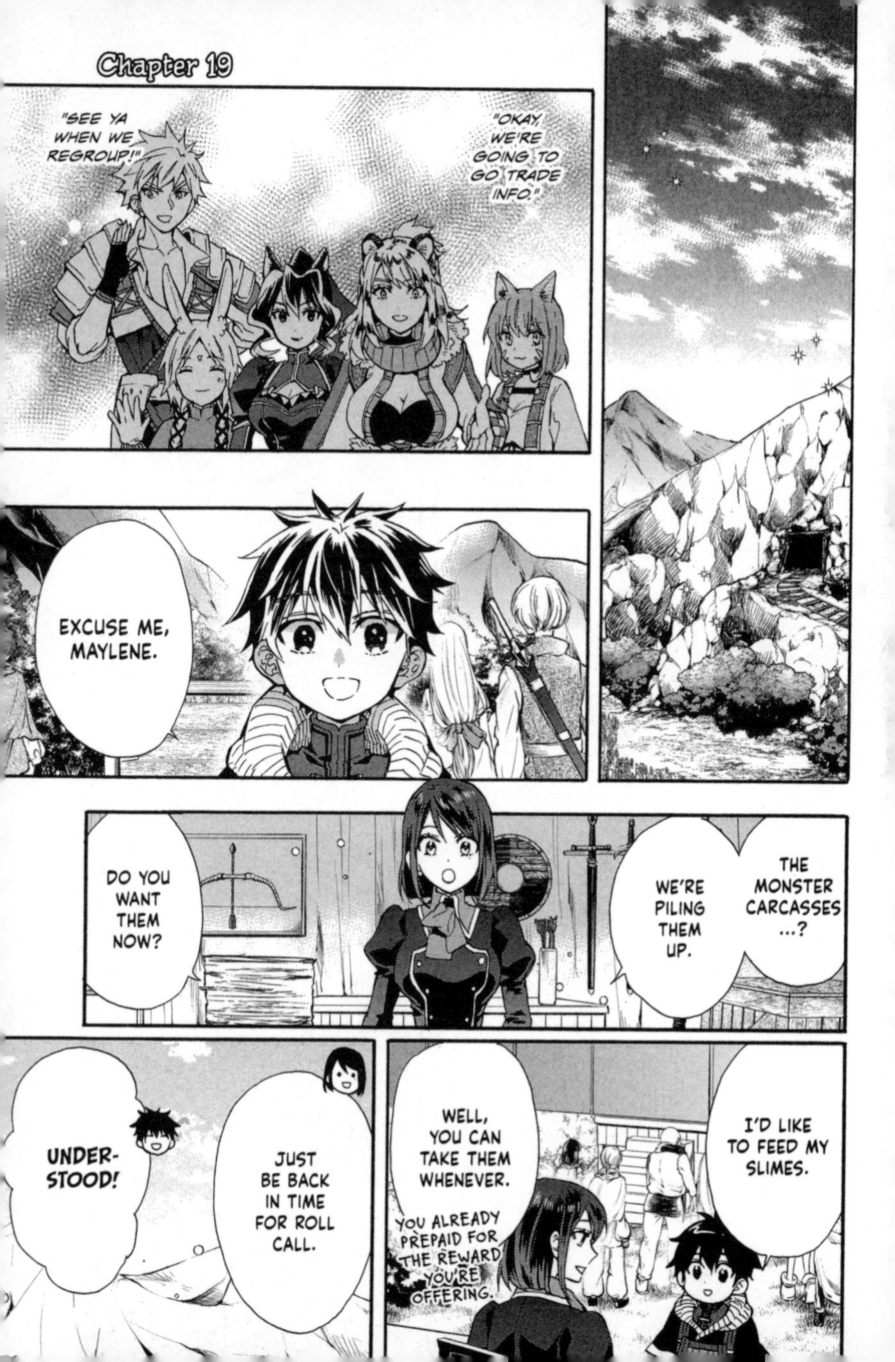
"OKAY, WE'RE GOING TO GO TRADE INFO."
"SEE YA WHEN WE REGROUP!!"
EXCUSE ME, MAYLENE.
THE MONSTER CARCASSES ...?
WE'RE PILING THEM UP.
DO YOU WANT THEM NOW?
I'D LIKE TO FEED MY SLIMES.
WELL, YOU CAN TAKE THEM WHENEVER.
YOU ALREADY PREPAID FOR THE REWARD YOU'RE OFFERING.
JUST BE BACK IN TIME FOR ROLL CALL.
UNDER-STOOD!

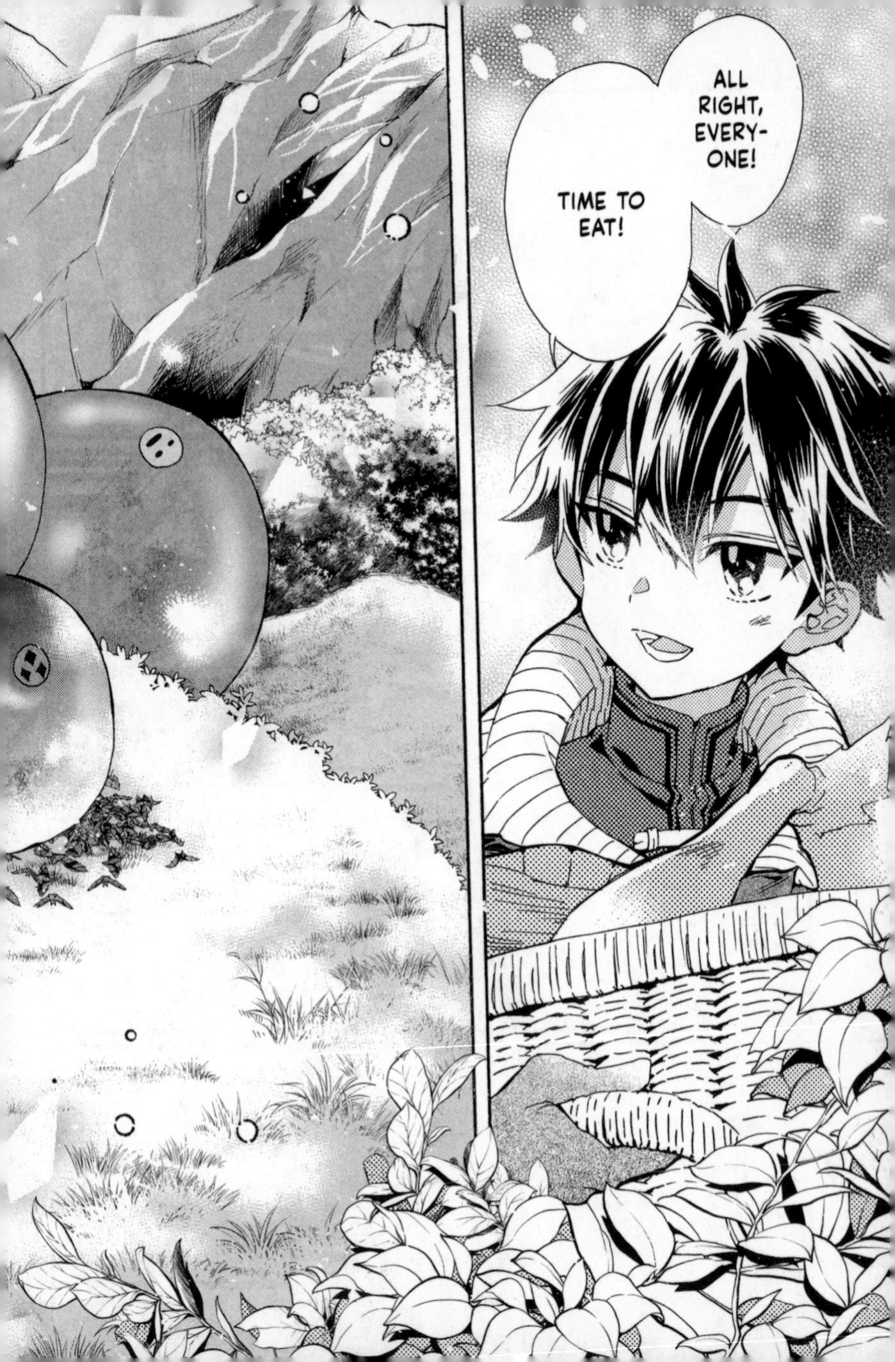
ALL RIGHT, EVERY-ONE!
TIME TO EAT!

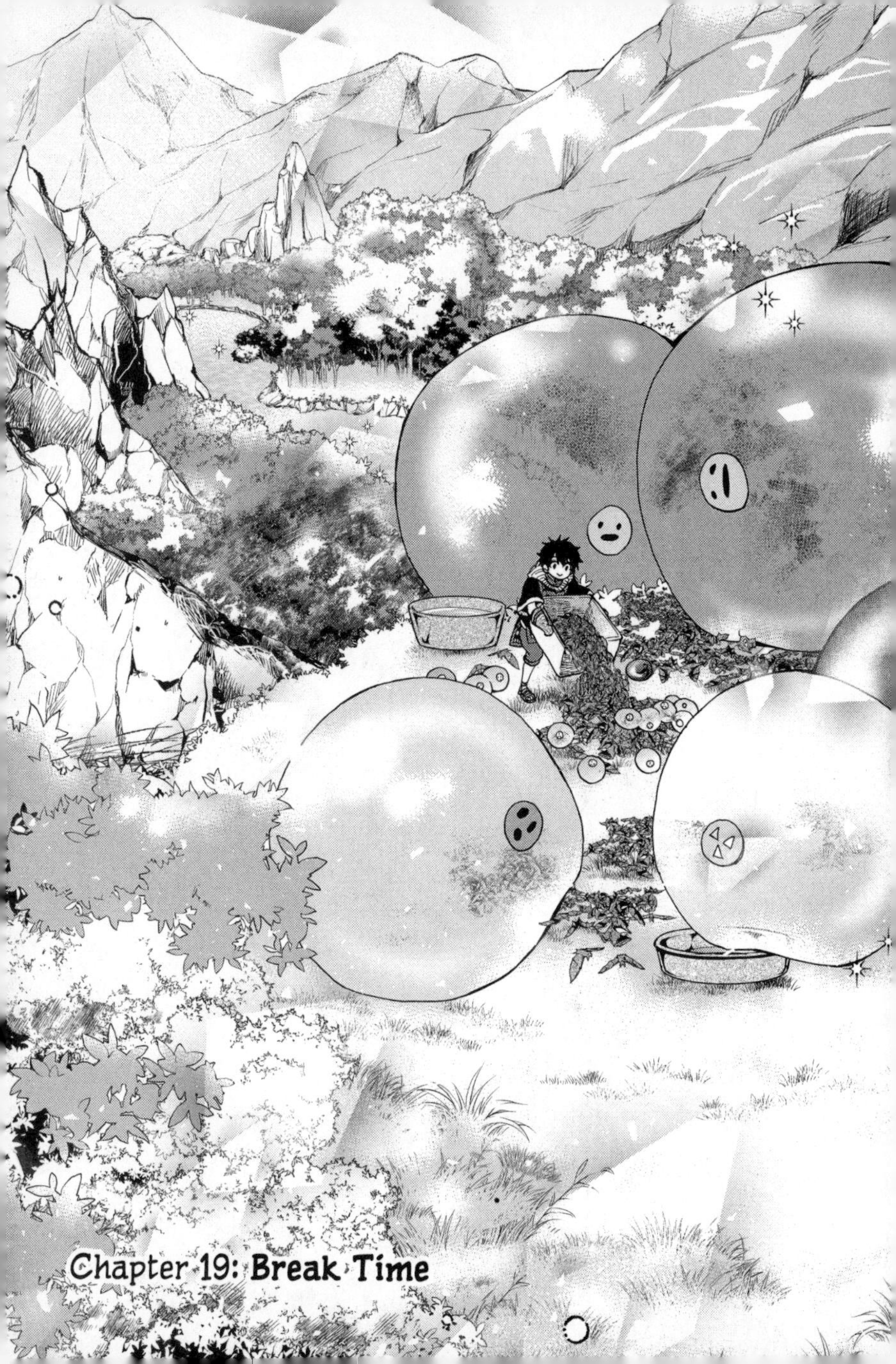

Chapter 19: Break Time

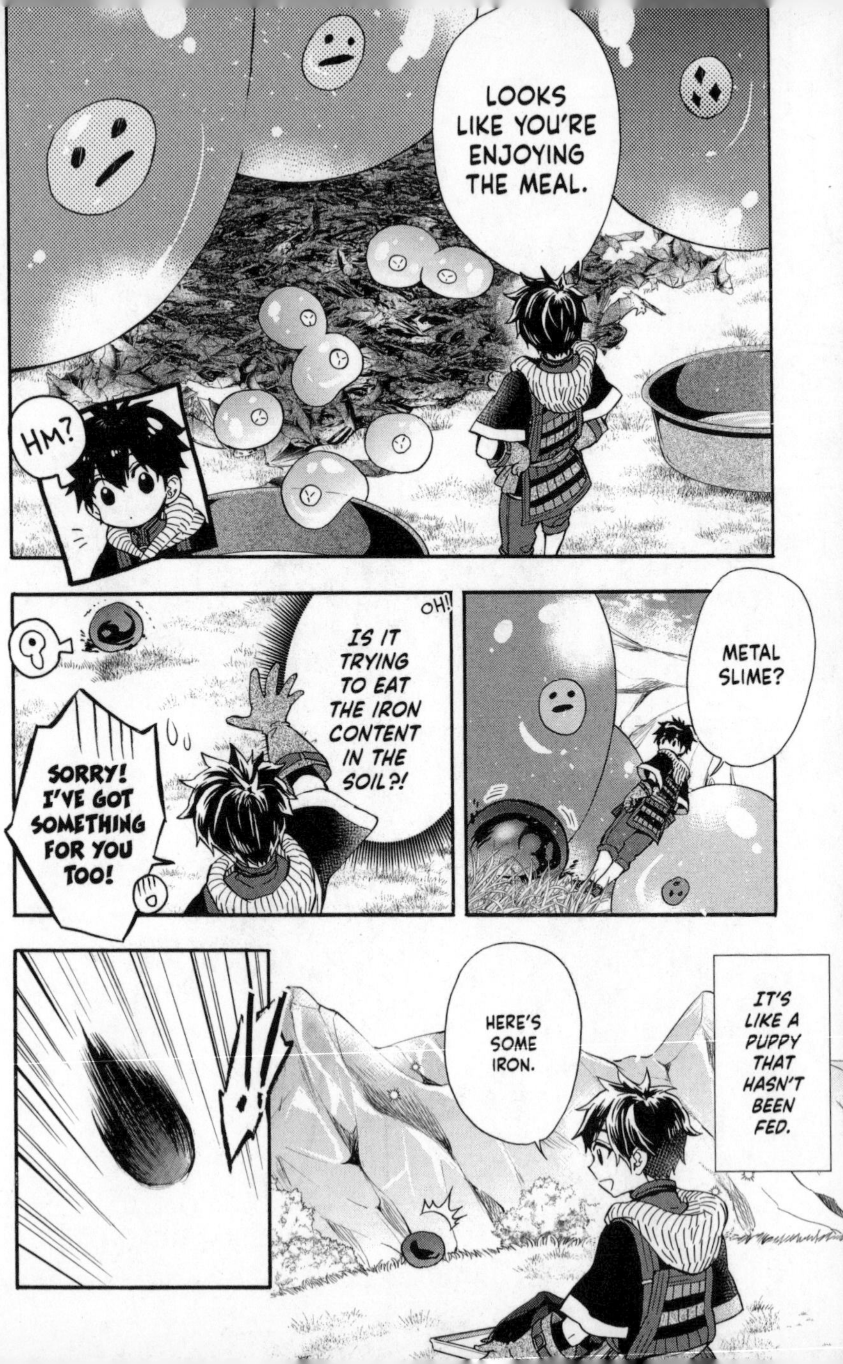

LOOKS LIKE YOU'RE ENJOYING THE MEAL.
HM?
METAL SLIME?
OH!
IS IT TRYING TO EAT THE IRON CONTENT IN THE SOIL?!
SORRY! I'VE GOT SOMETHING FOR YOU TOO!
IT'S LIKE A PUPPY THAT HASN'T BEEN FED.
HERE'S SOME IRON.

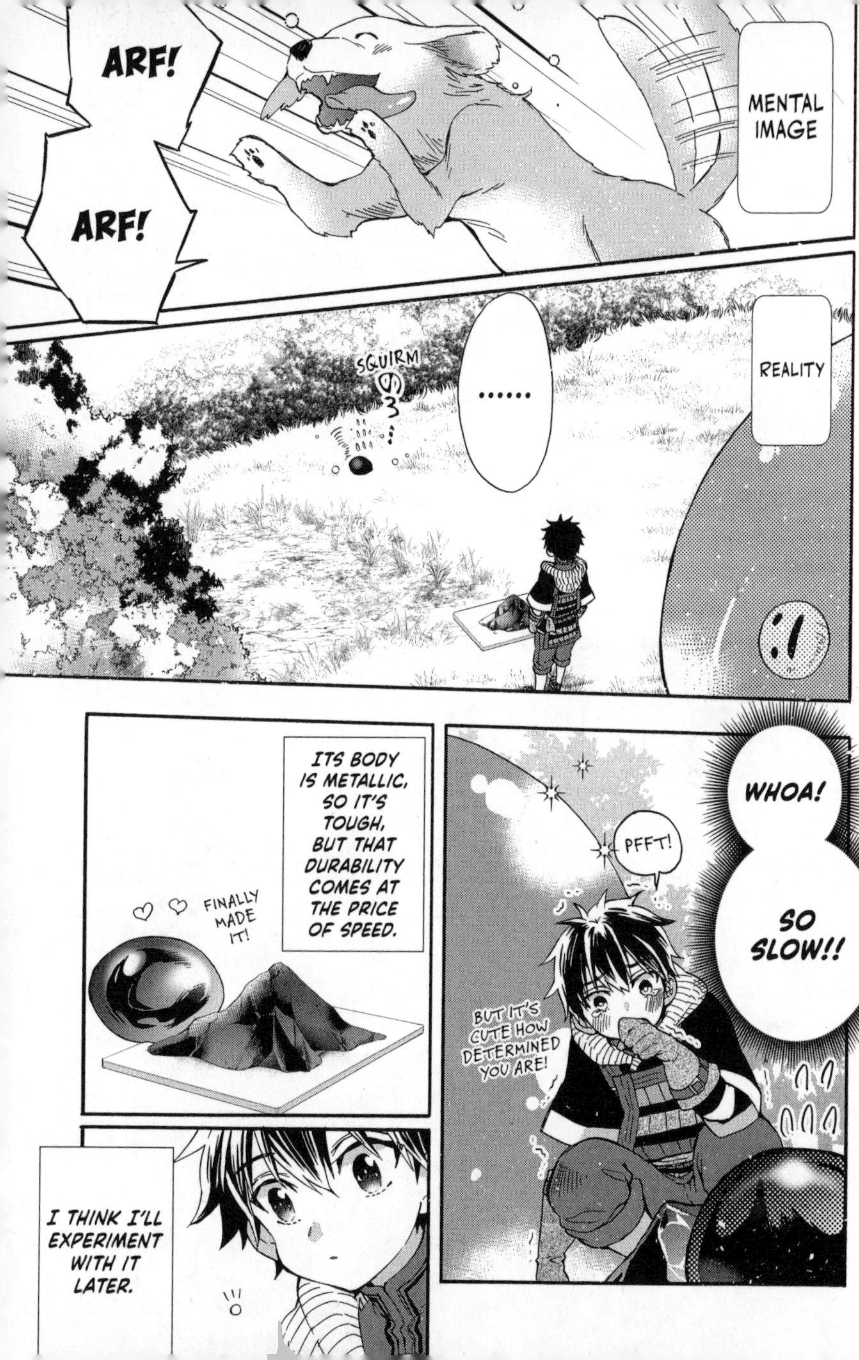
MENTAL IMAGE
ARF!
ARF!
REALITY
......
SQUIRM
WHOA!
SO SLOW!!
PFFT!
BUT IT'S CUTE HOW DETERMINED YOU ARE!
ITS BODY IS METALLIC, SO IT'S TOUGH, BUT THAT DURABILITY COMES AT THE PRICE OF SPEED.
FINALLY MADE IT!
I THINK I'LL EXPERIMENT WITH IT LATER.

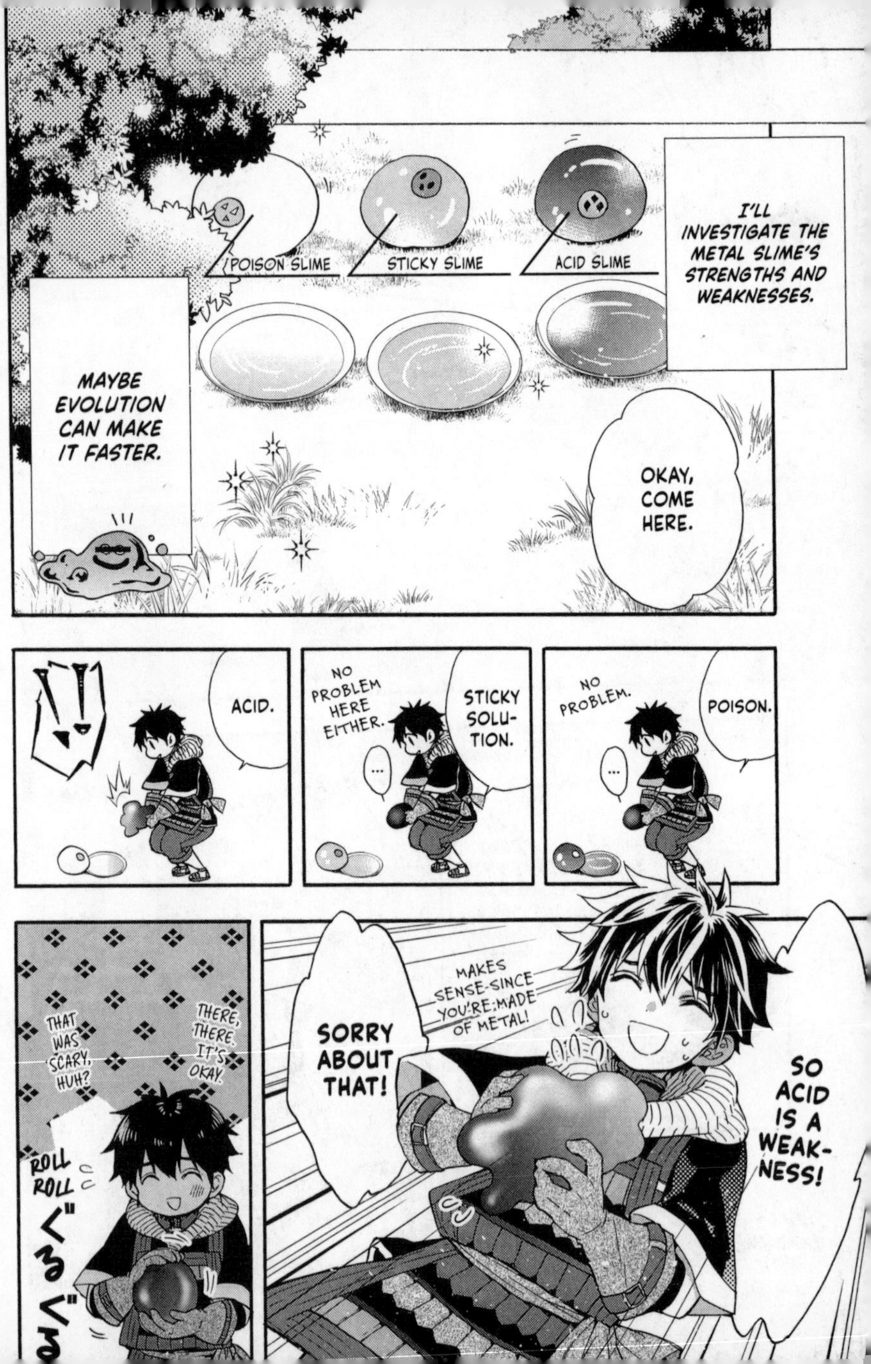

I'LL INVESTIGATE THE METAL SLIME'S STRENGTHS AND WEAKNESSES.
ACID SLIME
STICKY SLIME
POISON SLIME
OKAY, COME HERE.
MAYBE EVOLUTION CAN MAKE IT FASTER.
POISON.
NO PROBLEM.
...
STICKY SOLU-TION.
NO PROBLEM HERE EITHER.
...
ACID.
!!
SO ACID IS A WEAK-NESS!
SORRY ABOUT THAT!
MAKES SENSE SINCE YOU'RE MADE OF METAL!
THERE, THERE, IT'S OKAY.
THAT WAS SCARY, HUH?
ROLL ROLL

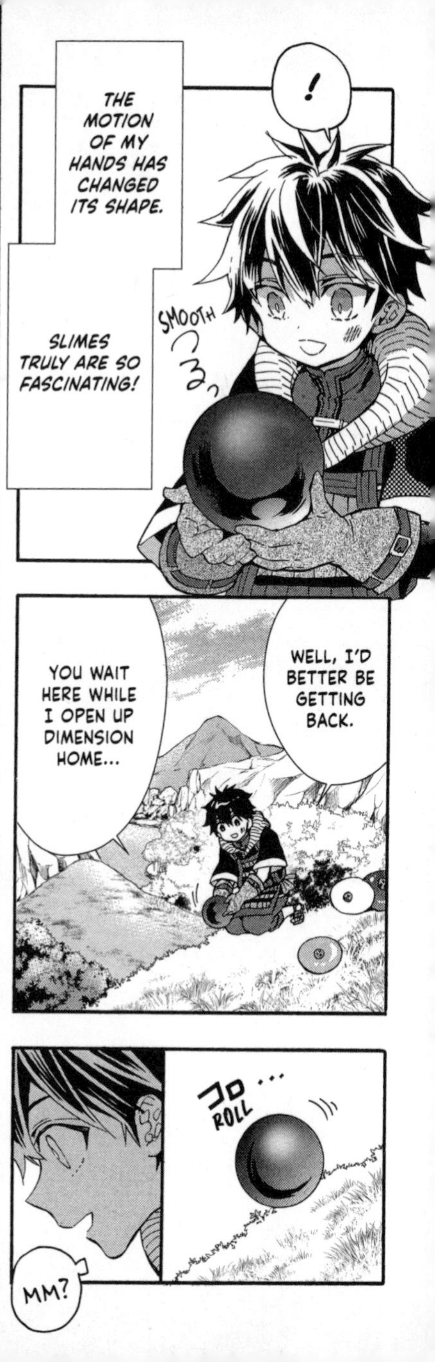
!
THE MOTION OF MY HANDS HAS CHANGED ITS SHAPE.
SMOOTH
SLIMES TRULY ARE SO FASCINATING!
WELL, I'D BETTER BE GETTING BACK.
YOU WAIT HERE WHILE I OPEN UP DIMENSION HOME...
コロ... ROLL
MM?
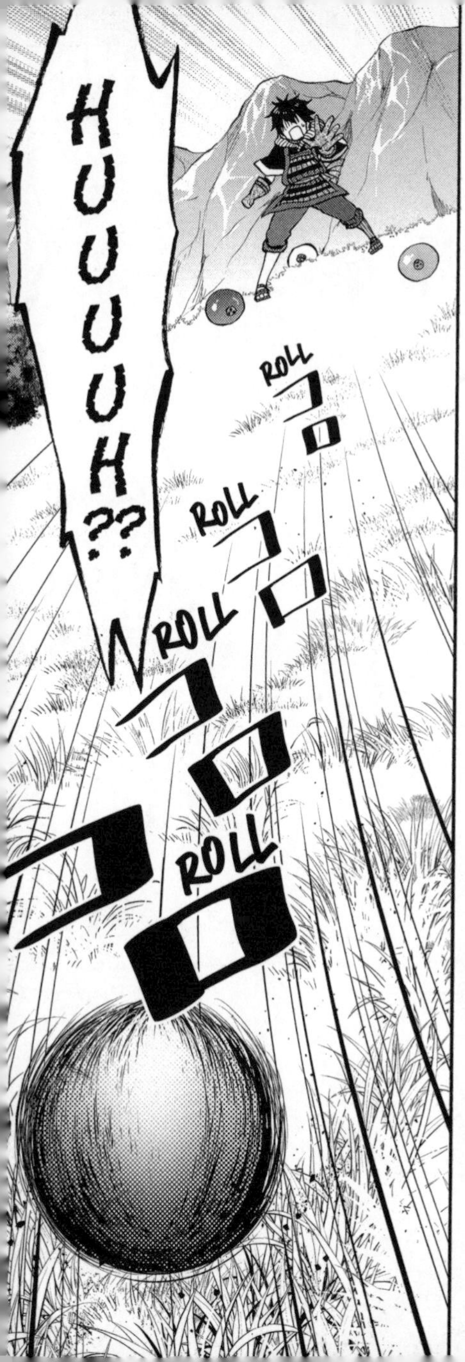
ROLL
ROLL
ROLL
HUUUUUH??
ROLL

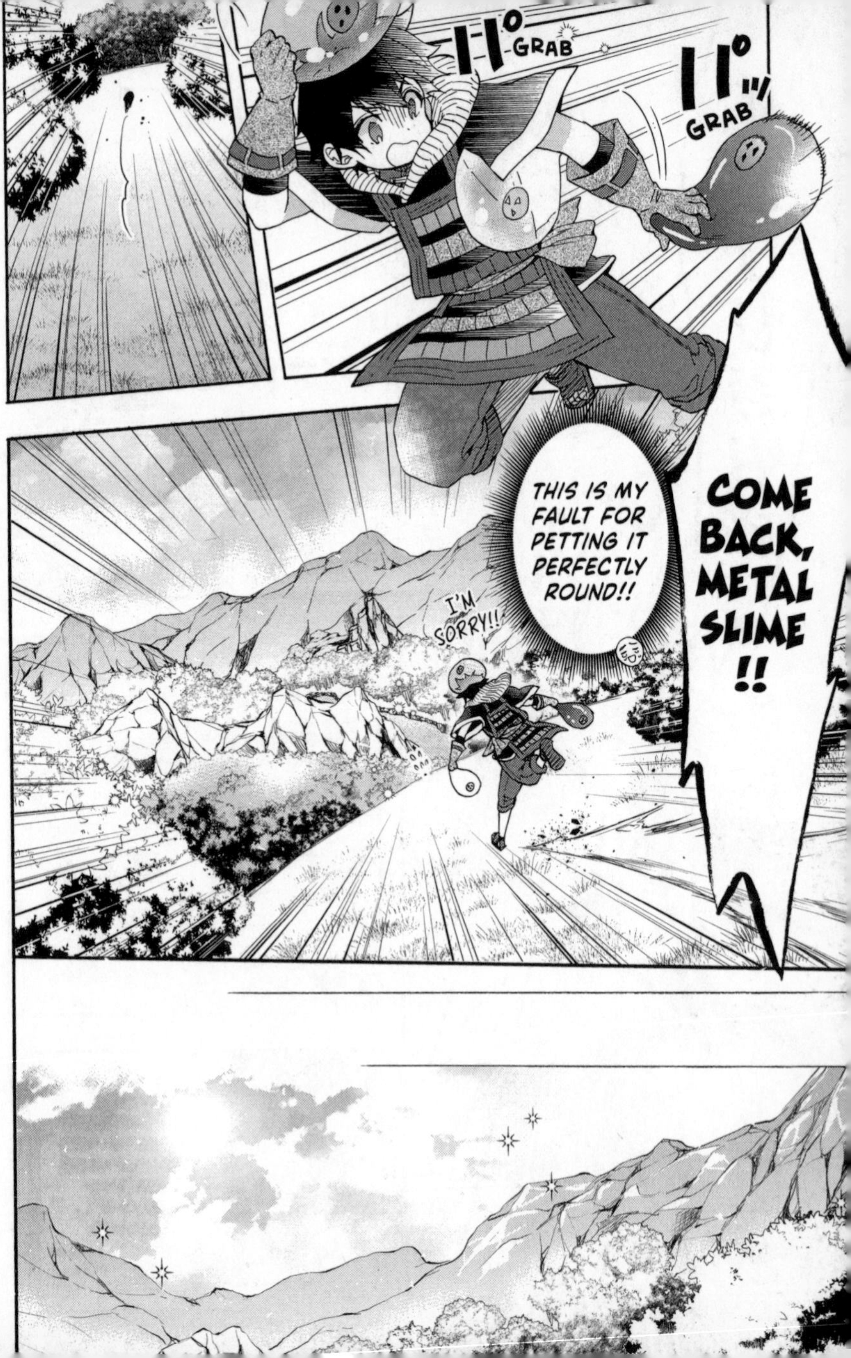
GRAB
GRAB
COME BACK, METAL SLIME!!
THIS IS MY FAULT FOR PETTING IT PERFECTLY ROUND!!
I'M SORRY!!

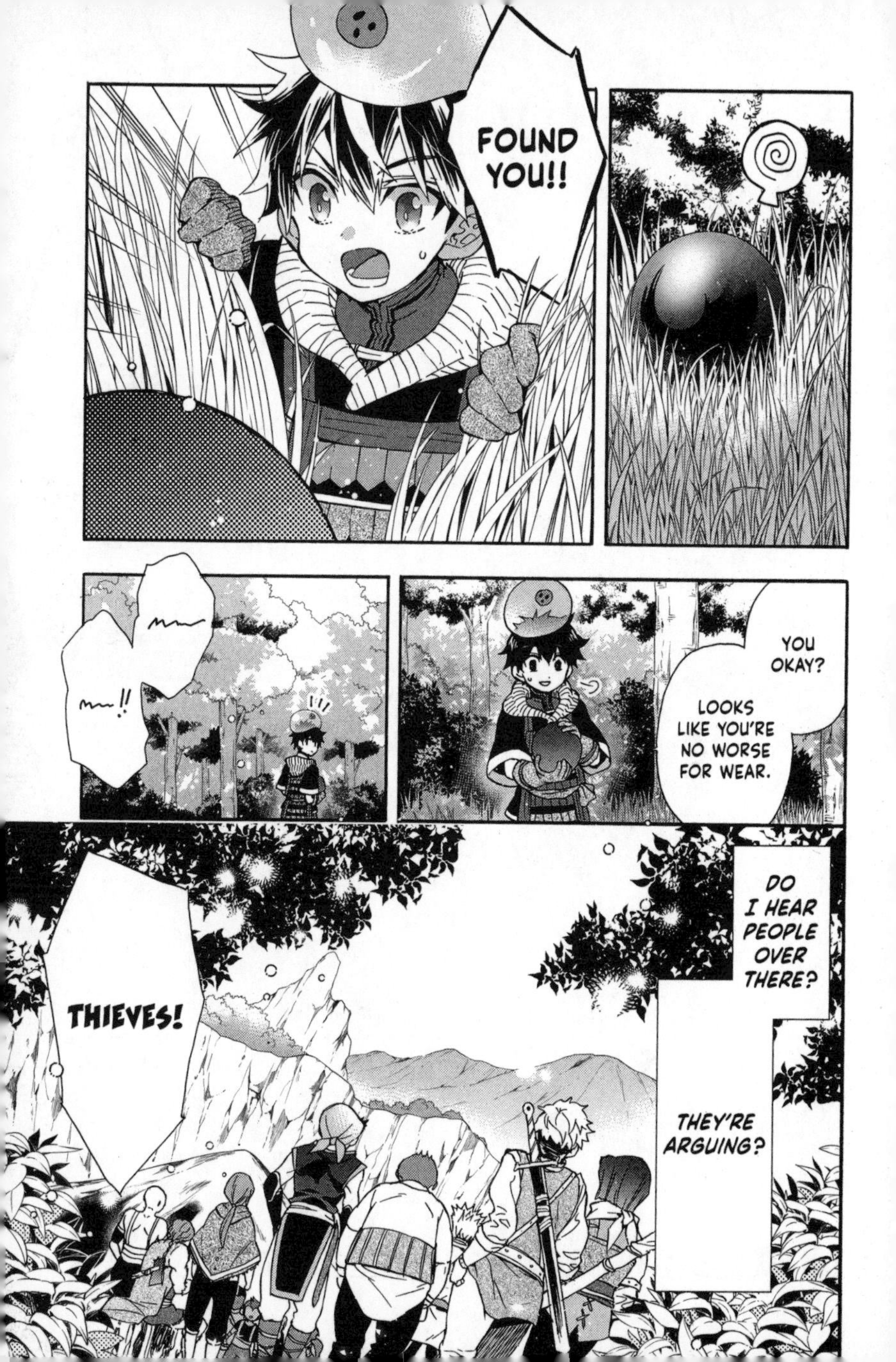
FOUND YOU!!
YOU OKAY?
LOOKS LIKE YOU'RE NO WORSE FOR WEAR.
mm~
mm~!!
DO I HEAR PEOPLE OVER THERE?
THEY'RE ARGUING?
THIEVES!

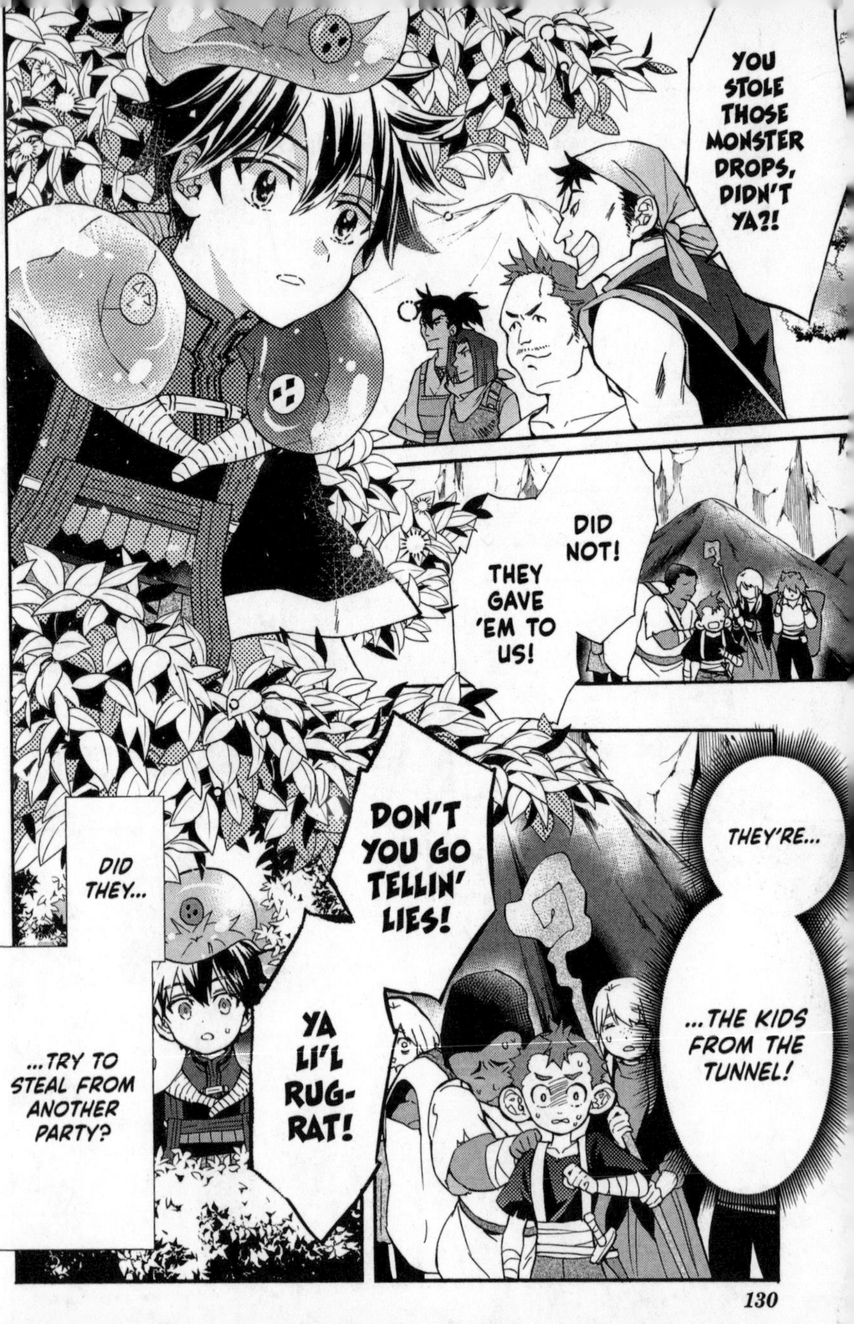
YOU STOLE THOSE MONSTER DROPS, DIDN'T YA?!
DID NOT!
THEY GAVE 'EM TO US!
THEY'RE...
...THE KIDS FROM THE TUNNEL!
DON'T YOU GO TELLIN' LIES!
YA LI'L RUG-RAT!
DID THEY...
...TRY TO STEAL FROM ANOTHER PARTY?

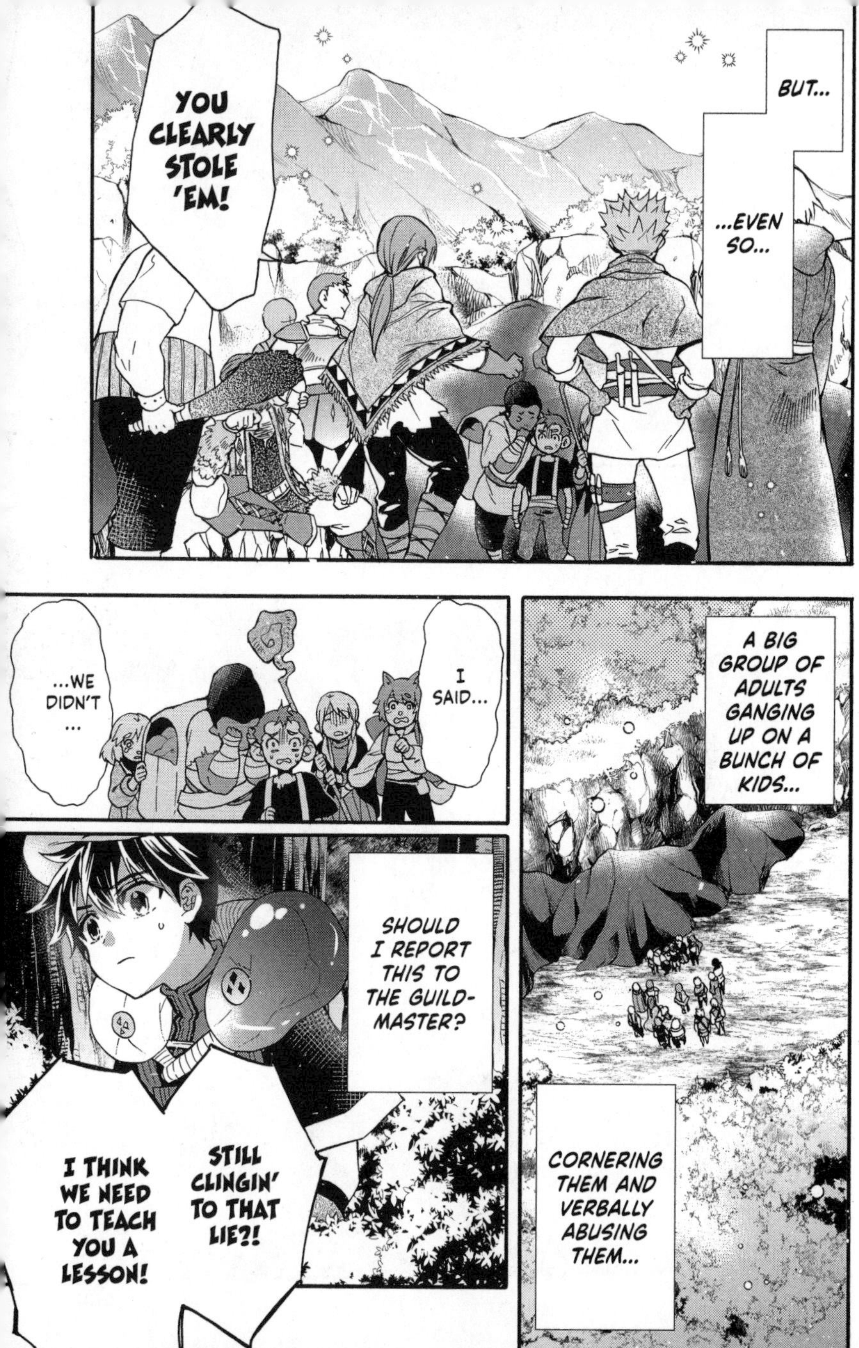
BUT...
...EVEN SO...
YOU CLEARLY STOLE 'EM!
A BIG GROUP OF ADULTS GANGING UP ON A BUNCH OF KIDS...
CORNERING THEM AND VERBALLY ABUSING THEM...
I SAID...
...WE DIDN'T ...
SHOULD I REPORT THIS TO THE GUILD-MASTER?
STILL CLINGIN' TO THAT LIE?!
I THINK WE NEED TO TEACH YOU A LESSON!

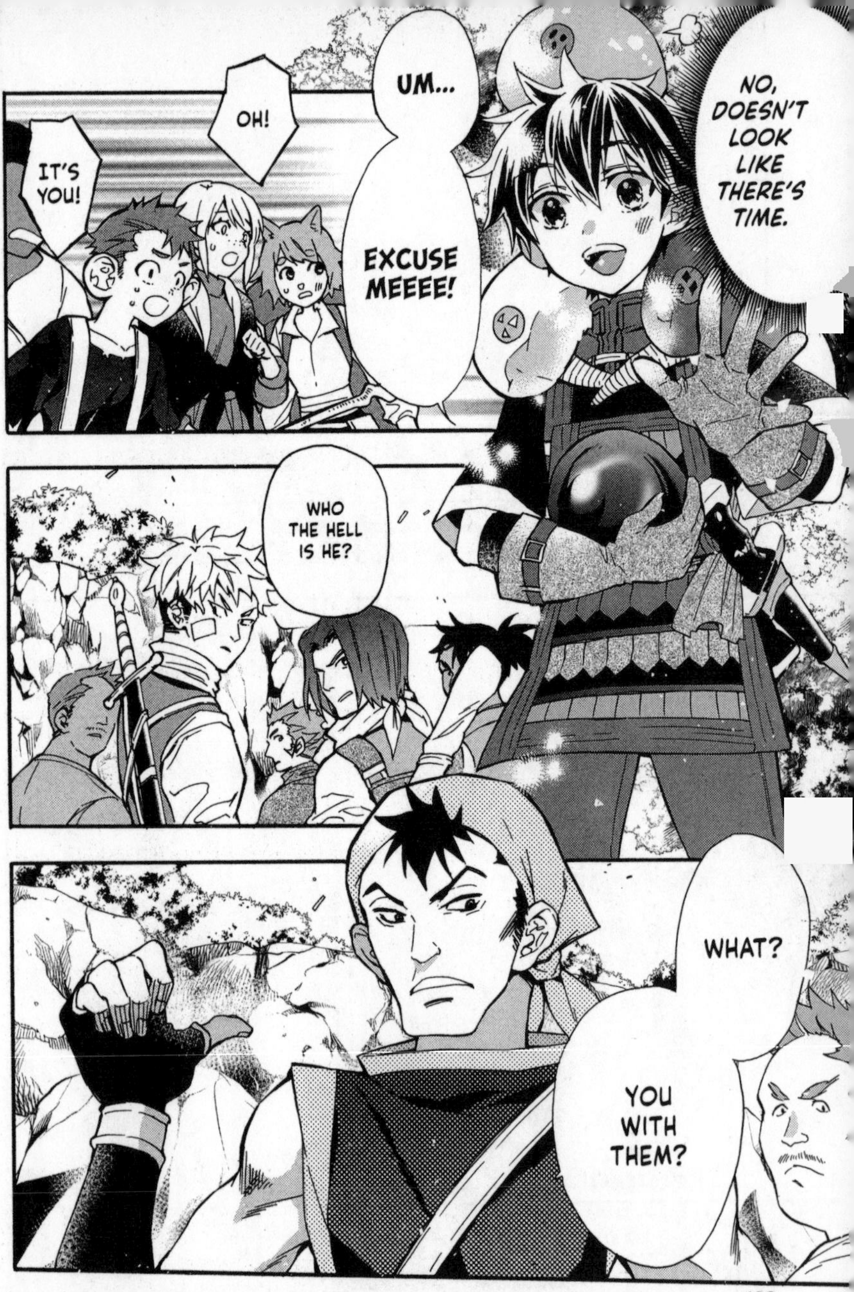
NO, DOESN'T LOOK LIKE THERE'S TIME.
UM...
EXCUSE MEEEE!
OH!
IT'S YOU!
WHO THE HELL IS HE?
WHAT?
YOU WITH THEM?

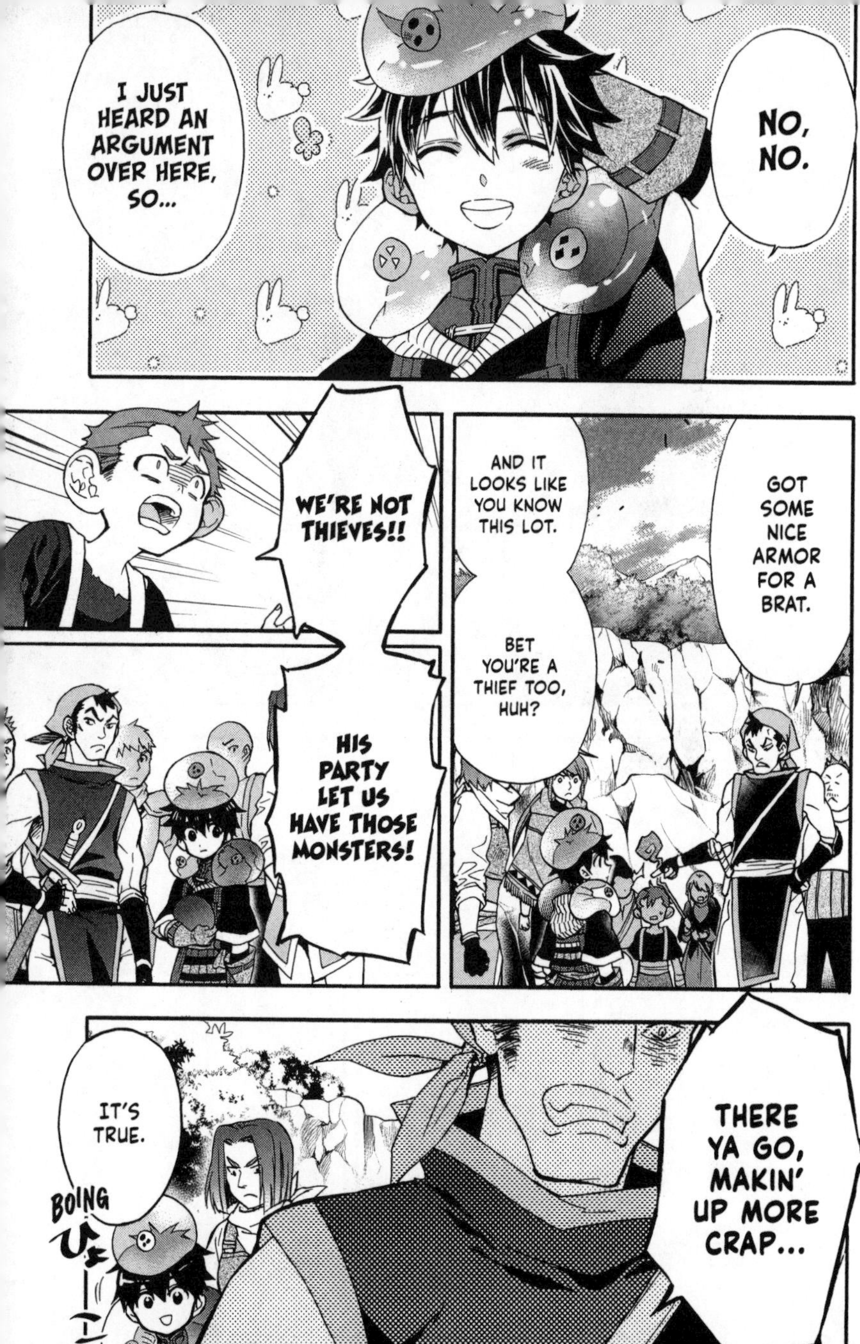

NO, NO.
I JUST HEARD AN ARGUMENT OVER HERE, SO...
GOT SOME NICE ARMOR FOR A BRAT.
AND IT LOOKS LIKE YOU KNOW THIS LOT.
BET YOU'RE A THIEF TOO, HUH?
WE'RE NOT THIEVES!!
HIS PARTY LET US HAVE THOSE MONSTERS!
THERE YA GO, MAKIN' UP MORE CRAP...
IT'S TRUE.
BOING

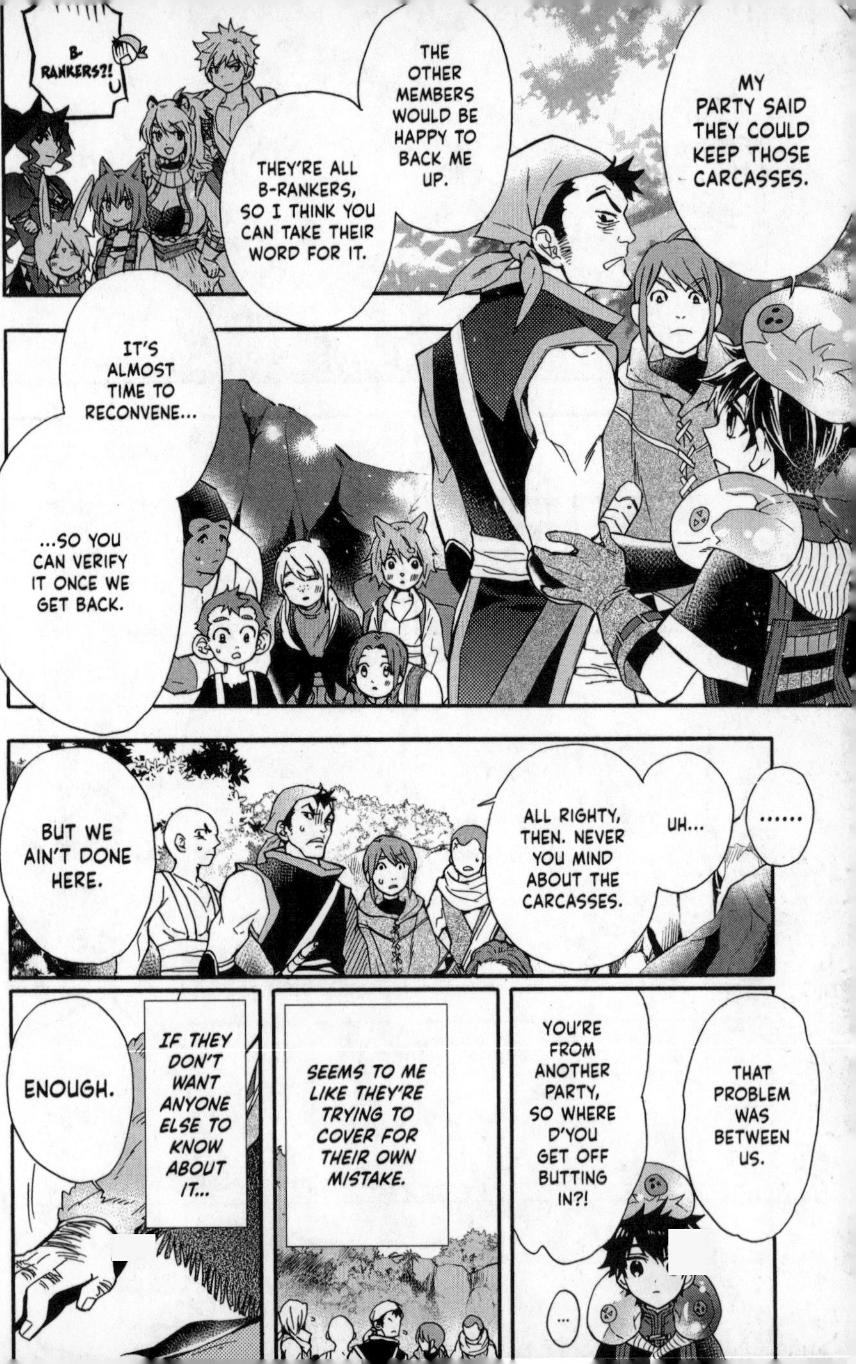
MY PARTY SAID THEY COULD KEEP THOSE CARCASSES.
THE OTHER MEMBERS WOULD BE HAPPY TO BACK ME UP.
THEY'RE ALL B-RANKERS, SO I THINK YOU CAN TAKE THEIR WORD FOR IT.
B-RANKERS?!
IT'S ALMOST TIME TO RECONVENE...
...SO YOU CAN VERIFY IT ONCE WE GET BACK.
......
UH...
ALL RIGHTY, THEN. NEVER YOU MIND ABOUT THE CARCASSES.
BUT WE AIN'T DONE HERE.
THAT PROBLEM WAS BETWEEN US.
YOU'RE FROM ANOTHER PARTY, SO WHERE D'YOU GET OFF BUTTING IN?!
...
SEEMS TO ME LIKE THEY'RE TRYING TO COVER FOR THEIR OWN MISTAKE.
IF THEY DON'T WANT ANYONE ELSE TO KNOW ABOUT IT...
ENOUGH.

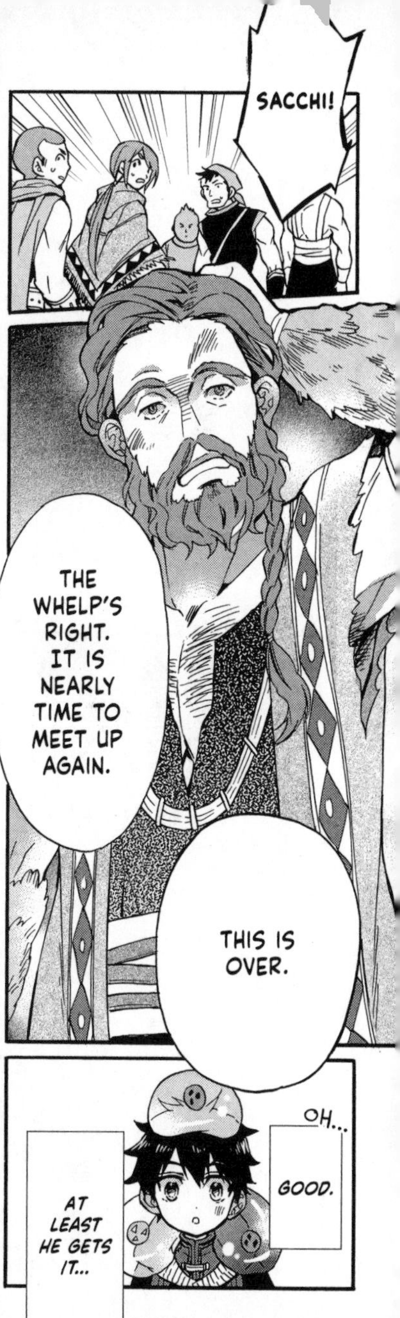
SACCHI!
THE WHELP'S RIGHT. IT IS NEARLY TIME TO MEET UP AGAIN.
THIS IS OVER.
OH...
GOOD.
AT LEAST HE GETS IT...
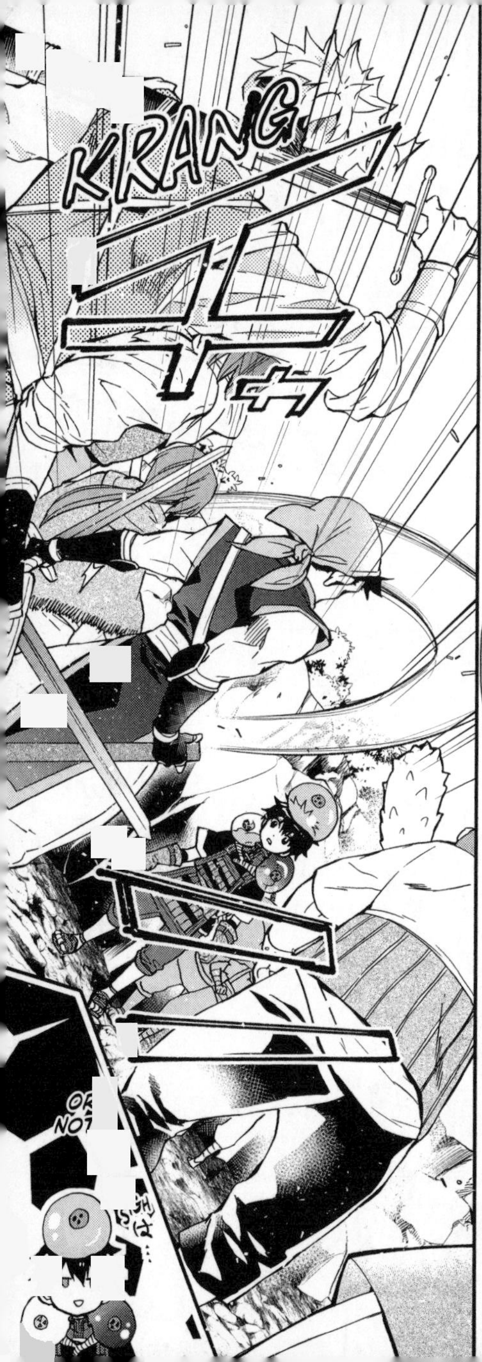
KRANG

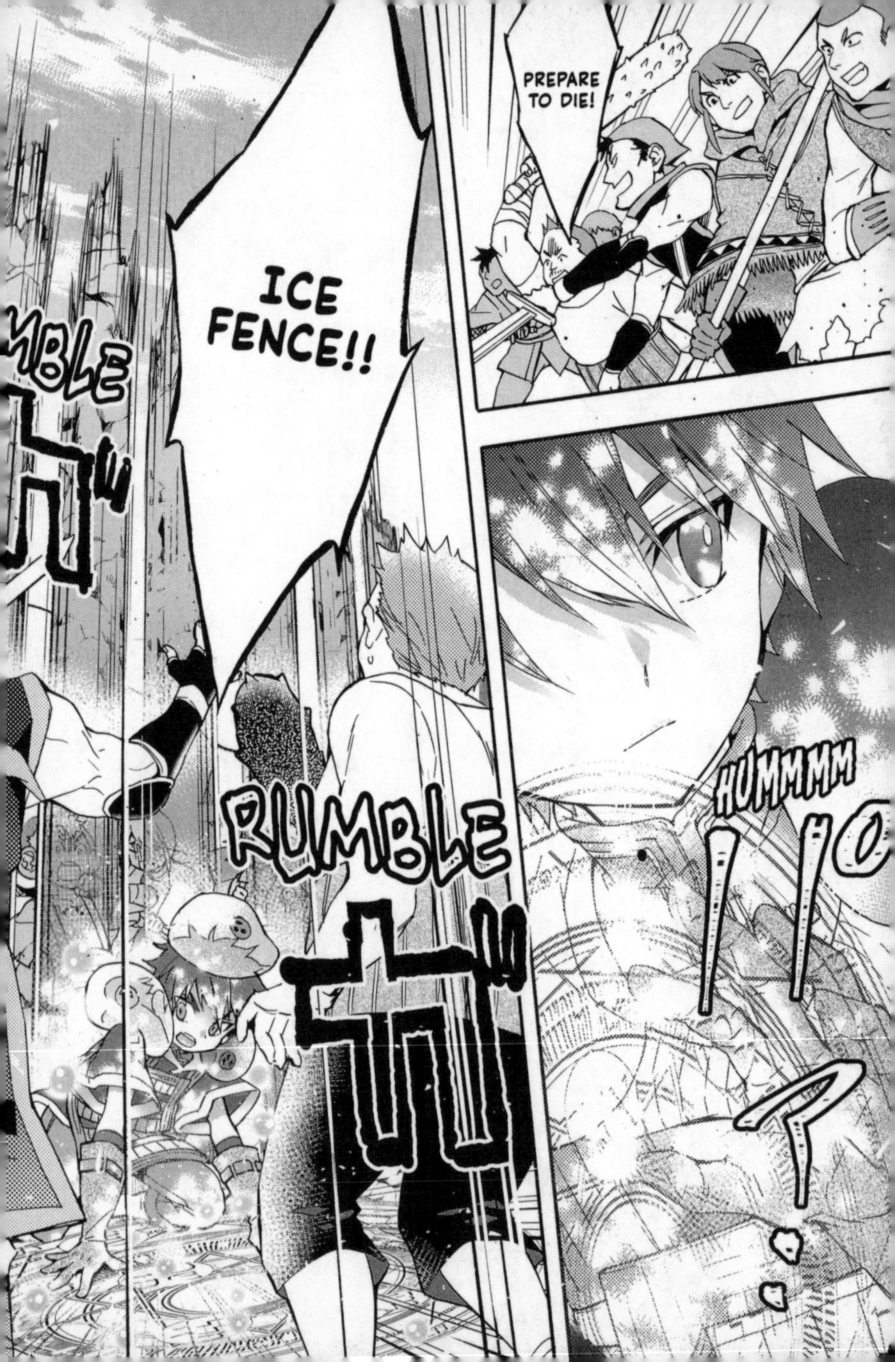
PREPARE TO DIE!
HUMMMM
ICE FENCE!!
RUMBLE

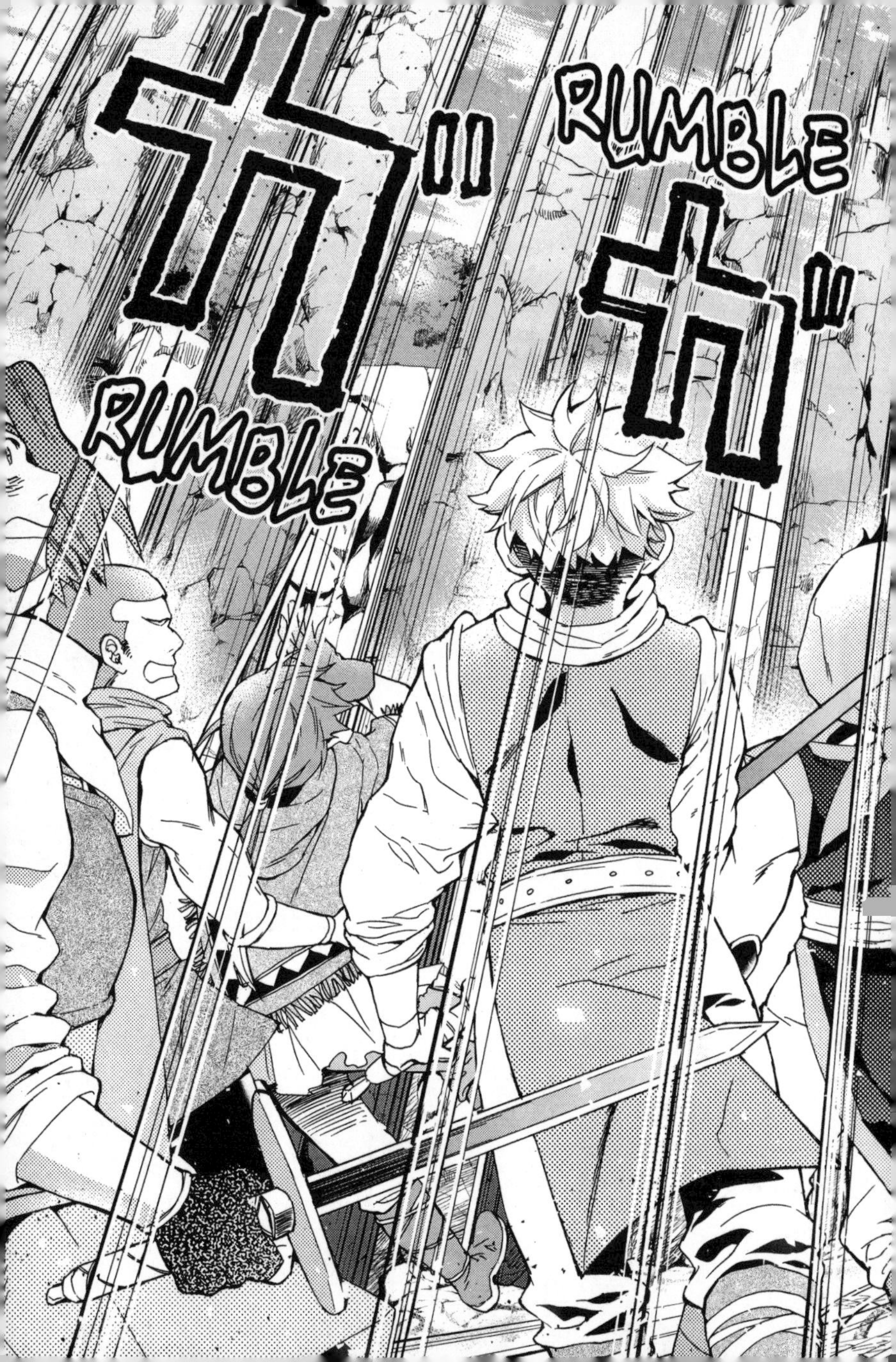
RUMBLE
RUMBLE

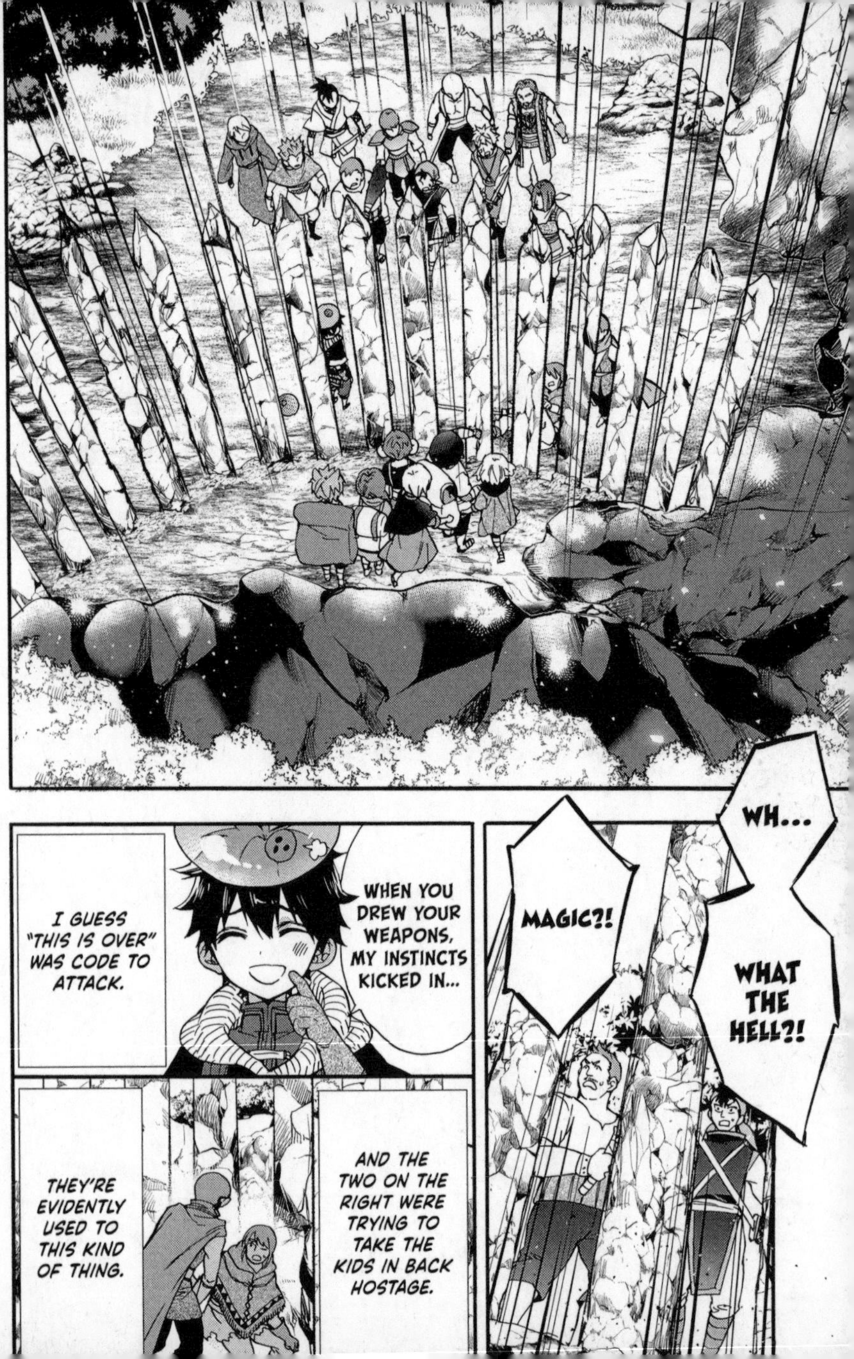
WH...
MAGIC?!
WHAT THE HELL?!
WHEN YOU DREW YOUR WEAPONS, MY INSTINCTS KICKED IN...
I GUESS "THIS IS OVER" WAS CODE TO ATTACK.
AND THE TWO ON THE RIGHT WERE TRYING TO TAKE THE KIDS IN BACK HOSTAGE.
THEY'RE EVIDENTLY USED TO THIS KIND OF THING.

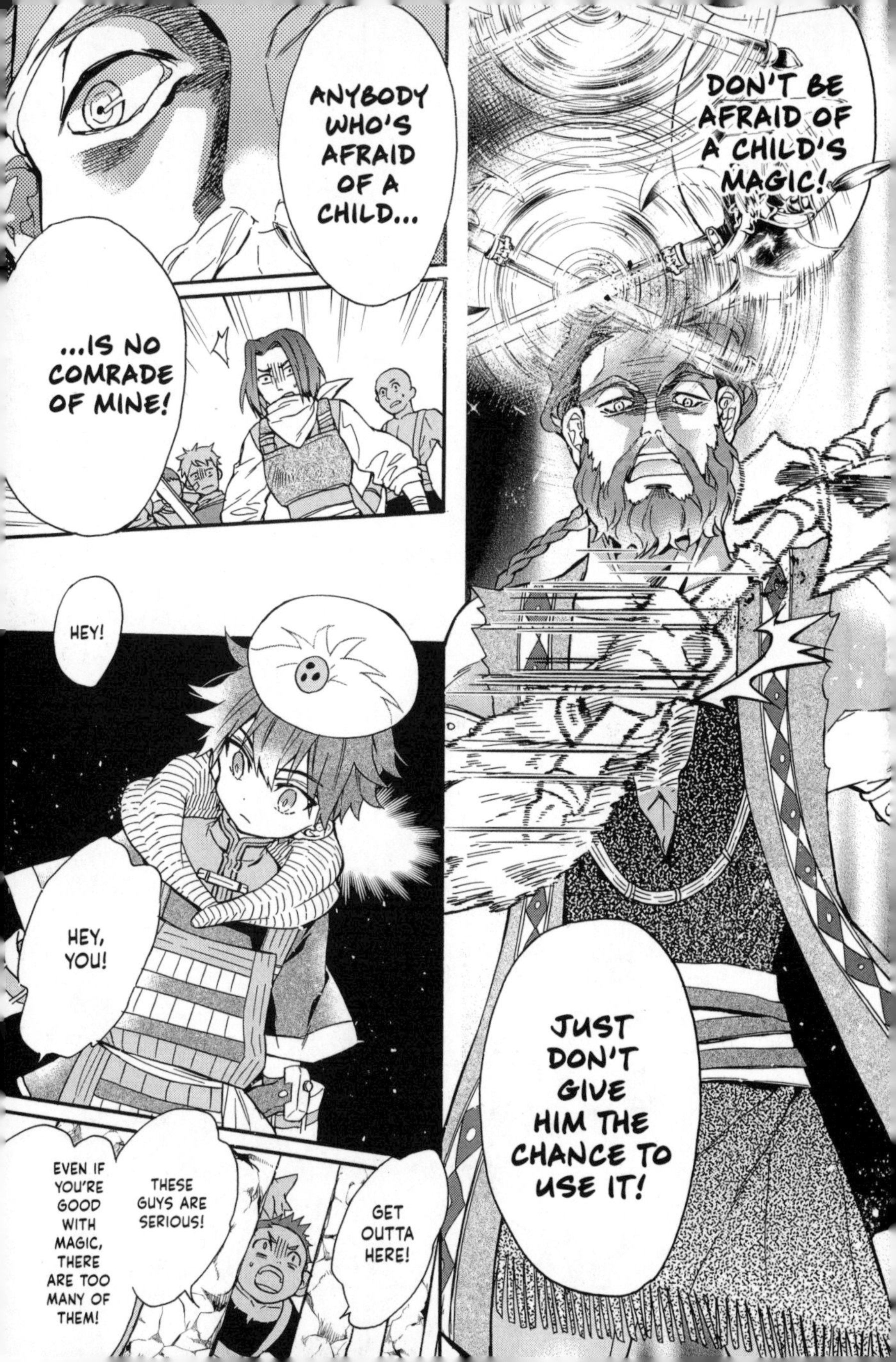
DON'T BE AFRAID OF A CHILD'S MAGIC!
JUST DON'T GIVE HIM THE CHANCE TO USE IT!
ANYBODY WHO'S AFRAID OF A CHILD...
...IS NO COMRADE OF MINE!
HEY!
HEY, YOU!
GET OUTTA HERE!
THESE GUYS ARE SERIOUS!
EVEN IF YOU'RE GOOD WITH MAGIC, THERE ARE TOO MANY OF THEM!

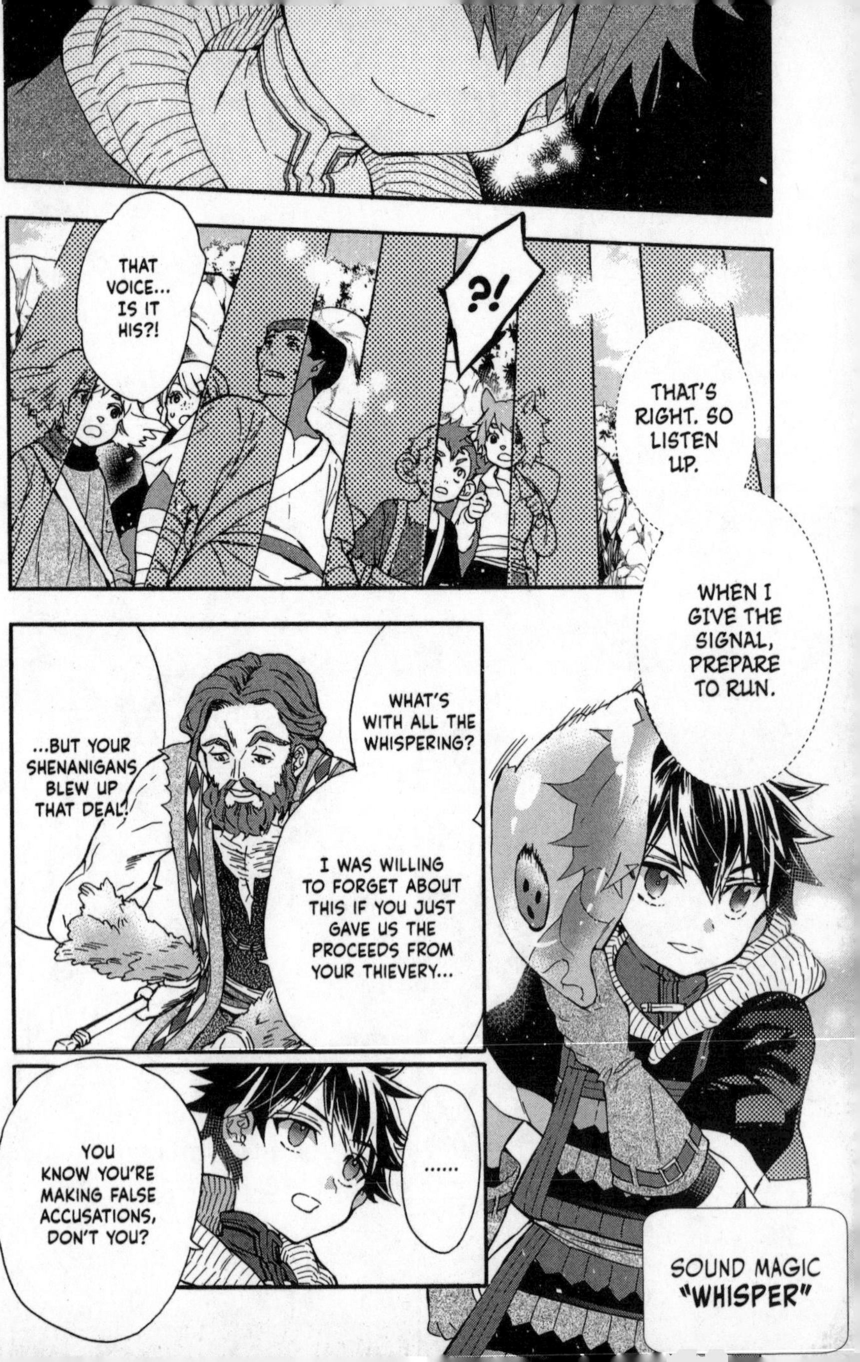
?!
THAT VOICE... IS IT HIS?!
THAT'S RIGHT. SO LISTEN UP.
WHEN I GIVE THE SIGNAL, PREPARE TO RUN.
SOUND MAGIC "WHISPER"
WHAT'S WITH ALL THE WHISPERING?
I WAS WILLING TO FORGET ABOUT THIS IF YOU JUST GAVE US THE PROCEEDS FROM YOUR THIEVERY...
...BUT YOUR SHENANIGANS BLEW UP THAT DEAL.
......
YOU KNOW YOU'RE MAKING FALSE ACCUSATIONS, DON'T YOU?

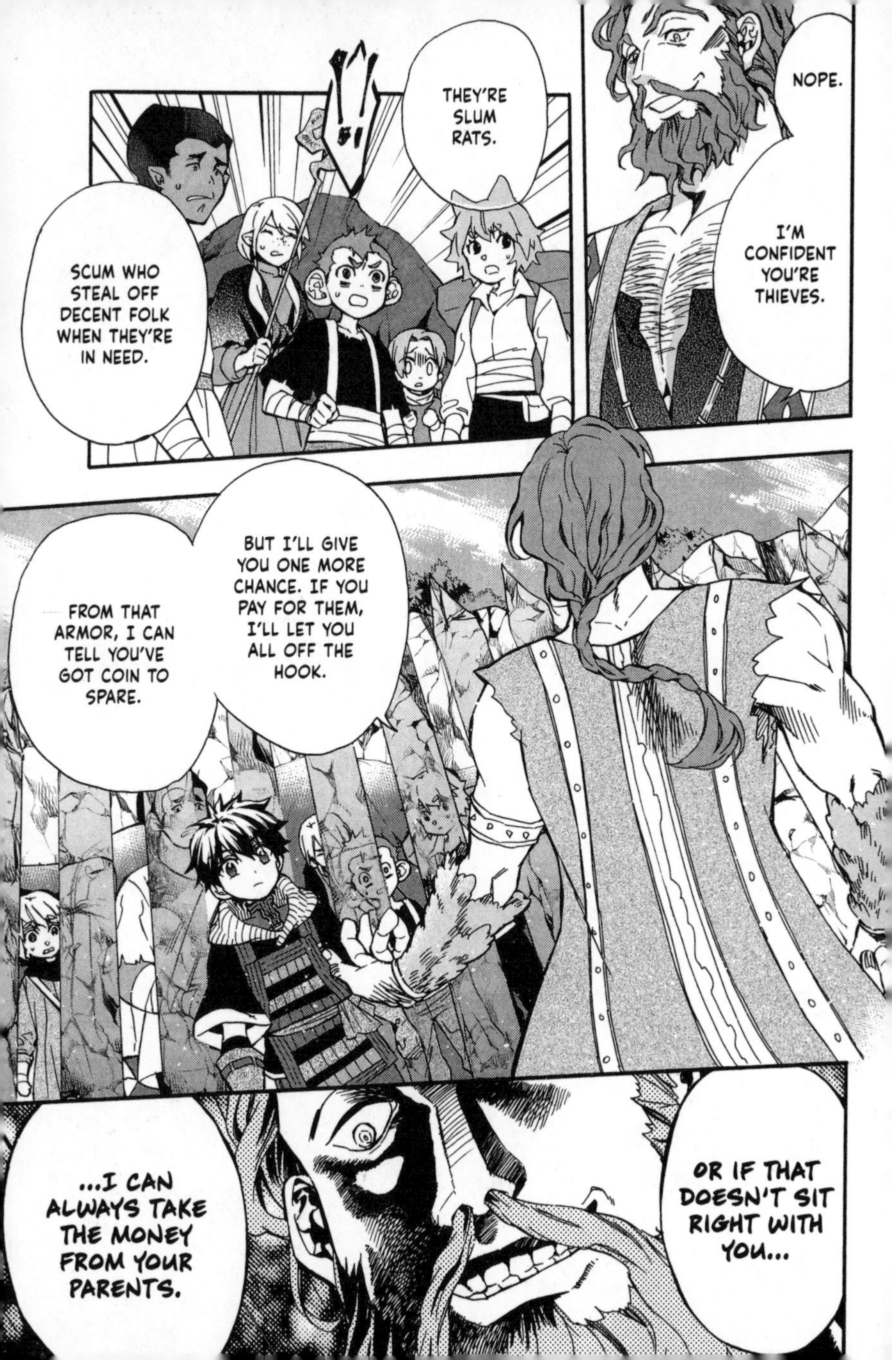
NOPE.
I'M CONFIDENT YOU'RE THIEVES.
THEY'RE SLUM RATS.
SCUM WHO STEAL OFF DECENT FOLK WHEN THEY'RE IN NEED.
BUT I'LL GIVE YOU ONE MORE CHANCE. IF YOU PAY FOR THEM, I'LL LET YOU ALL OFF THE HOOK.
FROM THAT ARMOR, I CAN TELL YOU'VE GOT COIN TO SPARE.
OR IF THAT DOESN'T SIT RIGHT WITH YOU...
...I CAN ALWAYS TAKE THE MONEY FROM YOUR PARENTS.

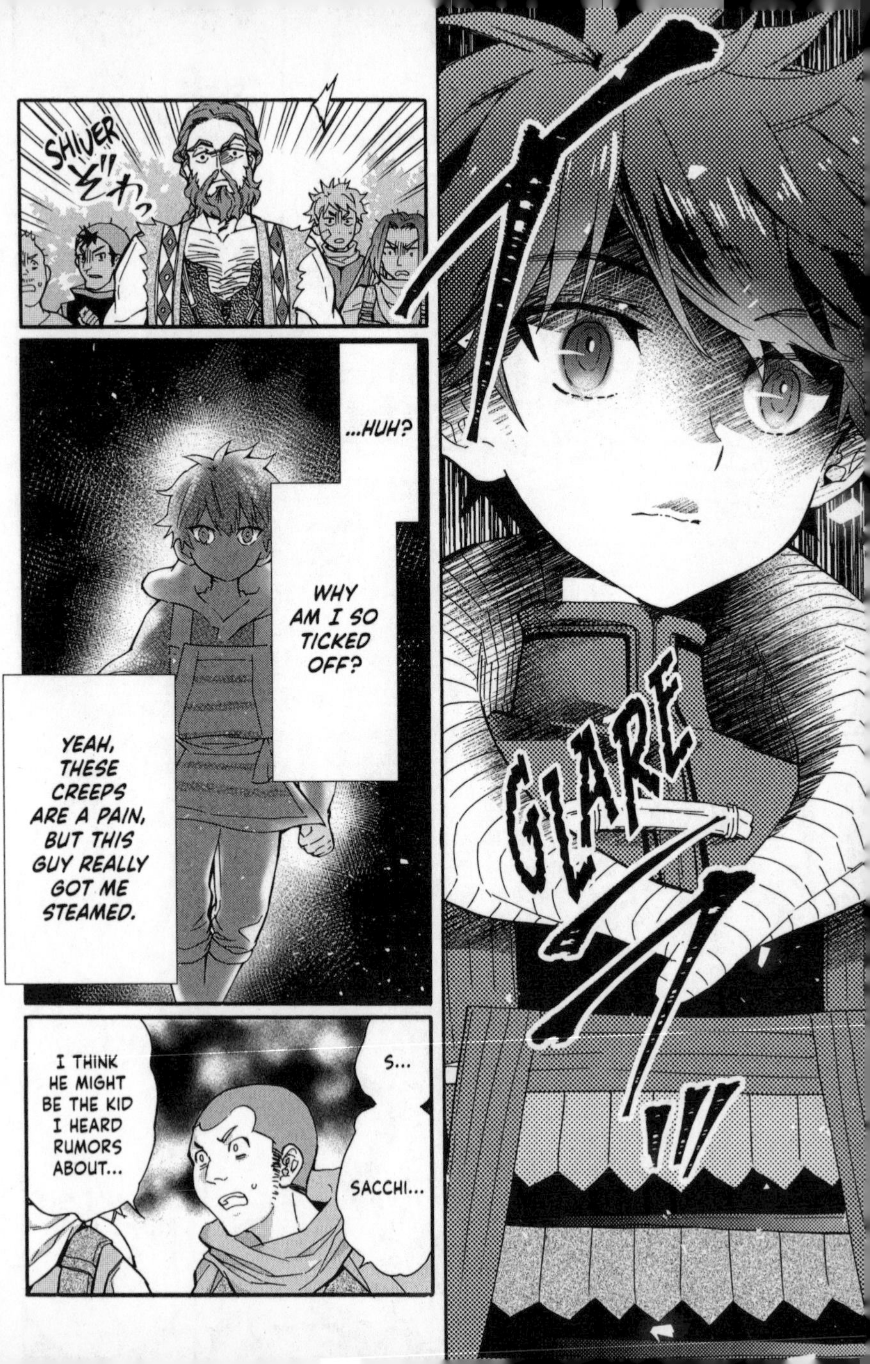
GLARE
SHIVER
ぞわっ
...HUH?
WHY AM I SO TICKED OFF?
YEAH, THESE CREEPS ARE A PAIN, BUT THIS GUY REALLY GOT ME STEAMED.
S...
I THINK HE MIGHT BE THE KID I HEARD RUMORS ABOUT...
SACCHI...

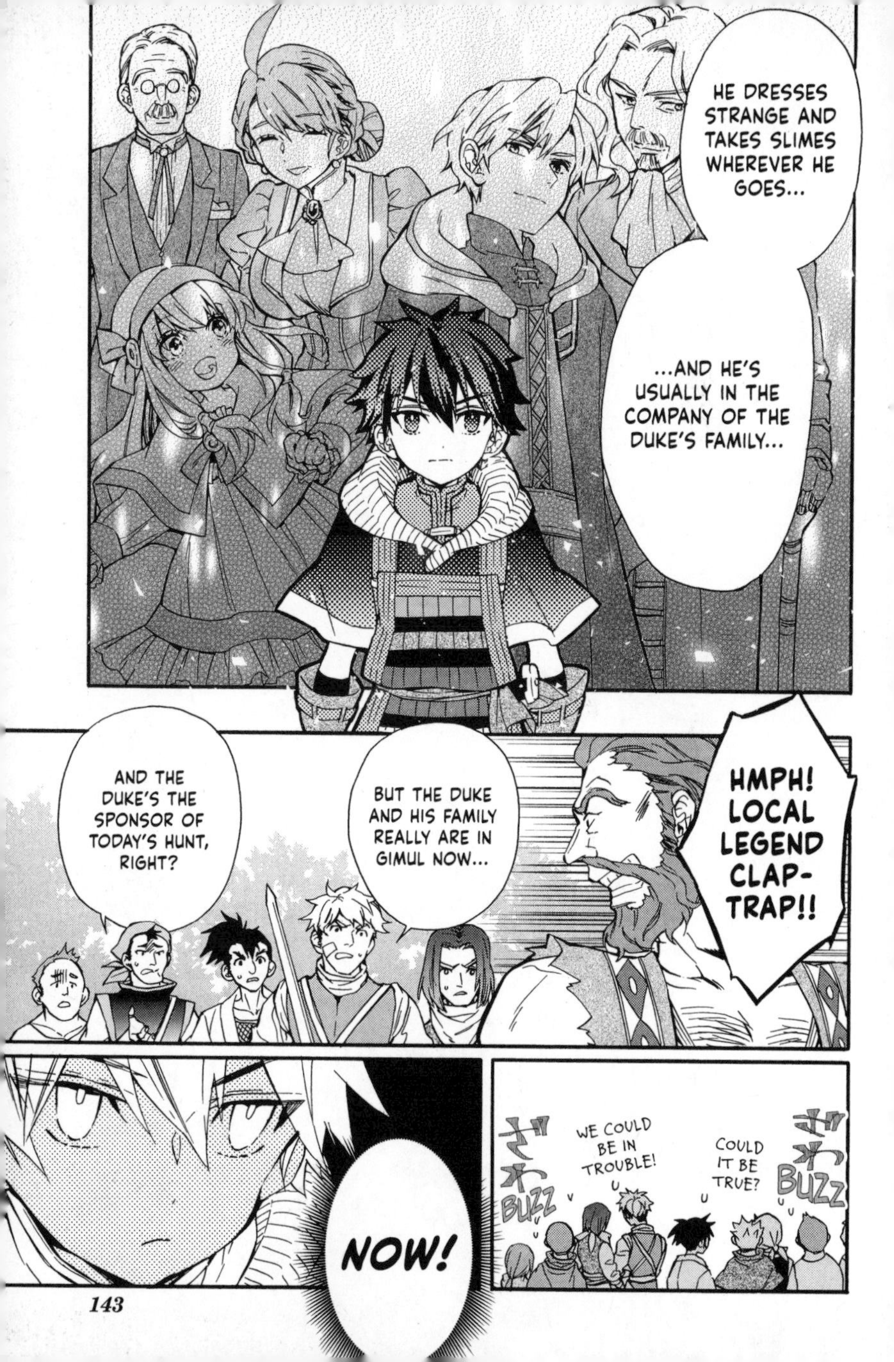
HE DRESSES STRANGE AND TAKES SLIMES WHEREVER HE GOES...
...AND HE'S USUALLY IN THE COMPANY OF THE DUKE'S FAMILY...
HMPH! LOCAL LEGEND CLAP-TRAP!!
BUT THE DUKE AND HIS FAMILY REALLY ARE IN GIMUL NOW...
AND THE DUKE'S THE SPONSOR OF TODAY'S HUNT, RIGHT?
BUZZ
COULD IT BE TRUE?
WE COULD BE IN TROUBLE!
BUZZ
NOW!

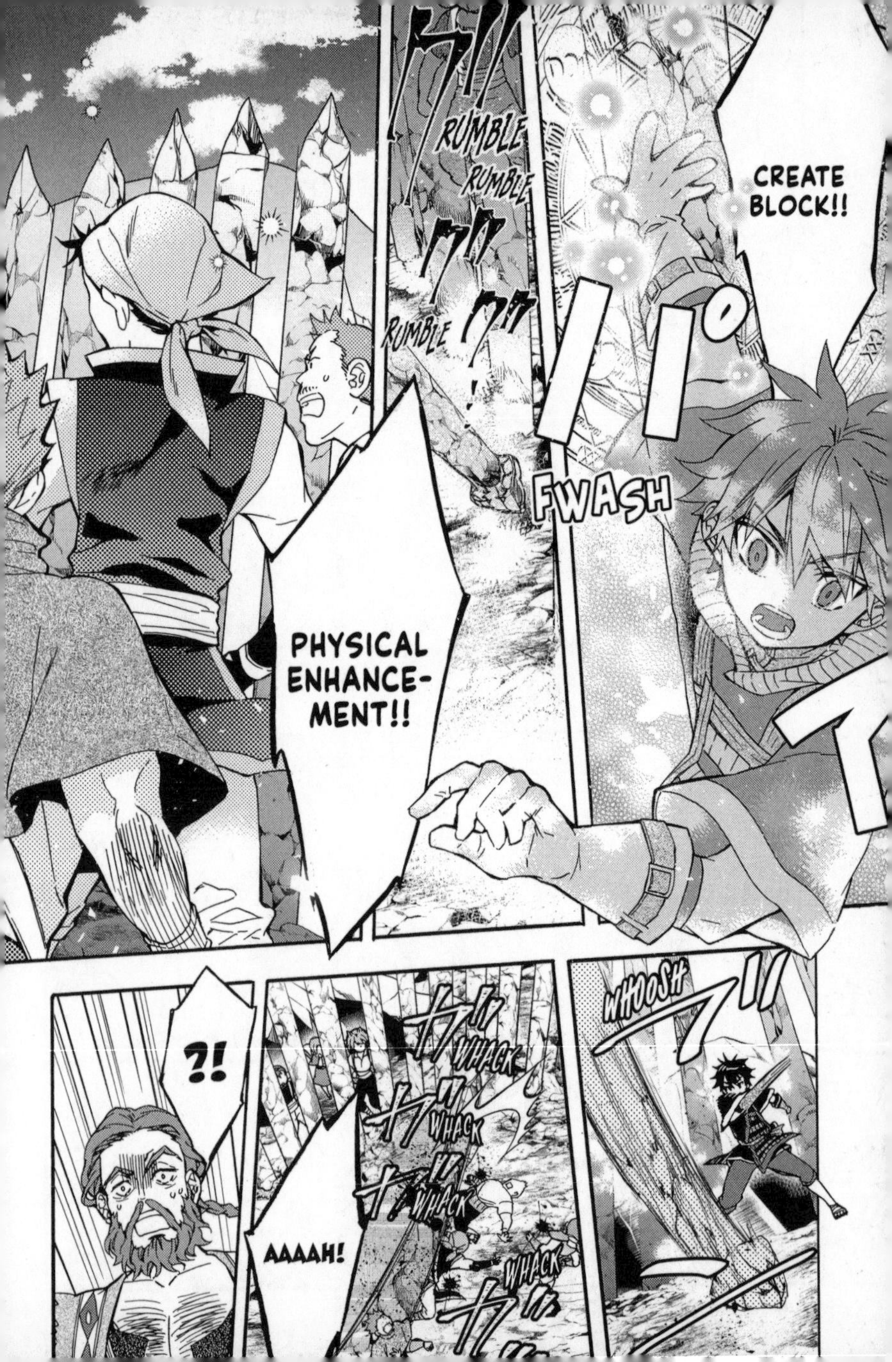
CREATE BLOCK!!
FWASH
RUMBLE
RUMBLE
RUMBLE
PHYSICAL ENHANCE-MENT!!
WHOOSH
WHACK
WHACK
WHACK
WHACK
AAAAH!
?!

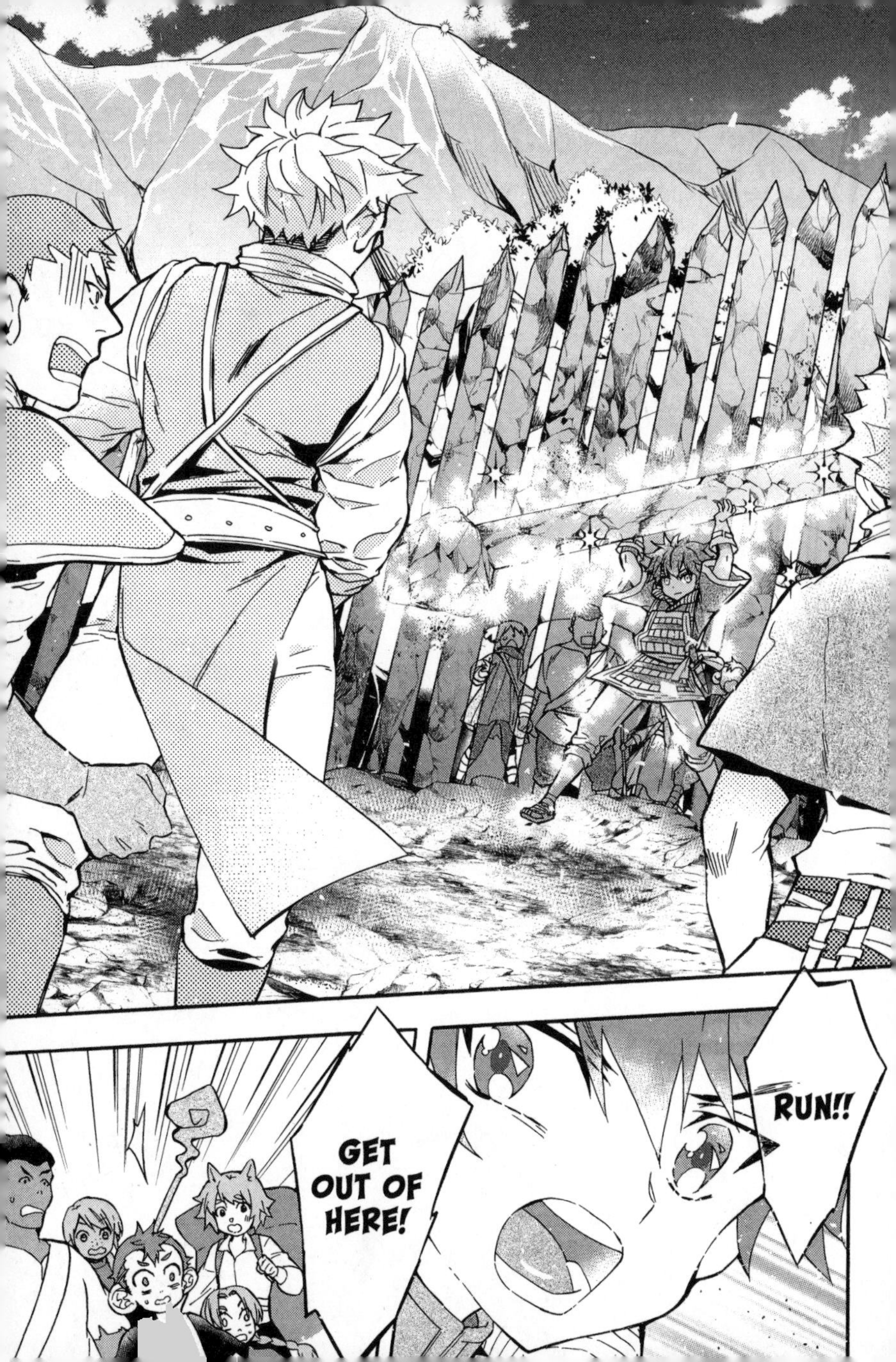
RUN!!
GET OUT OF HERE!

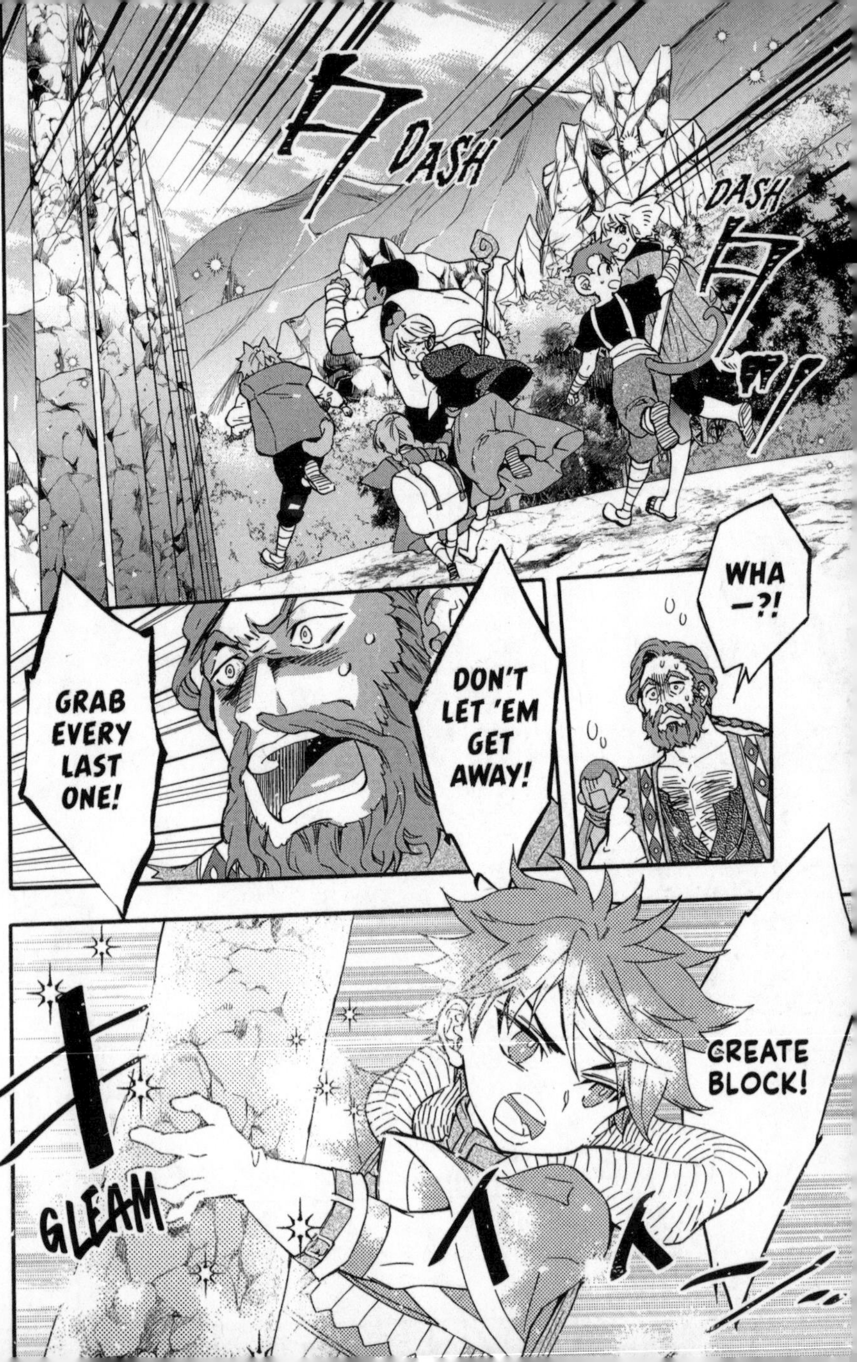
DASH
DASH
WHA—?!
DON'T LET 'EM GET AWAY!
GRAB EVERY LAST ONE!
CREATE BLOCK!
GLEAM

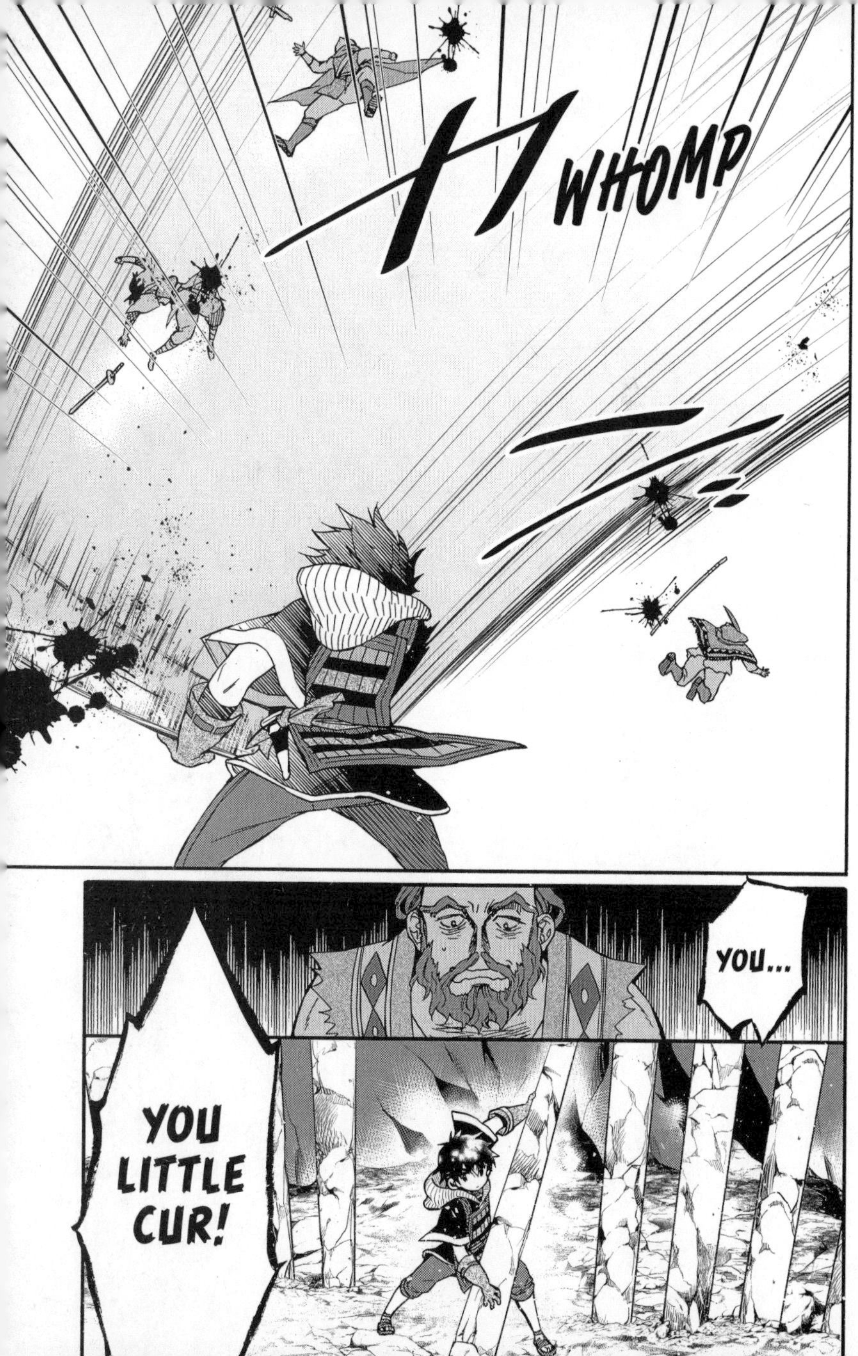
WHOMP
YOU...
YOU LITTLE CUR!

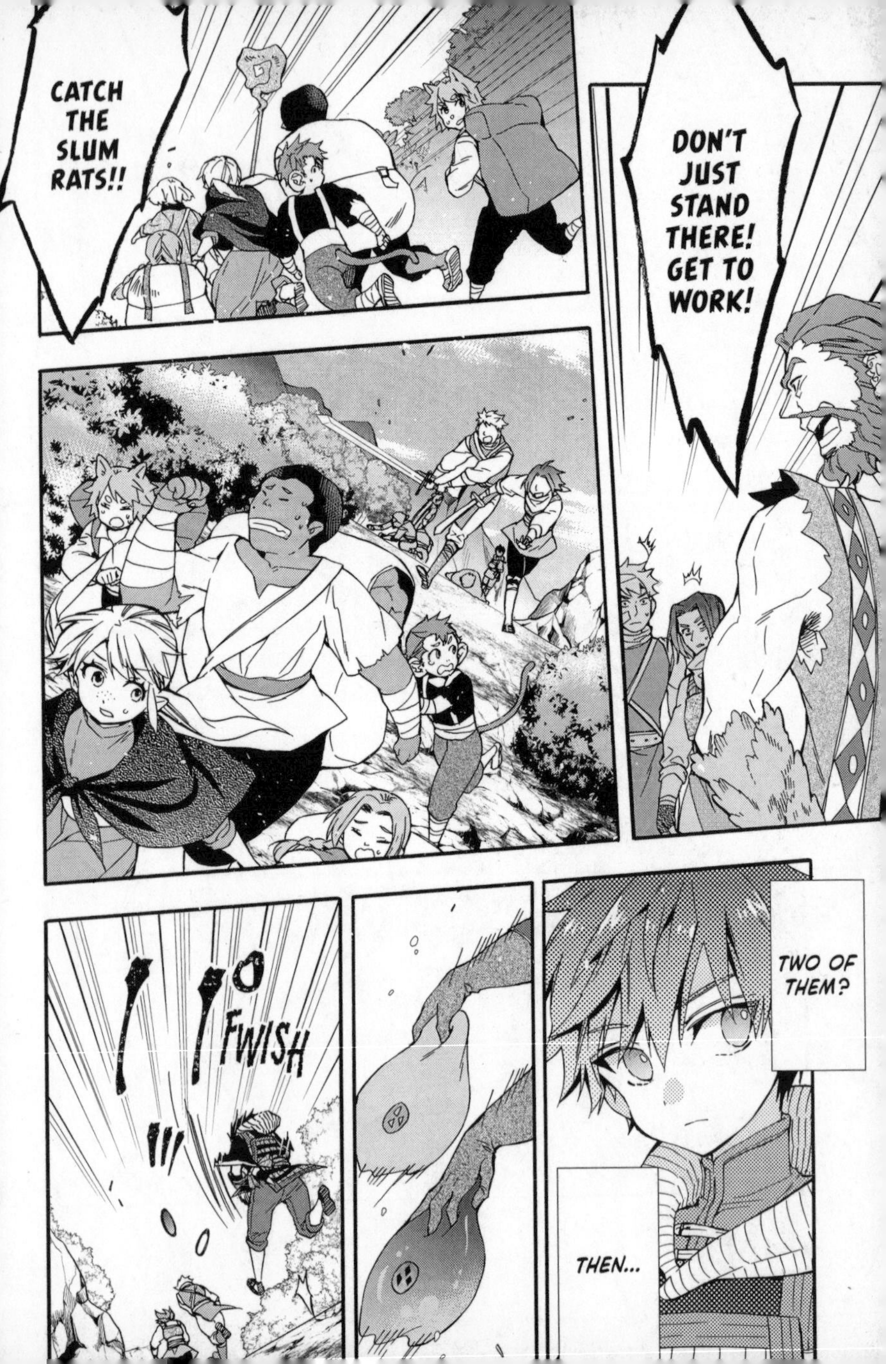
DON'T JUST STAND THERE! GET TO WORK!
CATCH THE SLUM RATS!!
TWO OF THEM?
THEN...
FWISH

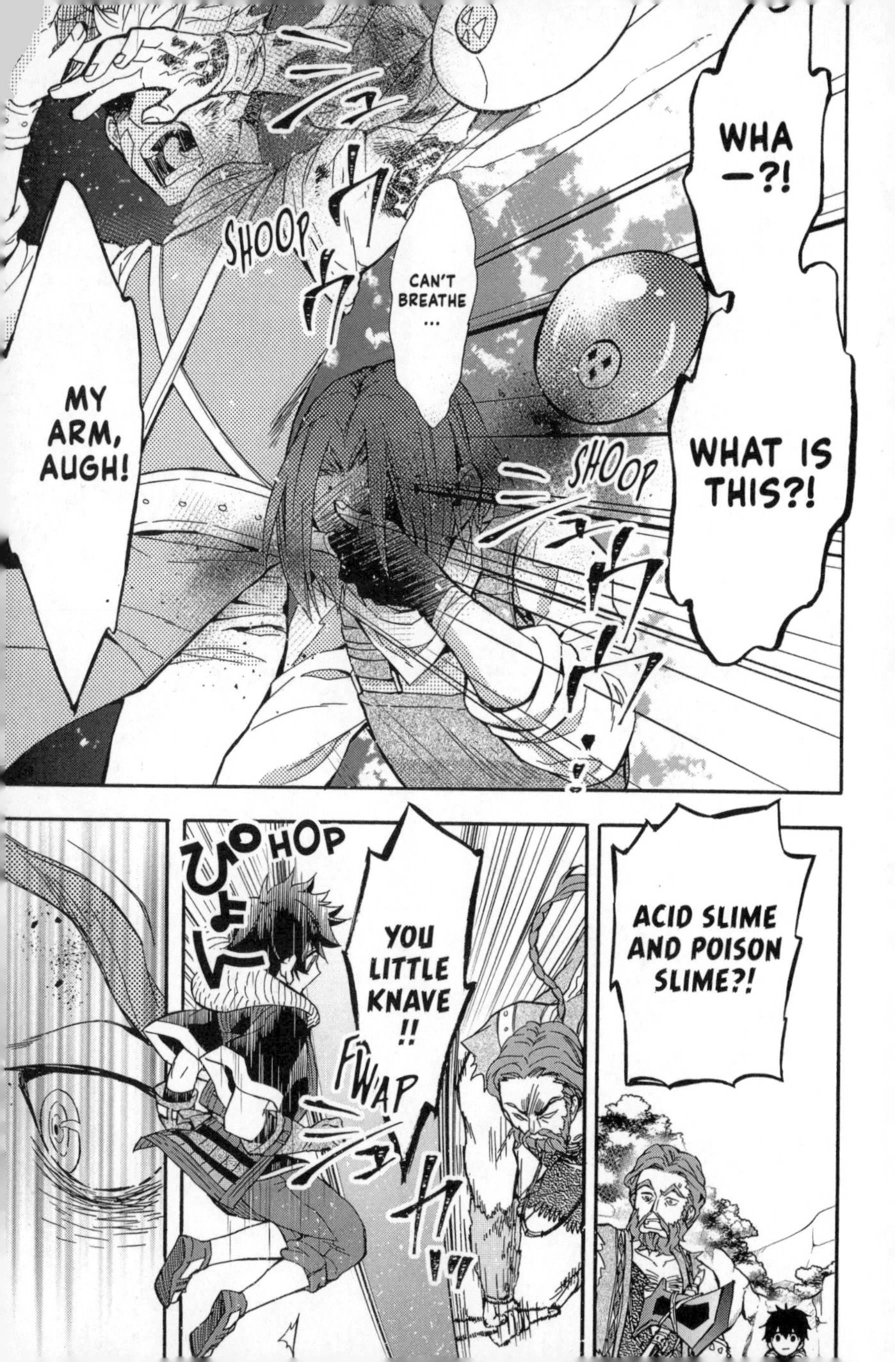
WHA—?!
WHAT IS THIS?!
SHOOP
CAN'T BREATHE ...
SHOOP
MY ARM, AUGH!
ACID SLIME AND POISON SLIME?!
YOU LITTLE KNAVE!!
FWAP
HOP

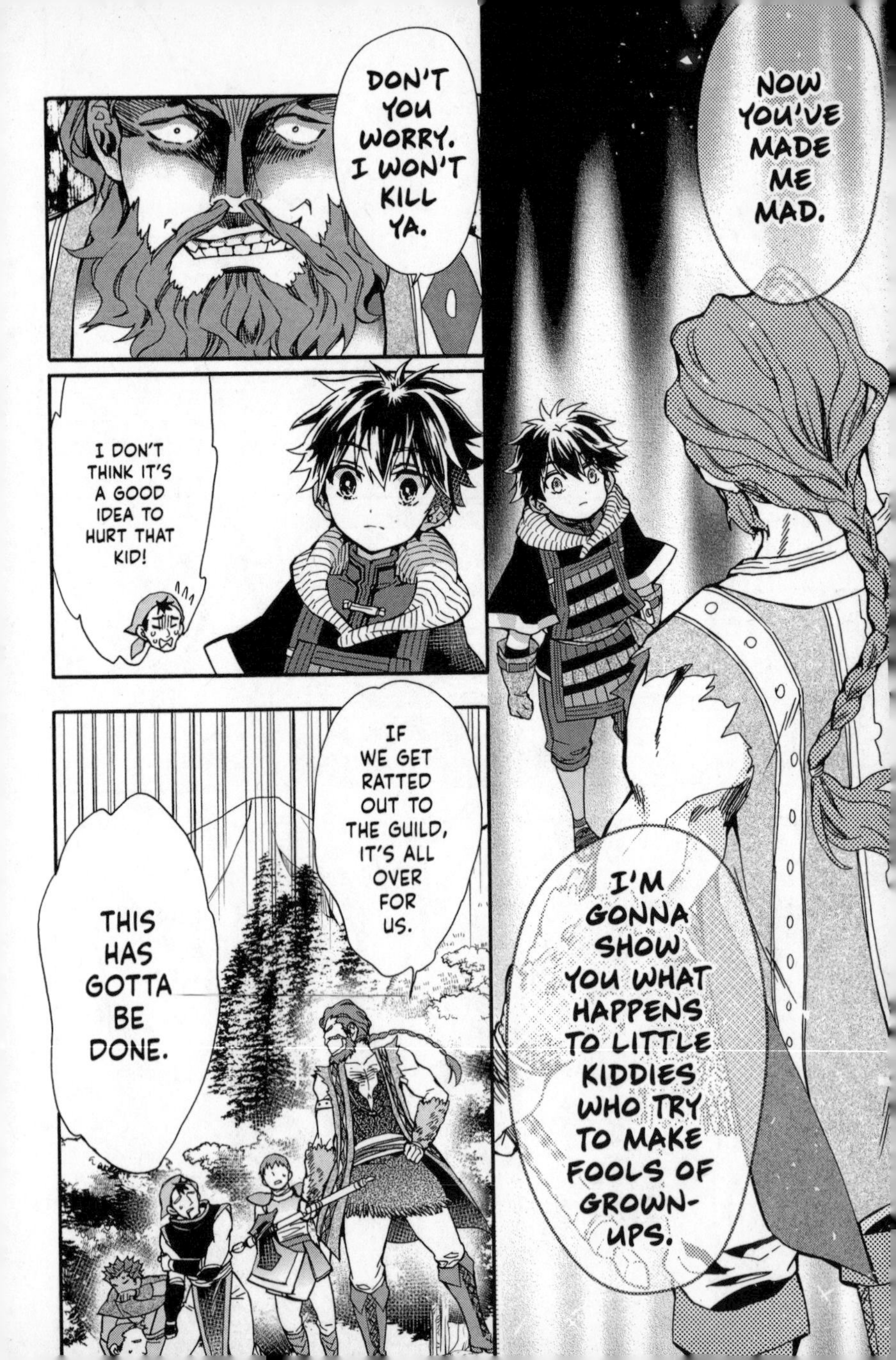
NOW YOU'VE MADE ME MAD.
I'M GONNA SHOW YOU WHAT HAPPENS TO LITTLE KIDDIES WHO TRY TO MAKE FOOLS OF GROWN-UPS.
DON'T YOU WORRY. I WON'T KILL YA.
I DON'T THINK IT'S A GOOD IDEA TO HURT THAT KID!
IF WE GET RATTED OUT TO THE GUILD, IT'S ALL OVER FOR US.
THIS HAS GOTTA BE DONE.

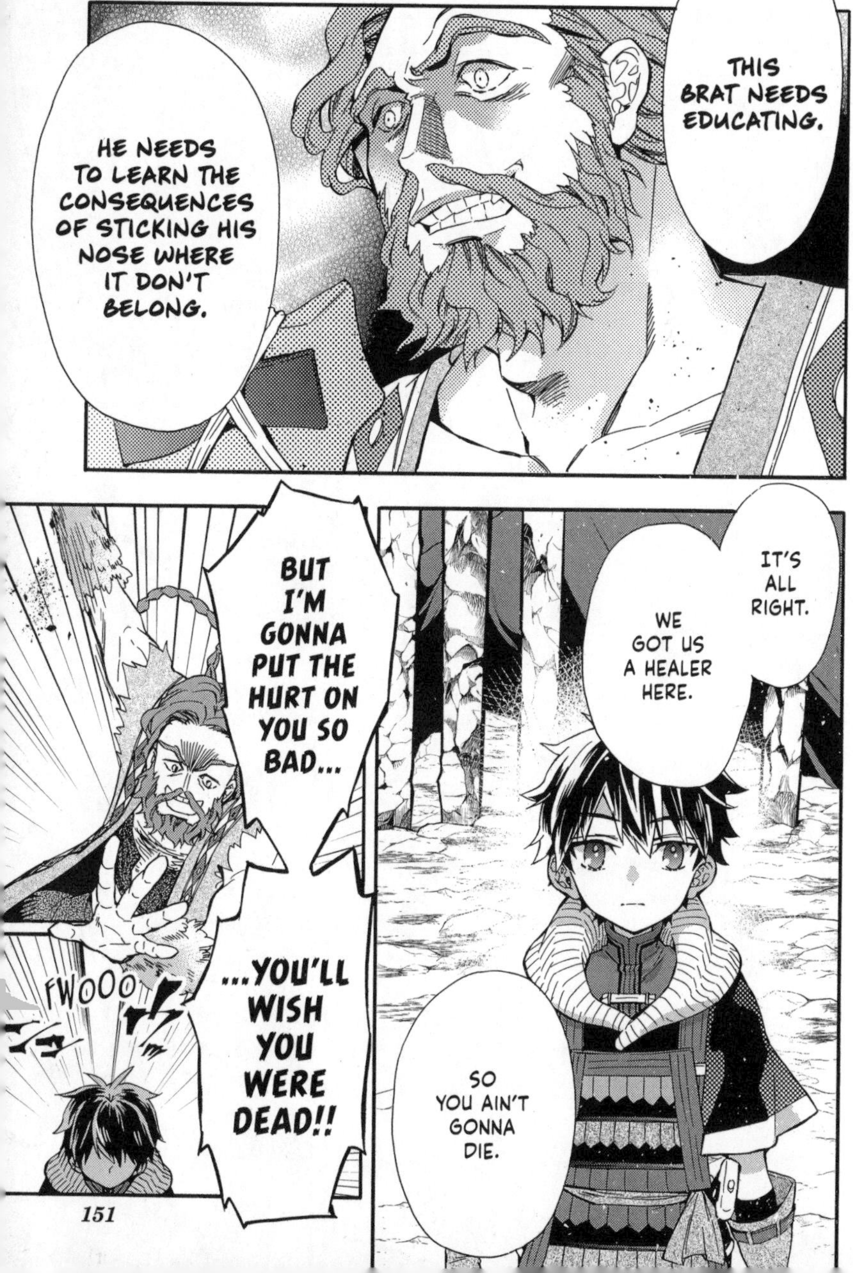
THIS BRAT NEEDS EDUCATING.
HE NEEDS TO LEARN THE CONSEQUENCES OF STICKING HIS NOSE WHERE IT DON'T BELONG.
IT'S ALL RIGHT.
WE GOT US A HEALER HERE.
SO YOU AIN'T GONNA DIE.
BUT I'M GONNA PUT THE HURT ON YOU SO BAD...
FWOOO
...YOU'LL WISH YOU WERE DEAD!!

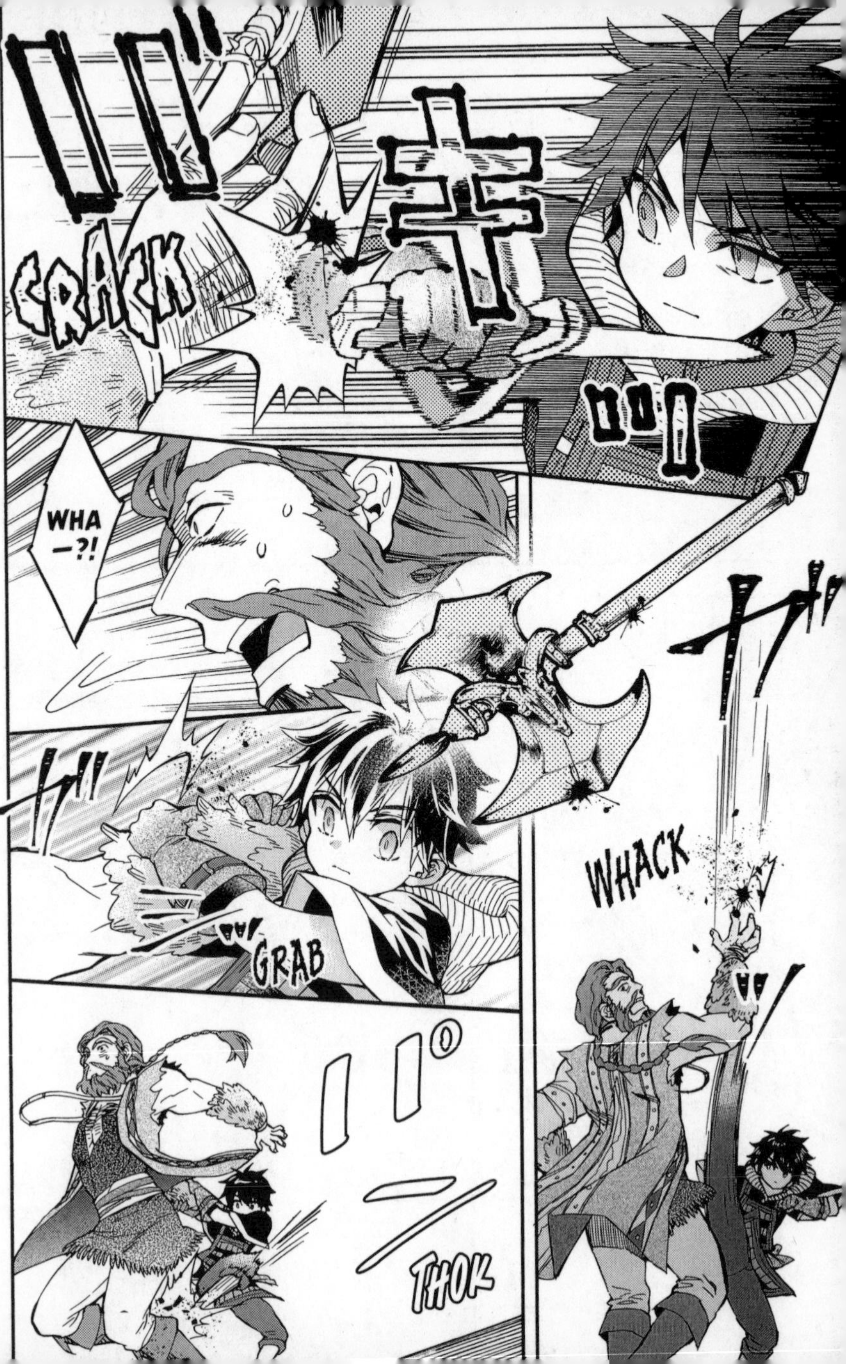
CRACK
WHACK
WHA—?!
GRAB
THOK

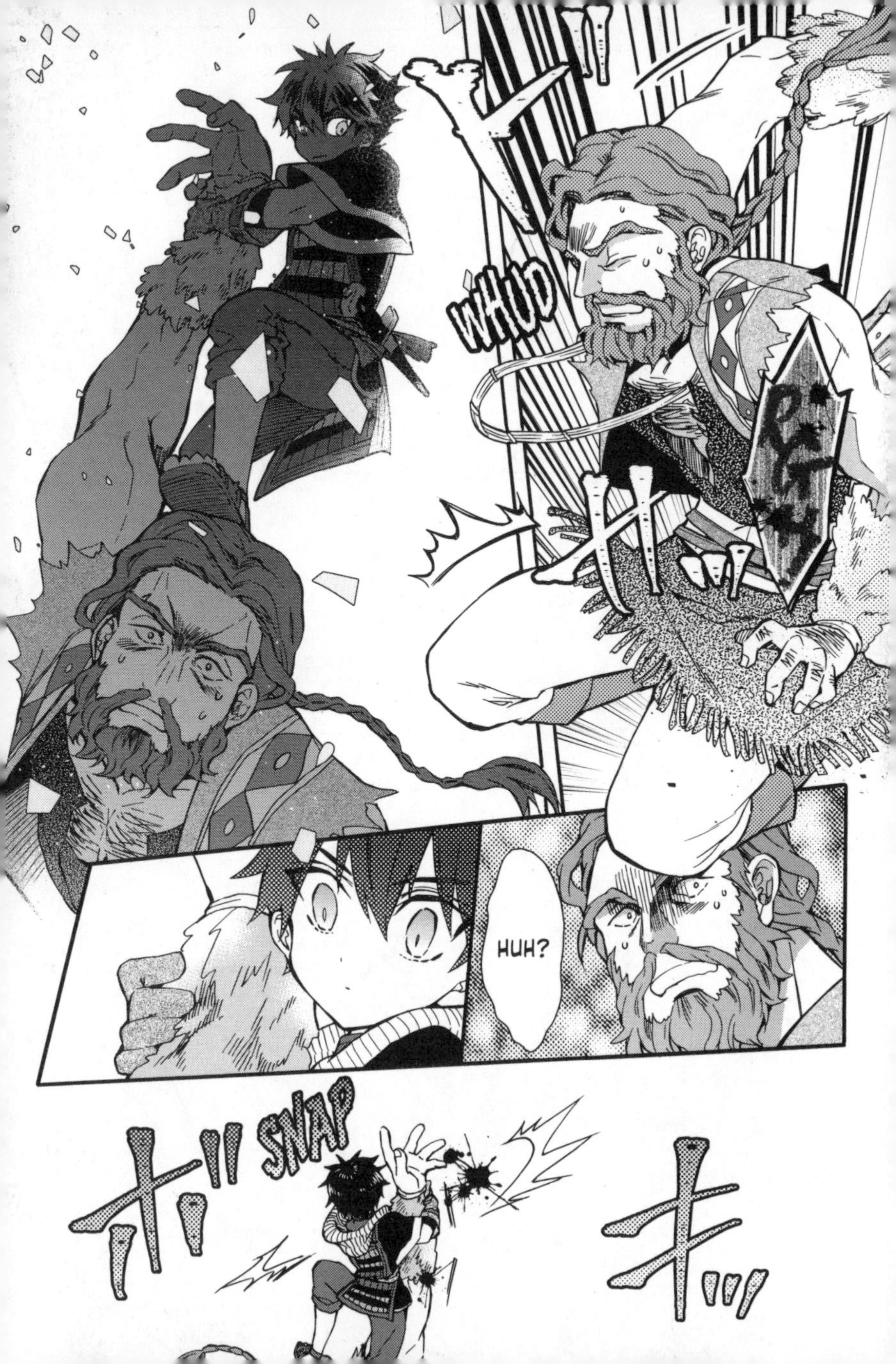
WHUD
HUH?
SNAP

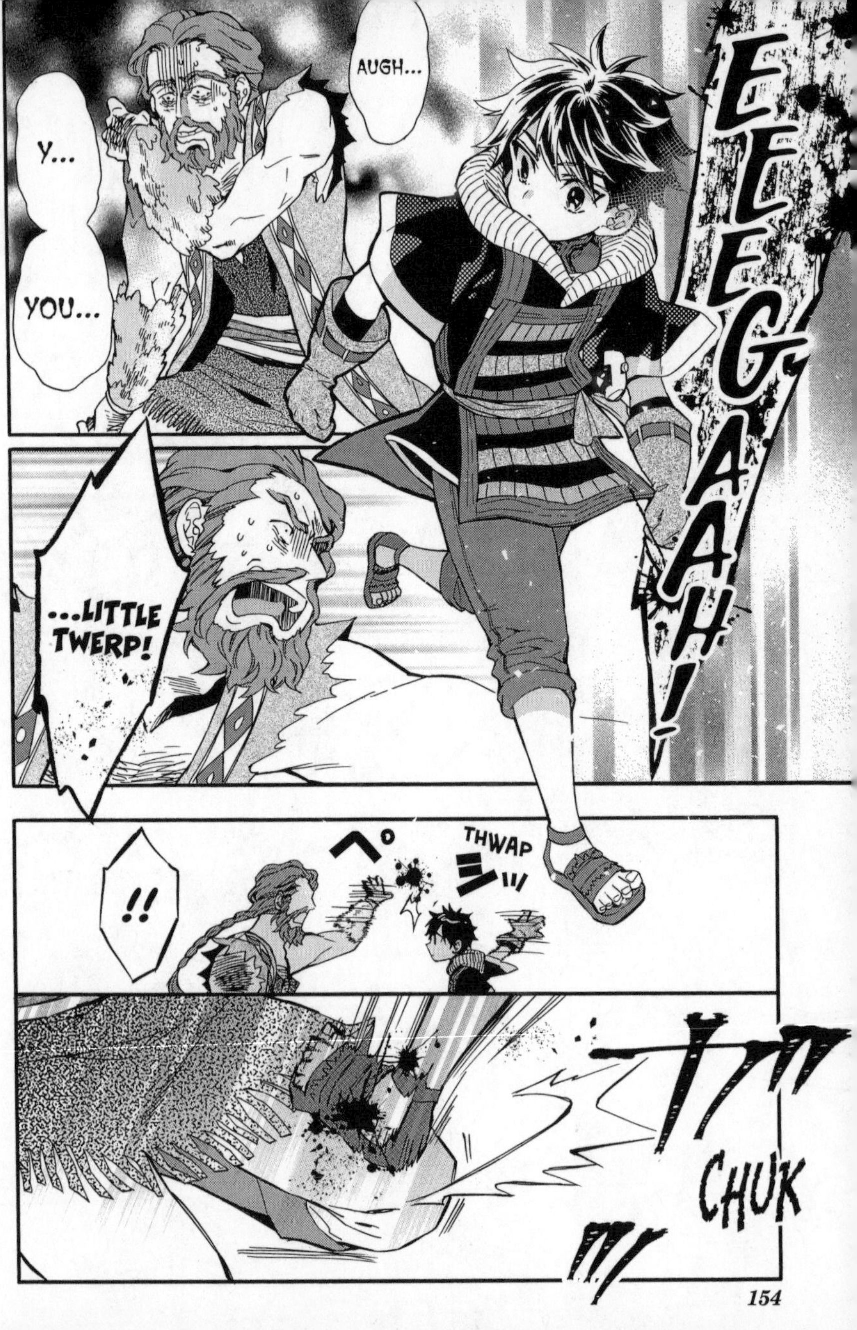
EEEGAAAH!
AUGH...
Y...
YOU...
...LITTLE TWERP!
THWAP
へ
!!
CHUK

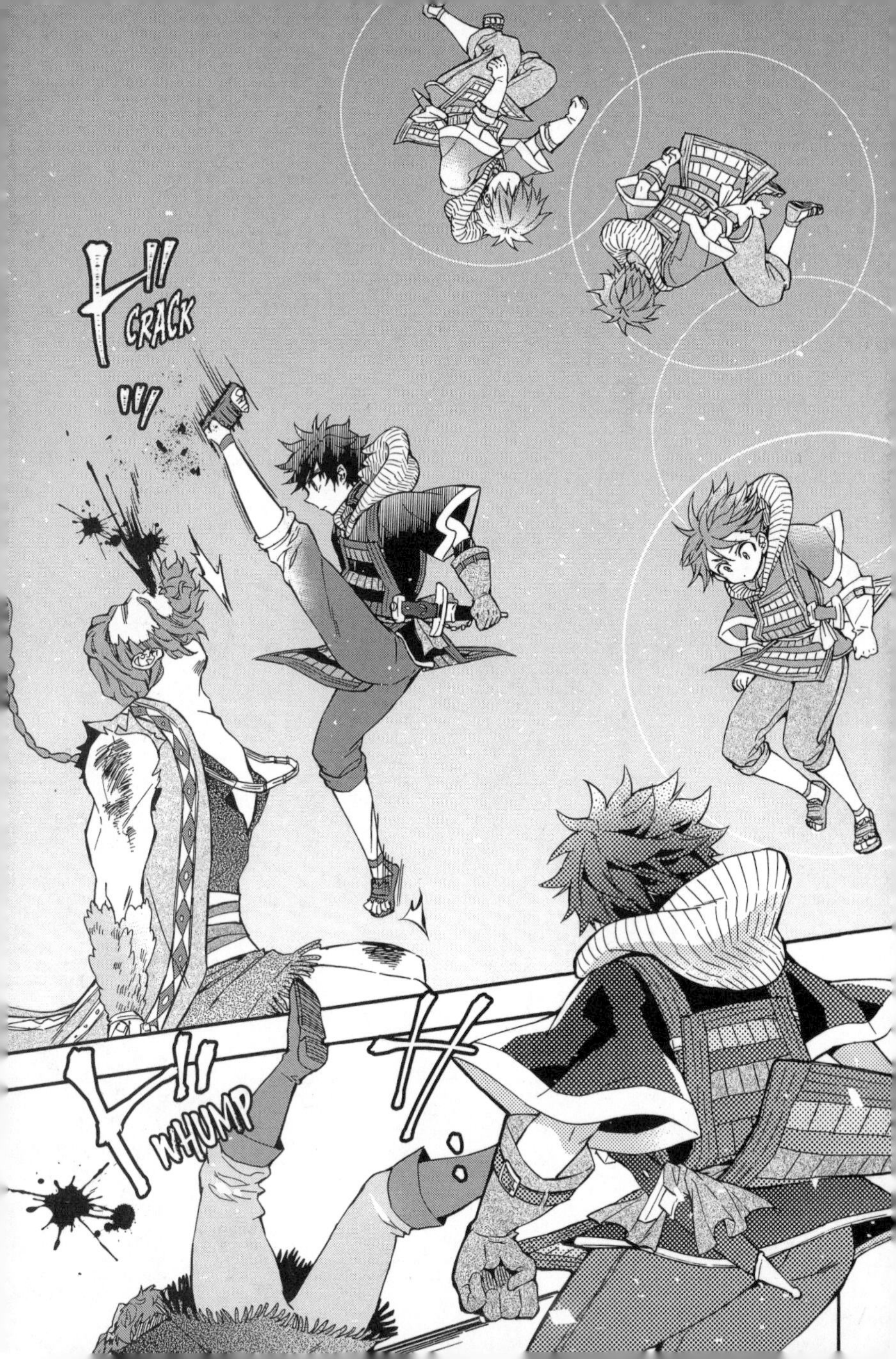
CRACK
WHUMP

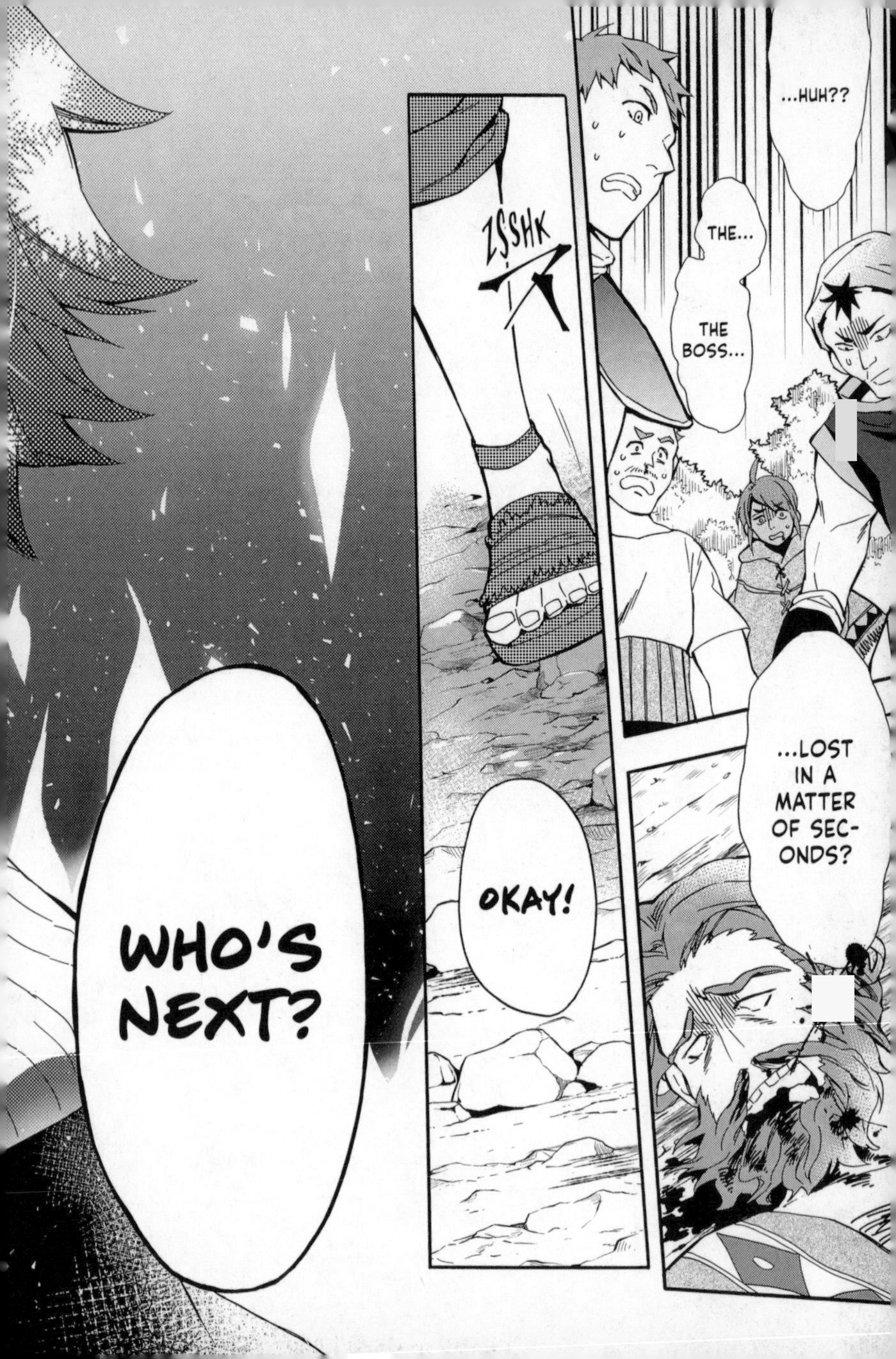

...HUH??
THE...
THE BOSS...
ZSSHK
...LOST IN A MATTER OF SECONDS?
OKAY!
WHO'S NEXT?

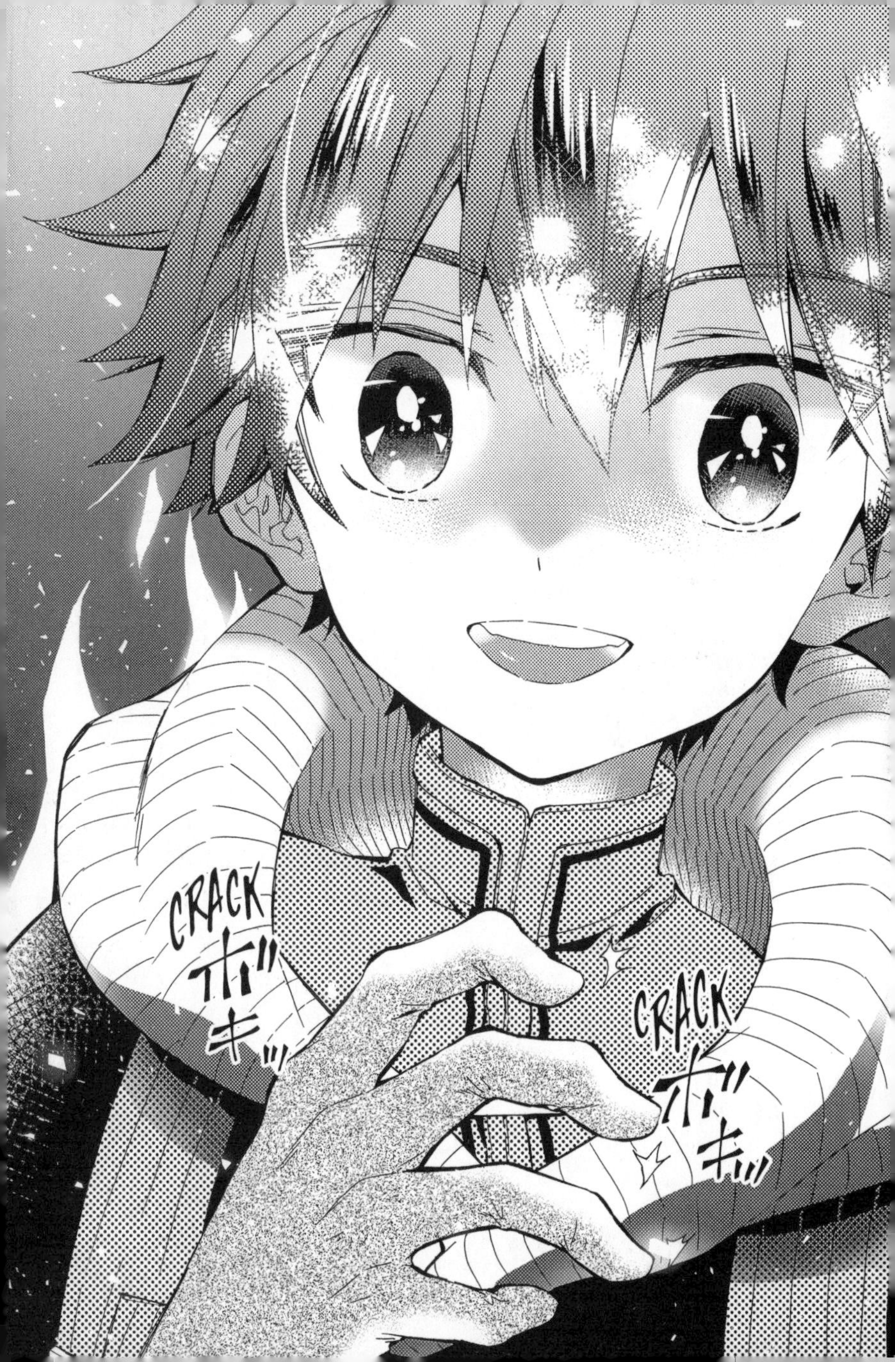
CRACK
ボギッ
CRACK
ボギッ

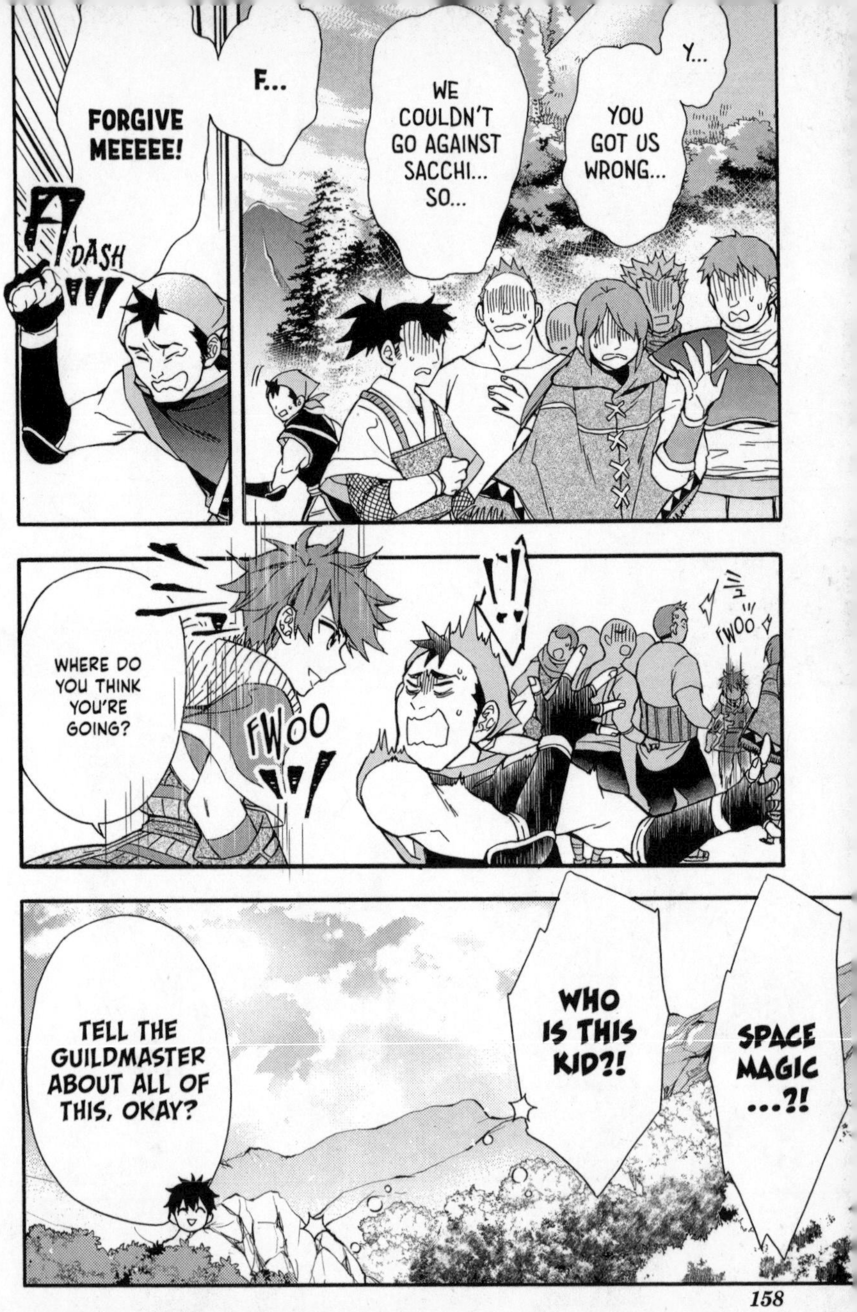
Y...
YOU GOT US WRONG...
WE COULDN'T GO AGAINST SACCHI... SO...
F...
FORGIVE MEEEEE!
DASH
!!
FWOO
WHERE DO YOU THINK YOU'RE GOING?
FWOO
SPACE MAGIC ...?!
WHO IS THIS KID?!
TELL THE GUILDMASTER ABOUT ALL OF THIS, OKAY?

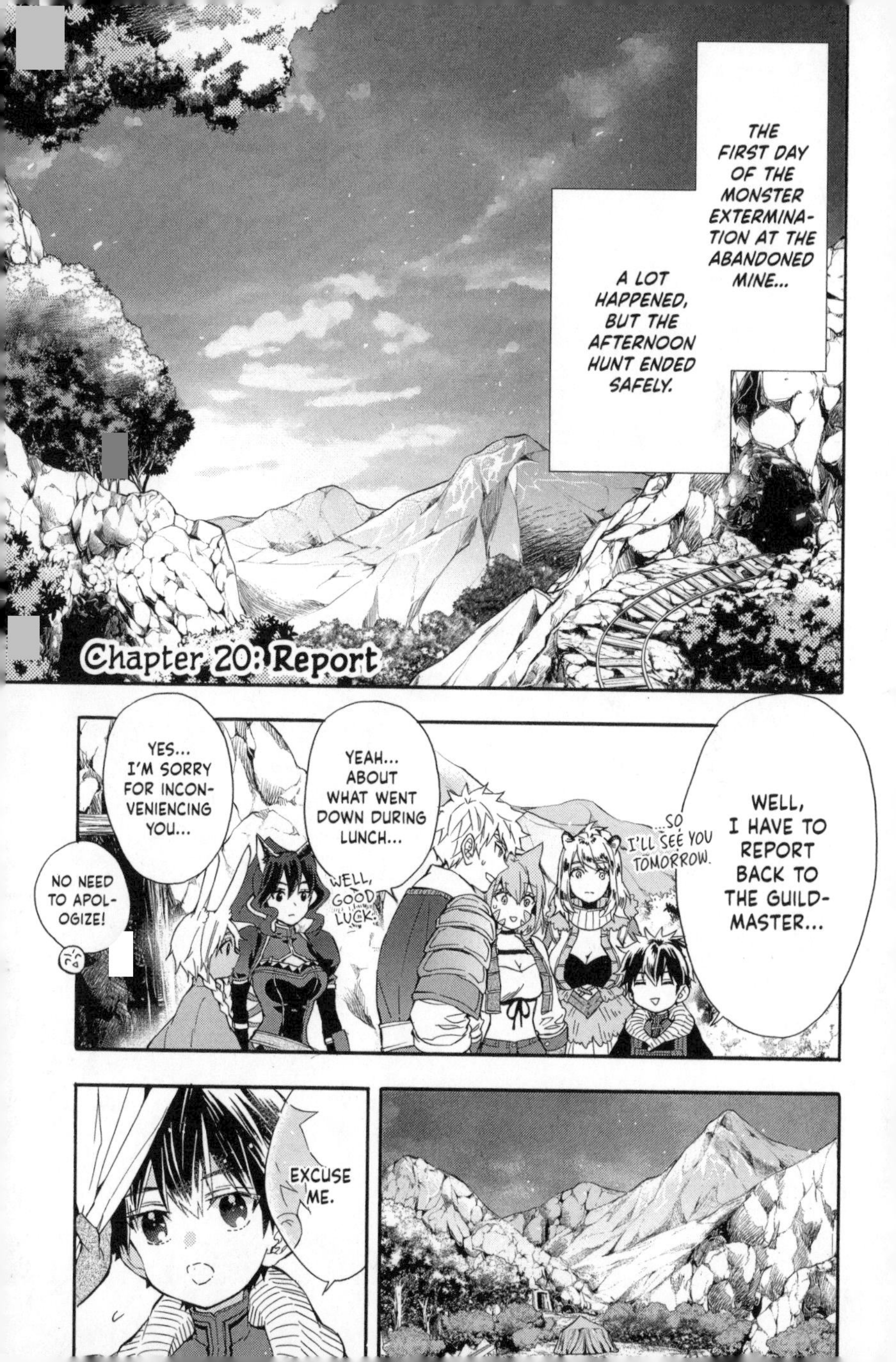
THE FIRST DAY OF THE MONSTER EXTERMINATION AT THE ABANDONED MINE...
A LOT HAPPENED, BUT THE AFTERNOON HUNT ENDED SAFELY.
Chapter 20: Report
WELL, I HAVE TO REPORT BACK TO THE GUILD-MASTER...
...SO I'LL SEE YOU TOMORROW.
YEAH... ABOUT WHAT WENT DOWN DURING LUNCH...
WELL, GOOD LUCK.
YES... I'M SORRY FOR INCONVENIENCING YOU...
NO NEED TO APOLOGIZE!
EXCUSE ME.

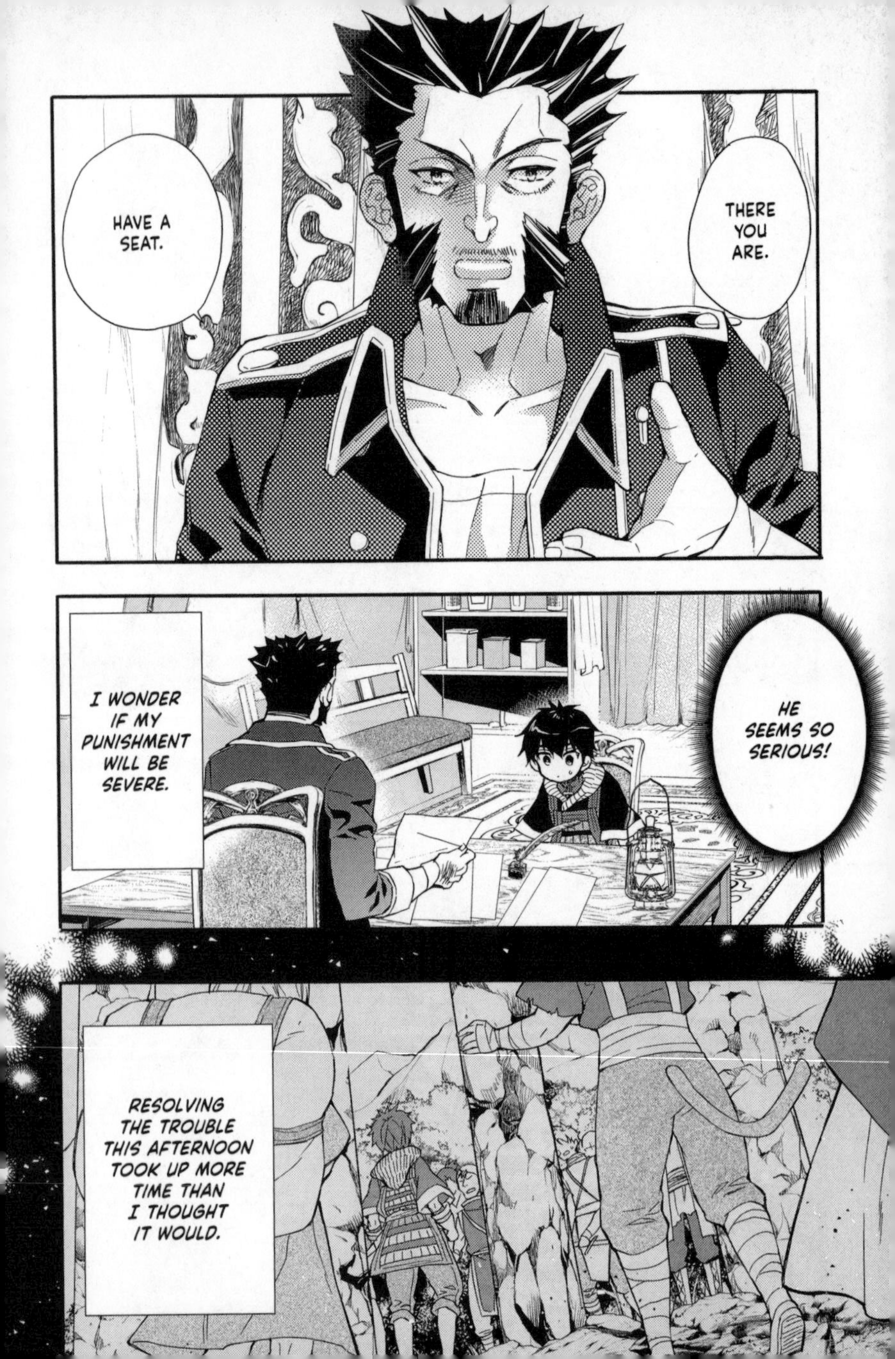
THERE YOU ARE.
HAVE A SEAT.
HE SEEMS SO SERIOUS!
I WONDER IF MY PUNISHMENT WILL BE SEVERE.
RESOLVING THE TROUBLE THIS AFTERNOON TOOK UP MORE TIME THAN I THOUGHT IT WOULD.

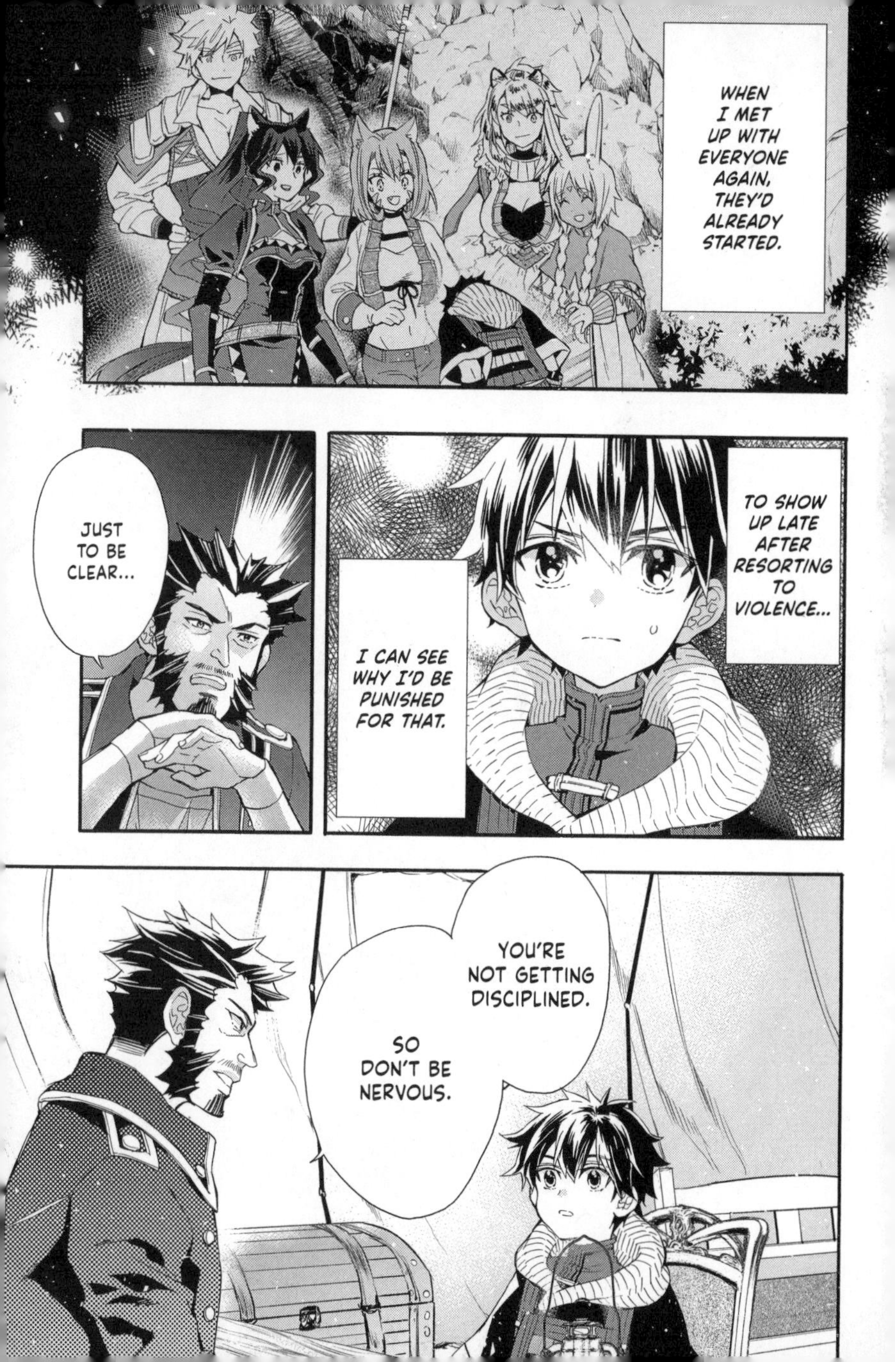
WHEN I MET UP WITH EVERYONE AGAIN, THEY'D ALREADY STARTED.
TO SHOW UP LATE AFTER RESORTING TO VIOLENCE...
I CAN SEE WHY I'D BE PUNISHED FOR THAT.
JUST TO BE CLEAR...
YOU'RE NOT GETTING DISCIPLINED.
SO DON'T BE NERVOUS.

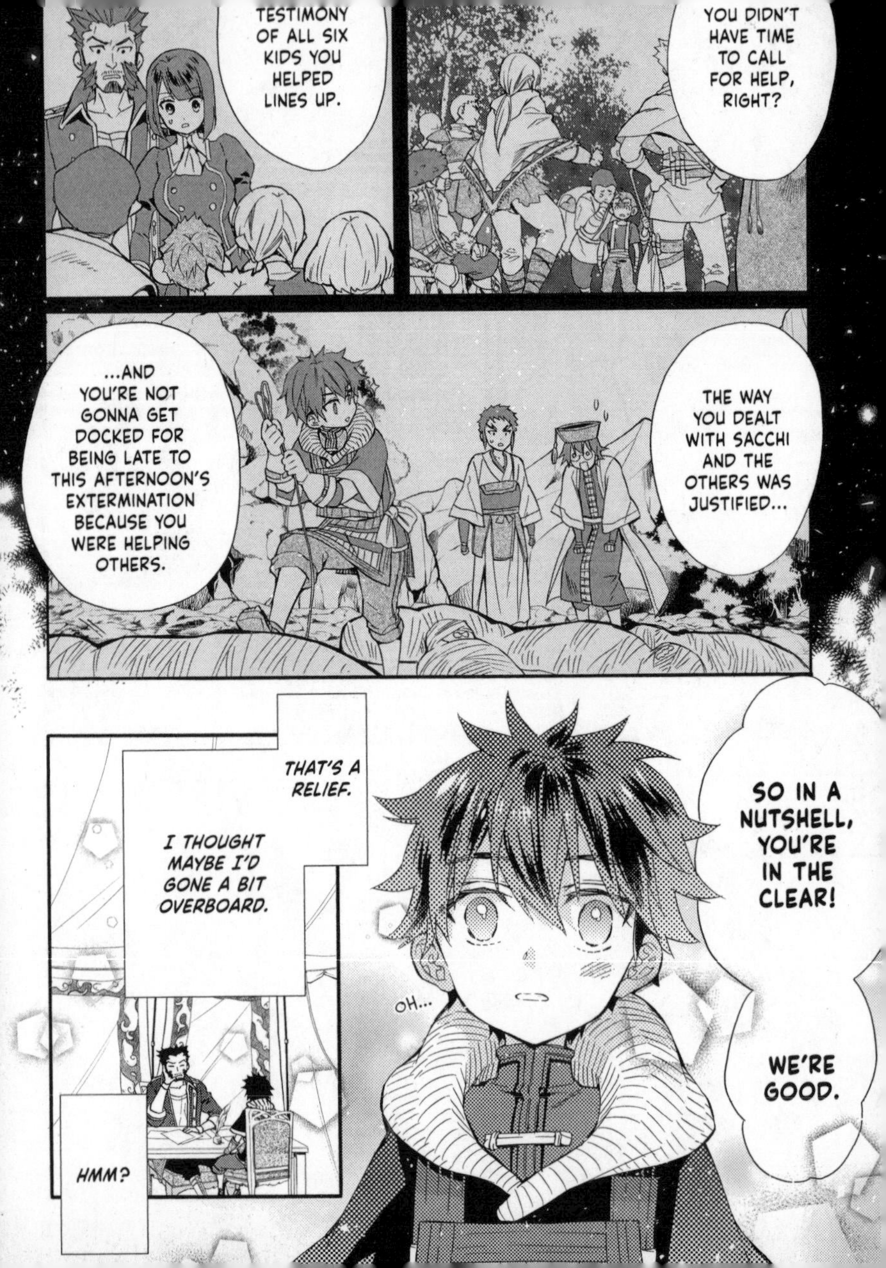
YOU DIDN'T HAVE TIME TO CALL FOR HELP, RIGHT?
TESTIMONY OF ALL SIX KIDS YOU HELPED LINES UP.
THE WAY YOU DEALT WITH SACCHI AND THE OTHERS WAS JUSTIFIED...
...AND YOU'RE NOT GONNA GET DOCKED FOR BEING LATE TO THIS AFTERNOON'S EXTERMINATION BECAUSE YOU WERE HELPING OTHERS.
SO IN A NUTSHELL, YOU'RE IN THE CLEAR!
WE'RE GOOD.
OH...
THAT'S A RELIEF.
I THOUGHT MAYBE I'D GONE A BIT OVERBOARD.
HMM?

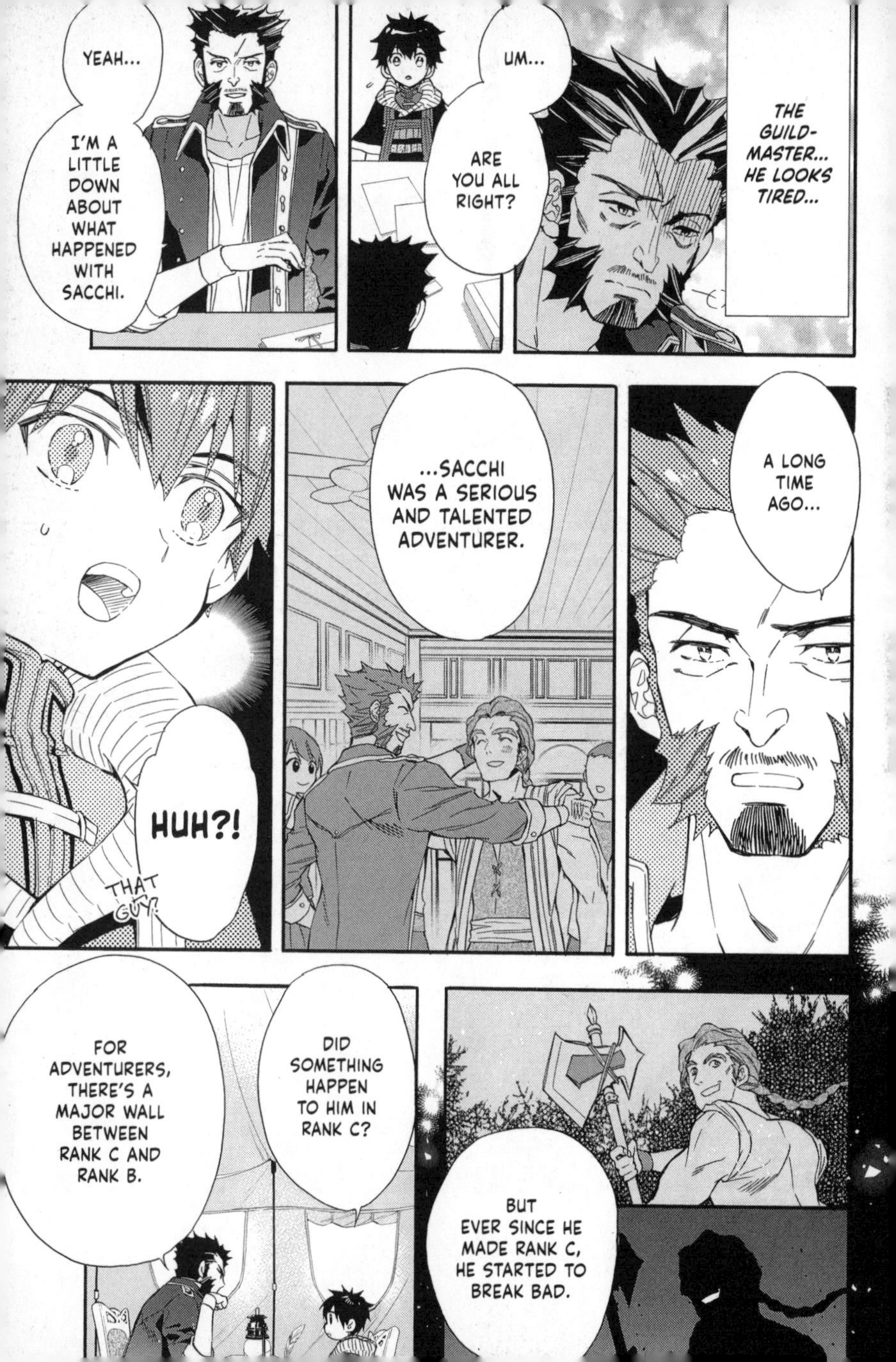
THE GUILD-MASTER... HE LOOKS TIRED...
UM...
ARE YOU ALL RIGHT?
YEAH...
I'M A LITTLE DOWN ABOUT WHAT HAPPENED WITH SACCHI.
A LONG TIME AGO...
...SACCHI WAS A SERIOUS AND TALENTED ADVENTURER.
HUH?!
THAT GUY?
BUT EVER SINCE HE MADE RANK C, HE STARTED TO BREAK BAD.
DID SOMETHING HAPPEN TO HIM IN RANK C?
FOR ADVENTURERS, THERE'S A MAJOR WALL BETWEEN RANK C AND RANK B.

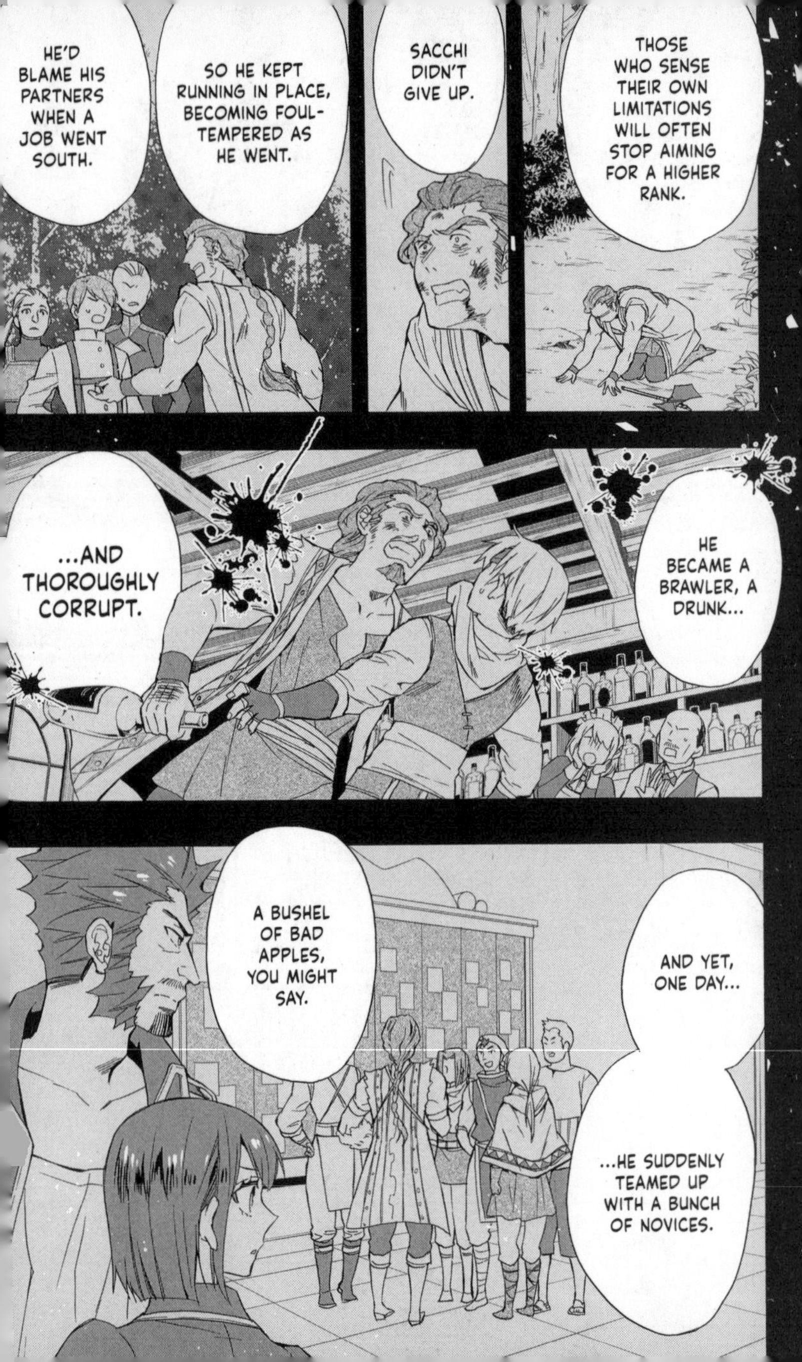
THOSE WHO SENSE THEIR OWN LIMITATIONS WILL OFTEN STOP AIMING FOR A HIGHER RANK.
SACCHI DIDN'T GIVE UP.
SO HE KEPT RUNNING IN PLACE, BECOMING FOUL-TEMPERED AS HE WENT.
HE'D BLAME HIS PARTNERS WHEN A JOB WENT SOUTH.
HE BECAME A BRAWLER, A DRUNK...
...AND THOROUGHLY CORRUPT.
AND YET, ONE DAY...
...HE SUDDENLY TEAMED UP WITH A BUNCH OF NOVICES.
A BUSHEL OF BAD APPLES, YOU MIGHT SAY.

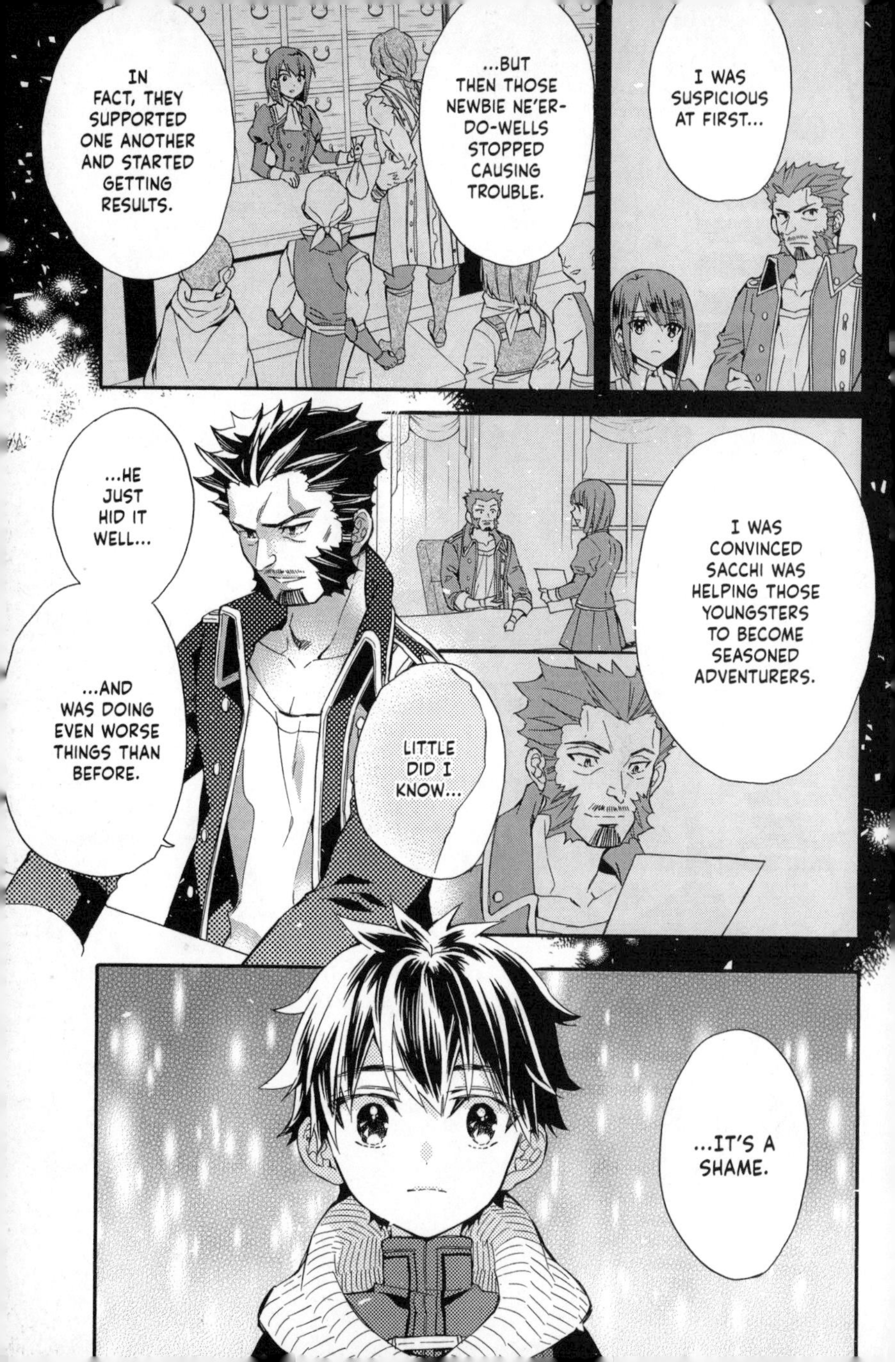
I WAS SUSPICIOUS AT FIRST...
...BUT THEN THOSE NEWBIE NE'ER-DO-WELLS STOPPED CAUSING TROUBLE.
IN FACT, THEY SUPPORTED ONE ANOTHER AND STARTED GETTING RESULTS.
I WAS CONVINCED SACCHI WAS HELPING THOSE YOUNGSTERS TO BECOME SEASONED ADVENTURERS.
LITTLE DID I KNOW...
...HE JUST HID IT WELL...
...AND WAS DOING EVEN WORSE THINGS THAN BEFORE.
...IT'S A SHAME.

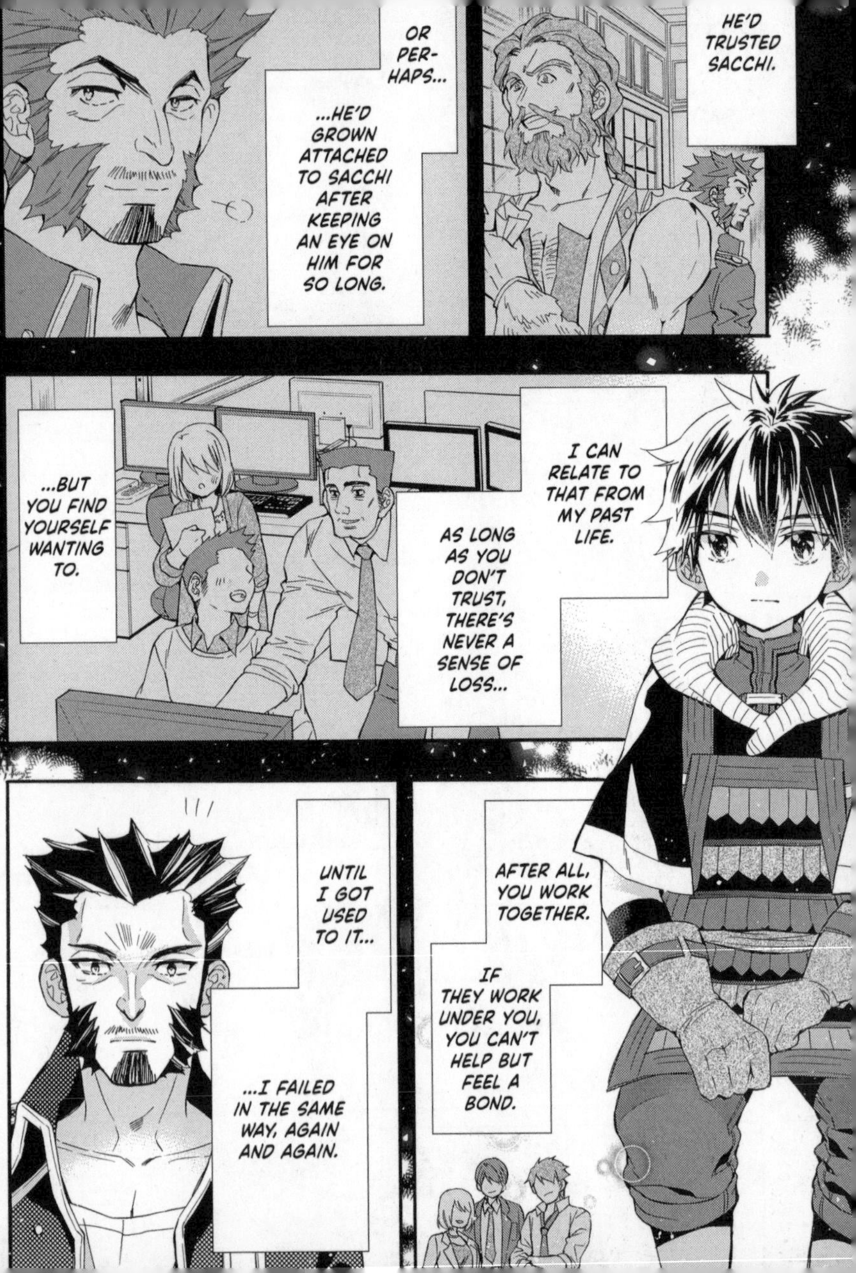
HE'D TRUSTED SACCHI.
OR PER-HAPS...
...HE'D GROWN ATTACHED TO SACCHI AFTER KEEPING AN EYE ON HIM FOR SO LONG.
I CAN RELATE TO THAT FROM MY PAST LIFE.
AS LONG AS YOU DON'T TRUST, THERE'S NEVER A SENSE OF LOSS...
...BUT YOU FIND YOURSELF WANTING TO.
AFTER ALL, YOU WORK TOGETHER.
IF THEY WORK UNDER YOU, YOU CAN'T HELP BUT FEEL A BOND.
UNTIL I GOT USED TO IT...
...I FAILED IN THE SAME WAY, AGAIN AND AGAIN.

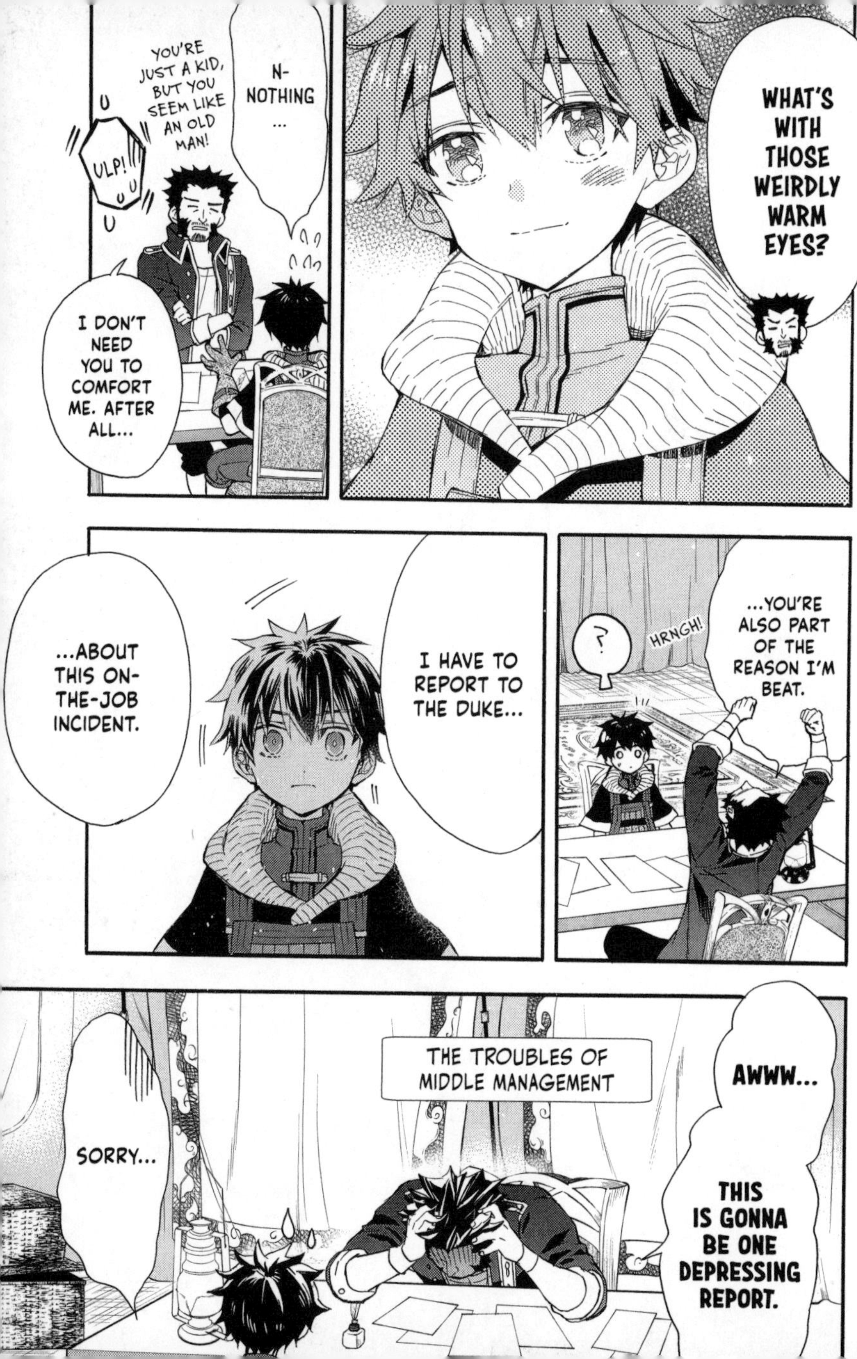
WHAT'S WITH THOSE WEIRDLY WARM EYES?
N- NOTHING ...
YOU'RE JUST A KID, BUT YOU SEEM LIKE AN OLD MAN!
ULP!
I DON'T NEED YOU TO COMFORT ME. AFTER ALL...
...YOU'RE ALSO PART OF THE REASON I'M BEAT.
HRNGH!
?
I HAVE TO REPORT TO THE DUKE...
...ABOUT THIS ON-THE-JOB INCIDENT.
AWWW...
THIS IS GONNA BE ONE DEPRESSING REPORT.
THE TROUBLES OF MIDDLE MANAGEMENT
SORRY...

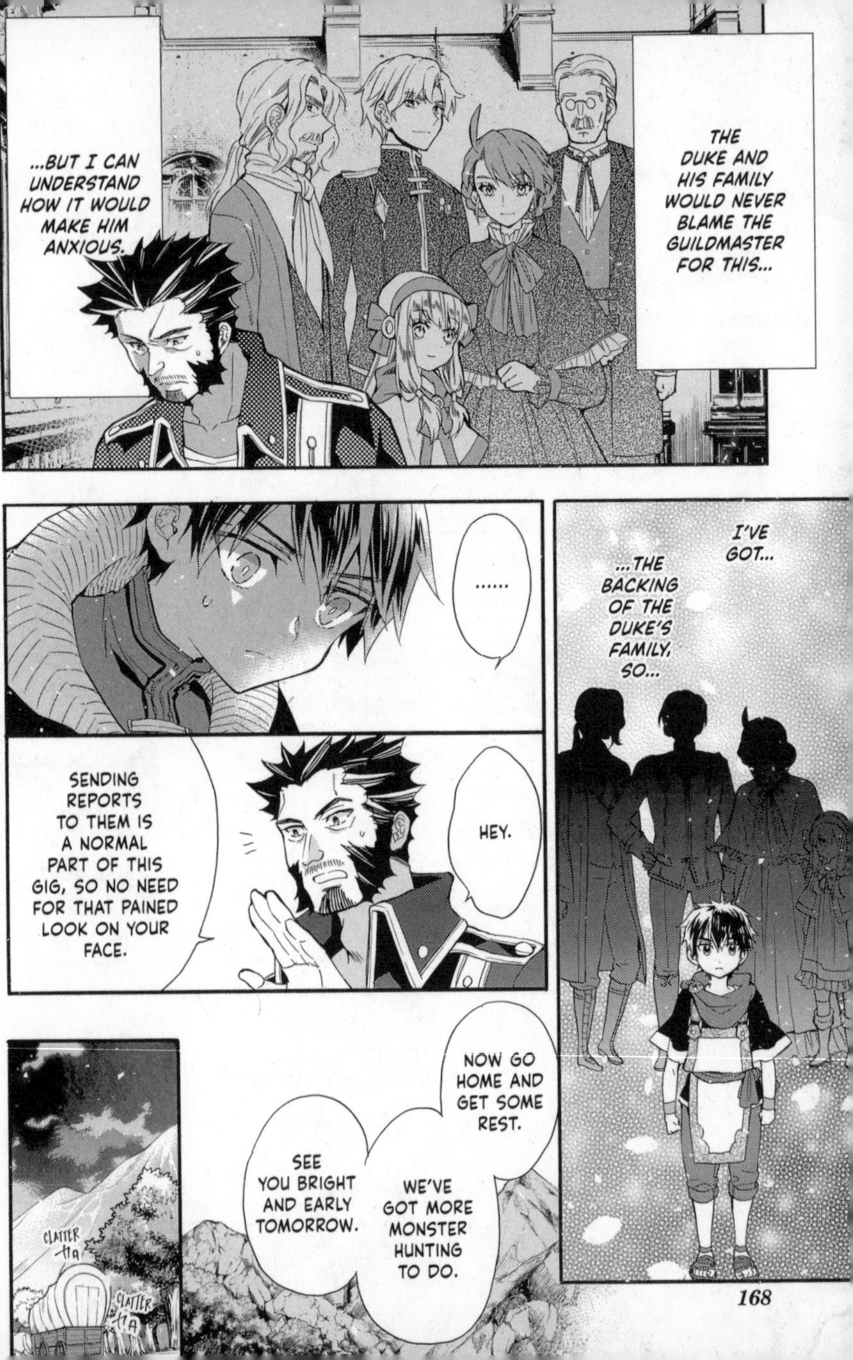
THE DUKE AND HIS FAMILY WOULD NEVER BLAME THE GUILDMASTER FOR THIS...
...BUT I CAN UNDERSTAND HOW IT WOULD MAKE HIM ANXIOUS.
I'VE GOT...
...THE BACKING OF THE DUKE'S FAMILY, SO...
......
HEY.
SENDING REPORTS TO THEM IS A NORMAL PART OF THIS GIG, SO NO NEED FOR THAT PAINED LOOK ON YOUR FACE.
NOW GO HOME AND GET SOME REST.
WE'VE GOT MORE MONSTER HUNTING TO DO.
SEE YOU BRIGHT AND EARLY TOMORROW.
CLATTER
CLATTER

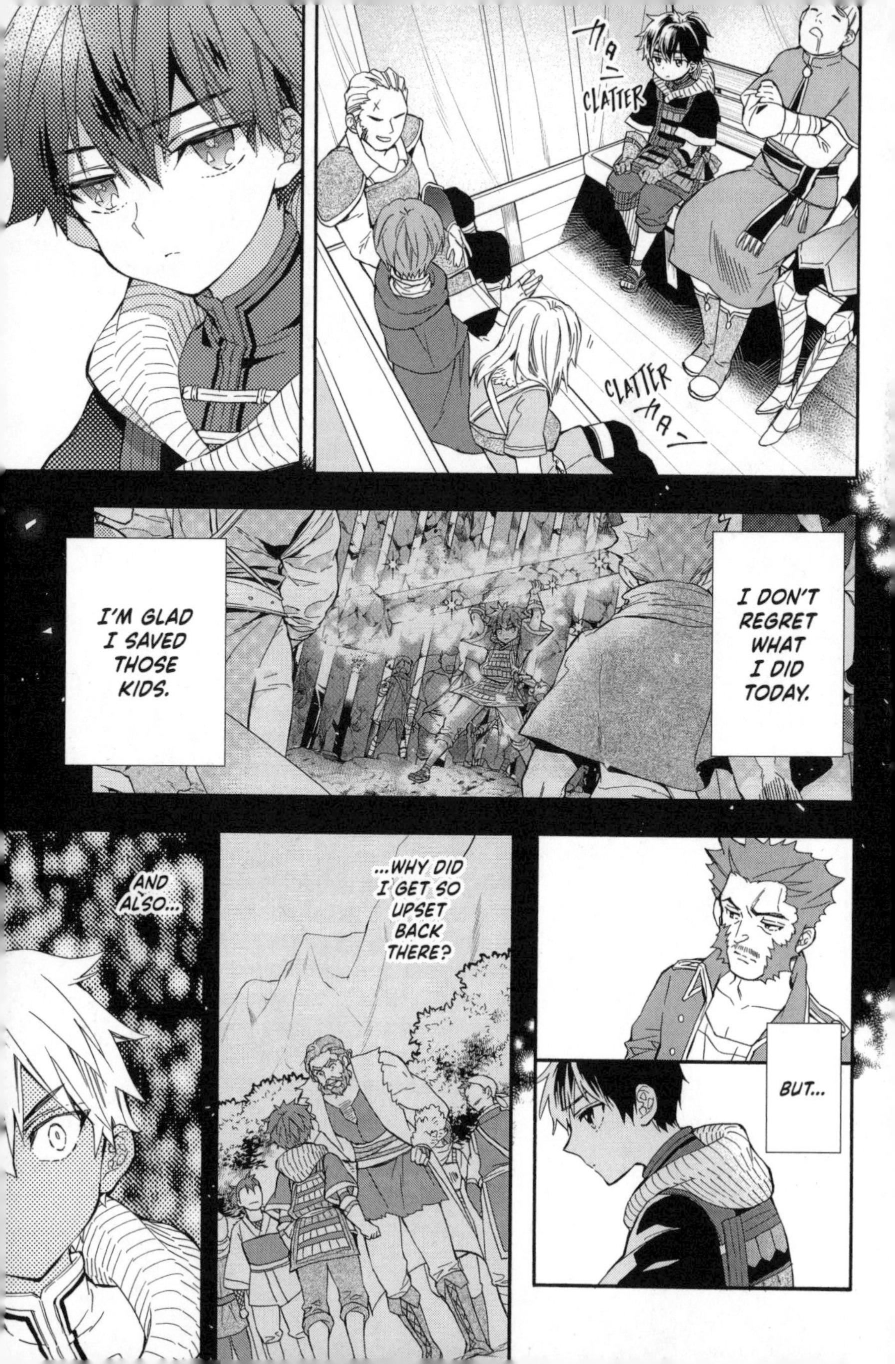
CLATTER
CLATTER
I DON'T REGRET WHAT I DID TODAY.
I'M GLAD I SAVED THOSE KIDS.
BUT...
...WHY DID I GET SO UPSET BACK THERE?
AND ALSO...

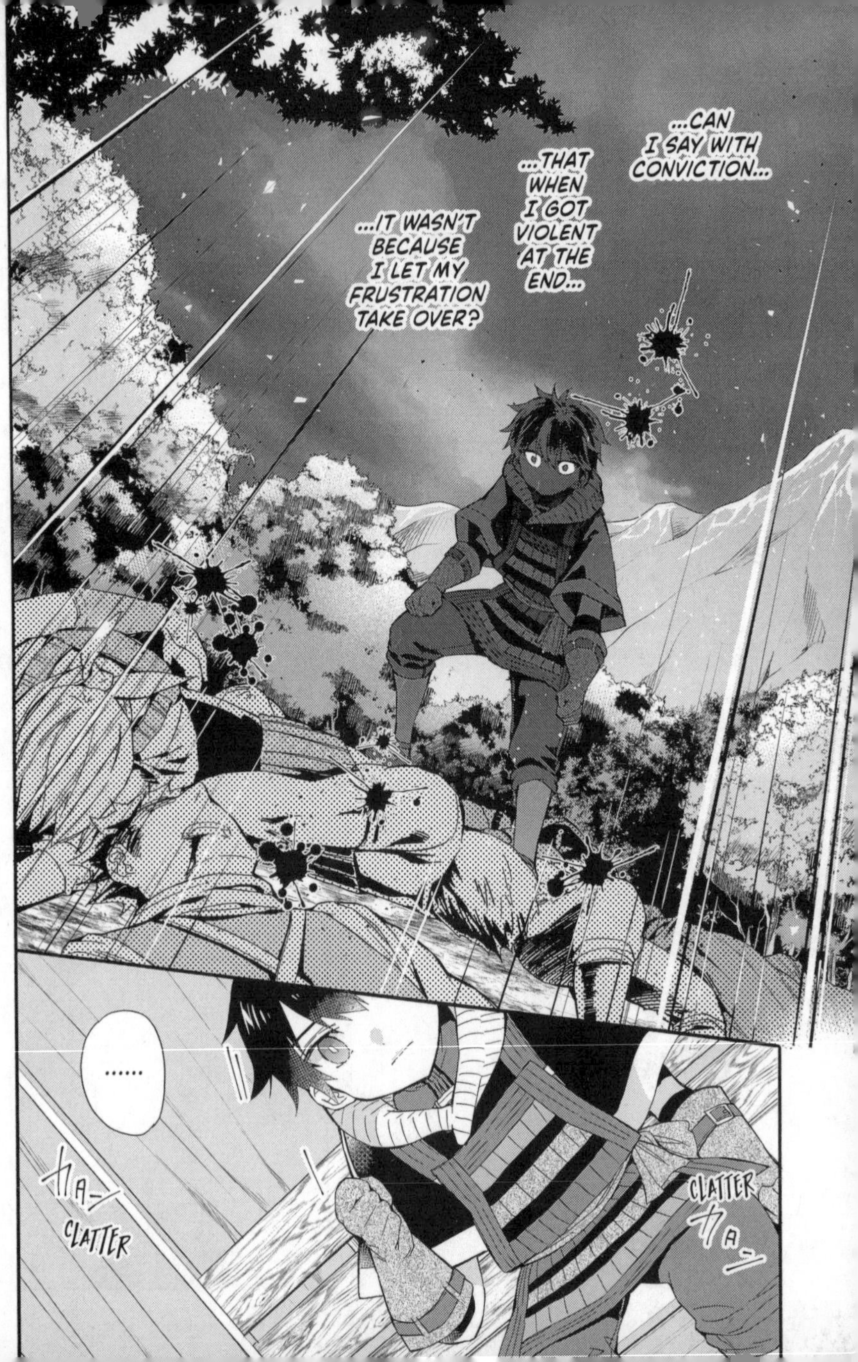
...CAN I SAY WITH CONVICTION...
...THAT WHEN I GOT VIOLENT AT THE END...
...IT WASN'T BECAUSE I LET MY FRUSTRATION TAKE OVER?
......
CLATTER
CLATTER

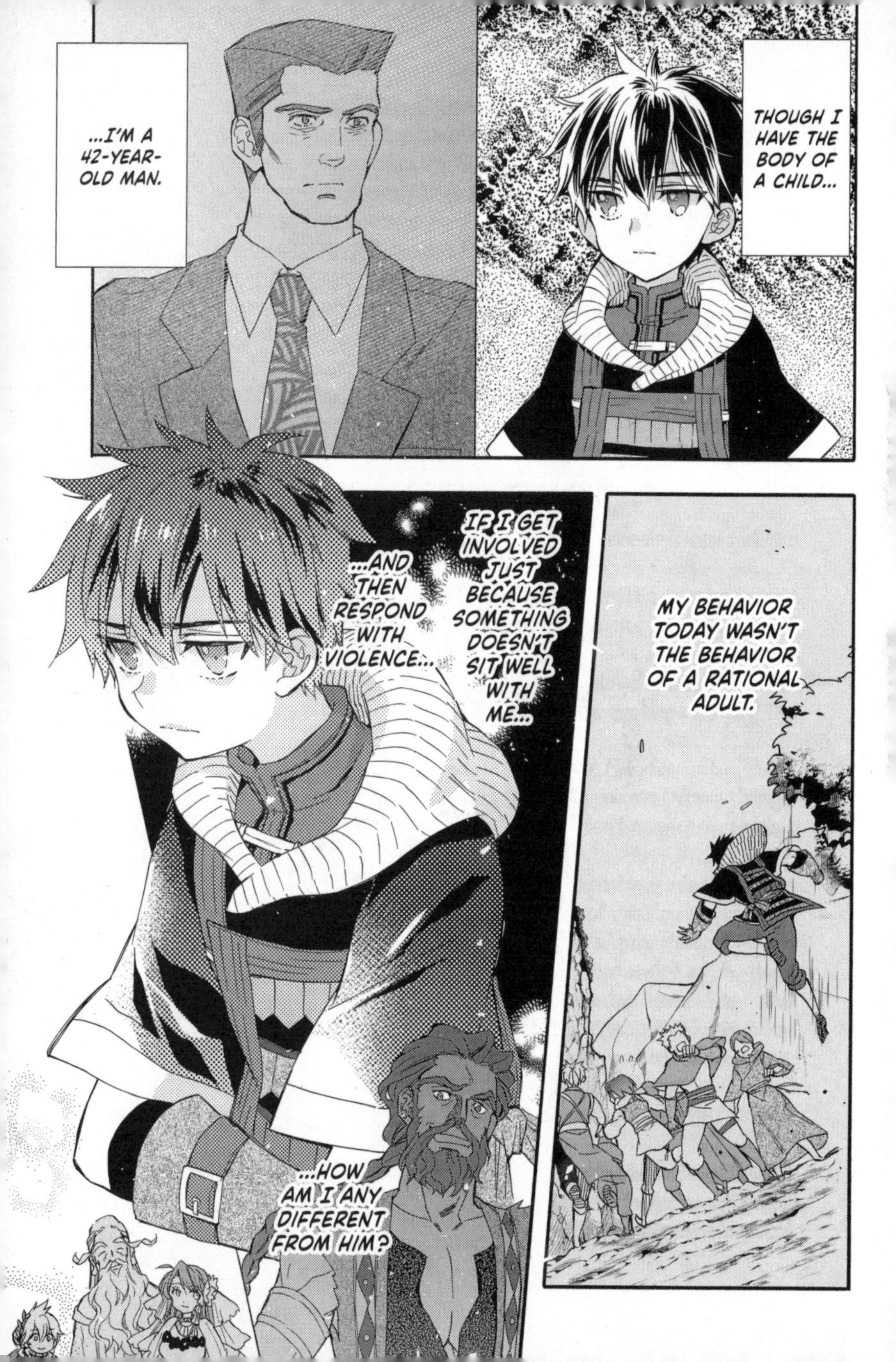
THOUGH I HAVE THE BODY OF A CHILD...
...I'M A 42-YEAR-OLD MAN.
MY BEHAVIOR TODAY WASN'T THE BEHAVIOR OF A RATIONAL ADULT.
IF I GET INVOLVED JUST BECAUSE SOMETHING DOESN'T SIT WELL WITH ME...
...AND THEN RESPOND WITH VIOLENCE...
...HOW AM I ANY DIFFERENT FROM HIM?

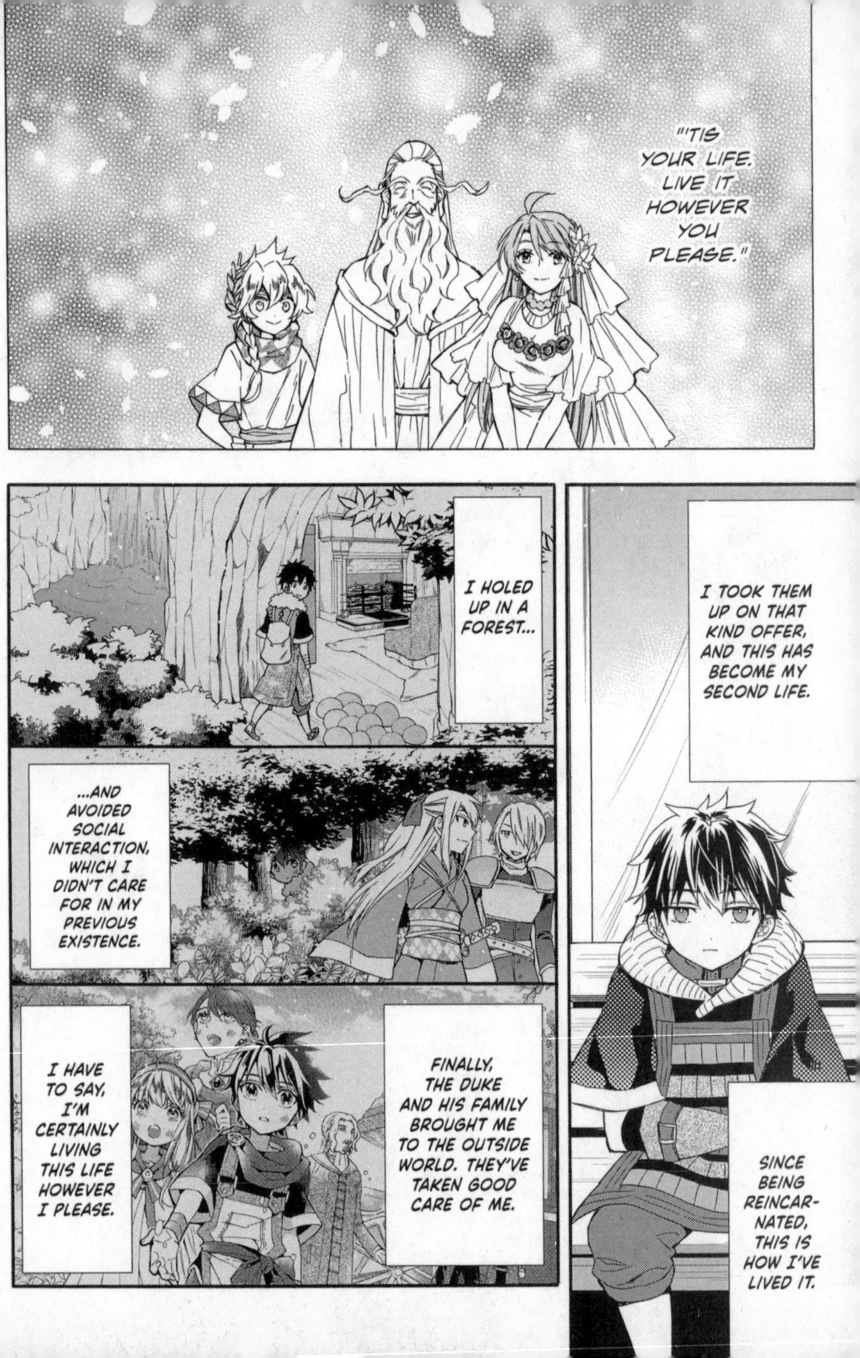
"'TIS YOUR LIFE. LIVE IT HOWEVER YOU PLEASE."
I TOOK THEM UP ON THAT KIND OFFER, AND THIS HAS BECOME MY SECOND LIFE.
SINCE BEING REINCAR-NATED, THIS IS HOW I'VE LIVED IT.
I HOLED UP IN A FOREST...
...AND AVOIDED SOCIAL INTERACTION, WHICH I DIDN'T CARE FOR IN MY PREVIOUS EXISTENCE.
FINALLY, THE DUKE AND HIS FAMILY BROUGHT ME TO THE OUTSIDE WORLD. THEY'VE TAKEN GOOD CARE OF ME.
I HAVE TO SAY, I'M CERTAINLY LIVING THIS LIFE HOWEVER I PLEASE.

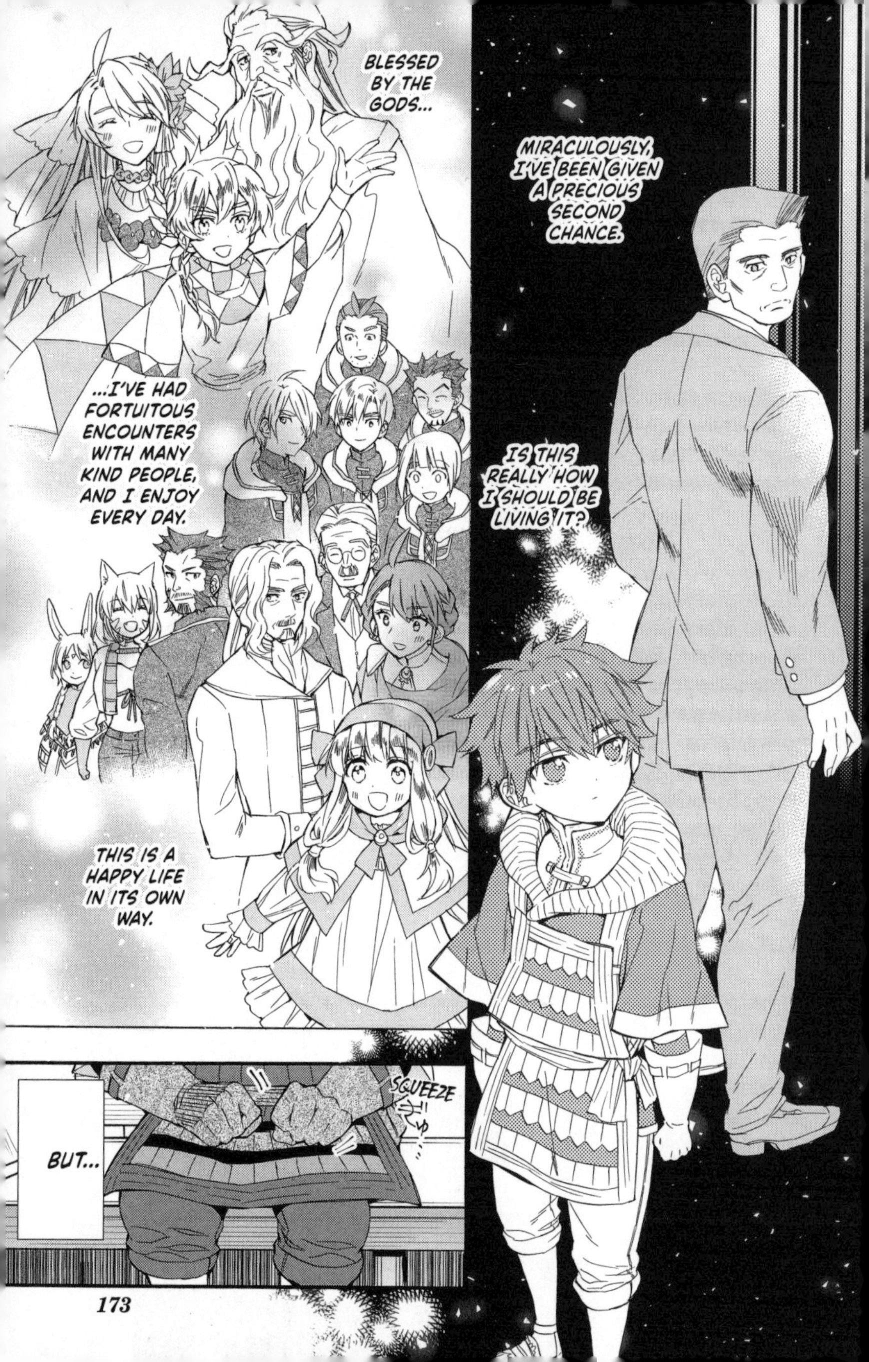
MIRACULOUSLY, I'VE BEEN GIVEN A PRECIOUS SECOND CHANCE.
IS THIS REALLY HOW I SHOULD BE LIVING IT?
BLESSED BY THE GODS...
...I'VE HAD FORTUITOUS ENCOUNTERS WITH MANY KIND PEOPLE, AND I ENJOY EVERY DAY.
THIS IS A HAPPY LIFE IN ITS OWN WAY.
SQUEEZE
BUT...

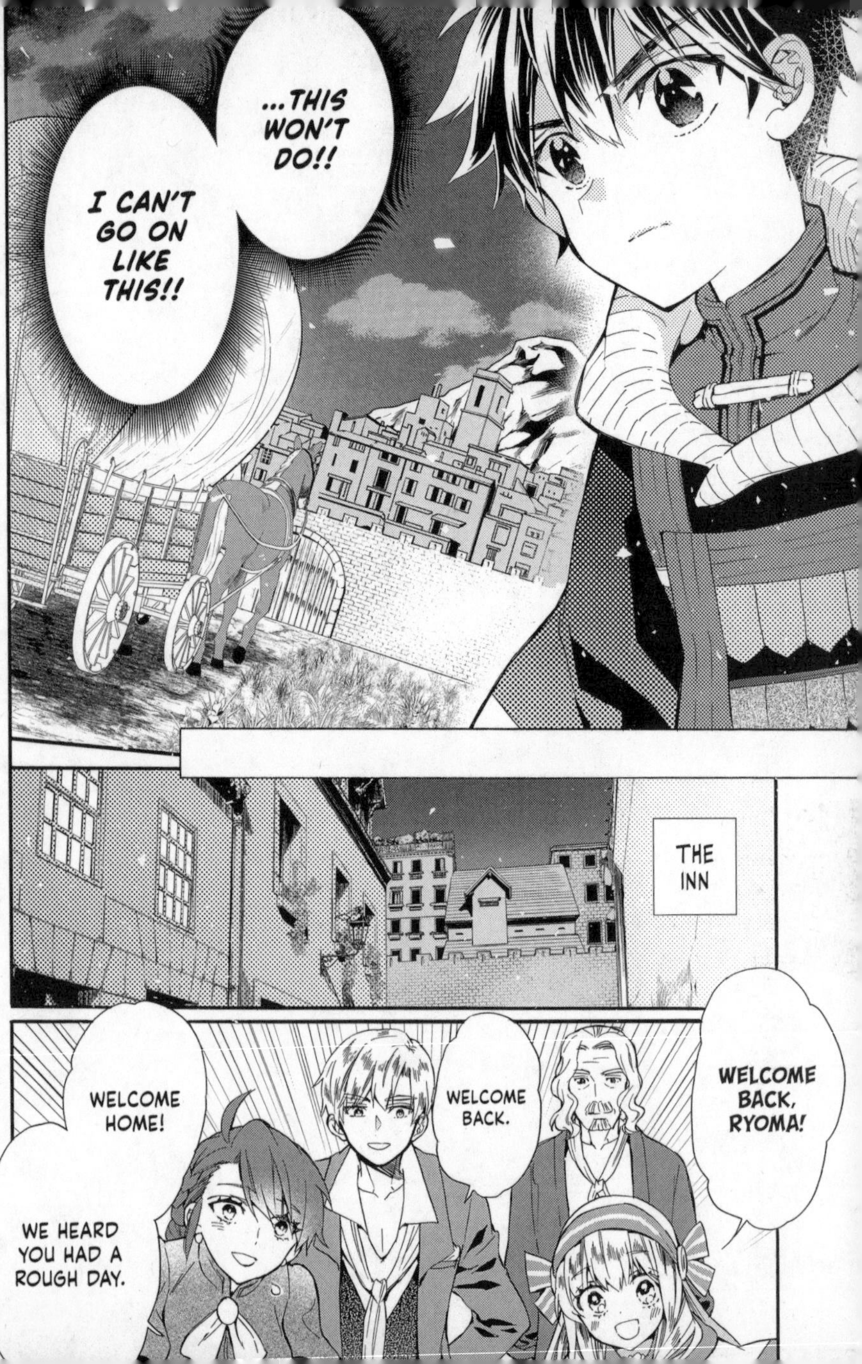
...THIS WON'T DO!!
I CAN'T GO ON LIKE THIS!!
THE INN
WELCOME BACK, RYOMA!
WELCOME BACK.
WELCOME HOME!
WE HEARD YOU HAD A ROUGH DAY.

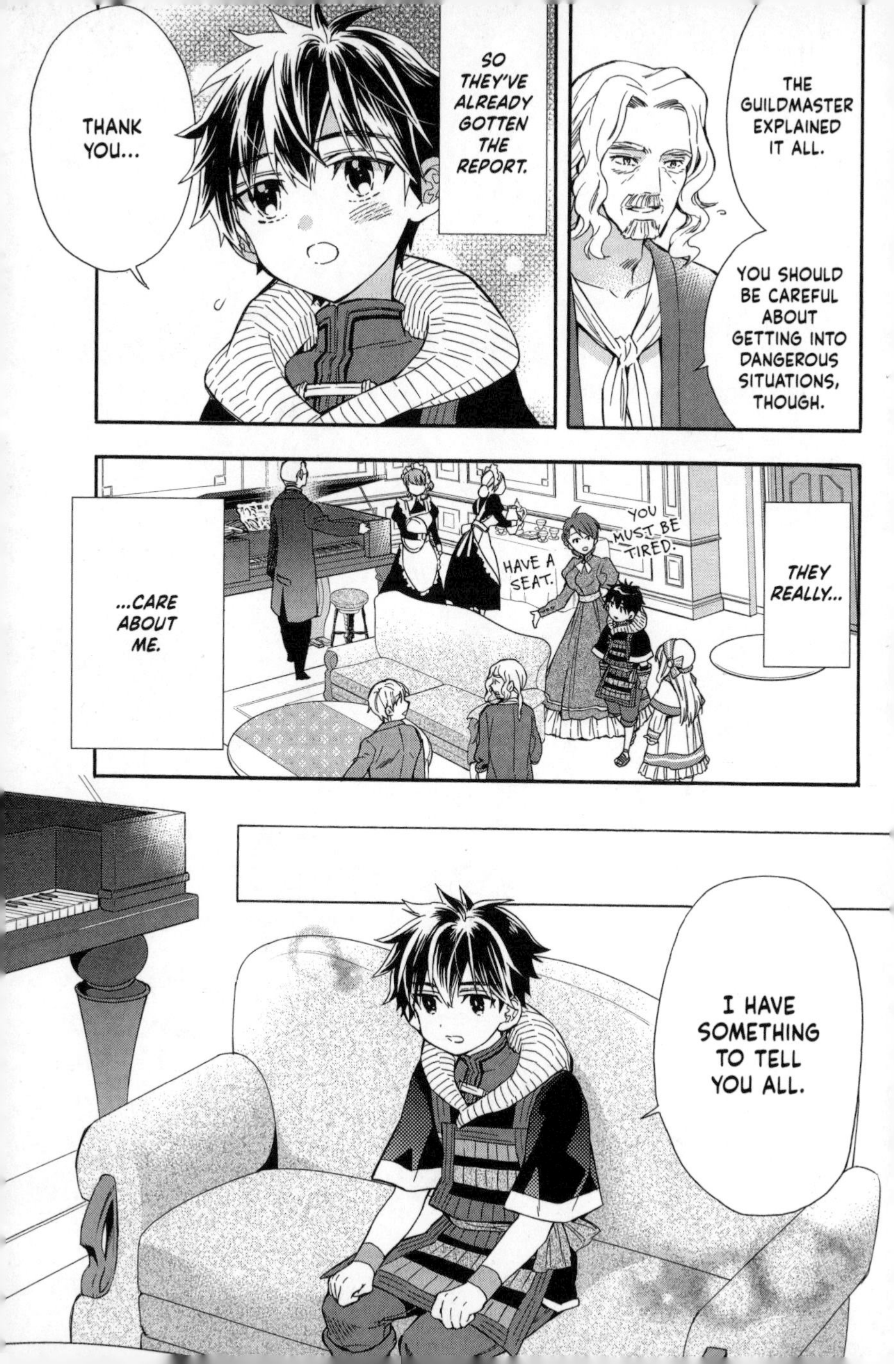
THE GUILDMASTER EXPLAINED IT ALL.
YOU SHOULD BE CAREFUL ABOUT GETTING INTO DANGEROUS SITUATIONS, THOUGH.
SO THEY'VE ALREADY GOTTEN THE REPORT.
THANK YOU...
THEY REALLY...
YOU MUST BE TIRED.
HAVE A SEAT.
...CARE ABOUT ME.
I HAVE SOMETHING TO TELL YOU ALL.

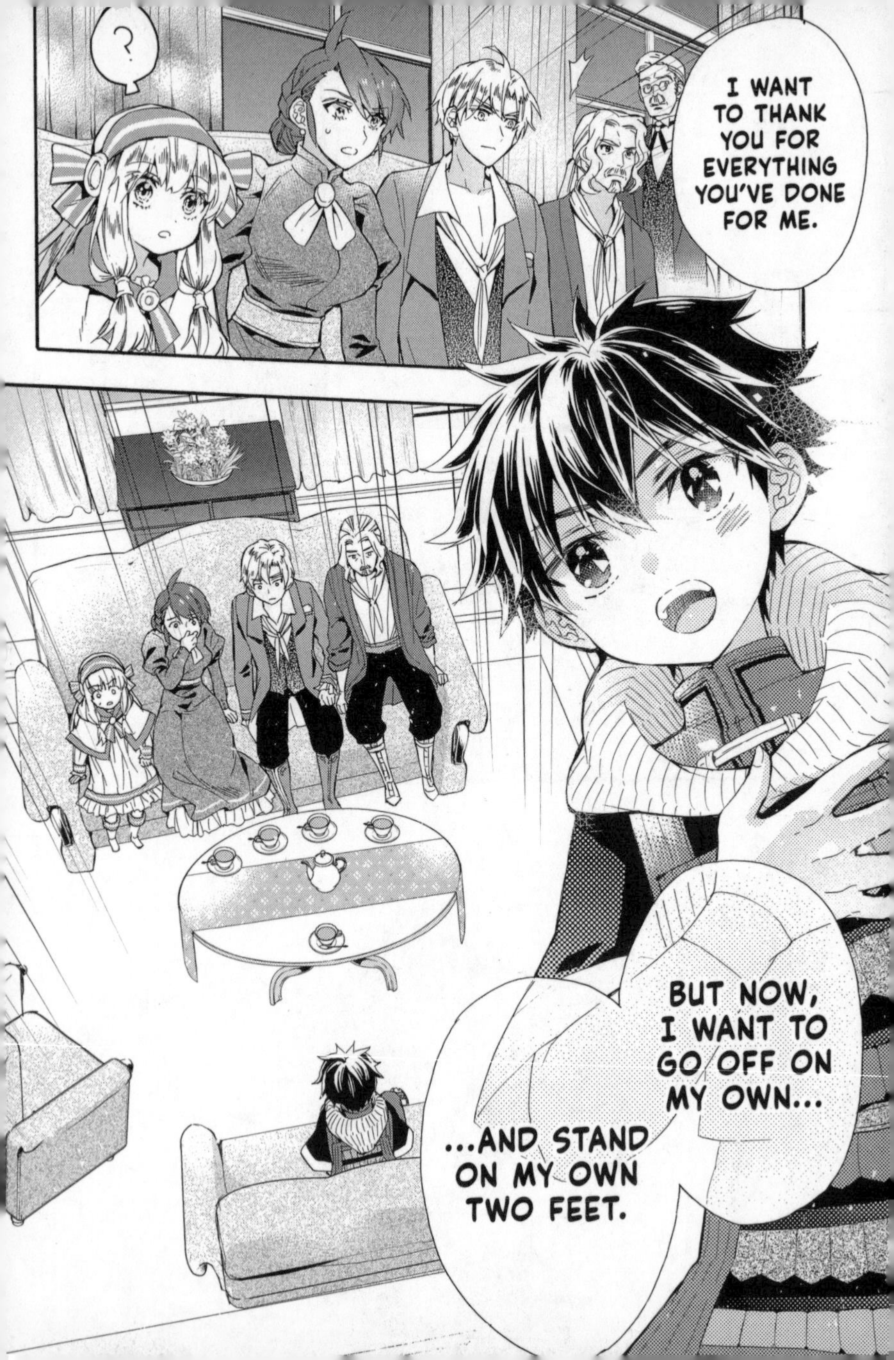
I WANT TO THANK YOU FOR EVERYTHING YOU'VE DONE FOR ME.
?
BUT NOW, I WANT TO GO OFF ON MY OWN...
...AND STAND ON MY OWN TWO FEET.

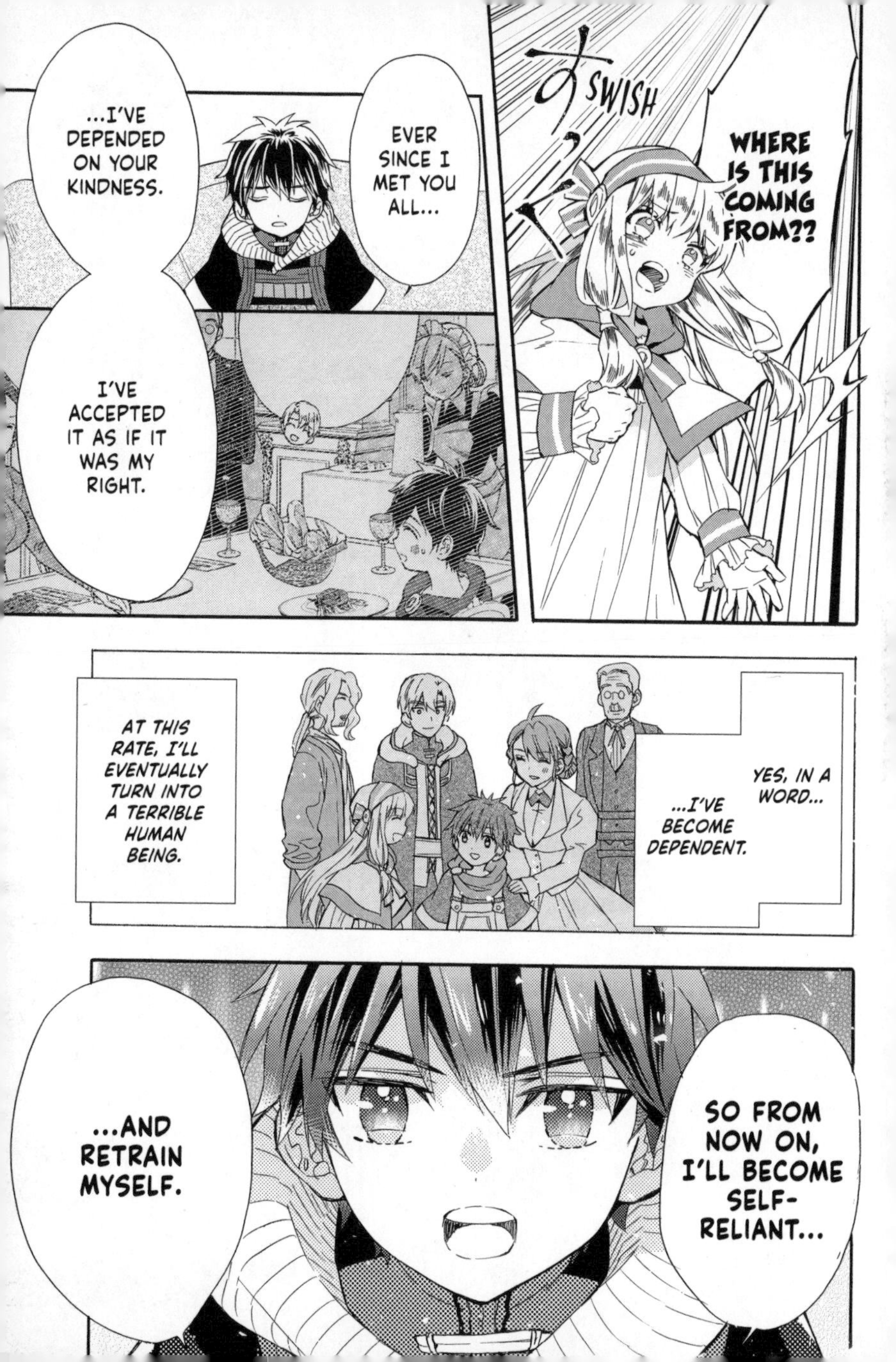
SWISH
WHERE IS THIS COMING FROM??
EVER SINCE I MET YOU ALL...
...I'VE DEPENDED ON YOUR KINDNESS.
I'VE ACCEPTED IT AS IF IT WAS MY RIGHT.
YES, IN A WORD...
...I'VE BECOME DEPENDENT.
AT THIS RATE, I'LL EVENTUALLY TURN INTO A TERRIBLE HUMAN BEING.
SO FROM NOW ON, I'LL BECOME SELF-RELIANT...
...AND RETRAIN MYSELF.

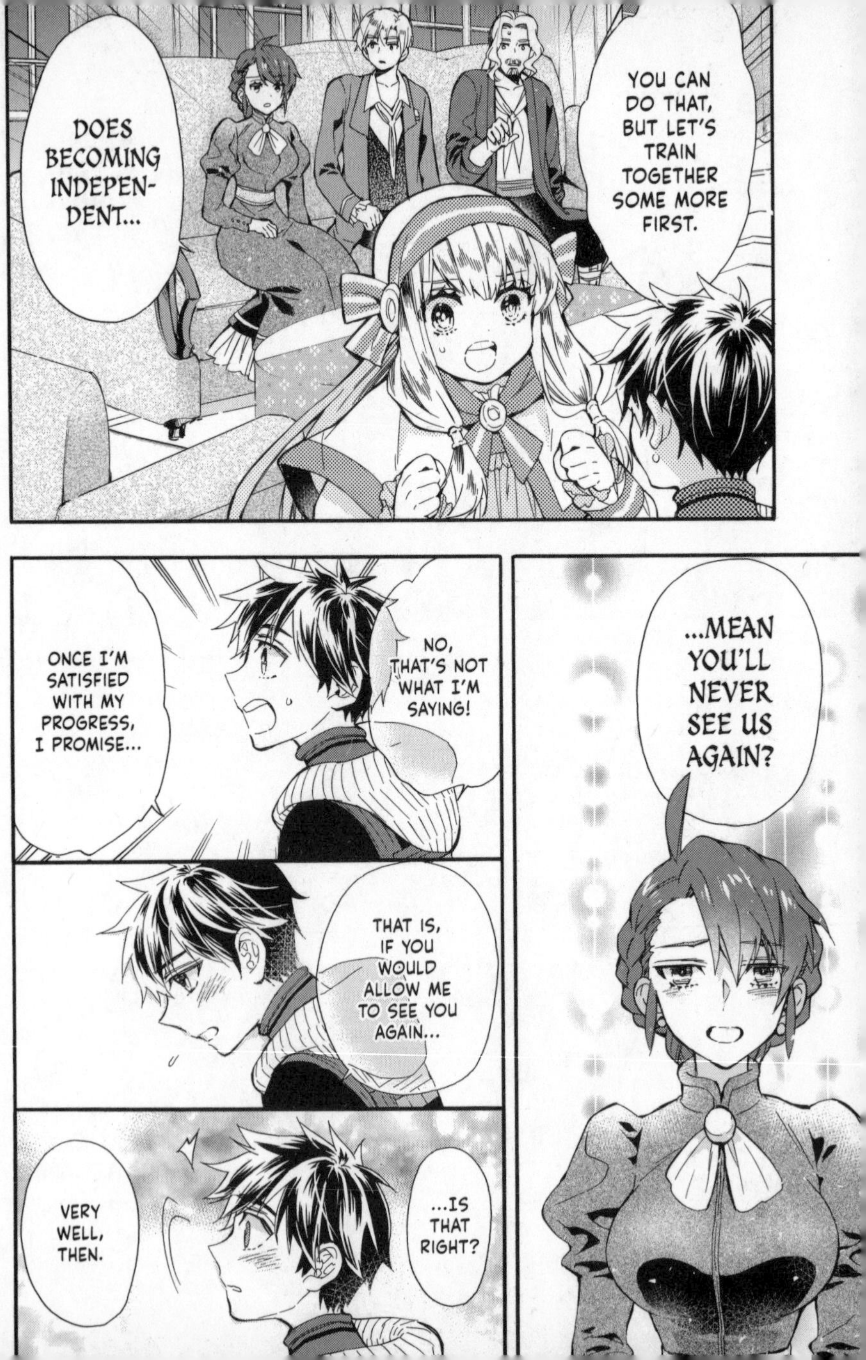
YOU CAN DO THAT, BUT LET'S TRAIN TOGETHER SOME MORE FIRST.
DOES BECOMING INDEPEN-DENT...
...MEAN YOU'LL NEVER SEE US AGAIN?
NO, THAT'S NOT WHAT I'M SAYING!
ONCE I'M SATISFIED WITH MY PROGRESS, I PROMISE...
THAT IS, IF YOU WOULD ALLOW ME TO SEE YOU AGAIN...
...IS THAT RIGHT?
VERY WELL, THEN.

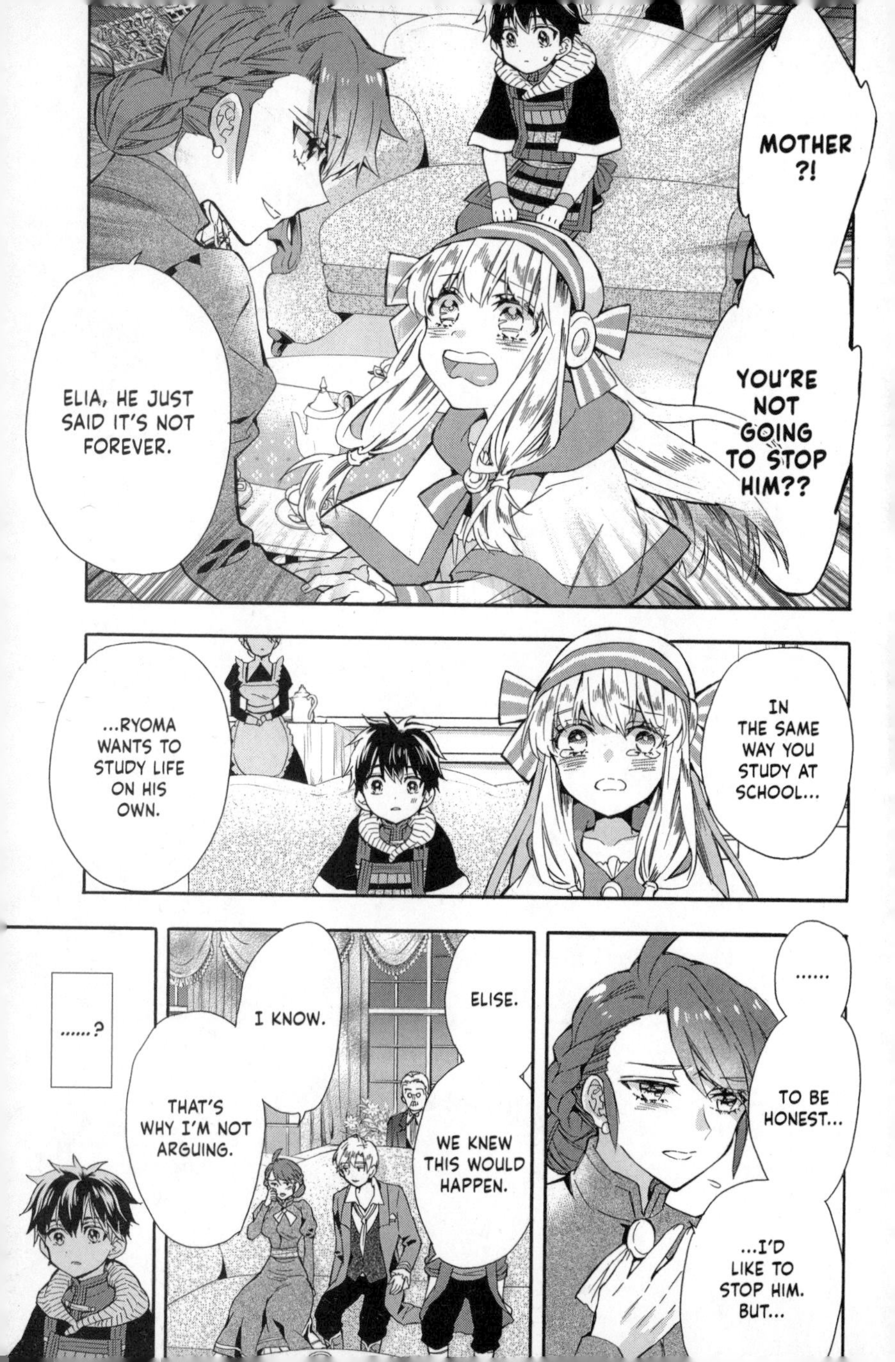
MOTHER ?!
YOU'RE NOT GOING TO STOP HIM??
ELIA, HE JUST SAID IT'S NOT FOREVER.
IN THE SAME WAY YOU STUDY AT SCHOOL...
...RYOMA WANTS TO STUDY LIFE ON HIS OWN.
......
TO BE HONEST...
...I'D LIKE TO STOP HIM. BUT...
ELISE.
WE KNEW THIS WOULD HAPPEN.
I KNOW.
THAT'S WHY I'M NOT ARGUING.
......?

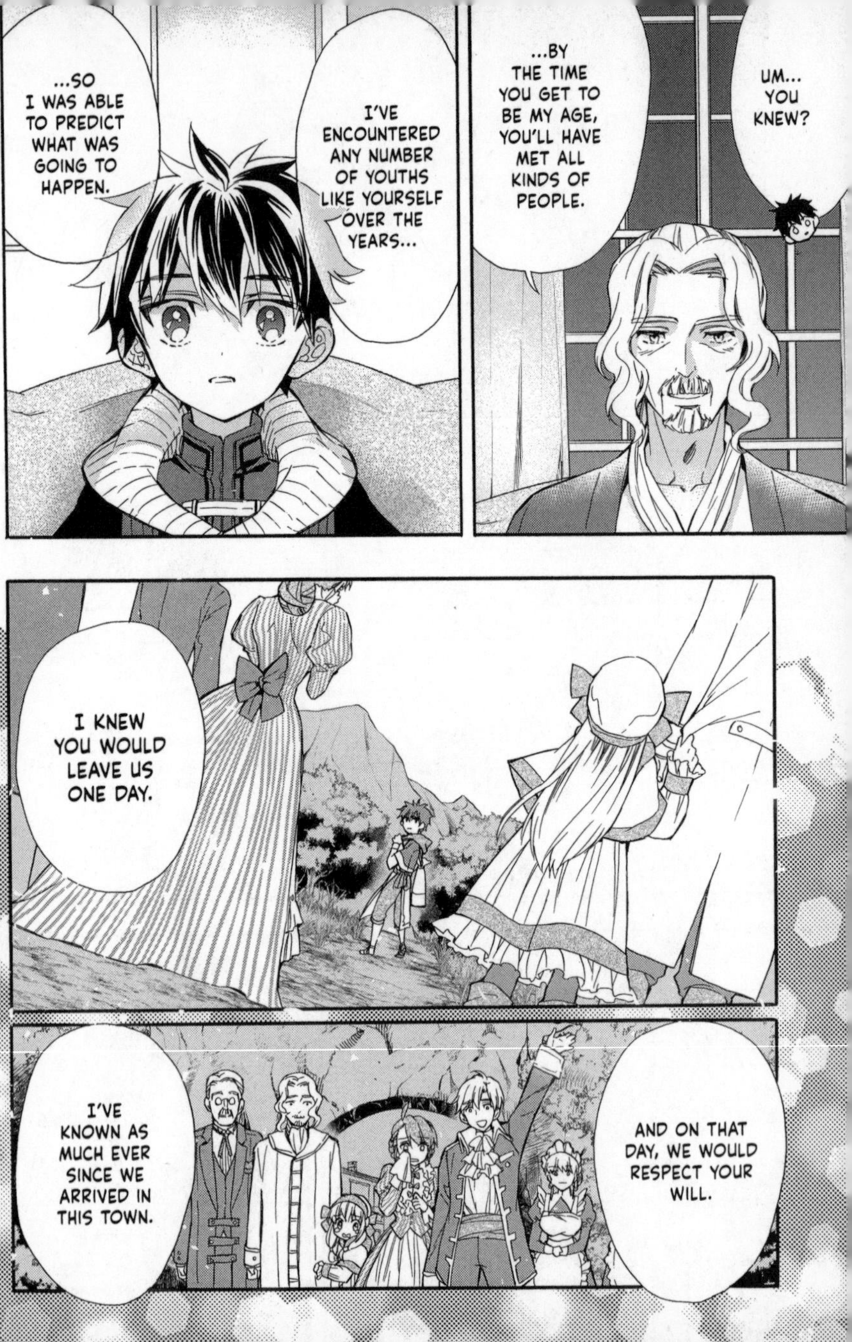
UM... YOU KNEW?
...BY THE TIME YOU GET TO BE MY AGE, YOU'LL HAVE MET ALL KINDS OF PEOPLE.
I'VE ENCOUNTERED ANY NUMBER OF YOUTHS LIKE YOURSELF OVER THE YEARS...
...SO I WAS ABLE TO PREDICT WHAT WAS GOING TO HAPPEN.
I KNEW YOU WOULD LEAVE US ONE DAY.
AND ON THAT DAY, WE WOULD RESPECT YOUR WILL.
I'VE KNOWN AS MUCH EVER SINCE WE ARRIVED IN THIS TOWN.

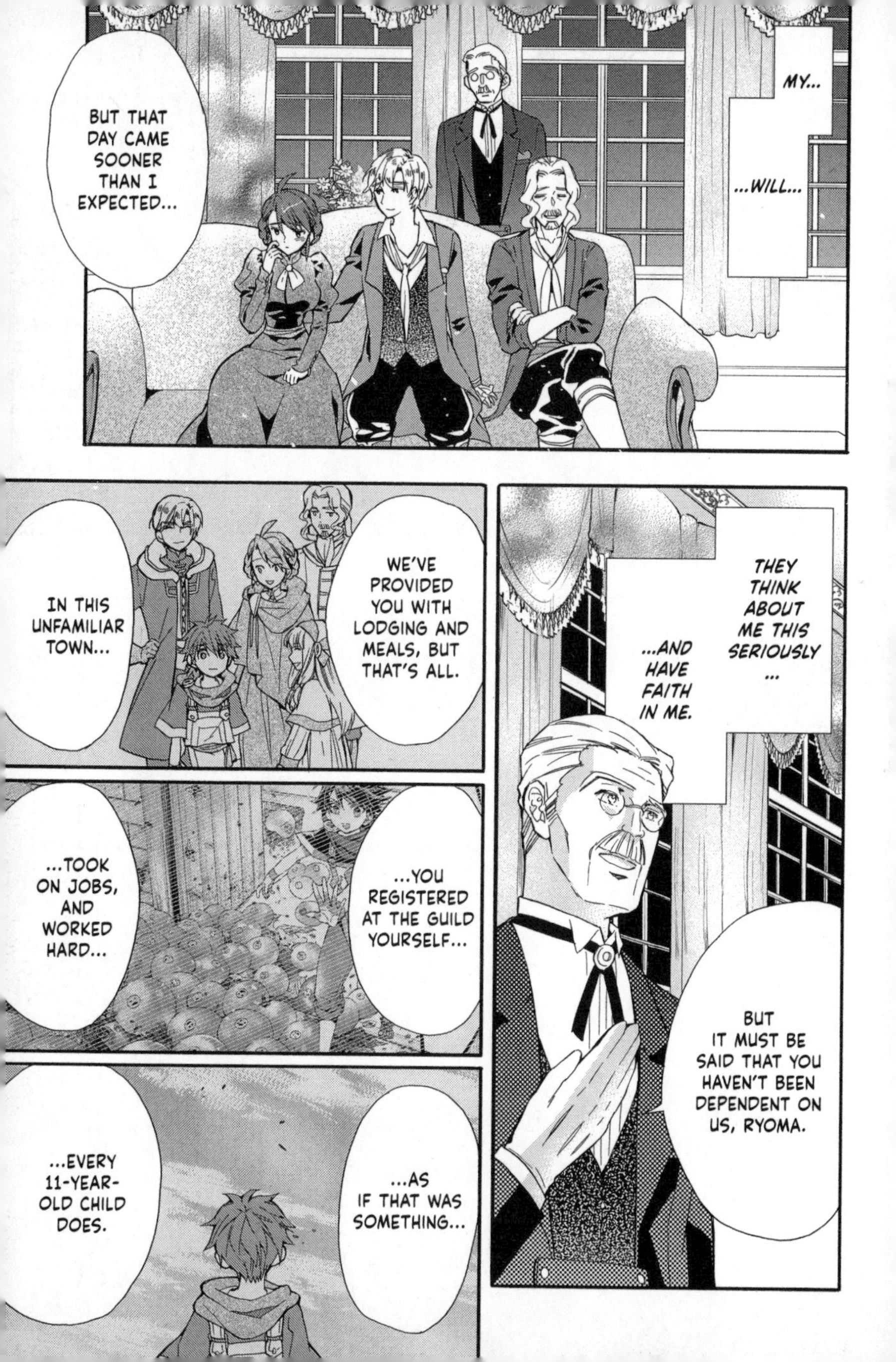

MY...
...WILL...
BUT THAT DAY CAME SOONER THAN I EXPECTED...
THEY THINK ABOUT ME THIS SERIOUSLY...
...AND HAVE FAITH IN ME.
BUT IT MUST BE SAID THAT YOU HAVEN'T BEEN DEPENDENT ON US, RYOMA.
WE'VE PROVIDED YOU WITH LODGING AND MEALS, BUT THAT'S ALL.
IN THIS UNFAMILIAR TOWN...
...YOU REGISTERED AT THE GUILD YOURSELF...
...TOOK ON JOBS, AND WORKED HARD...
...AS IF THAT WAS SOMETHING...
...EVERY 11-YEAR-OLD CHILD DOES.

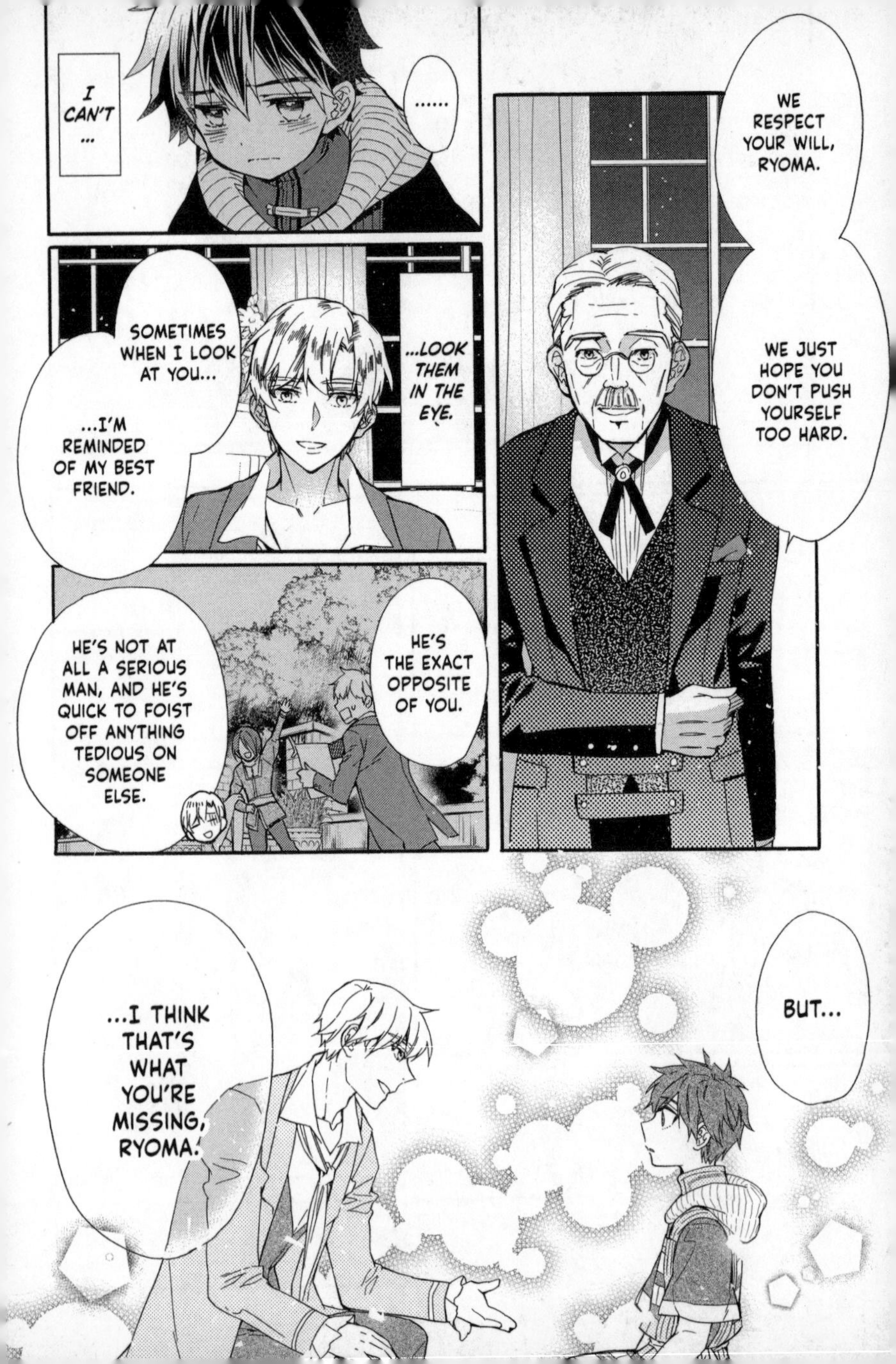
WE RESPECT YOUR WILL, RYOMA.
WE JUST HOPE YOU DON'T PUSH YOURSELF TOO HARD.
......
I CAN'T ...
...LOOK THEM IN THE EYE.
SOMETIMES WHEN I LOOK AT YOU...
...I'M REMINDED OF MY BEST FRIEND.
HE'S THE EXACT OPPOSITE OF YOU.
HE'S NOT AT ALL A SERIOUS MAN, AND HE'S QUICK TO FOIST OFF ANYTHING TEDIOUS ON SOMEONE ELSE.
BUT...
...I THINK THAT'S WHAT YOU'RE MISSING, RYOMA!

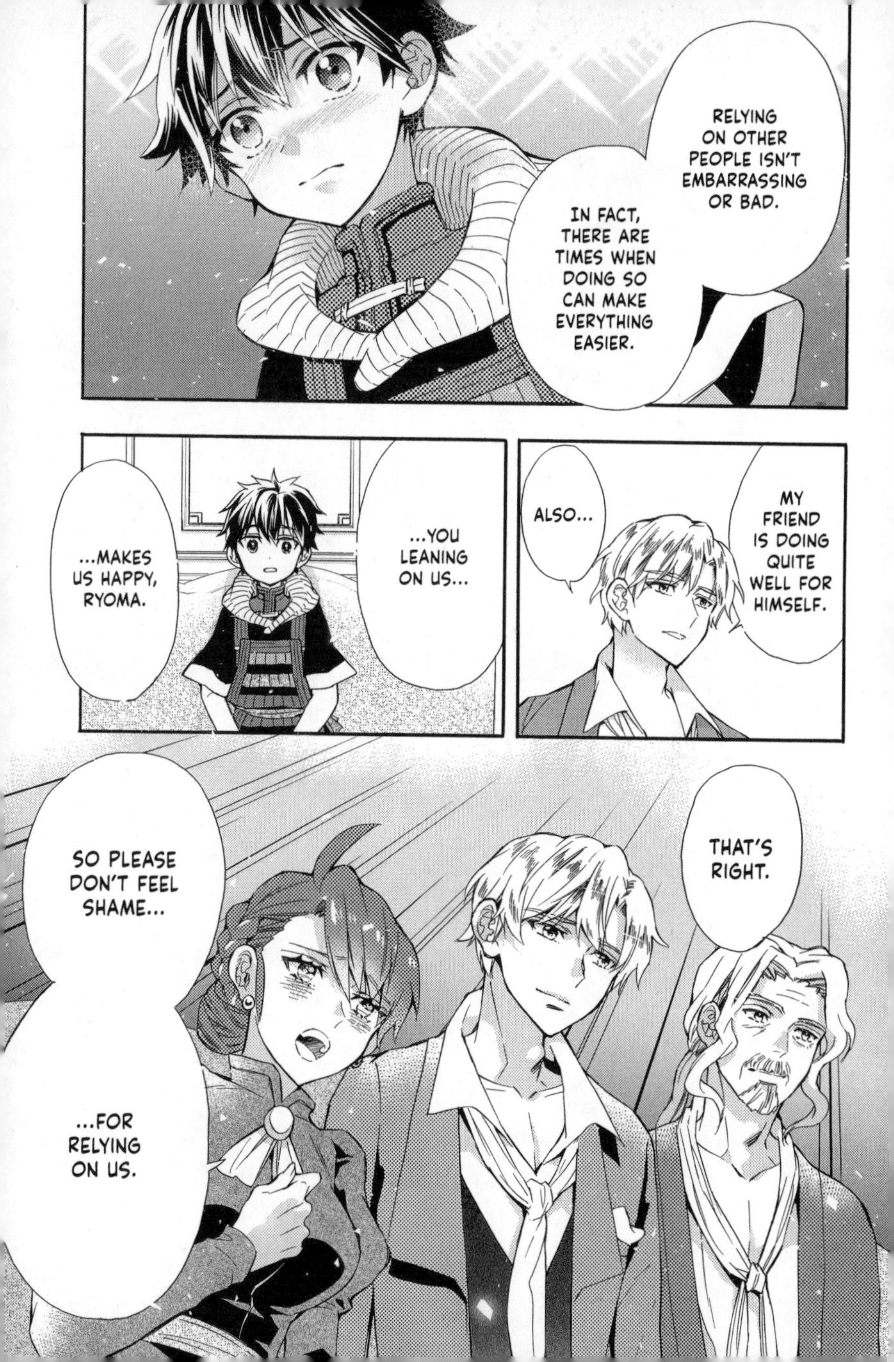
RELYING ON OTHER PEOPLE ISN'T EMBARRASSING OR BAD.
IN FACT, THERE ARE TIMES WHEN DOING SO CAN MAKE EVERYTHING EASIER.
MY FRIEND IS DOING QUITE WELL FOR HIMSELF.
ALSO...
...YOU LEANING ON US...
...MAKES US HAPPY, RYOMA.
THAT'S RIGHT.
SO PLEASE DON'T FEEL SHAME...
...FOR RELYING ON US.

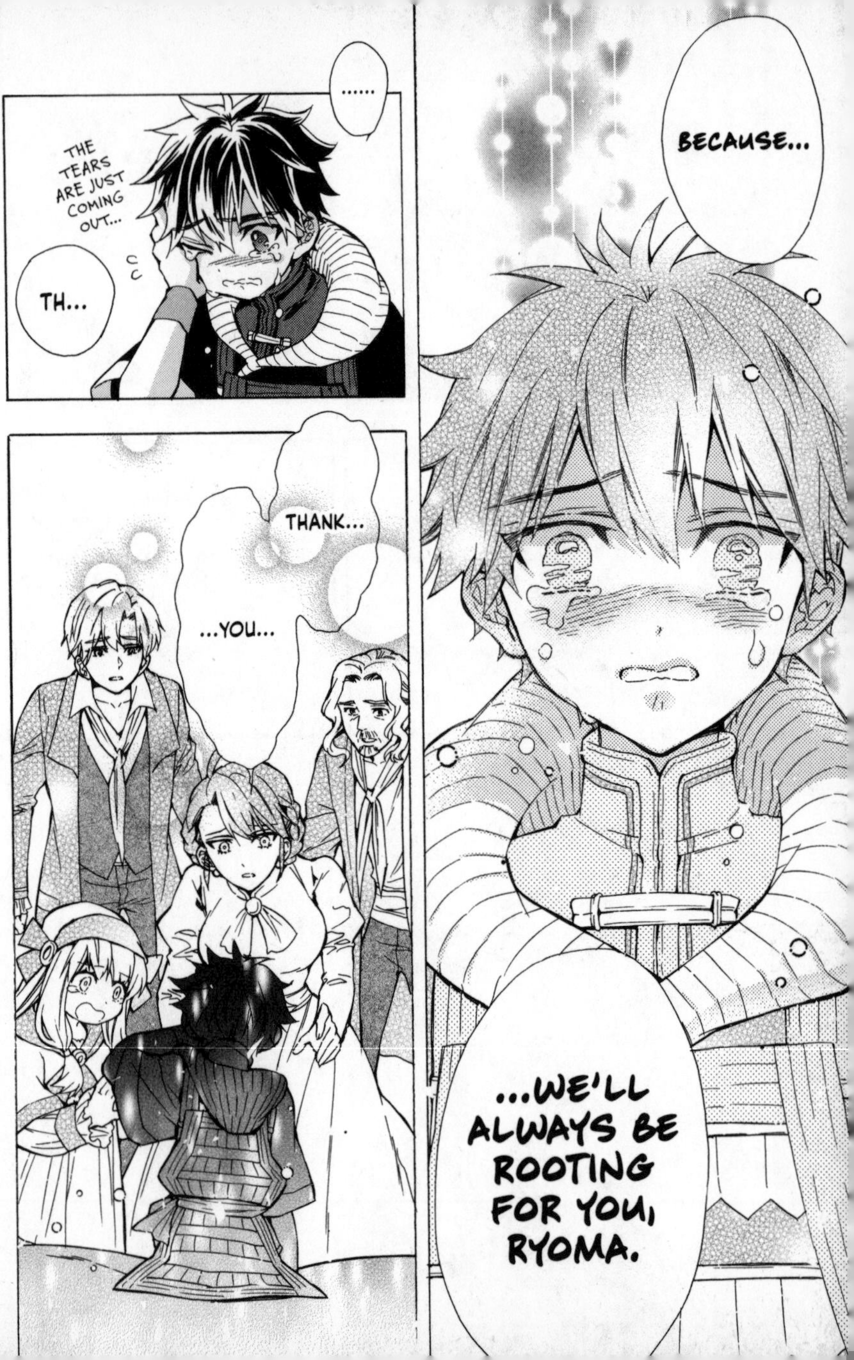
BECAUSE...
...WE'LL ALWAYS BE ROOTING FOR YOU, RYOMA.
......
THE TEARS ARE JUST COMING OUT...
TH...
THANK...
...YOU...

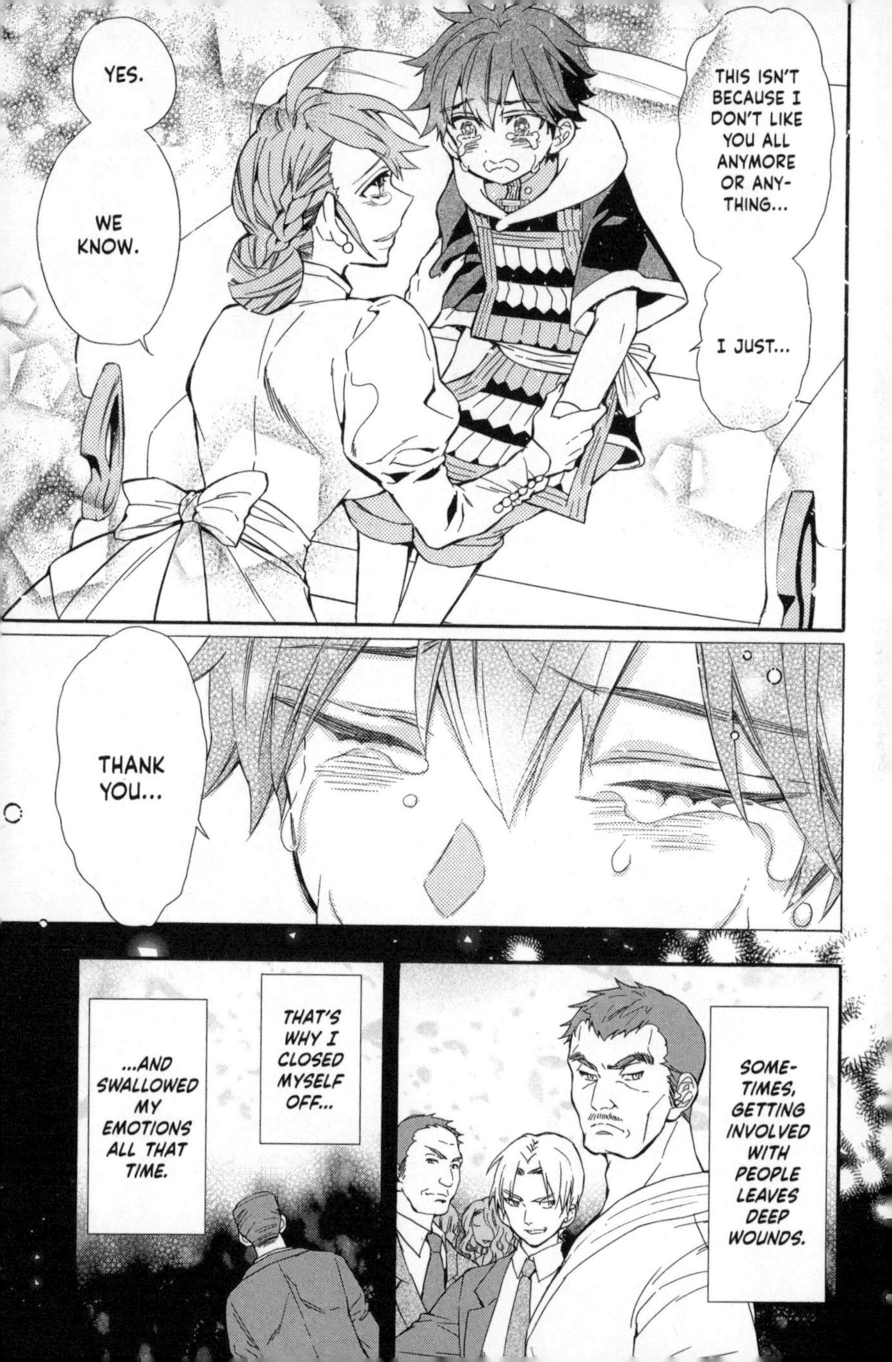
THIS ISN'T BECAUSE I DON'T LIKE YOU ALL ANYMORE OR ANY-THING...
I JUST...
YES.
WE KNOW.
THANK YOU...
SOME-TIMES, GETTING INVOLVED WITH PEOPLE LEAVES DEEP WOUNDS.
THAT'S WHY I CLOSED MYSELF OFF...
...AND SWALLOWED MY EMOTIONS ALL THAT TIME.

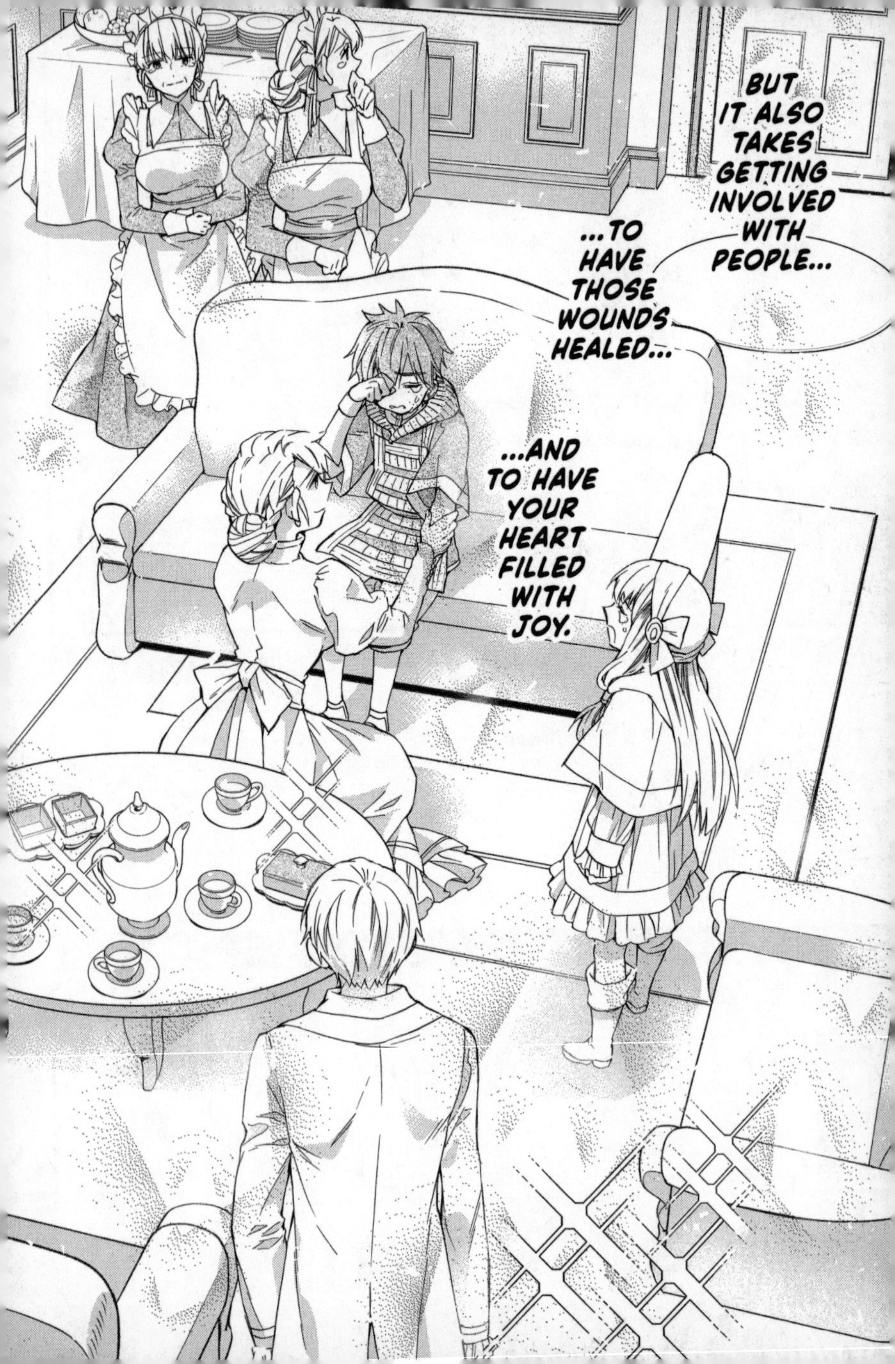
BUT IT ALSO TAKES GETTING INVOLVED WITH PEOPLE...
...TO HAVE THOSE WOUNDS HEALED...
...AND TO HAVE YOUR HEART FILLED WITH JOY.

ALL OF YOU...
...HAVE PROVEN THAT TO ME.
THAT'S WHY...
...I'D LIKE YOU TO LET ME GROW EVEN MORE.

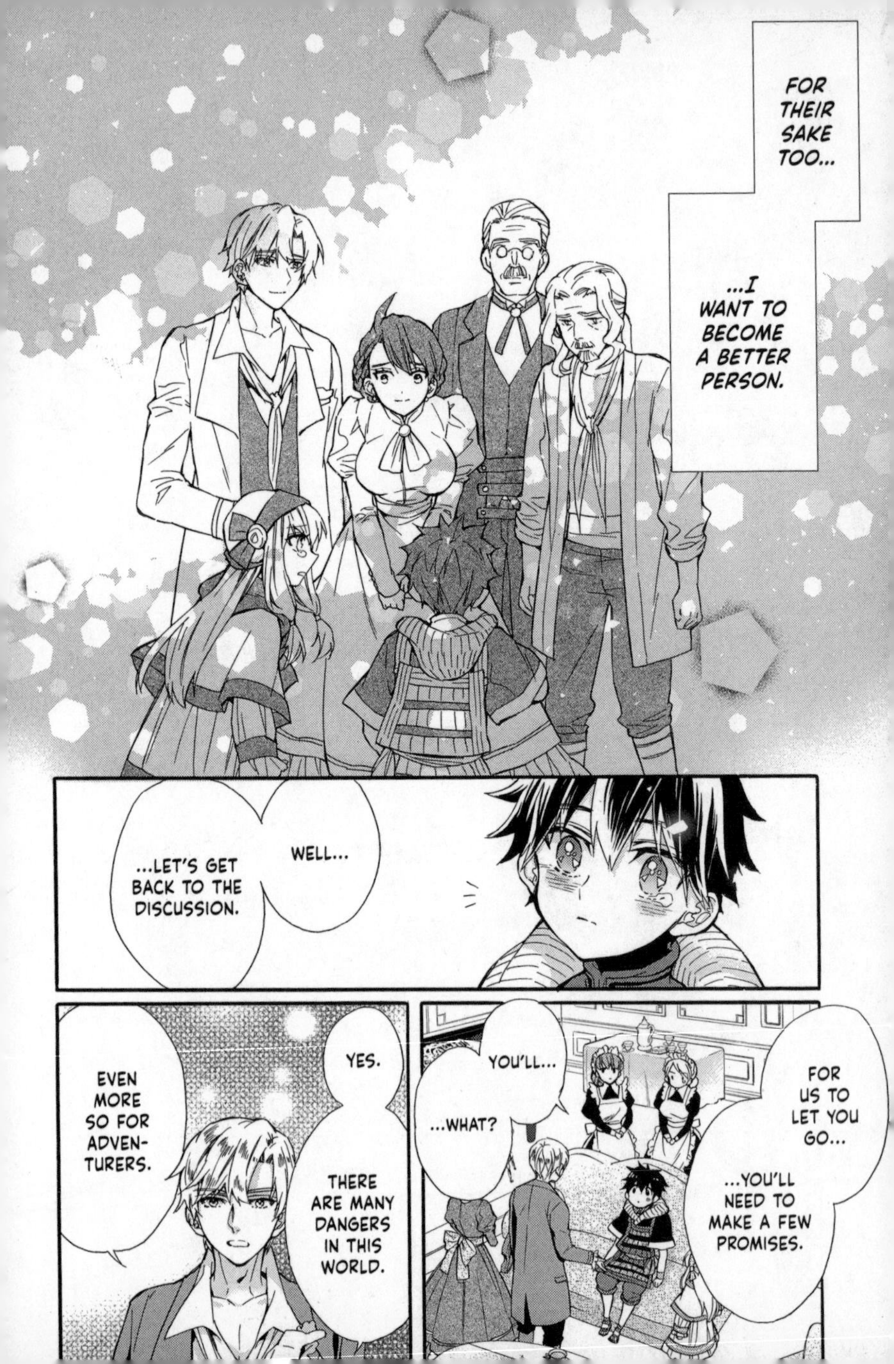
FOR THEIR SAKE TOO...
...I WANT TO BECOME A BETTER PERSON.
WELL...
...LET'S GET BACK TO THE DISCUSSION.
FOR US TO LET YOU GO...
...YOU'LL NEED TO MAKE A FEW PROMISES.
YOU'LL...
...WHAT?
YES.
THERE ARE MANY DANGERS IN THIS WORLD.
EVEN MORE SO FOR ADVEN-TURERS.

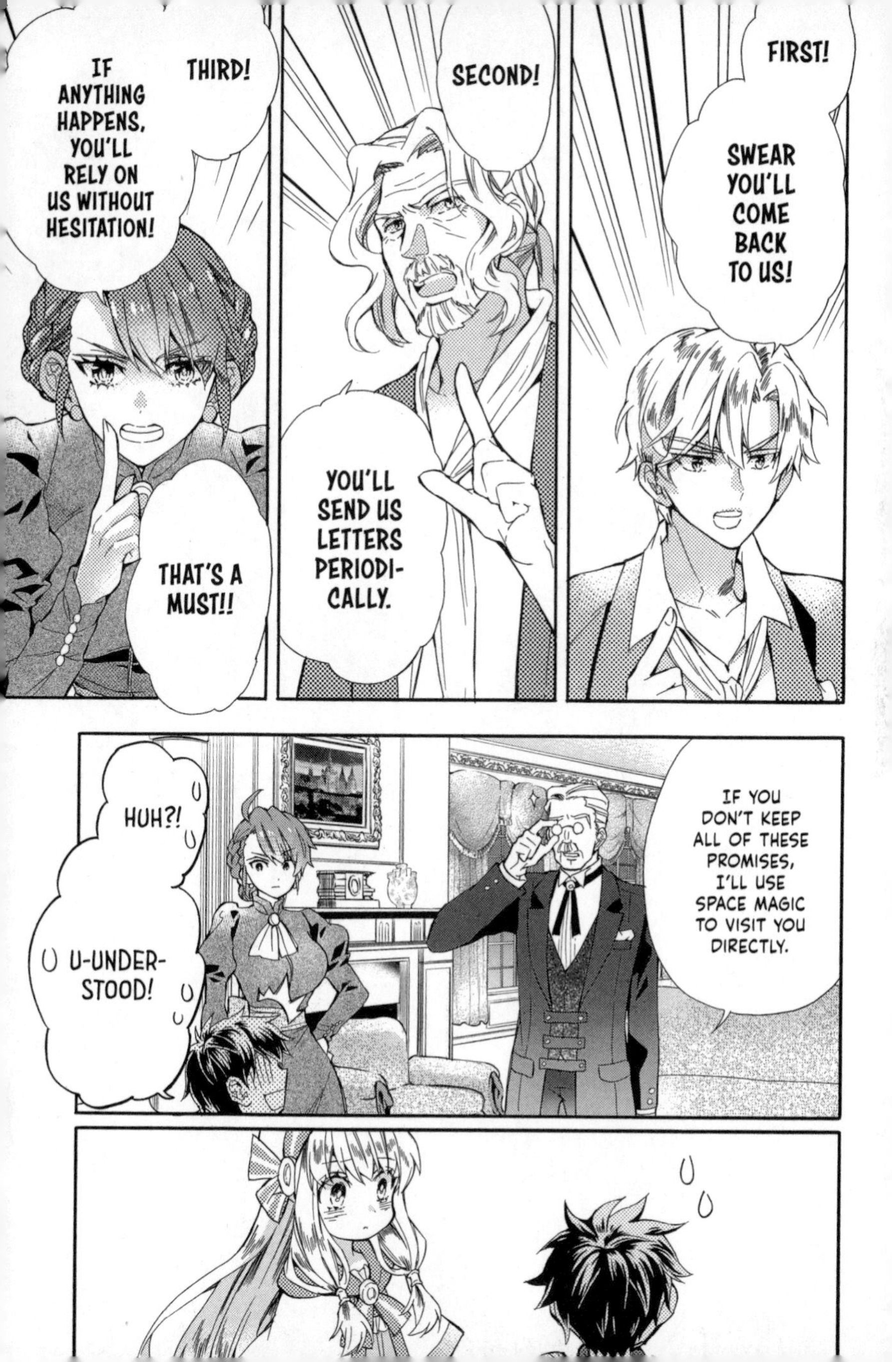
FIRST!
SWEAR YOU'LL COME BACK TO US!
SECOND!
YOU'LL SEND US LETTERS PERIODI-CALLY.
THIRD!
IF ANYTHING HAPPENS, YOU'LL RELY ON US WITHOUT HESITATION!
THAT'S A MUST!!
IF YOU DON'T KEEP ALL OF THESE PROMISES, I'LL USE SPACE MAGIC TO VISIT YOU DIRECTLY.
HUH?!
U-UNDER-STOOD!

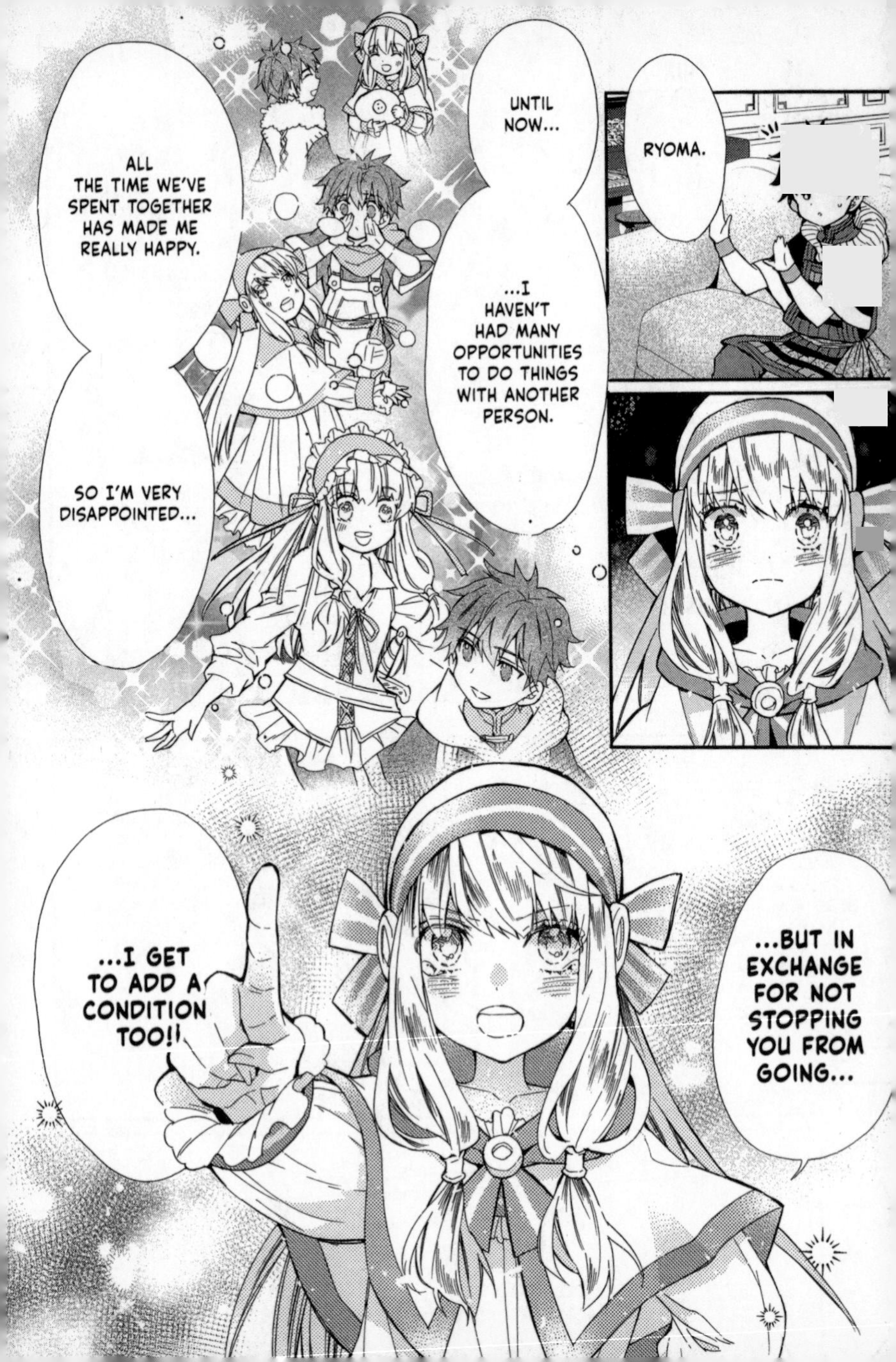
RYOMA.
UNTIL NOW...
...I HAVEN'T HAD MANY OPPORTUNITIES TO DO THINGS WITH ANOTHER PERSON.
ALL THE TIME WE'VE SPENT TOGETHER HAS MADE ME REALLY HAPPY.
SO I'M VERY DISAPPOINTED...
...BUT IN EXCHANGE FOR NOT STOPPING YOU FROM GOING...
...I GET TO ADD A CONDITION TOO!!

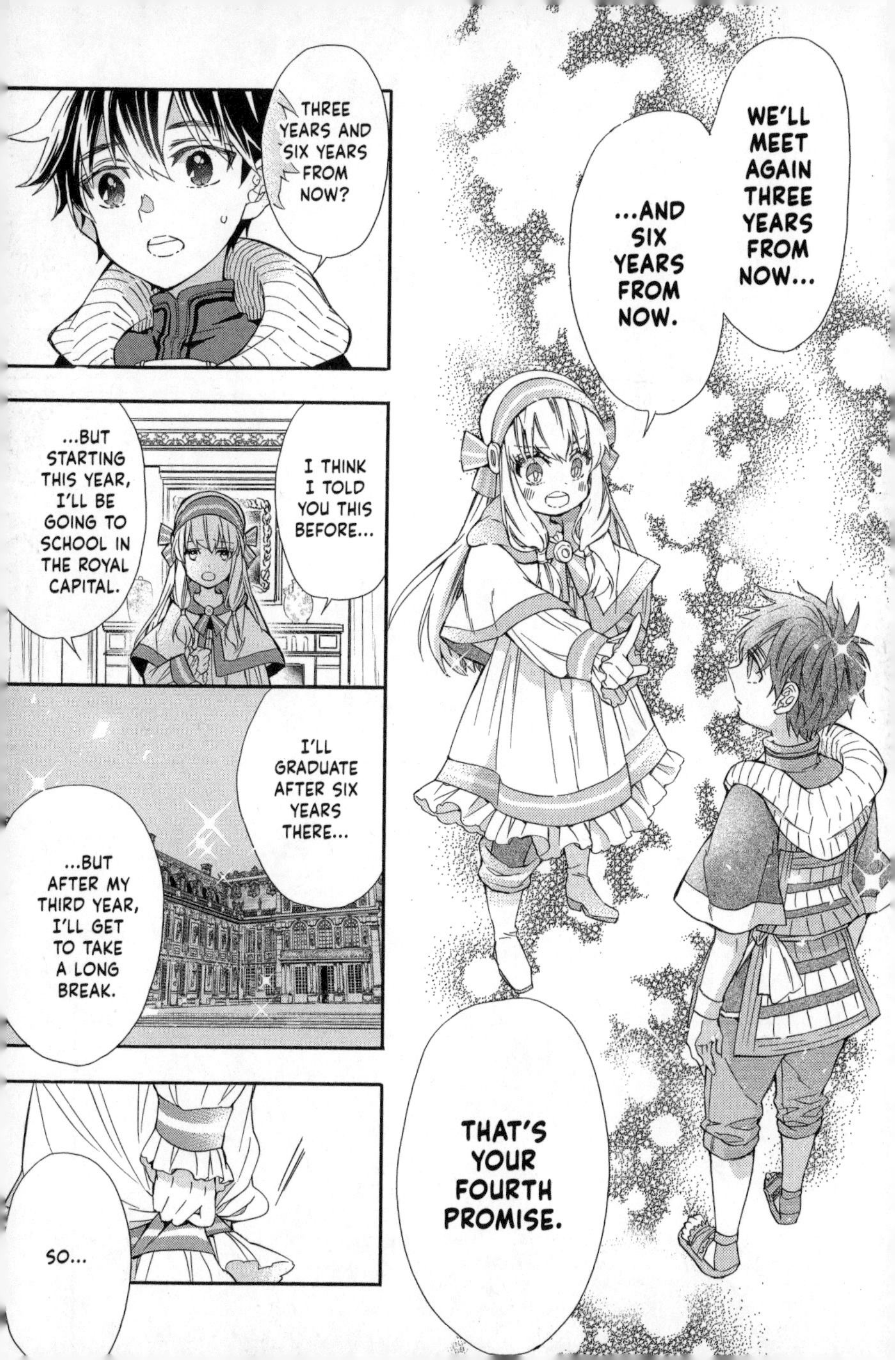
WE'LL MEET AGAIN THREE YEARS FROM NOW...
...AND SIX YEARS FROM NOW.
THAT'S YOUR FOURTH PROMISE.
THREE YEARS AND SIX YEARS FROM NOW?
I THINK I TOLD YOU THIS BEFORE...
...BUT STARTING THIS YEAR, I'LL BE GOING TO SCHOOL IN THE ROYAL CAPITAL.
I'LL GRADUATE AFTER SIX YEARS THERE...
...BUT AFTER MY THIRD YEAR, I'LL GET TO TAKE A LONG BREAK.
SO...

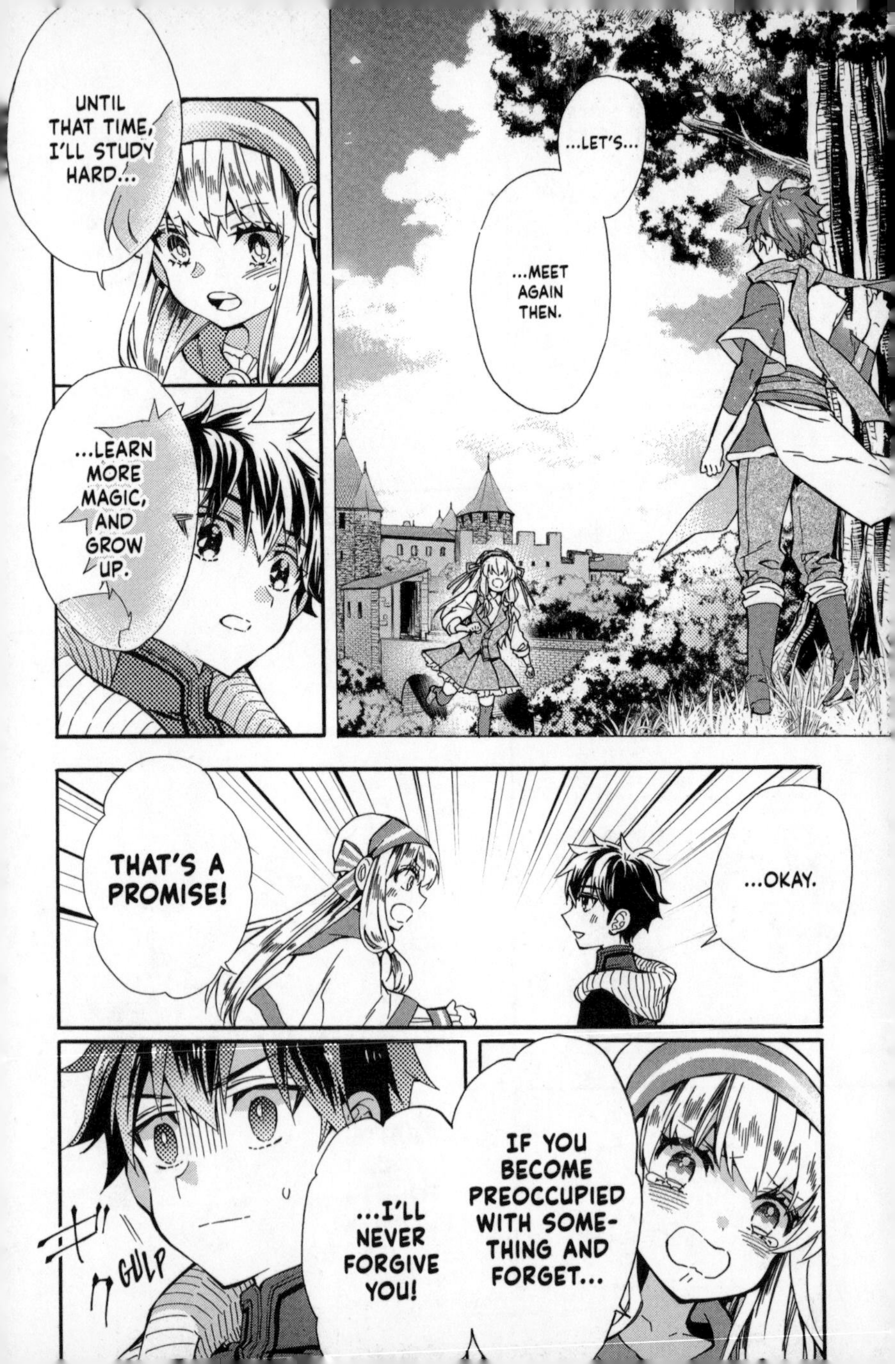
...LET'S...
...MEET AGAIN THEN.
UNTIL THAT TIME, I'LL STUDY HARD...
...LEARN MORE MAGIC, AND GROW UP.
...OKAY.
THAT'S A PROMISE!
IF YOU BECOME PREOCCUPIED WITH SOME-THING AND FORGET...
...I'LL NEVER FORGIVE YOU!
GULP

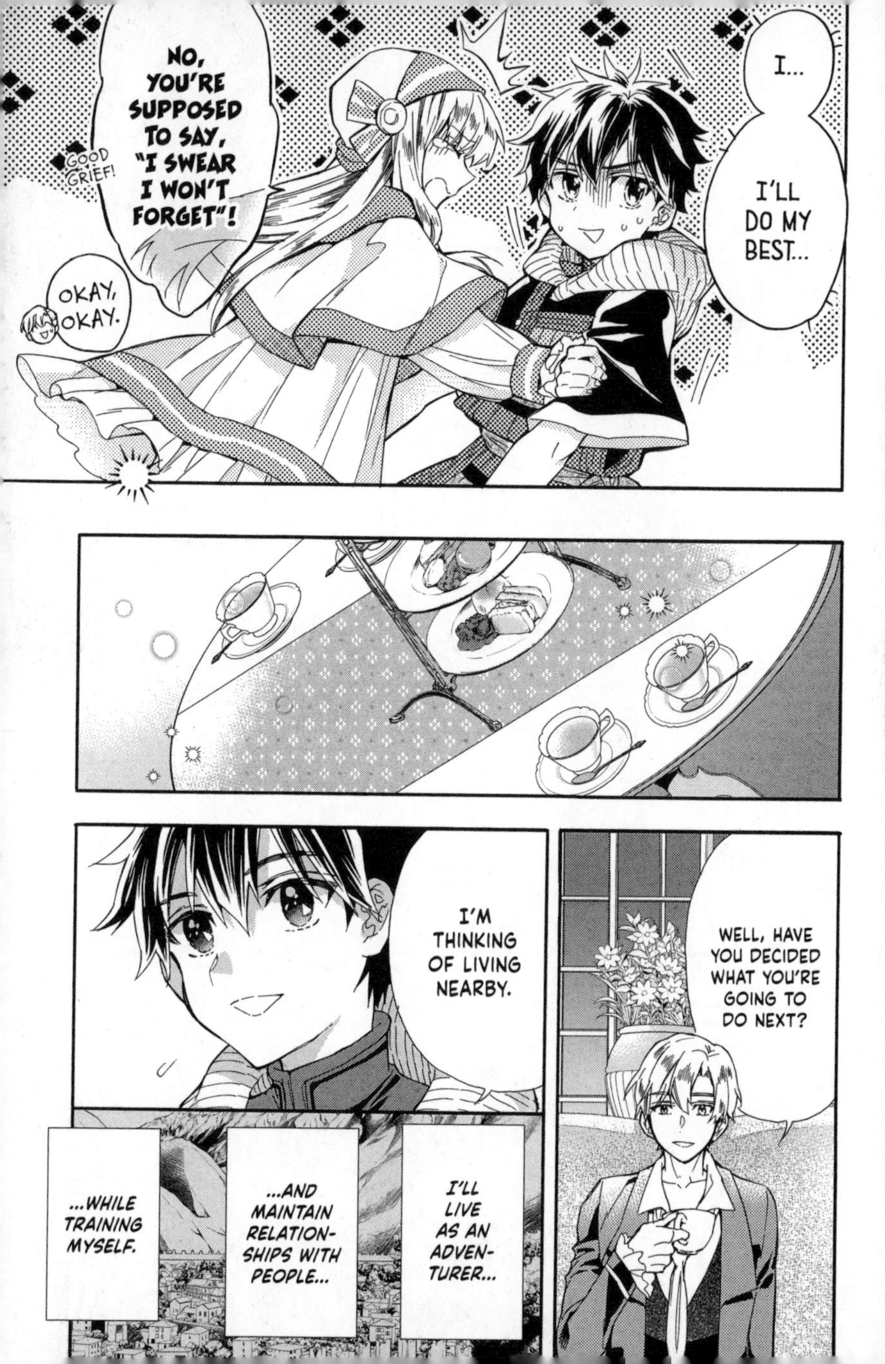
I...
I'LL DO MY BEST...
NO, YOU'RE SUPPOSED TO SAY, "I SWEAR I WON'T FORGET"!
GOOD GRIEF!
OKAY, OKAY.
WELL, HAVE YOU DECIDED WHAT YOU'RE GOING TO DO NEXT?
I'M THINKING OF LIVING NEARBY.
I'LL LIVE AS AN ADVEN-TURER...
...AND MAINTAIN RELATION-SHIPS WITH PEOPLE...
...WHILE TRAINING MYSELF.

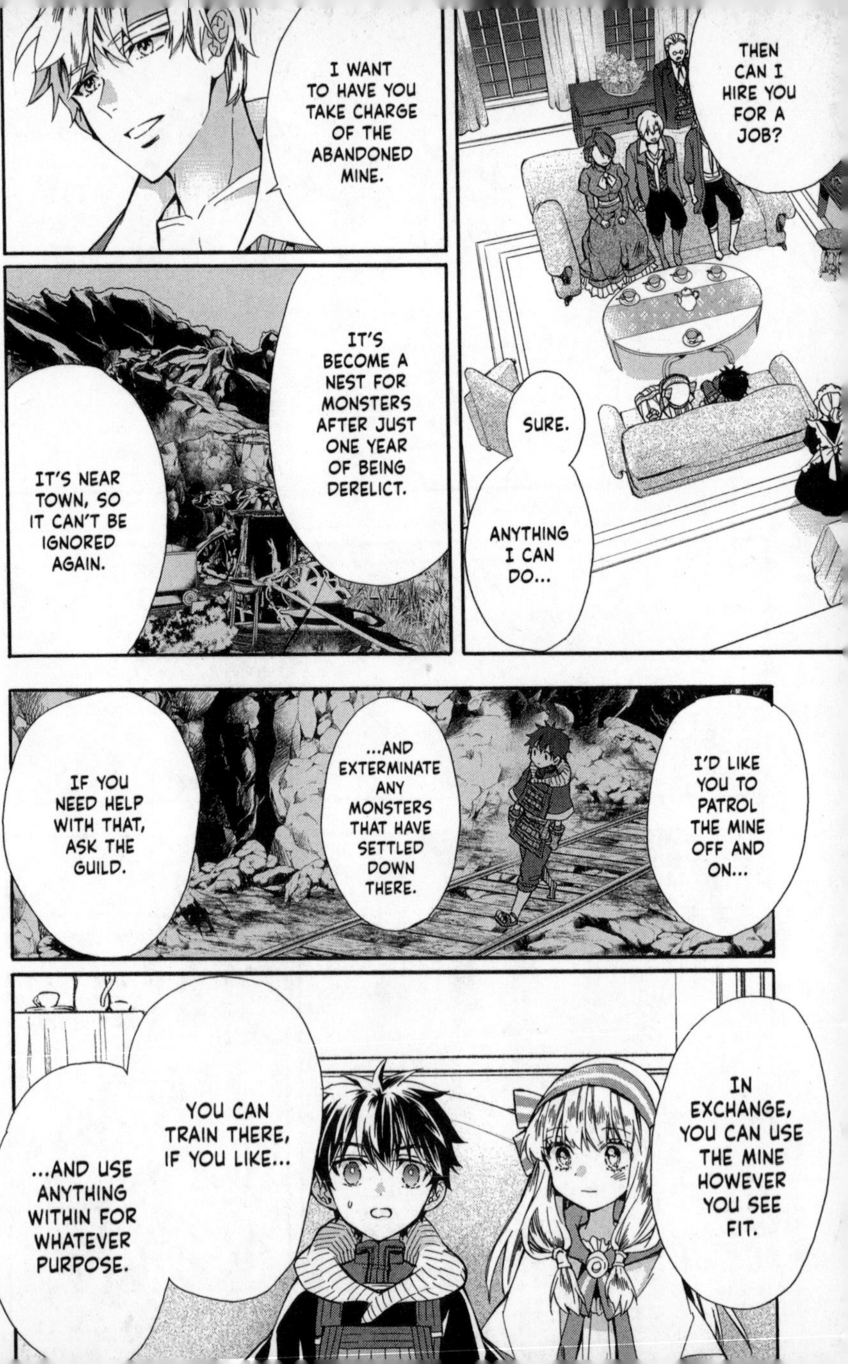
THEN CAN I HIRE YOU FOR A JOB?
SURE.
ANYTHING I CAN DO...
I WANT TO HAVE YOU TAKE CHARGE OF THE ABANDONED MINE.
IT'S BECOME A NEST FOR MONSTERS AFTER JUST ONE YEAR OF BEING DERELICT.
IT'S NEAR TOWN, SO IT CAN'T BE IGNORED AGAIN.
I'D LIKE YOU TO PATROL THE MINE OFF AND ON...
...AND EXTERMINATE ANY MONSTERS THAT HAVE SETTLED DOWN THERE.
IF YOU NEED HELP WITH THAT, ASK THE GUILD.
IN EXCHANGE, YOU CAN USE THE MINE HOWEVER YOU SEE FIT.
YOU CAN TRAIN THERE, IF YOU LIKE...
...AND USE ANYTHING WITHIN FOR WHATEVER PURPOSE.

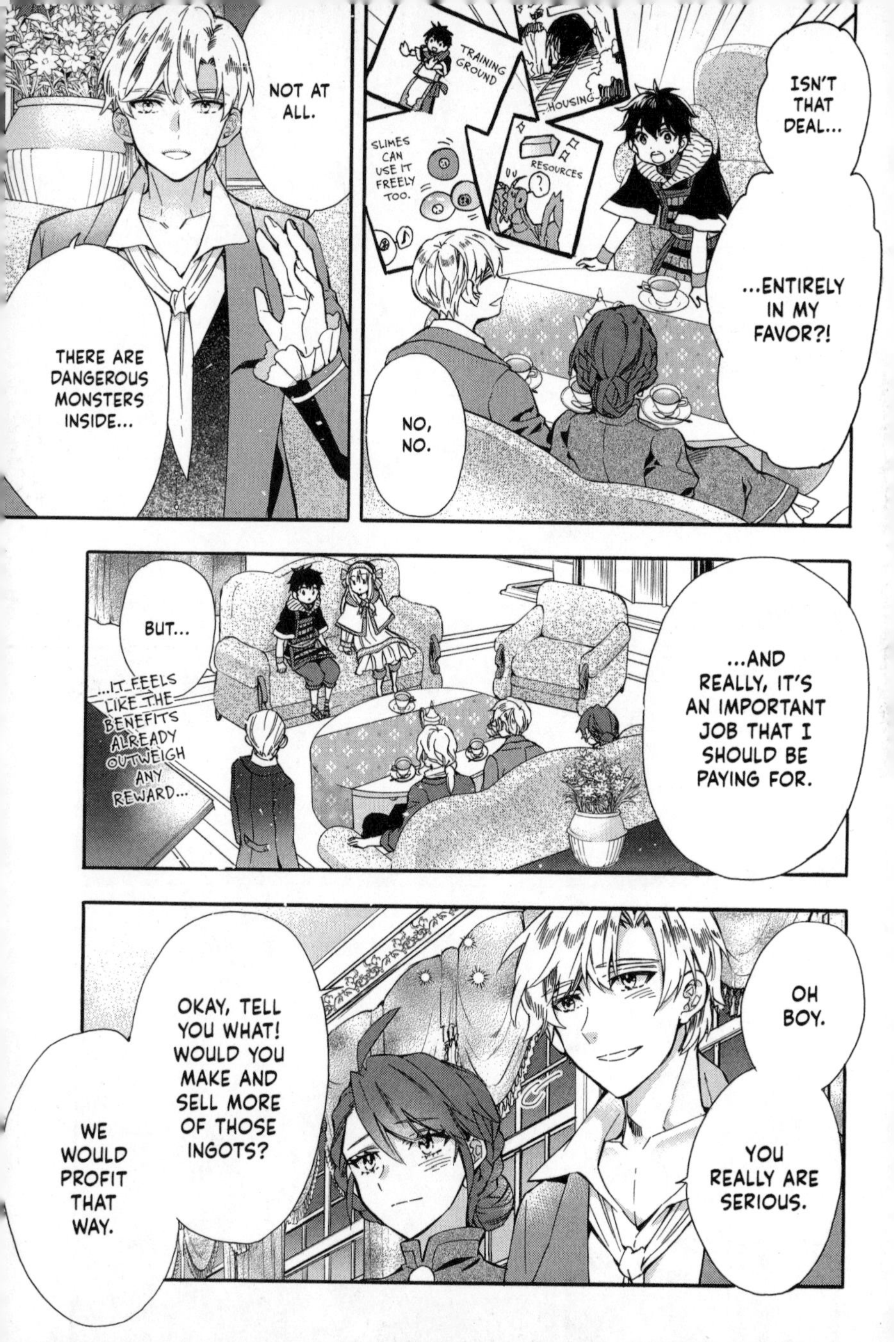
ISN'T THAT DEAL...
TRAINING GROUND
HOUSING
SLIMES CAN USE IT FREELY TOO.
RESOURCES
...ENTIRELY IN MY FAVOR?!
NO, NO.
NOT AT ALL.
THERE ARE DANGEROUS MONSTERS INSIDE...
...AND REALLY, IT'S AN IMPORTANT JOB THAT I SHOULD BE PAYING FOR.
BUT...
...IT FEELS LIKE THE BENEFITS ALREADY OUTWEIGH ANY REWARD...
OH BOY.
YOU REALLY ARE SERIOUS.
OKAY, TELL YOU WHAT! WOULD YOU MAKE AND SELL MORE OF THOSE INGOTS?
WE WOULD PROFIT THAT WAY.

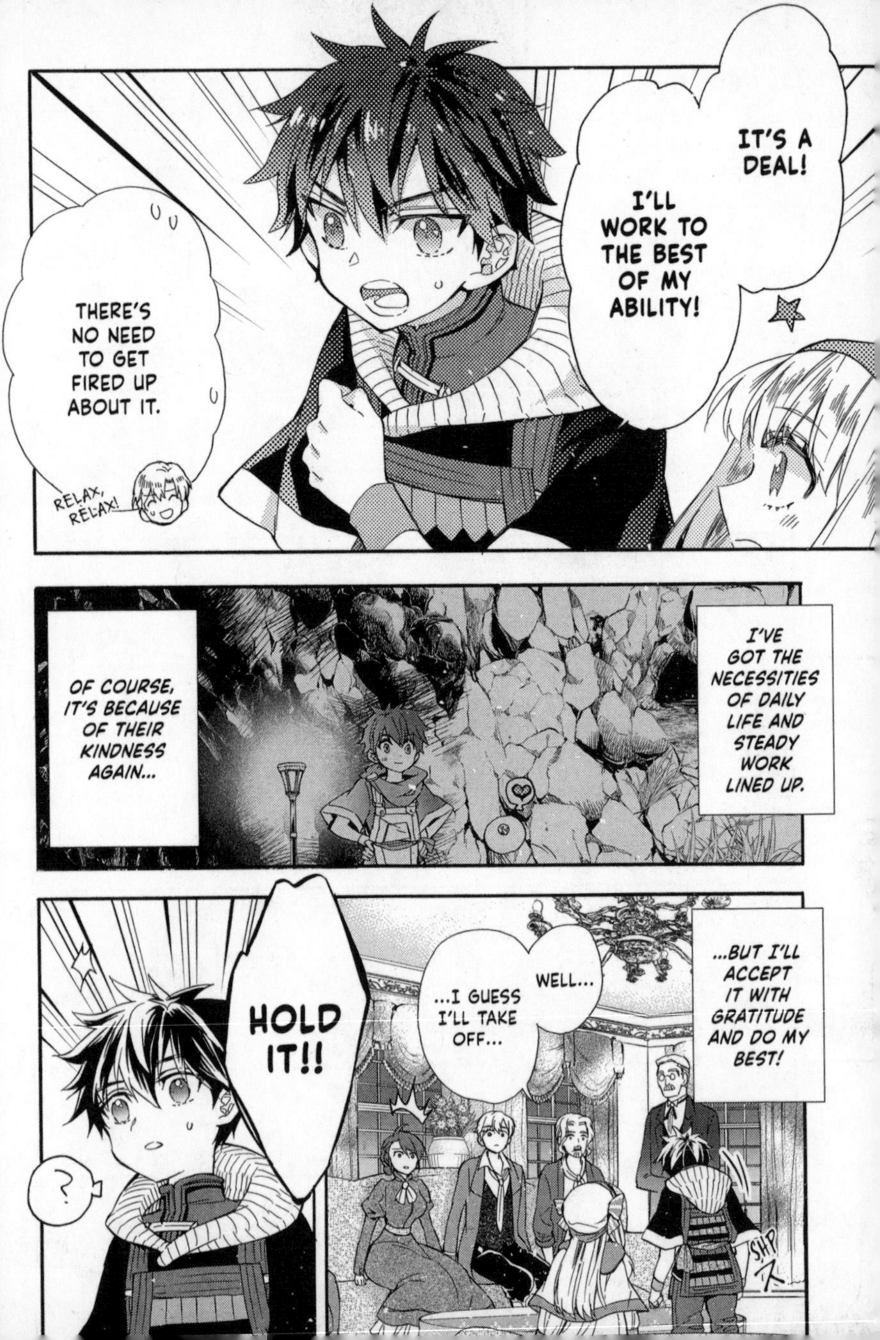
IT'S A DEAL!
I'LL WORK TO THE BEST OF MY ABILITY!
THERE'S NO NEED TO GET FIRED UP ABOUT IT.
RELAX, RELAX!
I'VE GOT THE NECESSITIES OF DAILY LIFE AND STEADY WORK LINED UP.
OF COURSE, IT'S BECAUSE OF THEIR KINDNESS AGAIN...
...BUT I'LL ACCEPT IT WITH GRATITUDE AND DO MY BEST!
WELL...
...I GUESS I'LL TAKE OFF...
SHP
HOLD IT!!
?

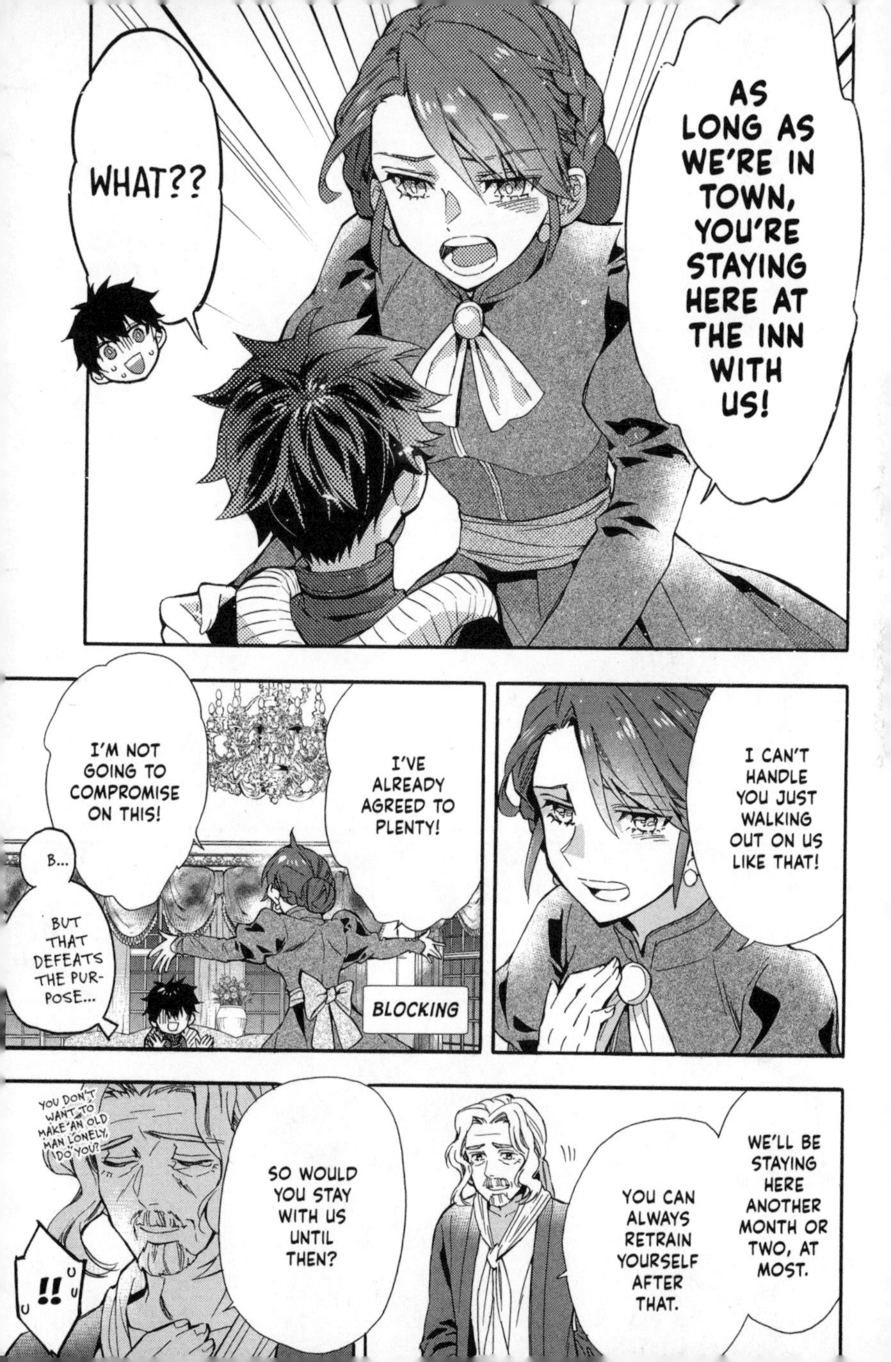
AS LONG AS WE'RE IN TOWN, YOU'RE STAYING HERE AT THE INN WITH US!
WHAT??
I CAN'T HANDLE YOU JUST WALKING OUT ON US LIKE THAT!
I'VE ALREADY AGREED TO PLENTY!
I'M NOT GOING TO COMPROMISE ON THIS!
B...
BUT THAT DEFEATS THE PUR-POSE...
BLOCKING
WE'LL BE STAYING HERE ANOTHER MONTH OR TWO, AT MOST.
YOU CAN ALWAYS RETRAIN YOURSELF AFTER THAT.
SO WOULD YOU STAY WITH US UNTIL THEN?
YOU DON'T WANT TO MAKE AN OLD MAN LONELY, DO YOU?
!!

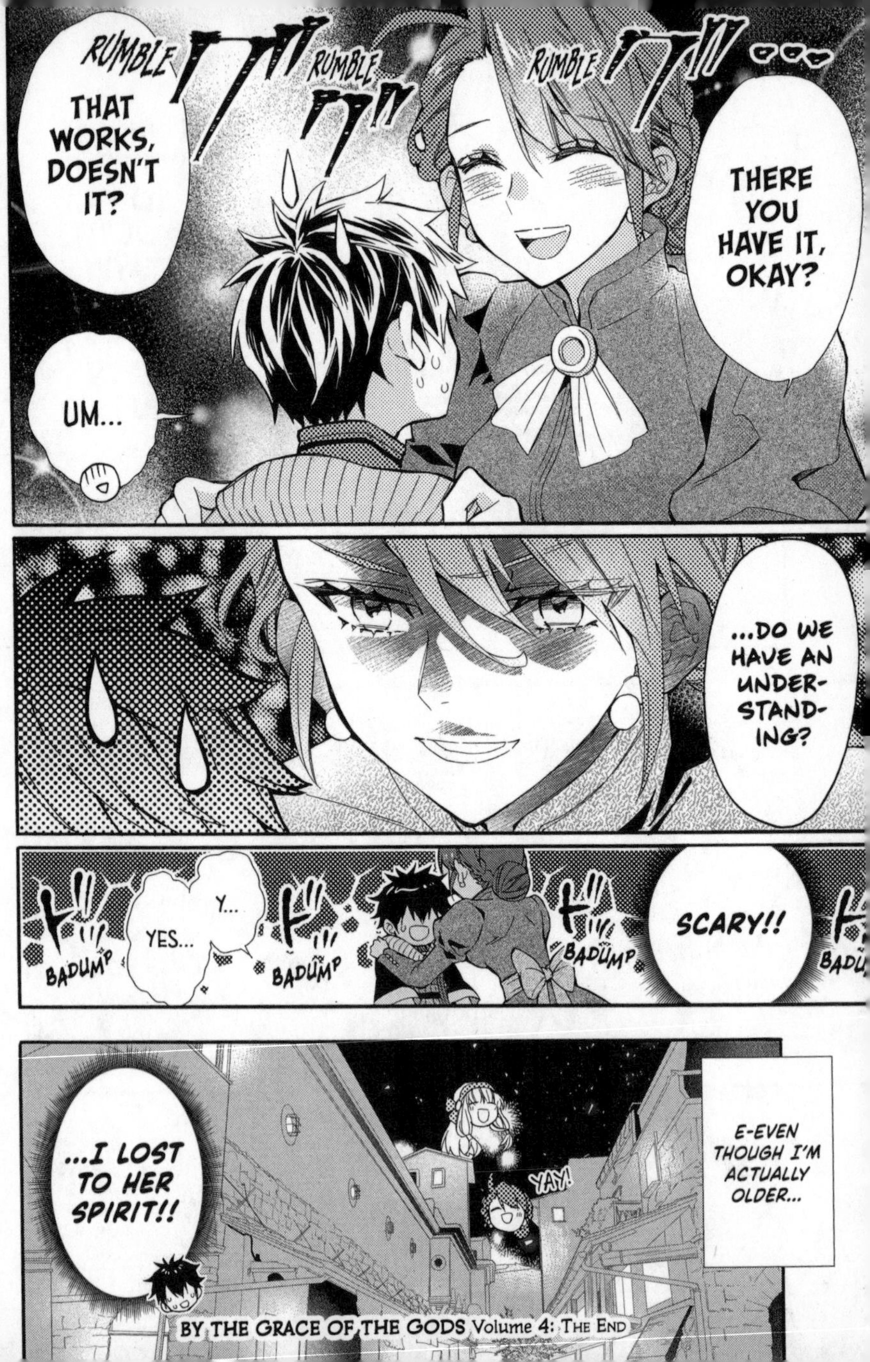
RUMBLE
RUMBLE
RUMBLE
THERE YOU HAVE IT, OKAY?
THAT WORKS, DOESN'T IT?
UM...
...DO WE HAVE AN UNDER-STANDING?
BADUMP
SCARY!!
BADUMP
BADUMP
Y... YES...
BADUMP
E-EVEN THOUGH I'M ACTUALLY OLDER...
YAY!
...I LOST TO HER SPIRIT!!
BY THE GRACE OF THE GODS Volume 4: The End

To read a brand-new short story by **ROY**,
the author of *By the Grace of the Gods*,
please turn to page 209 of this book,
where you'll find the story presented
in left-to-right reading order.

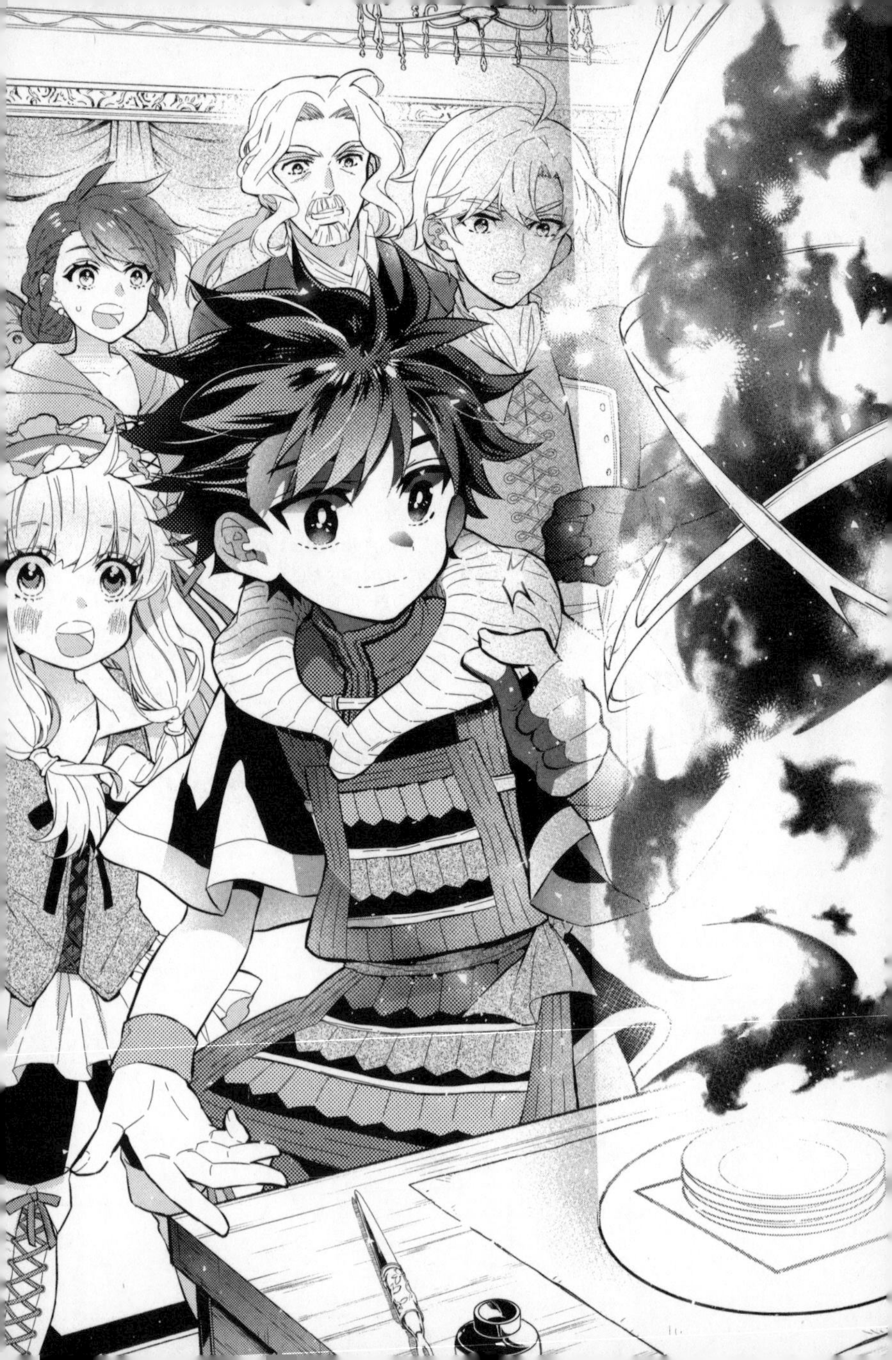

"Oh!"

"Er, you two?"

Unable to tolerate any more of the pair cheerfully discussing what would likely be top secret information, Reinhart interrupted.

"Sorry. I was a little too absorbed there."

"Oh. That's too bad. I was enjoying it!"

"Yes, it was definitely entertaining, but…"

"I'm not sure I should have heard all that."

"But now I understand why Ryoma sometimes uses eccentric magic and says things like 'I made that.'"

"Mm. As an alchemist, he has a deep understanding of the laws of the physical world. By the way, Ryoma, do you mind if I ask you why you created all that magic?"

"The fire and ice, you mean? Well, I wanted to heat up my bath quickly in winter, so that's how I came up with the magic to increase the power of a flame."

"Your…bath?"

"Yes. As for the ice… There was a period when strange weeds were growing all around my home. They were such a nuisance. They'd trip me up constantly. But there were too many to pull out by hand. So I thought up a magical solution. Surrounded by a forest as I was, fire magic wasn't the best option. Instead, I used ice to freeze them into large, hard clumps that I could then easily rip out."

"In other words, it was created as magic for weeding?"

Is that any way to use your knowledge of advanced magic?

That's what everyone else in the room wanted to ask Ryoma. Even Eliaria's smile was strained.

It had grown late, so the enjoyable meeting came to an end.

"Thank you for your hospitality."

"No, thank you for coming. I do hope to see you again soon."

The two children, especially Ryoma, were warned once more to leave alchemy out of their chatter on the way home. At the same time, Ryoma and the Jamils perceived the difference in their values, a realization that would lead them to become even closer.

But that's another story…

THE END

fires—a hearth used for cooking or a bonfire, for example—require something combustible like firewood, right?"

"So you prepare a substitute with an image, then! That reminds me. I've heard there's a place on a volcano where burning wind blows out of the ground! Right, Father?"

"Mm. Certainly, I've seen such a place."

"That's combustible natural gas. I think that's a good image. I tried to imitate that with wind magic once, but it unfortunately didn't work. I believe it's hydrocarbon, but maybe something was missing. I'd like to go to a volcano myself one day so I can get a better idea. Another combustible gas candidate is hydrogen. Hydrogen burns easily and explosively so I won't demonstrate it here, but you can extract hydrogen from water."

"It can burn even though you get it from water?"

"That's right. And there's one more thing you can extract from water—oxygen, which I talked about earlier. You could say that water is made up of hydrogen and oxygen. Oxygen and hydrogen gases are dangerous when mixed, but when they're combined into water, they're safe. Isn't that interesting?"

"It's fascinating!"

"It really is! Oh, I know. Have you heard of the phenomenon called 'supercooling'?"

"No, what's that?"

"For example, you can lower the temperature of water by using ice magic to make it freeze. But if you lower the temperature very slowly, the water won't freeze. That's the state of supercooling, which produces supercooled water."

Ryoma wanted to entertain Eliaria, who was keen on science, but his natural fanboy side kicked in too, and he dove into another experiment. He prepared a bowl of water and used magic to slowly lower its temperature, inducing a supercooled state.

"There. I used magic to create supercooled water. As with the fire before, I did it with a combination of basic fire and water magic."

"Now what happens?"

"Let's try stimulating the water."

Ryoma created a small ice chip and dropped it into the bowl. In an instant, the water froze.

"It turned to ice!"

"As you can see, supercooled water becomes ice with the slightest stimulus. If you combine this with water magic's 'Waterball' and fire it off, you can freeze a wide area!"

"That's wonderful! 'Fire,' 'Breeze,' 'Water'…the basics of magic, the very first things we learn! And yet, combining their images can have this much of an effect!"

Eliaria praised him with the first words that came to mind. Meanwhile, the adults were silent, stunned by Ryoma and his magic.

"Ryoma, if a practitioner of magic, particularly a researcher, heard about this, it would become a sensation."

"Magic is about using uncanny power and techniques to bend the laws laid down by the gods, to make the impossible possible."

"When you employ magic that runs parallel to these laws, it's called Ideal Magic and is the simplest and most efficient kind of magic. On the downside, it's difficult to explain such complicated laws, especially since they're invisible to the eye. Ryoma, this oxygen and its properties you spoke of are probably part of that. It's knowledge that many magic researchers seek out."

"Such knowledge might be akin to learning the mysteries of the world, going by how I think we're all feeling."

Hearing the observations from the adults of the ducal family made Ryoma recognize anew the usefulness and importance of scientific knowledge.

"Maybe another reason alchemy never took off was because of this hidden knowledge aspect. To use alchemy, perhaps having the knowledge you mentioned is a prerequisite."

"Ahh, a prerequisite. That's why you made it easy for us to grasp."

"Many scholars spend their lives trying to unravel these things. It's assumed that they understand it. There must be some incredible magic out there."

"Nowadays, magic has spread to the general populace, but in the field of research, secrecy is still the order of the day. Competing religious ideologies and sects often get in one another's way…"

At this juncture, the adults in the room grew aware of the deep divide between their and Ryoma's fundamental know-how and thought processes. They felt the need to protect him. Without delay, Serge peered out the door to make sure no one was eavesdropping. But Eliaria's curiosity and thirst for knowledge won out.

"Um, Ryoma? Is there anything else aside from oxygen? You've made me really curious!"

"Well, let's see… Where were we? You can increase a flame's power with not only combustible oxygen, but also by mixing it with a combustible gas. Magic fires can be fed with magic, but normal

"Eeeek!"

"Oh!"

"What was that?!"

"You didn't create large flames, but the small flame suddenly flared up."

Looking around, Ryoma could see wide eyes staring back at him.

"Oxygen is combustible. In short, one of its properties is helping a flame burn. I used alchemy to collect the oxygen," he explained.

"So you're saying that oxygen can make a small flame bigger in an instant."

Ryoma nodded with satisfaction at Eliaria's words.

"Incidentally, you know that a moderate wind increases a flame's energy, right?"

"Naturally. That's why I try to get wind to blow in the hearth when I'm cooking. Oh! When the wind blows, the flames increase in size and power. It's because there's oxygen in the air."

"That's right. Also, humans need oxygen to live. Even if there's air, we would die if it didn't have enough oxygen in it. And as fire burns and people breathe, oxygen in the air is consumed. When we did battle training in the abandoned mine this afternoon, we were warned not to use fire magic, remember?"

"Yes. In my magic studies too, I learned that you need to be careful using fire in cramped spaces. And I learned about the iron and steel industries as well. When you're in a mine, it's best to use a magic tool for light whenever possible. If miners use a torch or oil lamp, they could fall unconscious or even die. It must be because the oxygen in the air around them gets consumed."

"You catch on quick. By the way, if you're aware of the oxygen when you're casting fire magic, the flames will be more powerful."

He demonstrated by casting "Fire" on the dishes twice in a row. The difference was clear; the flames from the second cast were obviously bigger and brighter due to Ryoma's focus on the oxygen.

"And you used the same amount of magic both times?"

"Of course. To make the flames even stronger, I could combine it with wind magic's 'Breeze.' Water magic's 'Water' produces the equivalent amount of water, right? Taking that as inspiration, now I release oxygen and visualize that, along with the image of the flames surrounded by oxygen, to get 'Oxygen Burner.'"

The third time was clearly different from the others. A strong, blue flame stood straight up like a pencil.

context of the conversation, but it's a term I'm unfamiliar with, so I wanted to ask you about it."

She was 12 years old. Ryoma assumed she would still be in elementary school back in Japan.

"Think of oxygen as part of the air we breathe. You can't see it and may not be aware of it, but nitrogen, argon, carbon dioxide... It's mixed in with all those other components," Ryoma continued, trying to keep it simple.

As Eliaria had guessed, oxidized iron was the same as iron rust and was a combination of iron and oxygen.

What kind of materials existed in the world? What were their components and how could they be combined? And what could be combined with what to produce something else? That was how an alchemist thought, Ryoma surmised, and it was necessary information if one was going to use alchemy.

"It's difficult to explain...but do you understand?"

"A bit..."

Seeing that reaction made Ryoma want to perform a little experiment. He knew he wasn't eloquent to begin with, so he decided it would be easier to show rather than tell. And most of all, he thought that would be more interesting for her, particularly since she had been excited about his previous science experiments. After getting Serge's permission, Ryoma prepared an alchemy circle, the same kind he had used for his demonstration during the business portion of the day. Then he borrowed a number of cheap dishes and placed them within. Ryoma went about his preparations with efficiency.

"That's a Separation circle, isn't it? What are you going to extract?"

"I'm going to extract oxygen from the air and then explain it in a little more detail. First, watch this."

Being careful not to lean over the circle, Ryoma made his magic flow into it. As the circle began to glow, there was a brief, gentle breeze in the room.

"You can't see it, but I extracted the oxygen from the air within this circle. Now, cutting off the supply of magic to the circle, I'm going to bring a candle-sized flame over to it. Mr. Sebas, it should be all right, but if anything happens, would you douse the fire?"

"Certainly."

"Thank you. Now, everyone, this will be over in a moment, so please watch carefully. 3, 2, 1...Fire!"

familiar with market prices, and I could also tell by the way you answered questions during our business discussion. You let Lord Reinhart handle most of the negotiations. I apologize for being impertinent, but you don't have enough knowledge to be a trickster. It would have been easier for me to believe that Lord Reinhart was the ringleader."

"Oh, I see. That makes sense."

"Hey, that wasn't nice, Serge."

"Ryoma has no need to feel inadequate. All young people who come to town from the countryside are alike in that regard. If you feel self-conscious, I assure you that time will take care of it. But I was only speaking hypothetically anyway. Of course I didn't suspect you either, Lord Reinhart. You've long since earned my trust, and besides, had you wished to trick me, I'm sure you would have gone about it in a more effective way."

Reinhart and Serge. Their light banter gave the impression that they were close friends.

"Now, another reason is the product you prepared. It informed my judgment as well. To be sure, gold is a precious metal, but be it in jewelry or other goods, it's commonplace. Whether in a ring or a lump, you could easily procure some in advance. However, I've never seen or heard of 'pure iron' before, and try as I might, I don't believe I could've gotten my hands on such a thing. It's just not something I could see a cheat using."

This explanation also made sense to Ryoma.

An ingot of 100 percent pure iron. He himself had produced the ultrapure metal, which would have been impossible on Earth, even with its state-of-the-art science. Given the current opinion that alchemy was no more than a convenient pretense for fraud, he couldn't imagine the idea of crafting pure iron would be widespread.

"Finally, there was your behavior during its production. I don't know much about alchemy, but I can tell whether someone is working in good faith when I'm near at hand, looking on. When I saw all that, I decided I could trust you, Ryoma."

"Thank you. I'll work hard to live up to it."

Sensing that the conversation was winding down, Eliaria piped up.

"Ryoma, can I ask you a question too?"

"Yes, anything."

"You said something about 'oxygen' when making the iron. Does 'oxidized iron' mean iron rust? I more or less got the gist from the as I know, alchemy is capable of Separation, which is disassembling something and then extracting a substance it contains; Transformation, in which you change the form of something; Mixture, in which you mix two or more substances together; and Combination, in which you bring two or more substances together to create a different substance. Those four things."

"You must have used Separation for refining the iron, yes?"

"That's right. I separated out the oxidized iron from the derelict mine's soil, then split it into oxygen and iron. In the same way, if a certain rock contains gold, I think I'd be able to separate out and extract the gold."

"So you would just extract the gold. It's not as if you'd be turning the rock itself into gold, right?"

"Yes. As for an elixir of eternal youth... If we define that phrase as 'maintaining a youthful appearance,' I could extract ingredients that are good for the skin from various materials or even create them. If I just had the knowledge, I would be able to make something as effective as a beauty product you might buy in the market. And unlike normal medicines, some magical medicines can heal wounds in an instant or have other unbelievable effects... So I guess my waffling answer is that I can't be absolutely sure that it's impossible."

Ryoma's answer seemed to speak to the question that had popped into Elise's head as well.

"I see. But wouldn't it be safe to say this business of turning a stone into gold is a lie?" Reinbach muttered his question as if posing it to himself.

"That reminds me, Serge."

"Yes, Ryoma?"

"Our chat brought it back to mind, but what made you believe I'm an alchemist? I used iron instead of turning stones to gold, but isn't my magic similar to the scheme you experienced years ago?"

"True, the circumstances are similar..."

Serge cupped his chin with his hand and smiled while trying to think of how to explain it.

"First of all, it was more than just your demonstration that convinced me you're not a charlatan. I knew it the moment we met, from your attitude."

"My attitude?"

"Heh heh! You're not used to a shop like this, are you? Perhaps you're not even used to a big town like this one. You didn't seem and chanted some spell that sounded like gibberish. But when he opened his hand again, the pebble was gone, and a gold nugget lay in its place."

"Was it real?"

"It was, indeed. To show me that he was on the up and up, the fellow let me touch the gold and even allowed me to use Appraisal on it. The magic I mustered proved the nugget's authenticity. He had shown me a genuine gold nugget...one he had prepared beforehand to lend credence to his lie."

"Yes, I think I would've been surprised, but it wouldn't be enough to make me believe his whole story."

"As you say. I'm sure there aren't too many who would buy into it hook, line, and sinker just from that. But there are more than a few merchants who have been swindled by swindlers. Why is that? Because the swindler has a little trick, such as I've described, or perhaps they have a silver tongue, with which they gain the victim's trust bit by bit. There are masterful cheats who use a number of aliases and made-up social positions, depending on their purpose. I have even heard of those who spend years playing a 'long game,' bringing an even juicier proposal to their victim and then profiting from them until the money is all gone... Now, in my case, the fellow with his get-rich-quick scheme was of course a rogue. His pitch was ill-prepared, and he clearly used a spot of space magic for his gimmick. He was no alchemist."

Hearing that, Ryoma asked, "Um, so then is 'alchemy' just a pretext for fraud?"

"Good question... Certainly, there was an age long ago in which genuine alchemists amassed fortunes, but they also defrauded people. That's why it can successfully be used as a pretext for trickery. It's a pipe dream. But in recent years, I would say its popularity even as a pretext has waned."

Now, Ryoma saw the current state of alchemy differently.

Reinbach, who had also been listening, looked up.

"Ryoma. While he's correct about how alchemy is treated in the modern era, what kind of magic is alchemy, in fact? We heard the example of turning a stone into gold, but there's also creating an elixir that bestows eternal youth, and so on. Perhaps there is a possibility, however small, that these things exist."

Ryoma thoughtfully sipped his tea, then answered.

"I can only use the alchemy of which I'm aware. So I can't say with any certainty whether or not those things are possible. As far

⅄ The parlor of the morgan ⅄
trading company

They took a break following the close of their business discussion. The trading company president, Serge, offered Ryoma and the other guests a rare, aromatic tea and a cake that complimented it. The conversation flowed, and the topic eventually turned to the subject of alchemy.

"You may have given me the biggest surprise of my life today. I never imagined I would witness genuine alchemy performed before my eyes."

"Actually, I don't even know what 'fake alchemy' is. Could you give me an example? I've heard that it's used for scams, but…"

"The most famous one is turning a stone into gold, the alleged caveat being that the transmutation can't be done in the open. The victim says, 'I don't care if it'll fetch less than market price. Just go ahead. Turn it into gold behind closed doors.' The trickster boasts and has the victim prepare a great sum of money."

"And do people actually fall for that?"

"There will always be greedy individuals, while tricksters will always be thinking of ways to fool people. Once, when I was still a novice, someone tried to propose this very scam to me, but I said, 'I'd like to see you try.' Then I picked up a pebble from the ground and tossed it to him. What do you think the man did then?"

"I don't know. What?"

Eliaria leaned in and listened carefully, clearly fascinated.

"He nonchalantly held the pebble in the palm of his hand and said, 'Observe.' Then he closed his hand, grasping the pebble tightly,

BY THE Grace OF THE Gods {4}

Story:
Roy

Art:
Ranran

Character Design:
Ririnra

Translation: Sheldon Drzka
Lettering: Elena Pizarro
Cover Design: Andrea Miller
Editor: David Yoo, Tania Biswas

BY THE GRACE OF THE GODS Volume 4
© Roy
© 2019 Ranran / SQUARE ENIX CO., LTD.
First published in Japan in 2019 by SQUARE ENIX CO., LTD.
English translation rights arranged with
SQUARE ENIX CO., LTD. and SQUARE ENIX, INC.
English translation © 2021 by SQUARE ENIX CO., LTD.

ISBN: 978-1-64609-088-4

Library of Congress Cataloging-in-Publication
Data is on file with the publisher.

Printed in the U.S.A.
First printing, December 2021
10 9 8 7 6 5 4 3 2 1

SQUARE ENIX
MANGA & BOOKS
www.square-enix-books.com